HE'S AMERICA'S #1 M.D.
—AND HIS FILE COULD BLOW
THE WHITE HOUSE APART

Dan Lassiter's brilliant achievements rocketed him to the most influential medical office on Capitol Hill. His future seemed assured until his crusade to expose hospital corruption was shaken by an explosive past.

His marital difficulties, his affair with a TV newscaster, his link to a black terrorist group—all these were enough to shatter his career.

But Lassiter had one weapon left against the insidious Mafia sucking the medical profession dry. And he intended to light the fuse—even if it destroyed the President of the United States . . .

CRITICAL LIST
The Page-Searing New Shocker by
Marshall Goldberg, M.D.

Critical List

Marshall Goldberg, M.D.

CRITICAL LIST

A Bantam Book / February 1978

ISBN 0-553-11639-8

Published simultaneously in the United States and Canada

Bantam Books are published by Bantam Books, Inc. Its trademark, consisting of the words "Bantam Books" and the portrayal of a bantam, is registered in the United States Patent Office and in other countries. Marca Registrada. Bantam Books, Inc., 666 Fifth Avenue, New York, New York 10019.

PRINTED IN THE UNITED STATES OF AMERICA

Dedicated to:
My wise and wonderful mother, Ida Goldberg, and my darling daughter, Dara.

Acknowledgments

This novel was written during a particularly stormy period of my life. That it was ever completed, and published, is largely due to the advice, assistance and encouragement I received from the following people: Dr. John Knowles, President of the Rockefeller Foundation; Dr. Wilbur Cohen, Dean of Education of the University of Michigan and former Secretary of HEW in the Johnson Administration; William Oliver, Director of Fair Employment Practices of the United Auto Workers; Helen Hutchinson, Host of "CANADA A.M."; and Esther Margolis, Vice President of Bantam Books. I am especially grateful to Lieutenant Colonel (ret.) Kenneth Kay, a skilled novelist in his own right; my "literary security blanket," my sister, Dr. Toby Goldberg, associate professor of communications of the University of Wisconsin at Stevens Point; and Linda Price, my editor.

Humbly and deeply, I thank them all.

MARSHALL GOLDBERG, M.D.

Critical List

Prologue

The two men in the parked car outside the Department of HEW building meant this to be the last night of Artemus Hill's life. They bore no grudge against Hill. They hardly knew him. Apart from certain essential details, they did not want to know him.

The pair were professional killers, stalkers of human, preferably defenseless, prey, and the cigarette butts overflowing the ashtray, the empty coffee cartons stacked on the floor, attested to the fact that they had been waiting for Hill a long time. The waiting did not bother them. Each had his own drill for remaining relaxed and ready. Once they had waited for two days in the men's room of a federal courthouse before dispatching their victim, a corrupt judge about to turn state's evidence, with a cyanide spray.

Known to their clientele as "the brothers-in-law," they were independent operators, working at most once or twice a year and then only after the most thorough preparation. Tonight, though, was an exception, a rush job that they ordinarily would have passed up if the pay had not been so high, the risk low, and the weather to their liking. After a day-long rain Washington, D.C. was a presence of thin fog and streetlight glare at ten o'clock in the evening. Ground visibility was at a bare minimum at the airports and storm warnings were issued for boats on the Bay. District ambulance crews were geared for a steep increase in emergency calls and police for an outbreak of muggings and break-ins. It was a bad night to be out, to be traveling by land, sea, or air. But the brothers-in-law did not see it that way. Like surgeons, they had different instruments for different operations, and the weather spurred them on. For their purposes they could not have ordered a better night.

The silence that had lasted between the two men since one of them had said "cop car" almost an hour ago was now broken when the other said, "Hey, Rudy. The light in Hill's office just went out."

"About time," Rudy grumbled. "He didn't quit till nearly midnight last night. Must really be piling up the overtime."

"Must be, for all the good it'll do him."

"Ya. He got no wife and kids. Nobody, except his mother. Bet he don't even have a will. People should have wills, ya, Freddy?"

"Yeah." He wished his German brother-in-law would call him Fred, but he did not complain. It was better than what most of his friends called him. He detested the nickname "Squint" and the eye twitch he was helpless to suppress whenever anybody spoke to him. He could look any man square and steady in the eye, but he could not listen without squinting.

His father, a sadistic brute who had driven Fred's mother to desert shortly after his birth and whose words were so often followed by blows, was responsible. A breeder and trainer of watchdogs by profession, he had tried to instill the same blind obedience in his only child until Fred permanently pacified him by lacing his nightly bowl of chili with a mixture of roach poison and lye. Hiding behind the kitchen door, he heard his father's aah of pleasure after his first spoonful of the chili rise to an agonized howl as he rushed to the sink, panting like one of his dogs, and futilely tried to quench the liquid fire in his gullet. Remorselessly Fred watched him die, his eyes blood-red from retching, his body twitching and jerking as if jolted by electricity, his hands clutching his rapidly decomposing throat. Intuitively he knew the murder of one's father was a terrible thing. But his only regret was that it did not cure his squint.

Six stories above, Artemus Hill, acting chief of the computer analysis section of the Department of HEW, locked his office and headed toward the elevator. He had labored late each evening for three months now, and much as he looked forward to spending a restful two weeks at his small cabin in the Blue Ridge Mountains, he felt a curious mixture of triumph and letdown upon leaving his work. No matter what his future held in store, he knew it was unlikely he would ever again enjoy a more creative and exciting period. Had Einstein after originating his theory of relativity? Had Neil Armstrong after landing his Apollo spacecraft in the Pacific? Not that Artemus Hill seriously compared himself to such famous men. But he had accomplished something of note: He had single-handedly uncovered the greatest government theft of all time.

Born in Athens, Georgia, the son of an uneducated mill worker, Artemus discovered early in life that he had a good head for figures. He seemed to be able to visualize relationships between them that nobody else his age could. In high school his awed teachers called him a mathematical genius. At Duke University, where such a superlative is used more sparingly, he was called exceptional. After obtaining his Ph.D. there, he was offered a faculty position but turned it down. Much as he liked Duke, it lacked the new generation of computers essential to his research interests. So he went to work for the Department of HEW where his talents were wasted for years until his boss suddenly fell ill and he was assigned the task of programming their gigantic computer to project federal health expenditures for the coming year.

Artemus Hill did the job in record time. Then, since his mother had recently recovered from a stroke, he thought it might be interesting to compare the cost of the care given her by the Health Maintenance Organization in her north Georgia community with similar costs nationwide. To do this he had taken the unusual and laborious step of analyzing the mean hospital and clinic charges for her particular illness not only state by state and Professional Standards Review Organization region by region, but county by county. He expected to find minor differences in the per capita and per diem charges for those patients in large, sophisticated medical centers in the East and Far West and those in the small, Hill-Burton-created hospitals of the South, and he did—only they were the exact opposite of what he anticipated.

The differences surprised and challenged Artemus Hill. He knew how mischievous big computers could be, how easily they could mislead you if fed insufficient or indigestible data. But the HEW computer was the world's largest, with built-in safeguards against malfunction, and it had never lied before. So he tried again, enlarging his data base to include not only strokes, but the nine other most common adult afflictions, suspecting that because of the complex billing codes of some large metropolitan hospitals and clinics he might have omitted certain expenditures and that these extra measures should help balance them out, bring regional cost differentials closer in line.

Again he was wrong. It was almost exclusively in the rural South that the annual outlay per patient for Health Maintenance Organizations exceeded the national norm. The same was true for extended-care facilities, mental institutions, and old-age homes, even though food, labor, and similar costs were substantially cheaper there. More puzzling, these higher charges did not hold for the entire South but only in eighty-two counties of seven southwestern states and ten Louisiana parishes.

This apparent discrepancy did not fool Artemus Hill long. He concluded that it was strategic. If only the mean annual expenditures for the states and PSRO regions were analyzed, as was customary, it was unlikely such differences would be noticed. Looking closer, Artemus also discovered that those glaring clerical errors that all HEW personnel were accustomed to occasionally—the accidental recording of $5,500 instead of $500 for some standard-priced item—occurred much more often in the returns from these ninety-two regions. Someone, he surmised, was in cahoots with somebody else to defraud the government of public health monies. They were no small-time operators either. It took great organizational ability, as well as intricate knowledge of HEW auditing procedures, to have succeeded in so vast a swindle. Which meant their ringleaders had to be highly placed government officials. Artemus Hill was too cautious a man to spell out this last accusation in the report he had sent to the legal section of the General Accounting Office, but there could be no other conclusion.

The elevator in which he rode descended smoothly to the ground floor. Almost immediately after leaving it Artemus Hill paused, faced with a decision, a minor one, but a test of character as well.

With their intended victim due to emerge from the building momentarily, Fred got out of the car to take a quick look around. He scanned Independence Avenue in both directions, glad the fog was holding, the traffic was sparse, and the mud they had smeared on their rear license plate had not washed away. He sniffed the night air. It had a fresh, clean smell, a blossomy fragrance. Satisfied, he climbed back in the car.

At his nod Rudy released the emergency brake and started the engine of the Oldsmobile Toronado. Each of them had a preferred lethal weapon, and Rudy's was the automobile—statistically the most deadly device ever invented by an American. And just as a medieval executioner had his favorite axe, Rudy's favorite was his 1958 Studebaker Hawk. With its pointed hood he could spear his victim. But it was a collector's item now and too conspicuous, too easily identifiable. So he had chosen the Oldsmobile. Beneath him he could feel its powerful engine purr, waiting to roll.

Rudy peered intently ahead, clenching and unclenching the steering wheel, psyching himself up. Before his eyes a tall, bespectacled figure with a bushy Afro came out of the HEW building. The moment he stepped off the curb, Rudy's foot hit the gas pedal. The Olds hurtled forward until it was almost upon him before coming to an abrupt halt. The screeching tires made the man hunch his shoulders, shiver convulsively, and twist his neck and torso but not his legs, throwing him off balance. There would be no somersaulting over the hood or slipping off a fender now. Rudy had him in the sure-kill position. What happened next depended solely on density. The more densely packed molecules of the car would crush the less dense molecules of the human body. The ribs of the chest would crack under the weight of the wheels like pistol shots and the breastbone would collapse, squashing the heart like a melon.

Or so Rudy envisioned in his mind. It was what had happened to their last victim, what he meant to happen to this fellow, Hill, with the funny first name and the fifty-thousand-dollar payoff on his corpse, but it never did.

Their murderous mission was thwarted because of a fluke, because Artemus Hill, a polite and considerate black man, chose to leave the building through a side exit rather than tread on the night porter's freshly polished foyer floor.

Hungry and exhausted, Artemus Hill left the HEW building and carefully weaved his way between the trash cans and shipping crates cluttering the narrow alleyway until he reached the street. Yet no matter how much distance he put between himself and his computer-filled office, his thoughts remained rooted there.

Having sent a detailed summary of his findings to the General Accounting Office three days ago, Artemus was a little disappointed that he had not heard from them by now. No hurrahs, no howls, nothing. But they knew where to reach him if they wanted to, and he was sure they would.

To make certain that his explosive report did not get lost in any bureaucratic shuffle, he had added a dimension, a shocker, a bottom-line figure, to the swindle: *1.9 billion dollars.*

He knew the standard reward for tipping the IRS to tax fraud was ten percent of the amount recovered. Would the same hold here and the government hand him a check for 190 million dollars? Not very likely, he chuckled. Nonetheless, he was a firm believer in the fairness of the American system and felt confident he would be rewarded somehow.

"Well—?" Rudy ventured after many minutes of tense waiting.

"Well, what?" said Fred.

"Maybe he stopped off at the john?"

Fred snorted. "Or maybe he went out the side door."

"Why would he do that? It's dark in that alley."

"So's he. Practically invisible."

"You want to circle the block? See if we can spot him?"

Fred hesitated. Instead of wasting Artemus Hill they had wasted the evening. Now they were wasting words.

"Aw, hell," he said. "Let's go home. I always liked the mountains."

PART ONE

THE DEEPEST END

Chapter One

To Matthew Kinsella, steeped in Irish folklore from early youth, the shrill, startling whine of the heart monitor by his bed sounded like the dooming wail of a banshee.

A split second before the alarm triggered off he had felt a wrenching internal displacement, like a sudden ground-shift under his feet, sending him slipping and sliding toward some hazy, scintillating oblivion. He was about to let go, surrender to it completely, when a rib-rattling blow bounced him back against the bed. Something—a fist?—had just slammed into the center of his chest.

With a resounding *slap-thump* it pounded him again before he could open his eyes, grunt in protest. Blearily he perceived a white-jacketed intern hovering above, his tense, haggard face fading in and out of focus. Then a flock of other faces—nurses, orderlies, more interns—huddling around him until the senior on-call resident, the chief signal caller, broke it up by barking orders for certain drugs, certain emergency lab tests, a certain flow of oxygen.

Having been a hospital administrator most of his adult life, Matthew Kinsella was no stranger to the scene swirling around him. He knew intensive care units, knew cardiac arrest procedures, knew he must be dying.

Another upheaval in his chest, more violent than before, blacked him out momentarily. Again the heart monitor blared: the ultimate wake-up alarm. Buttons were pushed and the ululating note changed into a staccato beep-beep-beep in time to a heart now fluttering at a rate of two hundred beats per minute. Damned funny sensation, Kinsella thought: like a trapped bird wildly flapping its wings against his rib cage. Irrationally he wondered if they would have to cut open his chest to let it out.

In a more lucid moment, Matthew Kinsella, aged sixty-five and unlikely to grow any older, gathered breath to speak to his doctors. Feebly he grasped the intern's wrist to make sure he had his attention.

"Please," he rasped, "get me Dr. Daniel Lassiter . . . and a priest."

"He—what?" exclaimed Dan Lassiter. "Give me that again, Robby." And Dr. Neil Robinson, an intern at Boston's Commonwealth General Hospital, in a voice crisply informative but also highly respectful, as was proper when addressing the general director of an internationally famed twelve-hundred-bed medical center, repeated the patient's request. "Matt Kinsella asked for me and *then* a priest. In that order? . . . Well, I'll be damned. . . . Sure, I know him. I used to be his favorite whipping boy at one time. All right, Robby, I'll be right along."

Dan Lassiter hung up the phone with a bemused look. Will wonders never cease, he marveled. So stubby, pugnacious Matthew Kinsella wasn't a child of Satan after all, but a mere mortal like the rest of us. He had watched the adroit Kinsella wriggle his way out of almost certain condemnation and dismissal by his hospital board so many times that Dan had come to doubt it.

Ten years earlier Matthew Kinsella had been his employer and his scourge, but his mentor as well. It was he who had finally taught Dan why doctors could no more be allowed to run hospitals than generals run wars.

In their rapid growth and expansion after World War II, the basic purpose of American hospitals had undergone a subtle change. Unbeknown to the public, they no longer existed so much to heal the sick as to *be* hospitals: ends in themselves. Theoretically they remained nonprofit organizations, but actually they were not noticeably different from the automobile manufacturers in their wasteful rivalries and duplications, their spawning of satellite industries, their ever spiraling operating costs and swift obsolescence. Except that hospitals derived less and less of their revenue from consumer sales, from individual patients paying directly for services rendered, than from a plethora of insurance carriers and federal subsidies—the all-powerful *third-party payers*. Because of this, the control of all major hospitals had passed from doctors to teams of cost-accountants and lay administrators who knew little about patient care but were highly adept at keeping the hospital solvent by tapping each new wellspring of governmental largesse.

As a young, idealistic doctor, Dan had found this domination of medicine by dollars repugnant. But under Matthew Kinsella's unsparing tutelege he had finally learned his lesson. It was hammered into him so thoroughly in their five years together at Holmes Memorial Hospital in Springfield that, despite his love of clinical medicine, Dan had been irresistibly drawn from the bedsides of patients to the power-centers of the hospital's front offices.

Kinsella had been the prime mover for this change; unwittingly he was responsible for Dan's present lofty post and even loftier ambitions. But what in the world had possessed Matt to ask for him now? Did a dying cobra seek out the company of a mongoose in hopes of sparking a glimmer of compassion in its ancient enemy's eyes before uncoiling in a death rigor?

Robinson's call had reached Daniel Lassiter in his bachelor apartment on Boston's South Shore a little after 2:00 A.M. Late as it was, he was still awake. He had returned from California around ten, lethargic from a full day of airplane travel, and gone directly to bed. But he couldn't sleep. He seldom could anymore. Once he had prided himself on needing no more than four, five hours' sleep a night to function well, but now he was a hopeless insomniac and lucky to get even that. Was it fear of dying, the "worm at the core" of his being, as most psychiatrists held? Or was it merely too much tension?

His days were so hectic lately, so full of input, uncertainty, conflict, that his overburdened brain might simply have given up trying to sort things out, pigeonhole them in some orderly fashion at night. And without this sorting-out process, deep, dreamful sleep supposedly was impossible. Or was it his self-imposed isolation, the loss of his estranged wife's warm, comforting body from his bed at night that deviled him most?

His trip to Anaheim and meeting with the AMA Board of Trustees amid the phantasmagoric setting of the Disneyland Hotel had gone pleasantly enough. No acrimonious exchanges as in the past. But he expected nothing noteworthy to come of it; the rift between him and the elders of the American Medical Association was too deep.

It had galled Dan to have to make the pilgrimage to Anaheim, to extend the administration's peace pipe, or whatever the hell he was supposed to do. But Nelson Freiborg, the President's chief domestic advisor and Dan's sponsor for the newly created cabinet post of Secretary of National Health, had insisted. Nels was a crafty compromiser who knew that even for doctors times change, spheres of influence shift with the party in power, and history never quite repeats itself. Not only was the AMA still stigmatized in the public eye for its ruthless ditching of Dr. John Knowles for a similar appointment in the first Nixon administration, but they now had to contend with a popular Democrat President. And an uneasy awareness of a federal axe about to fall.

The enactment of National Health Insurance two years ago had made doctors busier and more affluent than ever. Yet the latest government survey had shown the health of the American citizenry worse than before. So something had to give and it might just be the rigidly doctrinaire leaders of the American Medical Association, Nels reckoned. Sensing that they might be ripe for some gentle political plucking, he had sent Dan to assure them that if his nomination for Secretary of Health was confirmed, they wouldn't all have to punch time clocks or work for wages. Not just yet anyway. . . .

Amid the noise and flurries of activity around him, Matthew Kinsella listened to the stream of oxygen hissing through pores in his plastic face mask and the steady, reassuring beep of his heart monitor and remained drowsily awake.

The priest he had requested had come and gone, Matt having largely ignored him. At first he had felt too weak and thick-tongued to confess properly. Then he turned defiant. Confess to what? Sixty-five miserable years clawing his way up from a Boston slum? Even if the intern had not been within earshot so much of the time he still couldn't have done it. Why be a hypocrite? He had never gone in for that ritual mumbo-jumbo anyway; not since toddler days when his proud parents took him to Mass Sundays and he thought God spoke only Latin. Besides, he really wasn't going to die, was he? Well, even if he was, he still couldn't have opened up to that one.

Despite his white hair, the priest was too young and worldly looking to suit him. Not his notion of what a giver of extreme unction should be at all. It wouldn't surprise Matt if that silvery hair sheen came out of a bottle and was meant to dazzle his lady parishioners. Or if the officious pup was screwing some poor mixed-up college girl, or worse yet, a novice nun—like so many of his heretical breed did these days. Scandalous!

Maybe I'd have had a more fulfilling life, Matt brooded, if I'd heeded my mother and gone into the priesthood myself. I'd have made a good one too; devout, obedient to orders, unyielding to my flock, and how it would have pleased my parents.

But as the only son of a poor, immigrant ditch-digger from County Cork, Matt had dreamed of becoming a doctor. And although none of the medical schools in Boston showed any interest in him, the United States Army had. They took better measure of his mettle, sent him to OCS, and commissioned him a second lieutenant in the Medical Service Corps. For the first time ever he had authority and he thrived on it. By war's end he was a major and upon being discharged went through Boston University's School of Business Administration on the GI Bill. With his degree and military background he seemed specially suited for the job of hospital administrator, and the board of trustees at Holmes Memorial in Springfield hired him instantly.

The doctors on the full-time staff there took their orders from him.

Suddenly aware that his surroundings had grown quiet, Matt Kinsella raised his head from the pillow to look around. But the sedatives drugging his brain made everything wavy, like heat rising, and he slumped back, idly wondering what page of the *Springfield Union* his obituary would make if he did die. After twenty-five years of dedicated civic service, he deserved a front-page spread. Doctors' deaths invariably made the front page. But he and the editor had been feuding for years, and it would be just like that SOB to bury it back in the want ads out of spite.

What the hell was taking Lassiter so long to get here? Was he out of town? Or was he such a big shot now he refused to see private patients and wouldn't come at all? No, he'd come, all right, Matt Kinsella predicted confidently. He couldn't possibly pass up this chance to lord it over me. Not in his own bailiwick of a hospital!

As Dan drove his car off the Weston Expressway onto Commonwealth Drive, the illuminated upper floors of the hospital came into view. As always, the twenty-story structure, jutting up from the low-lying Weston skyline like some majestic lighthouse offshore, stirred a warming glow within him, a pride of accomplishment that really belonged to his predecessor more than him, but, which as Gundersen's successor he had a right to share.

Dr. Curt Anders Gundersen had assumed directorship of the hospital in 1950 when it was a ramshackle, near-bankrupt municipal eyesore, a mere repository for the tubercular and alcoholic and insane, and with his medical reputation, his influential friends in government, his matchless powers of persuasion as a recruiter, had restaffed and relocated and rebuilt it in a single decade into a medical center whose prestige rivaled that of the nearby Massachusetts General.

Dan had been Gundersen's first chief medical resident at the new Commonwealth General Hospital—his protégé. An almost father-son relationship had existed between them until, in one of his inexplicable moves, Gundersen abruptly dismissed him. Whether Dan's clinical skill and popularity with the house staff were beginning to rival Gundersen's, or whether he simply wanted him to learn administration, Dan was never sure. All he knew was that one spring morning in 1965 Gundersen brusquely announced that he had recommended Dan for the newly created position of director of medical education at Holmes Memorial in Springfield, the state's fifth largest hospital, and strongly advised him to take it since Gundersen had already arranged to replace him as chief of the outpatient department with a Harvard man.

Thus on July first of that year Dan left Commonwealth General to deliver himself into the hands of yet another tyrant, Matt Kinsella.

The ninety miles from Boston to Springfield had been one of the longest, most doubt-ridden journeys of Dan's life. He could almost feel his ego shrinking along with the reflection of the Boston skyline in his rearview mirror. It seemed clear to him that his dreams of a career in academic medicine, a professorship or even departmental chairmanship someday, were finished. Certainly his already strained first marriage was. Lois wasn't about to leave cultured Boston for Springfield in the sticks.

Chapter Two

The various intensive care units at Commonwealth General Hospital were clustered on the eighteenth floor, sandwiched between the general laboratories and the operating room. The recently remodeled medical ICU was the largest and most efficiently designed. Instead of separate rooms or small wards, it comprised a semicircle of glassed-in cubicles around a central nursing station, affording each nurse maximum visibility of her charges. To its bed occupants, however, it was like being on display in an aquarium. They called it "the fishtank" and resented their lack of privacy. But it wasn't the fearful place the closed-off section at the end of the corridor was. The sign above its door read, SHOCK UNIT, but to those patients lodged nearby it was better known as the "death unit"—a forbidding chamber filled with blinking electronic gadgets and mechanical heart pumps: the final pausing place for the barely living on their way to the morgue.

The instant Dan pushed through the double doors of the ICU he began collecting medical personnel, medical facts about his patient, like a snowball rolling downhill collects mass. Word had spread that the general director was coming in and a large contingent of available house staff and medical students were gathering to observe the one-time medical boy wonder with the computerlike memory and uncanny diagnostic skills—the greatest since Chester Keefer, or even Gundersen, it was rumored—in action.

Neil Robinson, coming out of the kitchen with a steaming cup of coffee in one hand and a cigarette in the other, met him first.

"Where is he?" asked Dan.

"In the Shock Unit."

"You didn't tell me he was in shock when you called."

"He wasn't—then. But his blood pressure began to drop around ten minutes ago, so we moved him in."

Dan nodded at a trio of medical students who had joined them in the corridor and turned back to Robinson. "What's his pressure now?"

"Seventy over fifty."

"Pulse?"

"One hundred sixty. Atrial fibrillation, I think."

"You think!" Dan gave him a disapproving look. He despised such vague, sloppy medical locutions as borderline enlarged, questionably positive, a shade jaundiced. All they really told him was that the examining doctor had not taken the time nor pains to make sufficiently sure of the abnormality to report on it without hedging.

"Well," he demanded, "is it or isn't it?"

"He has an irregular irregularity of his pulse," Robinson replied. "I didn't see any P waves on his electrocardiogram. I also don't read electrocardiograms too well."

"Okay, I'll take a look for myself," Dan said, moving on.

The senior on-call resident was in the conference room writing a note in Matthew Kinsella's chart when the group entered. "Hi, Dr. Lassiter!" he said cheerily. "Sorry to get you out of bed."

Dan tried to remember his name. Was he Jewish? Israeli? To his chagrin he no longer knew his house staff as he should. He leaned across the table, sneaking a glance at the nameplate on the resident's frock. "What makes you think I was in bed, Sanbar?"

The resident blinked in surprise. "Law of averages, I guess. It's almost 3:00 A.M."

"Well, you're right about the time," Dan said. "But that's all you're right about! Depend on the law of averages to make your diagnoses, Sanbar, and *average* is all you'll ever be, understand?"

He was being hard-nosed, Dan realized, but justifiably so. A life was at stake, and the time for vague pleasantries, for relaxation in the ranks, was later—when the patient was out of danger. He stared hard at the Israeli and then smiled to soften his rebuff. "All right, let's get on with it. Who's presenting the case?"

Sanbar passed the chart to the intern. "Robby worked him up."

Neil Robinson cleared his throat and began the ritual of case presentation, as stereotyped in sequence and content as any litany and almost as sacrosanct: the cornerstone of the teaching of bedside medicine for over a century. ". . . This sixty-five-year-old Caucasian male entered the hospital two nights ago with a chief complaint of chest and abdominal pain . . ."

One year ago, on the second day of a Florida vacation, Matthew Kinsella had suffered a mild heart attack. Hardly anyone back in Springfield had known about it; he had not wanted them to. He had merely informed his two assistant administrators that he was extending his vacation from two weeks to four, and spent most of it in a Fort Lauderdale hospital.

Upon returning home, Kinsella consulted a cardiologist-friend in neighboring Hartford who placed him on long-term blood-thinner medication, though its actual value in preventing further coronaries remained in doubt, and ran a monthly blood test, a prothrombin time, on him to monitor its effect. But a protracted hospital crisis made Matt miss his last two doctor appointments and prothrombin checks, allowing the level of anticoagulant in his blood to rise too high.

Feeling no ill effects, apart from a mild nagging heaviness in his chest at times, Matt Kinsella kept to his usual routine and two nights before had attended the State Hospital Association meeting at Commonwealth General.

He seldom missed one of these bi-monthly get-togethers. His seniority, his superior political savvy among the membership, made them a highpoint of his solitary existence. But this particular meeting began poorly and ended even worse. Not only did the five fellow administrators at his table irritate him with their chummy garrulity, but the cabbage in the New England Boiled Dinner gave him indigestion.

Despite an Alka-Seltzer, the queasiness in his stomach grew steadily worse as the evening wore on. He longed to go to the men's room and vomit, but by then the guest speaker was launched on his talk and Matt was reluctant to draw attention to himself by squeezing through the rows of tight-packed tables between him and the exit.

So with his customary dour expression concealing his misery, Matt suffered in silence until a heavy drift of cigar smoke triggered a wave of nausea so intense he could hardly keep from retching. Racking gut spasms beaded his brow with cold sweat and made his head swim. Frantically he struggled to regain his composure, resist bolting the room, until crushing chest pain proved more than he could bear. He collapsed just as the guest speaker got his first good laugh of the evening. The glass-shattering noise and spectacle of Matthew Kinsella slumping face forward across his table swiftly cut the laughter short.

He regained consciousness on a stretcher in the hospital emergency room. Another coronary, he was told by the physician who had just examined him, but Matt thought he detected uncertainty in the young doctor's voice. Whatever it was, coronary or simple indigestion, his condition remained stable the rest of that night and under heavy sedation Matt had not worried about it.

His deterioration, thereafter, was marked by transfers: from a private room to the first available bed on the coronary care unit, to the intensive care unit. Finally, into an even more specialized area, one whose creation budget-watching Matt Kinsella might well have opposed had he been administering that hospital: the shock unit.

After Robinson had concluded his case presentation and Kinsella's X-rays and EKGs were reviewed, Dan led his entourage into the four-bed shock unit. The crowded room, resounding with a cacaphony of monitor chirps and bursts of computer clatter, reeked of pungent antiseptic and urine-soaked sheets. Awaiting them was Gene Detwiler, the cardiology fellow, who had kept watch over the patient while the intern delivered his briefing.

The group, now numbering eight, filed silently around Matthew Kinsella's bedside, reserving for Dan the space at the upper-right-hand side, the examiner's position.

Dan winced at his first glimpse of his old boss. With his cheeks puckered from the removal of dentures and a ghastly rim of white sclera showing under partially closed lids, the slumbering patient bore little resemblance to the ruddy-faced, jut-jawed Matt Kinsella he remembered.

Mentally he tallied the number of tubes that now nourished and drained Kinsella's corpus. Five in all. Not too bad, Dan reflected. The maximum number of different-type tubes the human body could accommodate was ten, but more than six usually meant that the attending doctors were stretching their heroic treatment to the limit to pull a patient's other foot from the grave.

Dan bent over and removed the oxygen mask from Kinsella's face. "Matt, this is Dan. Dan Lassiter," he shouted in his ear. Kinsella's eyes blinked open and his crusted lips parted. But when he tried to smile his mouth went awry and his jaw aquiver.

As Dan fit his stethoscope to his ears to confirm for himself the intern's findings, he continued to digest the information that had already been fed him, to weigh the possibilities. From what he had been told thus far, the clinical picture was confusing. With Kinsella's blood pressure so low and his urine output negligible, he was clearly in a state of shock. But after twenty-eight hours of hospitalization, innumerable laboratory tests, and reams of computer-analyzed data, why were his doctors still uncertain as to what type of shock it was: *cardiogenic,* from a failing heart pump; *hypovolemic,* from a sudden and profound loss of circulating blood or plasma; or *septic,* from the tissue-injuring toxins elaborated by an overwhelming bacterial infection? What might they be overlooking?

Except for an occasional request for instruments, promptly supplied by the nurse, Dan concentrated on the problem while he went on with a quick but thorough examination.

At last he straightened and turned to his audience. "All right, I agree with Robinson," he announced. "His heart is huge and his prothrombin time was way too high, so the odds are he's bled into his pericardium." He pointed to one of the medical students, a lanky, slouch-shouldered type. "Tell me all you know about cardiac tamponade."

The medical student went wide-eyed and ramrod straight, his face contorting as he tried to marshal his thoughts.

"Come on," Dan prompted. "Start with the commonest causes."

The student gulped and nodded. "The commonest causes are, uh, penetrating chest wounds, uremic kidney failure, ventricular blowout following a massive myocardial infarction or, in this case, the probable combination of a fresh infarct and excessive anticoagulation." He paused for breath.

"So far, so good," Dan said. "Now tell me what you know of the dynamics."

"That it usually takes 300cc or more of blood between the heart and pericardial membrane to significantly restrict its pumping ability, resulting in a high venous pressure, a low blood pressure, and various cardiac rhythm disturbances. It can also give you associated liver and kidney failure, I think."

"But if it's a massive bleed—a tamponade—" Detwiler interjected, "why aren't his right heart pressures higher? Why isn't he in frank failure?"

His fellowship status made Detwiler the senior member of the house staff group, and his pointed question drew an immediate response from Dan. Wheeling on him, abstractly taking note of Detwiler's sporty handlebar moustache and the fancy triple-headed stethoscope dangling from his neck, he said, "Maybe he's bled elsewhere?"

"But he hasn't!" Detwiler maintained. "If anything, his hemoglobin and hematocrit are on the high side."

"What about his blood volume?"

"Haven't measured it yet. Machine's not working. Just what are you getting at anyway?" he demanded, momentarily forgetting that this was no lowly intern he was disputing but the general director himself. Hastily he backtracked. "I mean, the computer doesn't indicate any—" Oh, God, he moaned inwardly. That was a dumb thing to say to an expert clinician like Lassiter.

"No, the *computer* doesn't!" Dan snapped. "It doesn't have an M.D. degree either. Ever read any Sherlock Holmes, Detwiler?" As he spoke, Dan remembered Gundersen once asking him that same question in a similar situation, shaming him into reading almost all of the collected works. If his former chief could only hear him now, he'd cackle gleefully. Still, the legacy of great teachers must be passed on.

"Sh—Sherlock Holmes, did you say?" Detwiler stammered. "Not for years anyway."

"Then let me refresh your memory: 'If you have eliminated the impossible,' " Dan quoted, " 'whatever remains, however improbable, must be the answer!' "

The soft moans and purposeless lip flutters that began to issue from Matt Kinsella with each exhaled breath diverted Dan's attention, made him realize he was violating his own cardinal rule by arguing about a patient's condition in his presence. He glanced at the monitor screen to make certain Kinsella's heart rhythm remained stable, then led the group away.

"All right," he told them in the outside corridor, "here's what I think has happened. . . ."

Matthew Kinsella emitted one loud, last moan as the effects of his sedative injection wore thin, raising his level of consciousness. Had Lassiter finally gotten here? Was he the one who had just examined him, or had he dreamt it?

If it actually *had* been him, where was he now? He wanted to see the great Dr. Lassiter, learn exactly what was wrong with him and whether he and his coterie of young geniuses could cure it.

For someone so severely stricken, Matt Kinsella didn't really feel too bad at the moment. His damaged body did not hurt a bit; indeed, felt light as a feather—as if he could float right off the bed if he chose.

But it was souls, not bodies, that floated out of beds, he realized, and he wasn't quite ready to give up the ghost. If second chances were ever granted men like him, he wanted one; he hadn't gotten nearly enough enjoyment out of life. He tried to concentrate, to restore strength and substance to his body. But he didn't exactly know how, whether through prayer or sheer force of will, and he was afraid that all the mental energy he was expending might be doing him more harm than good. One thing he did know: Never before in his entire life had he felt so babe-helpless. It was all beyond him, beyond the point where his natural guile and Spartan discipline could help him. Like a patient undergoing surgery, sniffing the brain-benumbing gas of the anesthesiologist, he had to rely on the mercy of others. And Matthew Kinsella found this dependency almost as hard to face as the fact of his mortality. Given the choice, he might have preferred to die in his long-ago war, not as a patient in a strange hospital. There was no dignity, no flag-draped coffin, no taps and musketry over the grave here, just an assembly-line conveyor belt from ward to morgue.

Suddenly, as if by some mischievous magic, he became aware of a pleasurable, earthy sensation rising up from his gloom and doom. An incipient erection. Jeez, he marveled. Hell of a time to get a hard-on, especially since he hadn't had one in years. Oh, well, no need to be embarrassed; the bedsheet concealed it. Might as well enjoy it. . . .

And he did, until out of some self-protective center of his brain a warning signal flashed and the significance of the erection dawned on him. The pathologist he employed, a crude sort with a ghoulish sense of humor, had once told him that this was a little-known sign of suffocation: a perverse response of the oxygen-starved brain that made the terminal agony of death by hanging or manual strangulation a little less unpleasant.

The realization of what was happening to his poor foolish flesh made Matthew Kinsella shudder, cry out for help. But either the words stuck in his throat or were muffled by the oxygen mask, because nobody responded. Even as his erection wilted, a noose of twitchingly tense muscle fibrils tightened around his throat. He began to pray, this time in fearful earnest: *Oh, my God, I am highly sorry for having offended Thee. I detest all my sins because I dread the loss of heaven and the pains of hell, but most of all . . . most of all . . .* What next? The words! Frantically he tried to recall the rest of the act of contrition. But it was so long since he had been to confession, and his mind was so muddled that he couldn't.

Dimly, as if filtered through smoked glass, Matthew Kinsella perceived a shadowy figure in a V-necked surgical scrub suit hovering over him with a glittering knifelike instrument in his hand. What was he doing in surgery? Why were they operating on him? Or maybe—could it be—that they thought he was dead and were performing the autopsy? Oh, dear God, have mercy. Stop them!

The cold touch of a steel blade on his chest electrified him with fright and panic. I've got to get out of here, he thought wildly, and struggled to rise.

Fortunately, before he could dislodge any of his tubes, do himself other damage, he passed out.

When Dan and his medical team returned to the bedside, the orderly had finished scrubbing and shaving Matthew Kinsella's chest. Dan pressed a button that raised the head of the bed to a forty-five degree angle, and bent over Kinsella until their faces were almost touching. "Matt!" he shouted several times, and when that failed to rouse him began slapping his cheek, gently at first, then harder. Finally Kinsella flinched, fluttered his eyelids aimlessly, and gave him a glassy-eyed stare.

"Matt, listen to me! To what I have to tell you!" Dan yelled. "I've got to stick a needle in your chest. It won't hurt, I promise. I'm going to freeze the skin first so you'll barely feel it. Just don't move, understand? Whatever you do, don't move!"

Dan nodded to the nurse who broke open an instrument tray and connected a 50cc syringe to a six-inch plastic-sheathed needle by means of a short metal tube containing a three-way stopcock. The technical name for what Dan was about to do was a *pericardiocentesis:* a strictly emergency bedside procedure to drain off blood or fluid from the heart sac, which, even in the best of hands, carried considerable risk. Should the plunging needle accidentally hit one of the serpentine coronary arteries that wound around the heart just underneath the pericardial membrane, the patient could die instantly.

On impulse Dan turned to Detwiler. "You want to do the honors?"

The cardiology fellow hesitated, aware of the pitfalls thrust upon him. To accept might be taken to mean that he thought himself better qualified to perform the delicate procedure than the GD. Or else foolishly eager. To refuse was embarrassing but showed the proper humility. "Maybe next time," he muttered.

Dan smiled faintly. Gundersen's influence again. His late chief never missed an opportunity to challenge the house staff, to keep them in a perpetual state of tense alertness. Such behavior by an attending doctor nowadays was called "roundsmanship," but Gundersen called it electricity: got to keep the current on, the juice flowing, your audience charged up. Instead of thinking for them, always make them commit themselves. Learn by their mistakes.

Jesus, he felt good, Dan suddenly realized. Despite the risky nature of the tap he was about to perform, his lack of sleep, he felt clear-headed and rock-calm. Having thrived for so long on just such late-at-night emergencies, he hadn't quite realized how much he missed them until now. But they and they alone satisfied a specific need that no amount of publications, committee chairmanships, or paper-shuffling behind his director's desk could. Without sick patients to heal, he felt morose, melancholy, only half-alive; no excuse for his insomnia, his celibate existence, his bouts of mindless depression. Now, back at the bedside, back in action, using his exquisitely honed skills to the fullest in order to preserve the life of his old enemy, he felt purposeful, worthy of his reputation and gifts, almost exultant.

Below him, under the long hypodermic syringe Dan held poised in gloved hands, Matthew Kinsella, wide-awake and eyeing the glint of the needle as he might a street-mugger's switchblade, did not share Dan's mood. In fact he was almost literally scared to death —his heart pounding so hard it seemed as if it might rip free of its moorings and jump out of his chest.

Finally the strain it labored under became too great. With one mighty, rib-shaking thump, his exhausted heart strove one more time to cast off the bag of blood burdening it, couldn't, convulsed from earlike auricle to apex, and gave up.

With his last, gasping breath, Matthew Kinsella experienced no great revelation, no vision of his life flashing past, no terminal terror. Instead, like a drowning man finally forced to open his mouth and drink in order to quench the scorching fire in his lungs, he felt a split second of blissful relief before an electrical brainstorm obliterated his capacity to feel at all. The next instant his eyes rolled up, his body went limp, and he died.

A brief demise.

Although real by every technical definition, Matthew Kinsella's death went unmourned and unrespected by those present, his passage into eternity stalled. In this modern-day temple of medical wizardry, a heart stoppage did not represent a finality, but merely another complication; not a cue for despairing sighs and shrugs of futility, but sudden warning shouts, a convergence of trained rescuers, the institution of vigorous countermeasures.

This time the specially programmed heart monitor did not whine, it shrieked. To Dan, a veteran of infantry combat, the piercing note always triggered the same shoulder-hunching wince as had the whistle of enemy bombs falling around his Korean foxholes.

His eyes darted to the oscilloscope screen on the monitor. The fluorescent white dot that had been dancing across its face with each heartbeat was an unwavering straight line. Cardiac standstill!

As Dan tore the cloth drapes from Matthew Kinsella's chest to begin external heart massage, he caught a revealing glimpse of Neil Robinson's face and accurately read his thoughts. The intern was exhausted. He had other critically ill patients to tend before the night was over. He almost wished Matthew Kinsella would go ahead and die. Instead of resenting it, Dan understood. He empathized. It was a natural way for a severely stressed young doctor to feel in passing about a dying patient who was basically a stranger to him. But *only* in passing.

Dan dug the heel of his left hand into the base of Matt Kinsella's sternum, reinforced it with his right and began a rhythmic compression of Kinsella's heart against his spine to propel stagnant blood from its chambers. With each pistonlike thrust of his powerful hands, he could feel the breastbone buckle and hear the attached rib cartilages creak. He pumped rapidly, hoping to restore muscular tone to the flabby heart, make it contract on its own.

At last it did: It began to writhe like a bag of worms.

"Now he's fibrillating!" someone shouted and simultaneously Dan heard a burst of static from the audio portion of the monitor. "Okay," he cried, "prepare to shock! Ready? Quick now!"

Dan stepped back to let Detwiler, holding a pair of ping-pong-sized defibrillator paddles in his hands, move gingerly past him to the bedside. He placed one paddle on Kinsella's left rib cage and the other below his neck. "All right, everybody back!"

Matthew Kinsella's spine arched and his chest leaped as the hundred-volt electrical charge passed through him. The fluorescent white dot shot off the top of the oscilloscope then reappeared in a zigzagging, downward course before it stabilized and began tracing regular heart complexes across the bottom of the screen.

"Normal sinus rhythm," Detwiler announced. "But his pressure is still pretty low. Seventy over fifty. Want us to start dopamine?"

Hastily Dan considered his options: fluids, heart stimulants, aortic balloon. Only one seemed to offer any chance of success at this extreme juncture—get the blood out!

Not bothering to replace the sterile drapes or disinfect the area again, Dan reached into the instrument tray, grabbing a small stack of alcohol-soaked gauzes in one hand and the 50cc syringe and needle in the other. He made a few swipes at Kinsella's breastbone with the gauzes, took quick but careful aim, and plunged the needle into his chest. Guided firmly, the beveled point slipped between the fleshy interspaces of the ribs until Dan felt a sudden give, an easing of resistance, as the engorged heart sac was punctured. Immediately blood under pressure gushed back into the barrel of the syringe, filling it to capacity within seconds.

"Bulls-eye!" cried Neil Robinson, his face brightening.

"How do you know?" Dan challenged. "How can you be sure I didn't stick the needle right through his left ventricle?"

"I can't, I guess. Not until we see whether the blood clots. But I'm too damned tired to do more than hope for the best right now. Besides, I have confidence in you, Dr. Lassiter."

Dan ignored the compliment. Turning the stopcock at the base of the syringe, he squirted the blood from the barrel into the metal basin the nurse held to it and again drew back on the plunger. "Give me a readout of his vital signs after every syringeful," he ordered.

In the next ten minutes Dan refilled and emptied the syringe repeatedly until the last free drop of blood was drained from the pericardial sac and the pint-sized basin full to overflowing. By the end of the tap, Matthew Kinsella's heart was beating slower, steadier, but his skin remained pale and mottled, reptilian cool, and his blood pressure dangerously low.

Earlier Dan had ordered a pint of blood to replace what he was removing. Now that almost all of it had run in without raising the blood pressure a millimeter, he ordered another.

A tense interval followed as the second unit of blood streamed out of its plastic bag into Matthew Kinsella's vein, each passing minute, each unchanged blood pressure reading, diminishing hope further.

Aware of the battery of eyes on him, Dan shed his rubber gloves and stepped over to study the latest computer printout. His diagnosis had been confirmed; Matthew Kinsella did have a massive pericardial bleed. But now that it had been drained dry, why was he showing no improvement? Had the corrective measure simply come too late?

Lowering the computer sheet, Dan glanced briefly at Robinson, bleary-eyed and drawn, but unlike the others around him, standing erect, on his own two feet, not leaning against walls or tables.

Their patient's puzzling lack of response, his impending death, must be as bitterly frustrating to the intern as to himself, Dan mused. But what more could they do? What other feats of medical magic remained to be tried? Dan had initially surmised that the excessive amount of anticoagulant drug in Kinsella had not only made him bleed into his heart sac, but into the wall of his gut or one of the hidden recesses surrounding his abdominal cavity as well. Now, however, he had to consider what other damage the drug might have caused that neither a pericardial tap nor a quart of transfused blood could remedy.

Ignoring the coat-rustling and shoe-creaking of his restive audience and his own mounting suspicion that some sort of invisible boundary line had been crossed, establishing death's victory beyond doubt, Dan concentrated on a multitude of possibilities until thoughts and instincts converged on an unlikely but not impossible explanation: adrenal hemorrhage.

The adrenals, a pair of triangular, thumb-sized glands sitting atop the kidneys, were the body's sole manufacturer of cortisone, the most essential of all hormones. Without this substance, neither blood pressure nor life itself could long be sustained.

"All right," Dan spoke sharply. "No use waiting around to see how he'll respond to more blood. Let's try something different, quicker-acting. That way, maybe, we can all turn in and catch some sleep. Perry," he barked at the nurse, a portly, gray-haired matron he had known since his intern days, "prepare an injection of 300 milligrams of Solu-Cortef."

The abrupt order, given without explanation, drew surprised looks from Dan's audience, particularly from Sanbar and Detwiler, its senior, most knowledgeable members. They exchanged quizzical glances: Did the general director have a specific indication for the hormone, one they had failed to deduce for themselves, or was he merely using "shotgun" therapy? Until recently, a hefty slug of cortisone was injected into virtually every end-stage shock patient in hopes that it might do more good than harm, reap some mysterious extra benefit—which it seldom did. Nowadays, however, it was used far more selectively, especially in such sophisticated shock units as this one. So why had Lassiter ordered it with such assurance, without even the tiniest hint that it was really nothing more than last-ditch desperation?

Finally Robinson, less status conscious or reluctant to admit his ignorance than the senior pair, asked the question for them.

"Why the cortisone?" said Dan, feigning astonishment at the query. "Oh, I don't know. Guess because last I heard it's still the standard treatment for bilateral adrenal hemorrhage secondary to coumadin therapy."

"But that's a pretty rare bird, isn't it?"

"That's right. Now that long-term anticoagulants aren't used so much, it's rare as hell."

"Then what makes you so sure that's what he's got?" Robinson persisted.

"Sure? I'm not sure at all. But it's 4:00 A.M. and I'm beat, and it's the only treatable condition I can think of that we might have overlooked. That's all I'm interested in right now—*treatable* conditions! If whatever he's got isn't that, I don't give a damn if I miss it or not. I can always find out what it was from the autopsy report." He paused and smiled slyly. "But bilateral adrenal hemorrhage—now there's a fancy diagnosis for you! Even has an esoteric ring to it. Don't you agree, Detwiler?"

The cardiology fellow nodded sagely. "It's, uh, it's a good thought, all right. I remember reading something about that complication in the older literature. We certainly should have considered it."

We, Dan thought wryly. Why so quick to share the blame? You're supposed to be the heart expert, the team leader. It gave him yet another reason to hope his diagnosis proved correct: to teach a super-specialist like Detwiler to get his nose out of EKG and computer tracings and pay more attention to his patients.

"Well," sighed Dan, watching the nurse inject the cortisone into the patient's intravenous tubing, "we should find out soon enough if that's the answer. Let me know. I'll be in my office."

Chapter Three

Slowly, ponderously, Dan climbed the two flights of stairs to his office. A muscle-knotting tension clung to his legs and pessimism to his mind. Even if the cortisone raised Matthew Kinsella's blood pressure temporarily, he was still doomed, Dan knew. Only in TV doctor shows did most cardiac-arrest victims survive; in actual practice it was less than twenty percent. And Kinsella was unlikely to be that fortunate. Everything that could possibly be done for him had been done—too late. Maybe if they had consulted him earlier, if Detwiler had been smarter . . . But now the clutch of death's bony fingers around Kinsella's heart seemed too tight to pry loose.

Strange, mused Dan, how he still personified death. It was an old, all but incurable habit developed back in medical school during the six months he had spent in the anatomy lab cutting up a cadaver in progressive stages of decomposition. Depending on his mood, his occupation, whether at the bedside of a critically ill patient or brooding in solitude late at night, he envisioned it in different guises: sometimes as a journeyman angel, doleful and misunderstood, a reluctant retriever of tortured minds and broken bodies; but more often as the traditional sack-clothed, skull-grinning reaper. And now . . .

Now that they had struggled over the body of Matthew Kinsella all night, he felt too benumbed to ponder it, to even consider what Kinsella's personal wishes might be.

Dan walked along the empty corridor, past the door with his name and title lettered on it, which led to his receptionist's desk, and unlocked the next one. The heavy door swung open to a room almost fifty feet long and twenty wide, with a bank of windows lining one wall and a frosted glass skylight, aglow with pale moonlight, in the ceiling.

In contrast to the small, quaint, steeped-in-tradition offices of most Boston hospital directors, this one was designed to fit his predecessor's style and ego. The forty-foot walk from anteroom to Gundersen's huge teakwood desk was intended to impress, even intimidate, visitors ushered into the Great Man's presence. But Dan found its dimensions wasteful and pretentious. Even after filling the forefront of the office with a long conference table he still felt dwarfed by it.

Dan flicked on the lights and walked past the deep leather couch in the center of the room to the alcoved bar and refrigerator behind his desk. A gleaming, stainless steel, foot-and-a-half-tall espresso coffeemaker stood on the shelf. It was of Swiss manufacture, costly and rare: an anniversary present from his wife to commemorate the glorious, month-long Paris honeymoon that had addicted them to French coffee. And even though the brew it spewed forth was so potent it sometimes made Dan's hand shake and his heart palpitate, the machine remained a cherished possession.

He plugged it in, waiting the customary five minutes for the steam pressure to build up by the windows. Outside the sky appeared to be paling as glimmers of dawn seeped through the purplish net of night. Or was he merely imagining it?

Dan had watched so many dawns break lately that he tended to anticipate the color changes as he might the next few bars of a familiar symphony. First the dark grays dispersed and the blues prevailed, illuminating the concrete shapes of buildings and rooftops and turning streetlights a penumbral blue. A peaceful color, soothing to the mind's eye, yet vaguely disquieting too, hinting of an eternal tide sweeping between this world and the unrealized dimensions of the next, tempting him to drift out.

The nearby leather couch lured him like the lifting arms of a woman, but he resisted its cool, soothing touch. Moving back to the espresso machine, he pumped a hissing steam of aromatic, mahogany-hued coffee into a mug and took it to his desk. Wearily he sank back in his leather-upholstered swivel chair, propped his feet up, and inadvertently dozed until the sudden backward slump of his head jarred him awake. Twisting his neck from side to side to work out a kink, Dan caught a glimpse of the life-size portrait of Gundersen that hung on the side wall.

No wife, no kin, no hope, he recalled with a groan. Even after all these years, Gundersen's terse, expressive suicide note still echoed hauntingly through his mind!

Dan had been back at Commonwealth General for a year in the minor post of director of the emergency room when Gundersen died. A night-shift scrubwoman had discovered his corpse and, possibly because Dan had always been so friendly to her, notified him first. It was there, on the same leather couch whose comforts had enticed him earlier, that Gundersen had lain, his color gray as the dawn. And on this desk that Dan had found his suicide note. For a brief, loving moment, he had been tempted to tear it up, to pretend Gundersen had died of natural causes. But all of his colleagues knew he was a victim of the relatively rare blood disorder, polycythemia; that he had not only borne this affliction stoically, but spent the last several years of his life seeking an effective cure. Thus his suicide represented a double tragedy: the loss of a man and of a medical genius for whom time and inspiration had finally run out.

To ward off drowsiness now, he summoned memories of Gundersen's wake; how, even in death, his medical mentor and model continued to exert a major influence on Dan's life. His undertakers, doubtless grateful that their client had chosen sleeping pills over a shotgun to end his life, had done an uncanny job of readying Gundersen for final exhibit, even to the extent of capturing a hint of his sardonic smile. And Paula, Gundersen's devoted spinster secretary, had seen to it that he had lain in state with all the grandeur of a national figure. Only the most elaborate and artistic of countless floral wreaths received were displayed; the rest were gratefully acknowledged but distributed among less renowned corpses in adjacent rooms.

With Paula in full command of final tributes to a man she had served so long and selflessly, may have secretly loved, the stigma of suicide vanished from the proceedings and the funeral services proved a model of dignity and decorum.

Perhaps too much so, Dan felt. Despite the undercurrent of excitement generated by the presence of so many famous people, it struck him as a curiously unemotional ceremony. All wore somber faces, but hardly anyone showed grief—as if none of the gathering had ever known Gundersen as a flesh-and-blood human being but only as a medical supereminence and doctor of last resort.

It was nearly closing time before Dan actually saw a mourner, a woman in her thirties, dab at silent tears as she filed past Gundersen's bier. The sight brought a trace of moisture to Dan's own eyes and made him feel a sudden sense of kinship toward her.

But it was more than her tears that caught his interest; any man would have turned for a second look. Under honey-blonde hair she had big, blue, hyperthyroid eyes, a broad but delicately chiseled Scandinavian face, and a shapely figure. Even more intriguing, she looked vaguely familiar. Who was she, a movie star, a TV news reporter, a mere socialite? he wondered, determined to find out.

He waited until she was alone at the bier before moving up beside her. She gave him a quick sideglance and then resumed gazing down at Gundersen's frozen visage.

Dan cleared his throat and said, "He—uh—was a great guy."

Surprisingly she turned to him with scorn. "Great guy, my foot! He was a cruel, unfeeling bastard. I should know. He was my professor once. Because of him I almost gave up medicine."

"But you didn't?"

"No more than you, Dr. Lassiter."

Dan's eyebrows lifted. "You know me?"

"I know *of* you."

"You flatter me."

Her lips curved mockingly. "Then you flatter much too easily. A lot of people know who and *what* you are, Dr. Lassiter."

"Care to explain that?"

"Not particularly. But since you ask, I hear the reason they picked you to succeed him is because you're right out of the same mold."

Dan sighed dolefully. "So I've heard too. Makes me wonder if I'll end up like him. . . . Who are you anyhow?"

"Kristina Torvald. *Doctor* Kristina Torvald. You see, I made it anyway. And now that you know, I'll say goodbye. But I'm glad I met you, Dr. Lassiter. I was curious—"

"About what?"

"About what you look like."

"Is that all? Doesn't your curiosity go deeper?"

She gave him a cool, appraising stare—a practiced put-down. "No, afraid not. Maybe if you hadn't been such a Gundersen protégé and carbon copy. I doubt I could contain my hostility over that."

"Oh, come on," Dan protested. "Why can't we commiserate together? Share hang-ups? Gundersen produced them in all his students."

"No, sorry. Not this time. *Good night,* Dr. Lassiter," she said firmly and turned away. "Good luck on your new job."

Dan caught up with her at the exit and took her arm. He knew she was unlikely to protest with grave, hollowed-eyed Paula, her hand limply extended, waiting to bid them a solemn farewell, and he was right. She let him hold onto her arm until they rounded the corner. Then she jerked free and confronted him.

"Just what the hell do you think you're doing, Doctor?"

"Hanging on."

"To what?"

"To a hope. Did you think I'd let you get away that easily when we have so much in common?"

"An M.D. degree, maybe. Not much else."

"You married?" he asked.

"Why do you want to know?"

"Because if you're not, I'll buy you a drink."

"And if I am?"

"Then I'll still buy you one, but maybe not as many. *Are* you married?"

"No. But I'll bet you are."

Dan shook his head. "Divorced. Almost six years now. Now how 'bout that drink?"

"No, really," she said after a moment. "You're nice, nicer than I might've thought, but too intense."

"Look," Dan began and immediately faltered. Without quite understanding it, his need for her had suddenly grown so great that his poise fled and he stumbled over words. "My God, Doctor—Kristina—Kris—whatever you'd rather I call you—haven't you ever felt so rotten and alone and sick of yourself you simply had to be with somebody? Well, that's how I feel now. I don't even know who I'm feeling sorrier for: Gundersen or myself, what I have to look forward to trying to take his place. And here you are, a doctor and a woman—a very attractive woman—who just happens to have some understanding of what I'm going through. So how about letting me unwind with you?"

Kris dropped her blonde head and then looked up with a deprecating smile. "What a line! But I guess I feel sort of the same way myself—enough so I don't really relish going back to an empty hotel room. . . . All right. This once."

Outside the funeral home a wintry wind burned their faces as they walked the long, ice-slicked block to where Dan's car was parked on the street. As Kris shivered beside him, waiting for the engine to warm up, he was tempted to take her in his arms, share the warmth of his heavier overcoat with her. She was not only physically desirable, but his curiosity was whetted. He had heard tales of Gundersen's sexual preferences. Never with a patient—he was as staunch as Hippocrates about the moral purity of the healing art. But he was not above trying to seduce certain well-favored female medical students or interns. Had Kristina Torvald been a conquest? Were her tears for a dead and faithless lover?

And by now Dan was remembering a great deal about her. He had read enough of her papers in medical journals to know that she was a brilliant endocrinologist, an authority on pituitary diseases. He had also heard some of her male colleagues in St. Louis discuss her. They conceded that she was a top-notch investigator, but aloof, ambitious, tough as nails on her subordinates, and safe as a poisonous snake to ignore on an editorial board or a curriculum committee. Nor was she above using sex to her advantage on occasion—although it was hard for her detractors to believe that even in the act of intercourse she would not be appraising her partner's sexual prowess with the same cool objectivity she judged the performance of her students in oral exams. Dan smiled inwardly at the realization that Kris Torvald's professional reserve and self-sufficiency made the two of them kindred souls.

They drove to the Boston Sheraton, where Kris was staying, and in a secluded corner of the mezzanine cocktail lounge clinked glasses like travelers about to embark on a long, arduous journey together.

"To Curt Anders Gundersen," intoned Dan over his whiskey and water. "May the good Lord take kindly to him."

"Suicides go to hell," Kris stated flatly. "Didn't you ever read Dante? They all go straight to hell!"

"But Curt wasn't exactly a suicide. He knew he was dying. Maybe he just wanted to spare Blue Cross some medical bills?"

"You don't *really* believe that, do you? He was just too vain to pay the penalties of dying slowly: the physical deterioration, the pity, the galling dependence on the judgment and mercy of others. Curt had been a doctor's doctor too long to accept the role reversal. Besides, he was always suicidal, if you ask me."

Dan's eyebrows arched. "Aren't you being a little hard on him?"

"You mean, speak no ill of the dead? Well, screw that. I don't care how Jesus-like he was toward his patients, he treated his underlings like dirt, like mere lumps of clay to mold in his own image. And those who didn't shape up he simply threw out. I know at least three and you probably know more. How do you think they feel about the great Gundersen now?"

"If you hate him that much, why the tears tonight? They weren't for the ones who didn't make it, were they?"

Kris dropped her gaze to the table. "No, I suppose not."

Boldly Dan asked, "Did you love him?"

"Love him?" she repeated distastefully. "No! His type of man repels me."

"Then what?"

"It's the *what* I'm not sure I want to talk about." She looked at him guardedly. Then she shrugged and said, "Oh, why not? It's not the most sordid story in the world. Just a mistake in judgment that I don't usually like to own up to. But I was younger then, entitled to a few mistakes, I suppose. Anyway—" Kris suddenly broke off to drain her drink. He signaled the waitress for more and waited for her to continue, unaware that he was holding his breath.

"I was his patient for a little while once," she began slowly. "My junior year in medical school. My father had died the summer before—literally amputated to death because of diabetic gangrene—and I was awfully shaken up by it; that horrible feeling of knowing something but not enough about what was happening to him. Then back at school, I couldn't settle down. Either I felt about to jump out of my skin in class or so wiped out at night that I couldn't study. It got so bad that I went to see Jerry Luby, the chief of psychiatry, and, bless his vestigial medical instincts, he took one look at me and said I didn't need a shrink at all, that I was simply hyperthyroid. Then he asked me what member of the medical department I'd like to treat me, and guess who I picked? . . . That's right. The big man himself."

"Why?" Dan asked softly.

Kris smiled wryly. "Oh, lots of reasons. Some pretty straightforward—you couldn't spend two years at *State* without hearing all the lore about our great Chief of Medicine. Some a little more devious. The year before, he had given a few lectures on physical diagnosis to my class and I was fascinated by him. During one of the sessions, he picked me to demonstrate the neurological exam and the way he looked me over, as if he could see straight through to my insides, the touch of his hand on my knee, sent shivers down my spine. Oh, sure, I'd heard what a lech he was supposed to be. A nurse who had once worked for him gave me an earful about the torrid affair Gundersen had with a female intern the year before that supposedly broke up her marriage. I guess you've heard those rumors too?"

Dan nodded.

"Well, this one happened to be true. Know who the intern was? Jan Tarrant. That's right, the same Jan Tarrant who took her training under G. W. Harris in London and now heads the neuroendocrine unit at the Brigham. I later heard from Jan herself that she'd not only had an affair with Gundersen, but a couple of other staff men that year, since her marriage was falling apart anyway, and that he personally had obtained her fellowship with Harris, making me wonder who had really used whom. . . . So when Luby asked me who I wanted to see for my thyroid condition, I thought why not? Why miss the chance to make myself known to such a great man of medicine. So I arranged to see him."

In the background a piano began to play ragtime. Dan leaned closer. "Tell me about it."

Her first appointment with Gundersen, Kris said, was nothing like she expected. It was scheduled for

6:00 P.M. after his office staff had left for the day. Imperiously he beckoned her across the room and pointed to the chair beside his desk. She sat down, smiled, waited for Gundersen to speak or at least stop staring so openly at her legs. "All right, Miss Torvald," he finally said. "Let's sum up. Your eyeballs are proptotic and your lids retracted, giving you a pronounced stare; the carotid pulse in your neck is beating at least one hundred twenty times per minute and I can see that you're having trouble cleaning the dirt from deep under your fingernails—all of which means you have hyperthyroidism. Dr. Luby made a pretty good diagnosis for a psychiatrist. But you're a junior, you ought to have been able to figure that out for yourself. Aren't we teaching you any endocrinology at all?"

"And what happened after that?" Dan asked.

"Nothing! Not for months. He put me on antithyroid pills and I saw him every couple of weeks for a brief checkup, but that was all. Then one day he mentioned he was giving a lecture on Grave's disease at Newton-Wellesley Hospital and offered to take me along. He even bought me a lovely lunch at Locke-Ober's on the way back. But much as I tried to get him to unbend, talk about something else besides medicine, he wouldn't open up. He was the high and mighty professor and I his adoring but inferior student. That's the way it was between us and that's how it stayed until a week or so later when he suddenly called me in the middle of the night. His voice sounded so weak and raspy that I couldn't believe it was Curt at first, which irritated the hell out of him, but he finally convinced me."

"W—what'd he want?" Dan asked.

"For me to rush out to his place. Because he was sick, really sick, from a reaction to a new drug he was taking and wanted somebody to check him over, find out how bad off he was. I was so stunned I was speechless. Why me, a junior medical student, instead of an experienced colleague? But before I could ask he hung up. So I went to him. Oh, I went all right!

That was Thursday night, and I didn't get back to my apartment until Monday."

Dan gulped, finding it almost painful to voice his next question. "Then what happened?"

Kris frowned as she studied him. "What's the matter with you? You look uncomfortable—as if Gundersen were your father or something and you can't stand hearing that he fooled around with girls. Don't deny it, Dan. I used to feel the same way about him. He even called me 'daughter' until I made him quit. I didn't particularly dig that Hemingway stuff and it only accentuated the difference in our ages. But I guess it does bestow a sort of brother-sister relationship on us, doesn't it? And if you want to hear anymore you'd better buy me another drink. . . .

"Well," she continued, a fresh whiskey in her hand, "I threw on some clothes, grabbed my black bag and *Merck Manual* and went to him. He lived about twenty miles out, on an isolated stretch of beach beyond Weymouth. The cab nearly got stuck in the mud a few times, and with the fog and drizzle and gusting wind off the Bay, the setting was almost gothic. But he was sick, all right. His bedroom reeked of vomitus and his toilet bowl was red from blood he'd thrown up. I wanted to call an ambulance, but Gundersen wouldn't let me."

"Why not?"

"Oh, vain as he was, I guess he just didn't want anybody to see him that way. God, he looked awful: pale and haggard, a thick stubble of beard on his face—he looked as if he'd aged ten years since I last saw him. But his voice, that commanding voice, stayed the same: 'Just don't panic, Miss Torvald, and do as I tell you. *Then* we'll decide whether or not I need hospitalization. Don't want to overutilize hospital beds, do we?' "

Dan grinned at the mimicry. "So what'd you do?"

"Do? Exactly as he said. First I took his blood pressure, both supine and standing, and when it showed no significant drop he decided he hadn't lost enough blood to warrant hospital admission. Then he made me go over him from top to bottom and report each finding." Kris smiled. "I balked at the rectal, but he insisted. Lectured me on it! So, with my face flaming, I pulled on a glove and made medical history of sorts: the first rectal ever done by a *State* medical student on its most illustrious professor. I desperately tried to keep my cool, be as tight-lipped about it as he was tight-assed, but I couldn't quite pull it off. All of a sudden I started to giggle. I simply broke up. And so did Curt. He grabbed his pajama bottoms with one hand and me with the other and said, 'It may be a little smelly and undignified, Miss Torvald, but there's nothing quite like it to break the ice!' Then he gave me that famous, all but irresistible Gundersen smile and said, 'Thanks for coming, Kris. I appreciate it. Stay with me awhile. I need you in my life.' And then . . ." She paused, her lips spreading taut. "Then he simply passed out."

Dan wanted to ask if Curt had made love to her, but he didn't quite dare. Instead he asked, "What happened after that?"

"He was really hitting the bottle hard around then, and every few weeks he'd call me to come and take care of him after one of his binges. And I came. I even bought an old jalopy I could drive out. I cooked for him, cleaned up his messes, listened to him rant and rave about the charlatans and incompetents who demeaned the sacred troth of the medical profession and had to be weeded out . . ." Kris stared morosely into her drink. "The only thing I wouldn't do was get drunk with him. Not after the first few times. Liquor brought out a funny quirk in him, made him try to tear down a person's defenses. 'The perilous game of truth,' he called it. And it was! If I drank with him, he'd badger me to reveal every intimate detail about my sex life, my fantasies, how I felt about the other med school professors and which ones had made passes at me. I finally realized what he was trying to do: strip me emotionally bare so he could completely control me. After that I wouldn't drink or talk about myself hardly at all. It made him even more surly and demanding, but I still stuck by him. I'd still drop everything and come running whenever he called."

"Why?" Dan asked gently. "Why'd you do it? You weren't in love with him."

"Why!" she exclaimed. "You of all people should know why. Those eyes! That hypnotic voice! That reputation! How could I—how could any ambitious med student—resist him? It wasn't any girlish romanticism either. I wanted to know his secrets! To be as great an internist as he was someday. I still want to and intend to, even if I am a woman and supposedly not tough enough to handle the pressures that go with the top jobs. Well, let me tell you," she almost snarled, "I had to be plenty tough to watch a man like Gundersen—a great man, really—systematically try to destroy himself. Talk about hang-ups—he had enough to fill the Boston Art Museum!"

"Did he know he had myelofibrosis then?" Dan asked, referring to the dread complication of polycythemia when after years of manufacturing too many red blood cells the victim's bone marrow turned to fat and fibrous tissue.

"No, I don't think so. But he was having a pint of blood drawn off him almost every month, so I guess he knew it would either end that way or in acute leukemia. Once I accidentally came across a chart he'd kept of his weekly blood counts over several years, but by then I didn't give a damn. I was through with him."

"Why?"

"Because for no reason the bastard had turned on me, tried to make my life in medical school a living hell."

Dan looked perplexed. "Why? What for?"

Kris grimaced and gulped her drink. "Why? Because he was paranoid, that's why. Thought I was a threat to him, for God's sake! Curt was more than a medical genius; he was also a genius at making an underling feel miserable. I was on my medical rotation at the time, and he not only assigned me the sickest cases, the ones that needed round-the-clock care, but was constantly on my back about them until I thought I'd lose my mind. Eventually it backfired on him, made the other students and staff men protective toward me. But that didn't stop him, only made him stoop lower by spreading the rumor that I was trying to lure him into bed so I'd be sure to pass his course. It was all a product of his four-plus paranoia, of course, but even so the looks—the actual leers—I got from others in the department nearly made me drop out of school. Finally I went to old Dean Westbrook who got me a transfer to Washington University in St. Louis for my senior year."

It was now 12:45—fifteen minutes before the bar closed. Dan ordered two more doubles.

"Well, there you have it," Kris said reflectively. "How a nice, corn-fed Norwegian girl off a Connecticut farm got loused up with the great Gundersen. How'd it happen to you?"

"Because I was once his student too," said Dan. "About ten years before you. He helped me out of a jam."

"What kind of jam?"

"I slugged one of his residents. Cold-cocked him. Best punch I ever threw."

"Tell me more!" Kris said delightedly.

"Well, one night when I was on my senior student rotation they admitted this old wino to the ward. He was so obtunded that it was hard as hell to get him to talk at all, but from what little history he gave me—headaches, blurred vision, vomiting—I figured he might have a brain tumor or subdural and called the neuro resident. His name was Schmitler, Schmidler, something like that—a real Kraut who'd taken most of his training in Germany, and even though he kept quiet about it must've been pure Nazi at heart. You could see it in the way he treated blacks and Chicanos, even the Jewish doctors on the staff. What he hated most, though, was being dragged out of bed in the middle of the night by a mere medical student. When he finally showed up on the ward, my old alky was barely conscious and not disposed to answering any more questions, no matter how loud we shouted them. So Herr Doktor Schmidler started slapping his face to bring him around. Only what he was dishing out weren't light taps but resounding blows like a Gestapo interrogator. I told him to take it easy, that the old guy was more sick than drunk, but he just snarled at me in German and whacked harder. So I finally put it to him: 'Look, Schmidler,' I said, 'hit him like that again and I'll hit you. . . .' "

"And?" Kris prompted as he paused for effect.

Dan grinned. "He did. So I did! Pow! The floor nurse happened to walk in just then and next thing I knew Gundersen materialized on one of his predawn visitations. He took one look at Schmidler sprawled on the floor, another at me looking scared but defiant, and ignored us both to examine the patient. . . . What saved my ass was that I was right about the old guy—they found a baseball-size meningioma pressing on his brain—and Gundersen was impressed. From then on he let me tag along on his after-midnight rounds, sent me to Boston City for my internship, and then took me back. Even took me along as chief resident when he moved to the new hospital. Like you, Kris, I got pretty close to him. Too close! Because in the end he dumped me too. Shipped me off to Springfield, Mass-ach-usetts, for five years before he brought me back to head the emergency room. . . . The rest you know."

"The rest I know," Kris said, slurring her words slightly, and yawned. Her heavy-lidded look made Dan fear she was losing interest in the conversation, that in her next breath she would thank him for a pleasant evening and retire to her room. Impulsively he asked, "How come a good-looking gal like you never got married?"

She looked up sharply. "Look, if you want us to part friends, knock off the nosy questions. You *do* want us to part friends, don't you?"

"I don't want us to part at all. Not tonight anyway," he said and waited for her to pick up the cue. She regarded him calmly. "How 'bout it, Kris?"

"How about what?" She yawned again. "Going to bed with you? Is that what you want?"

"Not exactly."

"Then be exact, goddamn it!"

"I will," Dan said. "What I want is to keep on drinking and talking with you until we're so bombed we fall asleep. Whether in the same bed or not doesn't matter. Just so we're not alone tonight and tomorrow morning. C'mon out to my place, why don't you? It's only a short drive from here and it's well stocked with liquor."

"Your place?" she muttered vaguely. Then in a harsh whisper, "*Your* place! Why, Dr. Lassiter, I not only hardly know you, I'm not even sure I like you—especially after Gundersen practically handpicked you to succeed him. Because I'm every bit as good an internist as you are. Maybe better, since I've had to contend with all those stupid male prejudices about women doctors all my life. So I'm afraid you're just plain out of luck. I've no intention of going to your place, understand? None whatsoever. You must be out of your mind to think I'd even give it a thought. And one more thing. Don't go judging my capacity for alcohol by your own. I may be a little tipsy right now, but I'm far from drunk. So if you're dumb enough to think you can outlast me, you'll just have to get that bartender to sell you a bottle and bring it up to my room."

"Your room!" Dan exclaimed happily.

"Shh. Not so loud, for God's sake! Let's see now . . ." Kris fumbled for the key in her purse. "Room 1505. Got it? . . . Good. I'll feel safer there."

"Why?"

She smiled slyly. "Twin beds."

In her room they drank and talked until past four when, still in his clothes, Dan fell asleep in the other twin bed.

His memory of their short time together the next morning was largely a blur. He had waked first, ordered continental breakfasts sent up, guzzled water from the shower nozzle, and tipped the valet ten dollars to press his suit for the 10:00 A.M. funeral. When Kris finally woke, she shared orange juice, aspirin, and coffee with him. The sight of Dan in only his underwear seemed to amuse more than embarrass her. His broad shoulders, dented nose, and blunt jaw made him look more like the boxer she vaguely remembered him saying he had once been than a famous man of medicine. Between sips of coffee she eyed Dan's shifting muscles with mild arousal, liking his physical side. Never before had she spent the night with a man without having intercourse with him. But she felt so relaxed and womanly right now it was almost as if they had.

Kris had to fly to Washington that morning to lecture, else she would have gone with him to Gundersen's funeral. Before they parted, Dan offered her a job: to head up the metabolic ward and diabetes research program at Commonwealth General. But Kris was already in charge of a similar, more established unit at Barnes Hospital in St. Louis and turned him down.

They did not see each other again for over a year.

In July, Dan went to Toronto for the International Diabetes Association meeting, arriving at the convention hotel in late evening. As he was registering, an old acquaintance, a brilliant and eccentric English researcher, rushed up and insisted on a nightcap at the bar. There a mutual friend and fellow diabetologist, Hal Selzer from Dallas, hailed them and Dan's heart leaped when he saw Kris sitting beside Hal in the booth. The four of them were soon joined by four more latecomers, serious drinkers all, and in time they moved to Selzer's hotel room to continue their boisterous discussions and general revelry. At 3:00 A.M., after two telephone warnings and one visit from the night manager, the party broke up. As if by design, Dan and Kris were the last to leave and found themselves alone at the elevators.

"Great seeing you again," Dan said.

She smiled at the hint of shyness in his voice and

manner—this from a man who only minutes before had been standing on a chair loudly denouncing the AMA, the British Health Service, and the mediocre officialdom of most of the world's scientific federations. "Great seeing you," she replied.

"I've thought a lot about you."

"I've thought about you."

"And just running into you like this, I—uh—sort of hoped—" His voice cracked.

Kris's smile widened. "You hoped I might want a roommate for the night? Your room or mine?"

"Mine!" said Dan emphatically. "It has twin beds."

This time, however, only one bed was used. Enhanced by an alcoholic glow, by the actual fulfillment of each's favorite fantasy, their lovemaking was sweet, relaxed, dreamlike, and so eminently satisfying that they later slept in one another's arms.

They woke late, stiff and hung-over, ordered up huge breakfasts from room service and showered together. The sharing of the shower stall gave Dan his first full look at Kris's nude body and even more to admire about her. Judging by her medical training she had to be at least thirty-five, but daily swimming and tennis had kept her breasts firm, her belly flat, her legs slender. He could hardly take his eyes off her.

Afterward Dan helped dry her off and lent her his terrycloth robe while he dressed in T-shirt and pants. Again he offered her a job at Commonwealth General, this time as vice chairman of the department of medicine. Her refusal, promptly arrived at and cheerily given, distressed and daunted him. Christ, he thought, I can't lose her now, can't spend every weekend flying out to St. Louis, and wondered for a wild moment if he dared go higher, boot Spencer Walt, his brilliant chief of medicine, upstairs to the higher-paying but professionally less-rewarding job of chief of research medicine and offer his job to Kris. Such a change would doubtless wound Spence's sensibilities, probably provoke him into moving elsewhere, but he would simply have to risk it, Dan decided. He was determined to keep Kris with him, and there seemed no other way, no other job that would interest her. Or was there?

The room-service waiter, an older man, beamed at the handsome couple as he served them the hotel's most nourishing and expensive breakfast, the Lumberman's Special. While Kris devoured the sizzling steak and scrambled eggs on her plate, Dan's stomach knotted and he merely picked at his.

"You're not eating," she observed after glancing at him a few times.

He shook his head.

"Then what are you doing?"

Dan sighed deeply. "Trying to get up the nerve to propose marriage."

She paused, eyeing the bite of meat on her fork. "Hmmm," she purred. "Is that what you're doing? Well, then, I accept." She smiled lovingly, leaned across the table to kiss him lightly on the lips, and then resumed chewing her steak.

Chapter Four

The blue and silver Dassault Mystère out of Fort de France, Martinique, came winging in across the Gulf of Mexico on a balmy summer's day to land at Tampa International. There were six passengers aboard: five black men and a tawny-skinned, Hispanic-looking woman of early middle age.

Four of the men sat facing each other while the woman, her head nestled on a pillow, dozed in the rear of the plane. The fifth man, Lemuel Harper, sat just aft of the pilot's compartment, two rows of empty seats separating him from the others. The gap was symbolic as well as intentional. He was their leader, indisputably and overwhelmingly, and command travels in solitude. Moreover, this commander had a deep dread of flying and preferred that his followers not know it. Each dip and jounce of the incoming plane sent spasms through his gut and made him grip the armrests tightly with his gnarled hands. It was not that Lem Harper was afraid to die—he had come to terms with that inevitability long ago in the Korean War and in half-a-dozen bloody African revolutions since then. But he abhorred dying for no useful purpose simply because an airplane fell out of the sky.

Following tower instructions the Mystère landed, taxied around to Airside C, and parked on an empty Pan Am apron for its passengers to clear U.S. Customs. The nattily uniformed Martinique aircrew went into Operations to file a flight plan on to the Raleigh-Durham Airport, and a Department of Agriculture technician in white coveralls came aboard to spray the cargo compartment with an aerosol insecticide bomb. He was followed by a bright-smiling blonde airport security guard in a brief, black skirt and policeman-blue shirt with a silver badge pinned over her left breast.

"M'sieurs and Madame," she began haltingly. "Bienvenue à l'Aeroport de Tampa—"

"That's all right, young lady," advised Lem Harper. "We all speak English."

"Well, good," said the girl, thinking what a huge, fearsome-looking black man he was with his oversized head, skull-shaped face, and shoulders wider than the seat back. She watched him stretch, exuding power and authority like a languidly stirring lion.

But when he stood up, ducking his grizzled head to miss the cabin roof, and moved forward, she saw that he limped and winced with pain at every step.

"This way to Customs, sir," she said, feeling a stab of compassion for the crippled giant. "It won't take but a few minutes to clear, you-all being the only overseas flight in right now."

In the rear of the plane, the woman lithely uncurled her body from the pair of seats and sat up. "Eh, Andy," she called to the man nearest her, "we have arrived?"

Lanky Andrew Sims, watching her add a turbaned hat to her Parisian-smart ensemble, grinned and said, "Monique, baby, y'ask me you arrived a long time ago."

She smiled back. Although they had never been lovers, Andy attracted her more than any of the others in Lem's globe-circling retinue. A novice killer herself, she was curious to know how multiple killings might change one's outlook on life, and ex-gangster turned Detroit vigilante Andrew Sims had slain scores of men. But she had not yet found the courage to ask him. That was a subject best broached in bed, and Lem would never condone it, not because he laid any sexual claim to her, but because sex could be disruptive to the smooth working relationships of his group. Oh, well, she thought philosophically, traveling like this provided other excitements. Many!

The passengers collected their hand baggage and filed out of the airplane, across sun-scorched tarmac, and into an air-conditioned terminal building until they entered a vast room with yellow walls and acoustic-tile ceiling. Except for rows of chrome and plastic chairs along its walls and three steel-topped baggage counters, the room was empty. Their blonde guide had vanished, and by some underground route their baggage had preceded them from the Mystère's cargo compartment and now stood racked neatly on the middle counter. Two Customs men, one a young redhead, the other middle-aged and bald, stood behind it.

"Welcome to the United States, folks," said the older agent. "American citizens check in with me please, and foreign nationals with Agent Bosworth. Have passports and Declaration Certificates ready."

The woman and the youngest male passenger turned to the redhead and the other four, Lem in the lead, to the older agent. He took Lem's passport, scanned it, and glanced up admiringly. He was a good-sized man himself, but Lem towered a full head higher.

"Well, Professor Harper," the agent remarked pleasantly, "looks like you got back home just in time. Your passport's about to expire."

"You are correct, sir," Lem acknowledged in his deep, resonant voice. "I fully intend to renew it in Washington."

"That your destination, Professor?"

"Not right away. But when I get there, I'll be sure to make it up to that passport office."

"You going back to Martinique then?"

Lem's thick lips curved, giving his saturnine face a look of wry amusement. "Does the United States Treasury Department really need to know that?"

The agent shrugged. "Far as I know they don't. Just making conversation, Professor. But your passport shows you spend more time in Martinique than anywhere else. Not that you don't get around . . ." He riffled the passport pages. "London, Hong Kong, Pyongyang, Paris, Tokyo . . . And places I never heard of: Botswana, Gabon, Benin . . . Goodness!"

Harper sighed. "Those are the names of new nations in black Africa. They're all in the United Nations,

I assure you. As you can see under *occupation,* I am—or was—a teacher of political science. I'm retired, but I still lecture to political and academic groups whenever I'm asked, and some are in far corners of the earth. And I'm not a member of the Communist Party, the Detroit DDD, or any other organization on the Attorney General's subversive list. The only drugs I'm carrying are painkilling pills for a bad hip prescribed by my personal physician, Dr. David Farragut Brattle. I don't know what's in them, codeine maybe, but you can ask him if you want to since he's standing right behind me. All I have to declare is a bottle of dark Martinique rum that's a gift for an old friend in Boston. . . . Anything else you'd like to know?"

The agent grinned and stamped his passport. "Not a thing. But I'll bet you're a real fine lecturer. I've enjoyed talking to you anyway. Not every day I meet a professor looks like he could play tackle for the Miami Dolphins." His grin widened. "You sure you ain't got a suitcase full of coke or a bale of Jamaican ganja hidden away? Something to liven up my day?"

"Of course not," Lem said tolerantly.

The agent nodded and scrawled chalk marks on Lem's bags without opening them. Of course not, he thought. Gretchen, the Customs Office's weimaraner with the sensitive nose, had already sniffed through the Mystère to make sure of that. Besides, it wasn't illegal drugs that had the FBI curious about Professor Lemuel Harper and associates. He had no idea what it was, but it wasn't that; Ferris would've told him. "All right, sir," he told Lem, "you're cleared. The tower will call down on the PA when your crew's ready to take off. Have a nice day and a pleasant flight."

"Thank you. Incidentally, where would I go to buy a newspaper?"

"Well, you take the escalator out there in the corridor up to the next level and then ride the shuttle car into the main terminal building and there's a newsstand. Oh, hell, Professor, you don't have to bother doing all that. Take mine. I'm through with it." He reached under the baggage counter and brought out a rumpled *Tampa Tribune.*

"I thank you again," said Lem Harper and, with the paper in his hand, limped off toward a plastic chair.

Behind him he heard the Customs agent's hearty greeting: "Welcome home, Dr. Brattle. Anything to declare?"

Lem sat down, grateful to take weight off his aching hip. That was a shrewd agent under all his cornpone garrulity, and it would take a slick smuggler to get anything past him. But he wouldn't be shrewd enough to sense the implacable hatred for him—for almost any uniformed white official—that burned behind David Brattle's bland professional gaze. If that agent knew how Brattle felt toward him he would shudder. The bravest man would. Because the saffron-hued, self-effacing little doctor with his ever-present black satchel was deadly as a mamba. He had proved that the one and only time Lem had let him: out of necessity, out of the conviction that the best deterrent to terror was worse terror—to so escalate your response that your enemies lost their nerve for more.

Lem Harper frowned as he spread and smoothed out the wrinkled *Tampa Tribune* pages. Fanatics like Brattle were valuable only in the early stages of a revolutionary movement. Later they invariably turned troublesome if not treacherous. Once the bloodletting is over, you need solid, sensible men to build a country with, not fanatics. With all that corrosive hate in him, how much longer would David Brattle be reliable? Was he now? Was David the one he had to fear?

Hate. Kenyatta preached that nothing good and lasting was ever founded on hate. Actually he preferred Charles Evers's words to the whites in Mississippi: "Don't you worry, we ain't goin' to do to you what you done to us. We just goin' to make *damn* sure you don't do it to us no more!"

Yeah, Charlie had done all right, better than all

right, and in one of the worst places imaginable. What he had done in Fayette was proof that with guts, know-how, the right political connections, you could work within the law to get what you want for your people. Evers had trailblazed the way for black politicians throughout the nation until recently, when all of a sudden his way seemed to have stalled. Well, I'm here to unstall it, Lem mused, to remind everybody what the alternatives are: Watts, the Detroit riots, even an Angolan-like revolt. They can take their pick. And while the resurgent white bigots sweated that, he had a bigger surprise to spring on them. . . .

Suddenly a paroxysm of pain exploded in Lem's hip. He squeezed his eyes shut and gritted his teeth as once again the plexus of nerves in his pelvis screamed at the stainless steel hip socket army surgeons had inserted after Sgt. Lem Harper, his left leg shot full of Gook slugs, was air-evacked home from Korea—home from the first war in American history in which niggers were judged good enough to fight alongside white boys.

Jesus! he moaned, rocking in agony. These days every attack hurt worse. He fumbled a painkiller from his pocket and swallowed it dry, knowing it would take time to work.

Brattle thought it was poison from his hip seeping into his system, eating his kidneys away. What had he called it? Amy-lord? Amy—something? David had given him a lot of fancy doctor talk about the condition, told him if he wasn't treated with a new Russian drug soon it could kill him. Unless, Lem mused morosely, pain waves sweeping across his brain like electrons across an oscillator tube, one of my faithful followers does it first.

Which one was it, he wondered, looking at the backs of his five disciples lined up before the baggage counter: at svelte, Haitian-born, Sorbonne-educated Monique Bouchet, tall as a Watusi princess beside squat, studious, Kikuyu tribesman Joseph Chekoba; at Andrew Sims, Vietnam vet and bodyguard of dope czar Henry Marzette until Lem got to him, turned him around, made him a co-founder of the Detroit-based Death to Dope Dealers; at burly Alphonso Beal, standing behind frail David Brattle, who had been the youngest black lieutenant of detectives in Philadelphia history until they floated him out of the department on a trumped-up bribery charge.

My loyal following, thought Lem, grimly seeking a diversion from the hammering pain: Monique, my secretary and official hostess; Joseph, my Kenyan protégé and economics expert; Alphonso, my chief of staff; Andy, my bodyguard and contact with the black underworld; David, my devoted personal physician—as able a personal staff as any minister of state could want. "The black Henry Kissinger," Chou had once called him. It made Lem smile through his pain. Even so, his dark foreboding lingered. Which of his loyal band had decided that the movement needed a dead martyr more than a live leader? One of them had. The same instinct that had kept Lem nimbly out of reach of an assassin for three tumultuous decades told him so.

But he had never before been this vulnerable. Though his five followers protected him from outside enemies, what protection had he against them? The next painkiller David Brattle prescribed might end all pain forever. That .38 Cobra nestled in Alphonso Beal's armpit could leap out at him instantly. The nine-inch, jewel-handled skewer from Cartier's that Monique stuck through her silver-brocade turban for a hatpin could slip between his ribs as deftly as it had the Boer masterspy's in Salisbury while he was sneaking his hand up her dress. And for sheer lethality Andy Sims's old-fashioned straight razor topped them all.

Suddenly Lem realized that his pain was completely gone. It happened that way sometimes after a particularly severe attack, a blessed respite that might last half an hour or half a day before it came flooding back. But for the moment a sense of well-being suffused him. Folding the newspaper under his arm, he rose and strode into the wide corridor leading to Delta and Pan Am boarding areas. They were deserted and Lem Harper stood at the window of one, looking out across an oil-streaked runway and sandy Florida flatland at a frieze of distant palm trees.

With grim derision he thought, this is my own, my native land. It was too. His father had been born and raised two hundred miles away on a worn-out cotton farm in the Florida panhandle. In his teens he had moved to Boston and learned to operate heavy earth-moving machinery, which made him a natural for the tank corps when the army drafted him in 1941. But war or no war, it was a racially segregated army in Louisiana, and an MP's bullet killed him when he led other black tankers in protest at their Jim Crow treatment. My own, my native land, mused Lem Harper. When is it ever going to be a fit place for all to live in? When will they finally realize that neglected people, like neglected trash, breed disease and spontaneous combustion?

He shook out the *Tampa Tribune* again and was not at all surprised to find on the front page a picture of the man he was flying to Boston to see. Why, hello, Doc, thought Lem, gazing at the faintly pugilistic face under the headline: LASSITER LEADING CANDIDATE FOR HEALTH SECRETARY POST. The AP story read:

> According to a reliable White House source, the President has selected Dr. Daniel Lassiter to fill the newly created cabinet post of Secretary of National Health and will formally announce his nomination soon.
>
> Dr. Lassiter is head of Boston's famed Commonwealth General Hospital and author of the controversial bestseller, *Medicine in Mississippi*.
>
> Once a strong proponent of national health insurance, Lassiter lately has become an outspoken critic of the way the program is being run. He is particularly critical of what he considers the excessive proportion of health funds spent by the nation's hospitals, an un-

usual position for a hospital director to take but one that is shared by the majority of experts in the health field.

Although an uneasy truce presently exists between Dr. Lassiter and leaders of the AMA, his Senate confirmation is expected to meet stiff opposition, especially from Arkansas Senator Alvin Balbridge. The two clashed so bitterly during Lassiter's recent appearance before Balbridge's subcommittee on health that a rematch seems inevitable.

Lem Harper smiled faintly, remembering nearly a quarter of a century back when two young Korean veterans, one a medical student, one a crippled slum-bred black seeking self-education in Boston's public libraries, had been forced by chance and morbid circumstance into a brief, violent comradeship before parting, presumably forever.

Yeah, Doc, thought Lem, reverting in his mind as he often did to the vernacular of his boyhood. Be dog if you ain't doin' all right. You a big man now, Doc, gonna be even bigger if you do like I tell you. But if you don't, Lord help you, 'cause I'm goin' to make your life pure misery. I sure don't want to, not after what we once done for each other. But I will, if you force me.

"So! There you are!" Monique Bouchet cried from the doorway and he heard the click of her approaching heels. "I have been looking everywhere for you. Didn't you hear the announcement? The *avion,* it is ready."

"Okay, hon," Lem said good-naturedly and stuffed the newspaper in his coat pocket. "Lead on."

Five minutes after the Mystère had taxied off toward the run-up pad, the bald Customs officer was on the phone to Tampa-based FBI Agent Will Ferris. "Yeah, Will," he was saying. "It was Harper and his five fellow travelers, just like you described. Everything kosher—if you can call a bunch of niggers kosher. Airplane and crew all checked out clean as a whistle. The outfit's borrowed. Belongs to some big French exporting house in Martinique. And interrogating the captain and crew at Ops didn't open up much. What is this all about anyway? Or can't you say?"

"What did you think of Harper?" asked the FBI agent.

"Christ, he's big. Bigger'n a skinned mule. But polite. Nicely spoken. I couldn't see anything out of the way."

"You remember his full name?"

"Sure. Lemuel Duvalier Harper. Why?"

"His middle name. It's common in the French Caribbean. You've heard of Papa Doc and his son Little Doc in Haiti? No relationship. But a lot of places call your nice-spoken retired professor only by that middle name. And they don't pronounce it like we do. 'Devil-A' they call him."

"Lord's sake, why?"

"Tell you what, Hal. You buy me a steak at Licata's sometime and I'll tell you stories about that black Goliath would curl the hair you ain't got. Right now, though, let it go at this. We'll be watching when he lands in Durham and again in Washington. Because the feeling higher up is Professor Lemuel Harper is just about the most dangerous man on United States soil right now."

Chapter Five

The first peal of his telephone made him stir, the second brought him shudderingly awake. Over the years Dan had developed an uncanny instinct for what these sleep-shattering calls portended about his critically ill patients. Now, though divining the news would be bad, he did not go so far as to steel himself for the announcement of Matthew Kinsella's death.

"Yeah, Robby," he mumbled into the telephone. "How bad is it?"

"Hard to say, sir. His blood pressure's up. Ninety over sixty. But we're having one hell of a time trying to break his arrhythmia."

"What arrhythmia and what rate?" demanded Dan, intolerant as ever of the guessing game that incomplete briefings like this made him play.

"Ventricular tachycardia, I suppose. At least we agree it's probably that, not atrial in origin. But he just keeps galloping along at one hundred sixty to one hundred eighty beats per minute in spite of everything we've tried to slow him down."

"And what's *that?*"

"Lidocaine, propranolol, the usual. We've even zapped him twice. Nothing!"

"Okay," Dan sighed. "What do you suggest we do next?"

"Detwiler wants to try overdrive pacing, but I'm a little leery. I just don't think his myocardium can take it."

Dan hesitated. Although overdrive electrical pacing of the heart, through a wire inserted into either its atrial or ventricular chambers, was no longer considered an experimental technique, he lacked firsthand familiarity with it. All the glittering new technology, he reflected wryly, that young house officers hungry for experience and expertise could not resist trying in place of the old, established methods. "Let's see now," he said, glancing at his watch. "It's been almost four hours since we shot in the cortisone. Not enough time for it to produce much of a shift in myocardial potassium content, but why don't we run a *stat* potassium and pH on him anyway."

"We have," Robinson reported. "His serum potassium has gone from 5.5 to 4.0 milliequivalents per liter. Not too bad a drop in view of a near normal pH."

"No, but it's not the absolute level as much as the change that's supposed to be the more important."

"Want us to run some in?"

Again Dan hesitated. Whose instincts should he heed, his or Detwiler's? The potassium or the overdrive pacing? Time had all but run out for Matt Kinsella and this decision could be final. "Yeah, go ahead and run in 30 milliequivalents over thirty minutes," Dan ordered with an assurance he did not feel. "I'll be right down to sweat it out with you."

Clinging to life by a rickety harness of wires and tubes, Matthew Kinsella grew progressively more feeble and exhausted as his nightmarish struggle against complications went endlessly on. He might have given up and gone under long before had not his cortisone injection, in some mysterious manner, suffused him with an artificial burst of vigor, a second wind to his will to live. But this euphoria did not last long. Within the hour, as the peak effects of the cortisone waned, so did Kinsella's life-sustaining cellular energy, again leaving him on the perilous edge of extinction.

But by now he was beyond fear, beyond caring if he lived or died; he was elsewhere. The strain of trying to absorb pain, suppress terror, had finally forced his mind to take refuge in hallucination.

He was seated in a burlesque house on Scollay Square—a dim, dingy, boisterous place resounding with brassy, bump-and-grind music, stinking of cold sweat and rancid popcorn butter. On the stage a scrawny stripper minced and preened in the footlight glare. Self-consciously he watched her jiggle her gourd-like breasts and rub a champagne bottle against her pubis until the cork somehow popped. The crowd howled, but Kinsella did not join in. Why should he? It was a disgusting spectacle, a degrading dive.

But from time to time an astonishing transformation occurred. A soundproof, domelike curtain would descend over the orchestra seats and under its effulgent shelter Matthew Kinsella felt pain-free and content, totally at peace with himself and with his fate. Although he hardly dared entertain so exalted a notion in the midst of such sleazy surroundings, he felt anointed by a heavenly balm, elevating him to a perfect state of grace.

But to his dismay and horror these blissful interludes never lasted long. Suddenly the curtain would lift, sirens would wail, and a searing pain across his chest practically knock him out of his seat and send him bolting up the aisle toward the red-gleaming exit sign. But before he could reach it, a bevy of bare-breasted nurses, grotesque in four-cornered caps and tassels swinging from their nipples, would rush up and drag him back to his seat. The band would blare, the audience cheer and catcall as the stripper pranced back on stage, and along with the deafening din a peculiarly pungent odor, like burning chicken feathers, would permeate the theater.

A sharp needle stab somewhere in Kinsella's groin wrenched a grunt out of him. He was about to reach up and yank out whatever was lodged in his throat that prevented speech and protest this latest indignity lustily when suddenly he heard the dreaded banshee wail of the monitor, a steep rise in the level of commotion around him, and above it all a voice groaning: "Aw, shit! There he goes again."

Matt Kinsella opened his eyes to the blurred outlines of faces, hands, and paddles converging on him. Oh, oh, electrocution time again, he thought in a sort of delirium and promptly reverted to hallucination.

"How many times does that make?" Dan asked Detwiler after the latest defibrillator shock had succeeded in converting Kinsella's chaotic heartbeat to a still rapid but less dangerous rate and rhythm.

"Three in the last half hour. Hope the potassium works."

Dan stared briefly at him and turned away, convinced that Detwiler's sentiment was sincere.

Twenty minutes passed in virtual silence as the potentially lethal potassium solution dripping into Kinsella's vein exerted a hypnotic hold on all their eyes. Dan remained at the bedside, periodically shifting his gaze from the intravenous bottle to the cardiac monitor. Purposefully he avoided Kinsella's face, grotesquely distorted by the plastic endotracheal tube that extruded from his mouth like a deep-sea diver's air line. He had seen the same snaky appendage on too many patients' stricken countenance to deny its deadly portent: It was the last tube before the last gasp, the mandatory end.

The last few cc of the potassium solution finally ran in and the watchers breathed easier. Dan ordered a bolus injection of lidocaine, and when it failed to slow Kinsella's racing heart personally administered another jolting electrical shock that took hold, terminating the abnormal cardiac rhythm and dropping the rate to 120 beats per minute.

As Dan fit his stethoscope to his ears and bent to listen to Kinsella's chest, he saw his eyes open, roll aimlessly in their sockets, and then focus on him. The look made Dan uncomfortable—the blank stare of a blanked-out brain? Or did he detect the barest glint of recognition? Then dispelling any doubt, Kinsella's hand came across the bedsheets, groping for his.

Jesus, marveled Dan. What a tough old Mick! With that strong a will to live we might just pull him through. Awed, he took Kinsella's hand and gave it a quick, reassuring squeeze.

Neil Robinson saw and was moved by the gesture. "How about a cup of coffee, Dr. Lassiter?" he suggested.

"Thanks. A little cream, no sugar," Dan said and sank into the chair by the bed. The sudden departure of the medical students from the shock unit and the noise of the chart cart wheeling in the outside corridor told him that Nan Forrester, director of the intensive care unit, had arrived on the floor to begin morning rounds. He smiled wistfully. That had been Kris's job once. During most of their marriage the ICU had been her responsibility, her whole professional life, until suddenly, unaccountably, after a heartbreaking failure to keep a courageous mother with incurable heart disease alive long enough to deliver a live baby, Kris had decided she wanted a baby of her own.

That had been three years and three miscarriages ago. Only the last of her pregnancies had gone beyond four months. And with each expulsion of huddled, purplish-gray fetal tissue from her womb, each cleanup D and C, Kris had grown moodier and more preoccupied by her paradoxical ability to preserve life but not create it.

Her last miscarriage had been the cruelest of all. Not only had the baby lived long enough for her to feel it kicking, but the premature separation of placenta from the wall of her uterus had triggered a profound blood-clotting abnormality from which she had nearly hemorrhaged to death. After that both Dan and Jim Neubeck, her obstetrician, had urged her to have her tubes tied. But Kris refused adamantly. The mere mention of such a finality could be counted on to produce either a stony silence or a tearful outburst from her.

Frustrated, and still shaken by how close she had come to dying the last time, Dan had persuaded her to at least take birth-control pills for a year until she was fully recovered. Or so he believed. But Kris was nearing forty and afraid her fertility was ending. Intentionally or not, she had taken the pills erratically if at all. So now she was in the sixth month of another pregnancy—the farthest she had yet gone. But Dan was no longer living with her, no longer there to share her fear lest a jounce of the car, a deep thrust during intercourse, might jar that precious nidus of embryonic life loose from the feeble grasp of her loving, nurturing womb.

The night Kris told him she was pregnant again they had quarreled savagely, resolving nothing. Either she didn't know or wouldn't admit whether the pregnancy had resulted from negligence or deceit on her part. And haunted by this uncertainty, Dan's chagrin, confusion, and deep sense of betrayal steadily worsened in the weeks of obstetric and endocrine and immunological consultations that followed.

He didn't really resent giving up sex at Kris's request, nor was he particularly bothered by his wife's furtive, anxiety-ridden behavior as the critical fourth month approached: the cigarettes she craved but did not dare smoke, the orange juice she downed by the pint though it gagged her with heartburn. What Dan found far more difficult to abide was her drastic personality change. Once so vivacious and energetic, Kris grew increasingly reclusive, refusing to work at or even visit the hospital. Then guilt-stricken over her idleness, she turned shrewish and distrustful, phoning Dan's office constantly to check on his whereabouts and accusing him of infidelity if he came home late at night. Unable to reason with her, Dan endured these tirades with a heavy heart until it became apparent that not only his marriage but his work at the hospital was deteriorating. He didn't recall which of them first suggested it; it didn't matter, he moved out.

That had been two long, lonely, insomniac months ago. Kris was well cared for in their large house in Sudbury by the live-in couple, housekeeper and gardener, who had previously worked for her in St. Louis. All he could do was wait and hope. There was no suggestion of divorce. Whatever feelings of abandonment Kris might harbor, she was not vindictive, and for Dan it was sufficient that he no longer added to the fierce struggle raging inside her between an indomitable maternal instinct and a mysteriously rebellious body.

Sitting now beside Kinsella, he resolved to phone Kris this morning, maybe even drive out to visit her that night. For all their differences, he knew she would be glad to see him. He also knew that with confidence growing along with her girth, she'd insist he put a hand on her belly to feel the stir of life inside. And he would—uneasy though this humoring made him feel. Until recently he had worried only about his wife's health, ignoring the doomed seed inside her, not daring to dwell on it in view of past misfortunes. But now that Kris was in her sixth month, nearing the stage of infant viability, he would have to think about becoming a father—add this to all the other unresolved issues burdening his mind.

Chapter Six

With one twisting motion Jimmy Dallesio raised his dug-in face from the pillow, flopped over on his back, and woke up from an unremembered dream with virtually the same look of scowling perplexity on his face that he had fallen asleep with the night before. Myopically he tried to focus on the digital clock by the bed, but without his thick eyeglasses its luminous numbers remained a blur. He sensed, without turning to see, that Nora was already up and in the kitchen fixing breakfast for him and the kids. Five more minutes. Jimmy gave himself this leeway to solve the mystery, possibly imaginary, that had left him stumped last night, even in the tranquil, twilight moments before sleep when he often did his best thinking.

Something had been amiss, some false note had sounded in his private chat with Charles Cheverton at the lawyer's home the previous evening, and his alert reporter's instincts had detected it. But whatever it was, its subtle nature eluded him. So he had slept on it.

Now he began to chase it down again with the confident anticipation of success that past triumphs had imparted. Cheverton knew how much he had wanted to interview him; it was, after all, the reason he had invited Jimmy and Nora to his dinner party. But Cheverton had avoided Jimmy during the cocktail-guzzling portion of the evening, had sent two of his Crime Commission deputies to keep him cornered in conversation. Then the phone call that wasn't—the flimsy pretext Cheverton had used to get the two of them alone in his den. Not much imagination there, Jimmy thought derisively. But why the den? Why that particular setting for their confidential little talk?

Jimmy pictured the room in his mind: the photographs of Cheverton's attractive family and the personally autographed political ones; the squash trophies and civic awards over the fireplace; the books, including two of Jimmy's, and the rows of calfskin-bound legal volumes on the shelves. A tape recorder softly humming somewhere? . . . No, the dignity. That was it! For Cheverton, the one-time law professor, the den that he had unlocked and admitted Jimmy to was his sanctum, the one haven in his twenty-room mansion where he could feel comfortably free from the crass politicians he was obliged to invite to his parties and cozy up to if he hoped to land the Republican nomination for Attorney General, or even Governor, two years hence. Cheverton had chosen the den merely to appeal to Jimmy's intellectual nature—one Harvard man's homage to another—nothing more.

So much for the stage setting then, the change of venue. Agnew had been capable of enormous dignity too, Jimmy recalled, and gelid-eyed John Mitchell had reeked of it along with pipe tobacco smoke. But why the special treatment, the confidential air surrounding what had turned out to be nothing more than Cheverton's routine pronouncement to newsmen that he stood with the angels?

What, after all, had Cheverton really confided to him? Simply that, election year or not, corrupt city and state officials still had to be prosecuted, no matter how an outraged electorate might overreact. "When you're gettin', get a'plenty," went the old Yankee saying, and scandals a'plenty were brewing in Boston's public monies pot.

As state chairman of Common Cause, the Governor's personal choice to head up his year-old special Crime Commission, Cheverton had pledged to expose and prosecute the culprits behind these scandals well before the November elections, no matter how unhappy this might make some of his incumbent GOP cohorts. He had promised it many times. But the rumors around town foretold a different outcome and Jimmy's instincts tended to agree. Cheverton's recent deportment contrasted sharply with the established style of most public defenders of Republican ilk. Give a Democratic DA with political ambitions the barest hint of malfeasance and he would shout it from every street corner until his voice gave out. But it was simply not the style of, say, an Ed Brooke or an Elliot Richardson, to offer so many public assurances before a trial date had even been set. Nor was Cheverton a known publicity hound. So what was behind all his mouthing off? And the persistent rumors?

Cheverton had spared Jimmy the need to ask. "Well, James," he had said with smiling earnestness, "let's not beat around the bush. I know you've heard rumors that I don't intend to seek indictments in the Park Plaza or oil refinery scandals until after the elections. That the public mood being what it is, my disclosures would incense people so they'd vote in droves for some wild-eyed reformer like Conaught . . . Well, don't you believe it. Not one word! Much as it would horrify me to boost the chances of an idiot like Conaught, who's not fit to be dogcatcher, let alone Governor, I'm determined to get those indictments to the Attorney General's office and before a grand jury no later than the end of next month. As long as my health holds out, nothing in the world can keep me from bringing this sordid mess before the bar of justice speedily. Nothing!" he had barked with such jut-jawed ferocity that Jimmy did not dare challenge him, despite his sneaking feeling that the whole ringing utterance was somehow more Nixonian than Churchillian.

With that particular rumor supposedly laid to rest, the two of them lingered in the den long enough to finish their brandies and that had been that. So what had seemed amiss? Jimmy wondered; what had roused his deep suspicion?

Stymied at last, he threw off his bed covers and was groping for his eyeglasses on the nightstand when his memory came into abrupt and revealing focus. *As long as my health holds out,* Cheverton had said, and then he had done one more thing. Offhandedly he had asked if Jimmy wanted to use his private lavatory off the den before rejoining the other guests. And feeling a sudden spasmodic pressure in his bladder—the power of suggestion?—he had accepted. So? . . .

So with its wall telephone and infrared heater-light and muffled toilet bowl flush, it was a pretty plush john. No concealed cameras or payoff envelopes or porno magazines to be found. But there was something in there Cheverton wanted him to notice—something a nosy news reporter could be counted on to check out.

Maybe James Dallesio, the nationally syndicated political columnist, would never take a peek into another man's medicine cabinet, but Jimmy the Digger might? Hell, *that* Jimmy never passed up any chance to snoop. And Cheverton had depended on him to do just that. His whole scheme was based on the presumption that Jimmy couldn't resist sneaking a look into that medicine chest. And what might he have seen there? Pills for heart, blood pressure, cancer? So that was his angle, Jimmy thought triumphantly.

The reason was obvious. Maybe it wouldn't sucker a Jack Anderson, but a sentimental Wop reporter like himself could never accuse a man of faking illness if, say, he suddenly checked into a hospital the week before a case he was prosecuting was scheduled to go before the grand jury. Not after he had stolen a peek at the man's medicines and knew how sick he really was. Hell, no, Jimmy thought, whistling at Cheverton's deviousness. He was almost sorry now he hadn't taken the bait and found out exactly what type of medication Cheverton was on. Heart pills seemed unlikely, considering that even in his late fifties Cheverton still played a fast game of squash twice a week. And cancer even more remote. Any good Irish Catholic stricken with that would undoubtedly be seeking forgiveness for his sins, not contriving to commit new ones. Jimmy made a mental note to ask Dan Lassiter, when he saw him later in the morning, if anyone at Commonwealth General was looking after Cheverton. Since they were all specialists of some kind, that might narrow the field.

At last Jimmy rose, stretched, and wandered into

the bathroom. He could hardly wait to have his suspicion confirmed so that he could tell his wife, Nora, and proud papa, Pasquale, about it. It was an appealing notion, but he knew that even to them he wouldn't actually boast. He was too modest a man. To this day, despite all that the intervening years had done to vindicate its judgment, Jimmy still found it astounding that Harvard College had ever agreed to educate him. What, he wondered endlessly ever after, could they possibly have seen in him at the time? Neither his background nor appearance nor high-school record presaged any special promise. Far from it. His father was an Italian immigrant typesetter with a small Boston printing firm, and Jimmy was a shy, gangling, generally shunned teenager condemned to view the world through thick eyeglasses.

At the age of eight Jimmy had nearly gone blind. The lenses of both his eyes had been dislocated by an otherwise minor tumble, and this ophthalmological oddity, together with his disproportionately long and spindly fingers, had made his doctor fear that he had Marfan's syndrome: an hereditary flaw in the body's connective tissue that more often than not progressed to early death. His case was sufficiently unique to gain the attention of specialists at the Massachusetts General Hospital where after many costly tests and consultations they concluded that Jimmy did not have the full-blown condition but a *forme fruste*—a medical ambiguity meaning that the few features he showed did not resemble the parent disease as much as a close cousin of it, sparing him from its deadly inheritance.

The verdict was tentative and couched in typically obscure medical phraseology which, for those who understood the lingo, simply meant, I've never seen a case quite like it so don't really know, but it came as God's personal mercy to Jimmy's devout parents. His father, Pasquale, promptly gave the church what the doctors had left of his meager savings and began working extra shifts at the printing plant so he could afford to send his only son to college someday. In the meantime he did something that ultimately proved even more beneficial to Jimmy's chosen career. In the mistaken belief that reading would further weaken his eyes, Pasquale Dallesio read to his son for hours each night, instilling in him a love for the classics and the printed word at an early age. So that when the time came, Jimmy did exceptionally well on the verbal parts of his college aptitude tests. Still, he never really expected Harvard to accept him. Actually he would have preferred a less tradition-bound, more freewheeling college like Antioch or Wisconsin. But to the everlasting credit of the Harvard College Admissions Committee of that year, and in particular the steadfast insistence of its one member of Italian descent, Jimmy Dallesio was admitted, educated, and duly graduated with the class of 1954—thereafter to go unrecognized and virtually unnoticed by his former classmates and teachers for years, even at the Harvard Club whose bland food and sallow lighting he despised.

At his class's tenth reunion, Jimmy still felt as unchummy and out of place as during his undergraduate years and vowed never to return. But Nora kept wheedling him about it until eventually he gave in, partly out of curiosity, partly on the hunch that his reception might be different at their twentieth reunion. He was right. Like some hitherto obscure painting or manuscript whose merit had recently been recognized, Jimmy was acclaimed on a par with once famous athletes and Kennedy-style politicians as he strolled, paper cup and plate shakily in hand, along the lawn in front of the Harvard Quad. And by the time the crowning, last-chance-to-make-your mark twenty-fifth reunion rolled around, Jimmy Dallesio was indisputably the most famous member of the class of 1954 on the premises.

It had taken no magical transformation for Jimmy to have reached this pinnacle; it was simply testament to the power of the press. And two-time Pulitizer Prize-winner James Dallesio, having a masterly grasp of the clout and drawing power of his nationally syndicated column, harbored no illusions about his celebrity. He accepted the adulation of old classmates, slavishly eager to refill his drink or plate, with wry forbearance, understanding their mentality and motives only too well. Almost to a man they had fallen victim to the "Harvard grad" syndrome: a near maniacal compulsion to prove themselves worthy sons of their famed Alma Mater and if at all possible worthier than their peers. Thus afflicted, they craved recognition—and how better to get it than to be portrayed as a personality, a pundit, a public benefactor, by Boston's most widely read columnist.

Jimmy's choice of subjects for his daily column was almost totally whimsical. One day he might interview the Secretary of Agriculture about the periodic beef shortages that drove up prices and made incensed housewives declare another butcher boycott; the next day a garbage collector on Beacon Hill to find out what the affluent were really eating. Trash collectors, bartenders, coin-laundry operators, barbers, and beauticians were his favorite sources, since he figured they knew best what the common people were thinking. It was a sound calculation. In twenty years, ever since his first column appeared in the now defunct *Boston Post,* Jimmy's readership had grown steadily and his syndicated column was now carried in over two hundred newspapers. Nowhere, however, was his influence greater than in his hometown of Boston.

Bostonians of all stripes, whether they read him on Back Bay terraces or in waterfront shacks, felt a special kinship and affection for him. Many put such store in his judgment that whenever any complex political or moral question arose they relied on Jimmy to clarify the issues before making up their own minds.

Popular as his column was, Jimmy flatly refused to appear on TV talk shows or accept invitations to lecture. Anonymity suited him personally and professionally, and it often came as a shock to people meeting him for the first time to discover that this lanky, round-shouldered, tousled-haired man squinting at them through thick lenses was the famous James Dallesio. Sometimes they never found it out. Unless Nora happened to be with him, he hardly talked at all, saving his best quips and observations for his column. This reticence did not reflect any inclination to be standoffish on Jimmy's part, it just came naturally. Better than anyone, he remembered his long apprenticeship as a second-string political reporter, too shy to elbow his way through a pack of his more vociferous colleagues to speak directly to a public figure. And even after the astuteness of his reporting came to be recognized and respected by his peers, they still kept him out of their clubby inner circle. Talented and dogged as he was in tracking a story, he was simply too quiet and cultivated for their drunken, womanizing roistering. They acknowledged his ability by calling him *Jimmy the Digger,* a not altogether flattering nickname in view of its rodentlike overtones, but that was all. It was years later, after it became painfully clear that he was the one newsman in town that politicians and other public figures truly trusted, the one they called upon first if they felt compelled to confide a guilt-generating knowledge or confess some grievous error, that the nickname was grudgingly changed to *Jimmy the Priest.*

Nowadays, of course, nobody but family and a few close friends called him Jimmy anything. The young reporters who flocked around him at the *Globe* or in the press galleries addressed him as *Mr.* Dallesio. Their deference amused him; he knew what they were after. Underrating his talent, not realizing how long and hard he worked, each hoped to discover and steal the special tricks he must have developed to make his column so popular, so feared, so unfailingly accurate in prediction and analysis.

It was all a crock, Jimmy mused as he thrust his thickly lathered face so close to the surface of the bathroom mirror that it was almost touching before he could see well enough to swipe at it with his razor. Someday when he was ready to retire he ought to write a how-to-do-it book for investigative reporters that would finally reveal his pet strategies and secrets. *The Art of the Artful Interview* by James Dallesio, he playfully envisioned; to be read by every journalism student and cub reporter as religiously as Strunk and White's *The Elements of Style.*

But that was mostly a crock too, he admitted, since so much of what he did was instinctive, more art than science, and true art was not teachable. Part was inherited and part acquired by long, hard experience. Nor did he have any real desire to teach it, even at Harvard. Not yet anyway; not until he had gotten the most fun and use he possibly could out of it.

"Congratulations," said Nora as Jimmy sat down to breakfast with her and their two sons: Paul (for Pasquale), age sixteen, and Danny, age fourteen.

"On the column?" asked Jimmy cautiously, having learned long ago to be wary of praise from his family on anything less than his most humorous or incisive efforts. Today's column, on the comeback of the wedding ring as a status symbol among cohabiting college couples in the Boston area, hardly seemed to merit his wife's accolade.

"No, on not cutting yourself shaving. The first time in a week, isn't it?"

Jimmy pondered the question with mock solemnity before nodding.

"I kind of miss those bits of toilet paper dabbed on your face," Nora continued. "Why don't you ever use the electric razor Danny gave you for Christmas?"

"Because Paul is always using it to remove that peach fuzz of his and never bothers to clean out the heads."

"Aw, Dad," Paul whined. "You never said nothin'."

"I never said *any*thing."

"Yeah," Paul exclaimed, brightening. "I knew I could get you to admit it! Trapped into a damaging admission by the clever ruse of his oldest son, James Dallesio today confessed that he had never said *anything* about the cleaning of his electric razor. Thus making his earlier statement on the matter inoperative."

"My, my," Nora remarked dryly, "aren't we all witty

today. Oh, for God's sake, don't ponder that, Jimmy. Just smile!" She looked at her watch. "You'd better get a move on if you're catching the nine o'clock shuttle," she warned, referring to the Boston to Washington flight Jimmy usually took each Tuesday and Thursday.

"I'm taking a later one," he said.

"How come?"

"Dan Lassiter wants to see me this morning. The President intends to announce his nomination to the Health post tomorrow, and I guess he wants to know how the wind is blowing around Capitol Hill."

"Tsk, tsk," clucked Paul. "Cliché."

"Yeah, Dad. Cliché," Danny echoed.

Nora shushed them. "How *is* it blowing?"

This time Jimmy really did ponder. "Something's up; something in Dan's past that worries the FBI Director—enough so he's got agents scurrying all over the country running it down. Just what, though, nobody knows. Either that or they're under strict orders not to say."

"Well," Nora said after a moment, "give Dan my love when you see him."

"Mine too," added Danny.

"And tell him I'm almost ready to take him on in handball again," Paul boasted.

Jimmy nodded as he rose from the table. Clearly the FBI investigation had done nothing to dampen Dr. Daniel Lassiter's popularity with members of the Dalesio household.

Chapter Seven

Bleary-eyed, unshaven, the freshly laundered white coat he had donned earlier now rumpled and blood-splotched, Dan Lassiter was still on the ICU when a mid-morning lull settled over the unit. Kinsella's admission had filled it to capacity, and all twenty patients had been bathed, fed, bled by the laboratory leeches, and examined by now. A pair of scrubwomen, starting at opposite ends, were hurriedly mopping the corridor before it became too congested with tray carts and gurneys lining up to carry patients to X-ray and other departments of the hospital. The nurses were back at their desks, catching up on their charting while simultaneously watching the central monitor console.

Although this slack spell usually occurred between 9:30 and 10:00 A.M., it was not invariable; many mornings it never came at all. Nor did it ever last long. But while it did a waiting kind of hush fell over the floor, which some of the veterans on the staff found unnerving.

Dan was one. Now that Matthew Kinsella's vital signs had remained stable for the past few hours, most of the nervous energy that had sustained him through the night was spent, and as he waited for Nan Forrester to finish rounds so he could brief her on Matt's case, Dan felt limp and edgy.

Six feet tall, two hundred plus pounds, hefty, handsome Nan Forrester was an imposing figure, physically and professionally. She had been Kris's close friend and colleague at Barnes Hospital in St. Louis, her personal choice as new director of the intensive care unit, and in less than a year her sharp wit and no-nonsense approach to house-staff training had made her one of Dan's favorite people at Commonwealth General. Much as they might argue over minutiae at medical conferences, and much as Dan suspected she disapproved of his leaving Kris, a warm and easy camaraderie existed between them.

Now she stood, arms akimbo, while Dan described the complications Matt had survived in the night. When he finished, she sighed and said, "Not bad. Not bad at all for a paper-pushing general director who hasn't been around sick people that much lately. . . . All right, Dan, I guess you've proved you can still be taken seriously as a doctor. So run along to your committee meetings and let the real pros take over."

"Aw, Nan—that all you got to say?" He hung his head, pretending to be crestfallen.

"To you—yes. I'll have a few choice remarks for Detwiler later on."

The next instant Dan was called to the telephone where Hedley, his private secretary, informed him his first visitor of the morning had arrived.

The dazzling sunlight striking Dan's retina as he entered his office made him blink and sneeze. He recognized the sneeze as some reflex, and when his hazy vision cleared he recognized Jimmy Dallesio sitting on the couch, hunched over a cup of coffee. Dan shook his hand, poured coffee for himself, and sat opposite him in silence.

Finally Jimmy asked, "You sent for me?"

Dan grinned. "Oh, sure. A Pulitzer Prize-winning journalist! I also sent for David Broder, Scotty Reston, and Teddy White, but you're the only one who showed up. How's the family?"

"Fine. Nora wants you to come for dinner Friday night."

"Oh? How's her fettuchini these days?"

Jimmy could not help grimacing. "As bad as ever. More paste than pasta. But what the hell, grab a bite to eat beforehand and come anyway."

"All right, I will."

"Tomorrow's the big day, huh?" Jimmy ventured after another silence.

"Yeah, tomorrow. At the press conference. . . . How's it look anyway?"

Jimmy started to speak, faltered, and sipped coffee.

"All right, let's hear it," Dan demanded, alerted to trouble by the obvious stall. "Give it to me straight."

Jimmy did. When he had finished telling him about the spate of rumors rising out of the FBI investigation, Dan shuddered with nervous fatigue. "So they're after me," he growled. "Hell, for all I know I'm on their ten-most-wanted list. Now suppose you tell me why?"

"You knew you'd be investigated thoroughly. Every candiate for cabinet rank is. It's routine. But assigning so many agents to the job without more top people in the Justice Department knowing why—*that's* not routine. So you tell me. Any deep, dark secrets in your past I don't know about? You know," Jimmy said in a feeble attempt at humor, "any unexplained corpses in your morgue?"

"There might be," Dan said menacingly, "if you don't stop diddling around and tell me what *you* make of it."

Jimmy gestured futilely. "I swear I don't know. I've done my damnedest to get a line on it for two days now. Talked to all my best sources, including the attendant in the Senate Cloak Room, and nothing! You've simply got to clue me in some."

"How?"

"By thinking back. Remembering. After all, you haven't led a monk's existence all these years. You must've done a few things in your life you're not exactly proud of. Everybody has. What could one of them be?"

Dan stared at him bewilderedly as if trying to grasp the reality of the situation. *All right, Lassiter, come clean!* an authoritative voice boomed in his brain. Whose voice—his long-dead father's, the FBI Director's, that of his conscience? Come clean to what?

Abruptly he rose, strode to a window, and gazed down at the tar-black rooftops of hospital buildings below. Did he have secrets so shameful and ignominious that he had repressed them? Was the FBI onto something he had hidden from himself? But what?

What could they possibly know or suspect or simply want to rule out that would impinge on his political fitness to be Secretary of Health?

Mental illness? He had come close to it, particularly his first year of medical school when he had been caught in a mental maelstrom that nearly cost him his career, his sanity, his very life. In some bizarre way he had become emotionally involved with his anatomy lab cadaver, with the then nameless corpse of a young man who had died violently and whose remains had been disposed of, presumably forever, in that noisome, gloom-ridden place. Maybe if his cadaver had come from an insane asylum or old-age home, as had the others in that year's collection, he might not have felt so compelled to learn his name. And if he had been less clever in finding that out, none of the rest would have happened. But there was so much about Rick Ferrar he could identify with—his youth, his boxing, his rootless existence—it had made the transference that much easier. Not only had Dan tried to take over Rick's girl and his best friend, but he had carried his compulsion so far that he'd almost died like Rick.

But he hadn't, Dan reminded himself. He had overcome and banished this temporary aberration and with it a dark side to his nature. Apart from that, and the periodic fits of depression he mastered alone, he considered himself as well balanced as any man. So it could hardly have to do with anything mental.

Adultery? Yes, he was guilty of that too. Not since marrying Kris; he had been faithful to her. But a few times with his first wife, Lois. One-night stands mostly, except for one notable exception: Catherine Colbine. Kit Colbine, then a top NBC news reporter, had been substituting for Barbara Walters on the *Today* show the day they interviewed Dan on his book *Medicine in Mississippi*. Now she co-hosted that show and was as bright, as lovely, as admirably feminine as ever, though she had never married. His brief affair with Kit might make a juicy tidbit for the gossip columnists, but it hardly justified unleashing the bloodhounds of the FBI.

Malpractice? No, either by luck or simple competence he had managed to evade that bugaboo of doctors. So what did that leave—murder?

The ugly word seemed to jar something loose from deep in his mind. It was so long ago, so covered up and layered under by the years, it was almost as if it never happened. But it had. As the ultimate penalty he had been made to pay for his obsession with his cadaver, Dan had killed a man once. He had been one of the two hired hoods who had beaten Rick Ferrar to death and then cleverly concealed the crime by slipping his body into the medical school's collection of cadavers. One of them—the gray-faced man—was called 'Turk' something, but what was the name of his partner, the one Dan had killed? From out of the dregs of dim, distant memory he conjured up an image of the man who had waylaid him outside Kim Chatfield's Beacon Street apartment: burly, broad-shouldered but nattily dressed in a Chesterfield coat. An Italian-sounding name, he recalled, groping for the first syllable. D'Mata! That was it. He had killed D'Mata and nearly himself by precipitating a fatal auto accident. And Lem Harper, Rick's great buddy before he had befriended Dan, had prevented Turk from retaliating by killing him somehow, thereby finally avenging Rick's death.

"Well—" Jimmy prompted. "Come up with anything?"

Dan turned away from the window to look at his friend and confidant's blurry brown eyes behind the distorting thickness of the lenses he wore. "Jimmy . . ." he began haltingly, "it just came to me. I killed a man once."

"You what!"

Dan nodded numbly. "I'd almost forgotten; made myself forget. No, it wasn't murder exactly. It was an auto accident that killed him. But I caused it."

"An auto accident? You ran into him?"

"No, we were both in the same car."

"Then how did you cause it?"

"I hit the gas pedal . . . On purpose. I know it

sounds wild, but he and another Boston hood were trying to abduct and probably kill me."

"Dio mio!" Jimmy's eyelids fluttered in astonishment. "Why would they want to do that?"

"Do you remember a local society and sports figure named Walter Chatfield?"

"Chatfield? Yeah, vaguely. Owned a string of racetracks and boxing arenas around the state, didn't he? What about him?"

"Well, this was when I was in medical school and dating his stepdaughter. Chatfield didn't like it so he sicked these two hoods on me."

"To *kill* you? Christ! What were you doing to his stepdaughter?"

"*That* wasn't it," Dan said testily. "Look, I've already told you it's a pretty weird story—one hardly anybody knows about. Not even Nora, even though she had a small role in getting me involved in it."

"Nora? My Nora?" Jimmy was well aware that Dan had known his wife longer than he, the two having met when he was a medical student and she a single newspaper gal. But Nora had certainly never mentioned anything to him about murdered cadavers! "Well, don't stop there, for Chrissake!" he demanded. "Tell me about it!"

Dan sighed wearily. "It happened back in 1954, when I was taking freshman anatomy. That's when each medical student gets to spend half a year hacking up a corpse—or at least they did in my day. Anyway, I drew a young cadaver and developed this morbid curiosity about who he'd been in life. You aren't supposed to do that with cadavers, of course, but with the help of Nora's newspaper connections I found out he'd been a local boxer named Rick Ferrar and he'd probably been murdered."

"Murdered? How?"

"A whack on the head. We discovered that when we sawed his skullcap off and found an enormous blood clot—what's called a subdural hematoma—on top of his brain. I was a pretty mixed-up kid then—a lot of what I'd seen in Korea still haunted me—and I literally became obsessed with the guy. It simply wasn't enough for me to learn his anatomy but all I could of him as a person: who his friends were, how he'd lived, and especially how he'd died." Dan shook his head ruefully. "I did too! I got in so deep I nearly flunked out of medical school, nearly got killed myself. But in the end it was good for me. Along with learning all I did about Rick Ferrar, I learned a lot about myself."

"Like what?" asked Jimmy, intrigued.

"Well, the main thing was that I really wanted to become a doctor. I wasn't all that sold on it before." Dan yawned deeply. "Anyway, that's the story."

"The hell it is!" Jimmy protested. "That's only the barest outline. But the big question is, could the FBI possibly be on to this hoodlum killing?"

"I don't see how," Dan said. "Only two people ever knew I was in that car. And one, the partner of the guy I killed, was dead before the week was out."

"And the other?"

Dan closed his eyes briefly. "The man who killed him. He had more reasons for doing it than just protecting me, so he's not about to talk."

"Let's hope not," Jimmy said. "But there's one connection I'm not making. What did your dating Walter Chatfield's stepdaughter have to do with it?"

The Chatfield connection, thought Dan, feeling a surge of anger for the man and sorrow for his beautiful ill-fated stepdaughter, Kim. Chatfield was a self-made millionaire who owned a stable of boxers and treated them as if he were a Roman patrician and they his gladiators. Because his eighteen-year-old stepdaughter had dared defy him and fall in love with a slum-bred boxer like Rick, he had ordered him beaten to death.

Lem Harper had long suspected that Chatfield was behind the murder and Kim later confirmed this to Dan at the end of their tumultuous love affair. So Chatfield had sent the same two thugs to silence him. But this time they'd failed. In one of the most reckless acts of his life, Dan had escaped, killing D'Mata in the process and setting up his partner, Turk, for Lem to eliminate later on.

If Chatfield had not suffered a stroke shortly thereafter, which totally invalided him, Lem would've killed him too. Kim had not fared much better. Dan had read of her two failed marriages and occasional drunk-driving arrests in the newspaper but made no attempt to see her again. Then fifteen years ago, he had heard from a mutual friend that Kim had died of liver failure in Rio de Janeiro. Her death, much as it saddened him, eased Dan's guilt over the grief he had caused her and nearly erased the entire episode from his mind.

"Chatfield was responsible for all of it," he told Jimmy. "But it's too long and involved a tale to go into now. So let's save it for Friday, okay? I'll tell you the whole thing then."

Jimmy shook his head in wonder. "Sounds like some yarn, Doctor! I can hardly wait to hear it. Nora too, I'll bet."

"Yeah," Dan said dully. "It was through Rick I met Lem Harper. You know, that brilliant black professor you've heard me talk about. Even though Rick was white, the two of them were childhood buddies, almost like brothers." Dan paused thoughtfully. "You don't think this FBI thing is connected with my work in Mississippi, do you?"

Jimmy deliberated briefly and shook his head. "I doubt it. That's pretty much public knowledge, I'd say. Especially after that book you wrote about it. Anything unusual happen to you down there that didn't go in the book?"

"Nothing earthshaking."

"You sure?" Jimmy persisted. "Some pretty strange things have happened since."

"Like what?"

"Like those four Southern sheriffs being blinded a couple of years ago. Two in Mississippi, as I recall." Jimmy shuddered with revulsion. "That sure as hell was a demented thing to do. Not only the work of a madman, but of a medically trained one too."

"What makes you say that?" said Dan, surprised.

"Because of how it was done. The FBI never publicized it, but they're virtually certain a laser beam blinded those men."

"Yeah, I've heard that." Dan shrugged. "It's just rumor. Besides, it doesn't take a doctor to know how to operate a laser. Almost anybody could've done it."

"Not quite anybody. For one thing, the guy had to be a fanatic. A black fanatic, most likely, and one who knew his psychology. Knew what a devastating impact blindness has on a man's masculinity."

"That's one I never heard before. How do you know that?"

" 'Cause I almost went blind myself once. And puny kid that I was, I tried to build myself up by weight-lifting at the 'Y'. I was really amazed how many blind guys worked out regularly down there until I finally got up the nerve to ask one about it and he explained it to me."

"Explained what?" Dan asked.

"That even though they couldn't see their bulging muscles, the stronger they got the better they could defend themselves if they had to, and it gave their girlfriends something to admire. Those were their two big hang-ups: self-defense and women. So whoever blinded those swaggering, he-man sheriff-types knew that; knew what a terrible psychological blow it would be to them. Which it was! Every cop south of the Mason-Dixon line was a nervous wreck for months afterward. I know. I was on a story down in Jackson around then and it's all they talked about. As one deputy sheriff told me, 'Keerist, I'd rather have some crazy nigger cut my nuts off than blind me!' That's how they had it figured—the work of a cop-hating madman. But if you ask me, Dan, it was planned; it was a calculated form of intimidation, and no matter how sick-minded, it worked. There was a lot less harassment of black voters by red-neck lawmen the next election. Not like the first few times Evers ran for office in Mississippi. Tell me again how you got involved with him? You were a little vague about that in your book."

"Through this Lem Harper. He and Charles Evers were buddies. And one day Lem phoned me to meet him in Fayette at some music festival. So I flew down. Lem was gone when I got there, off on one of his mysterious junkets, but he left word with Charles Evers to look out for me. This was right after Evers's big breakthrough in getting elected mayor of Fayette, and in the week I spent there he really opened my eyes to the unbelievably bad medical care—if you can even call it that—blacks in Mississippi were getting. But you know all that. You read my book."

Jimmy smiled. "Yeah, I reviewed it for the *Globe*, remember? Got them to put it on the front page of their Sunday book section. But that was just returning a favor. Besides, it was a pretty good book. Never would've believed a doctor could be that literate."

Dan eyed him mockingly. "Don't patronize me, pal. The way I hear it, all those misspellings in your columns aren't typos. You just can't spell."

"That's right," Jimmy said cheerfully. "And neither can my copy editor."

Suddenly Dan's smile turned to a grimace as anxiety welled within him. "For God's sake, Jimmy," he pleaded, "don't hold out on me. What the hell could the FBI be after? You must have *some* clue."

Jimmy scowled. "Nope. Not a one. But I'll try again today. Get ahold of Herb Boyers, the congressional liaison with the FBI, and find out what he knows. You're not really all that worried, are you, Dan?"

"Damned right, I am! It's bad enough to have the AMA and practically every Southern senator lined up against me! Now the FBI?"

"Could be just a fishing expedition," Jimmy suggested.

"Well, even if it is, the President would know. Given them the go-ahead. That's what really gripes me. Why put the FBI on me when all he has to do is pick up the phone and ask me whatever he wants to know?"

"Probably because he wants to use it to keep you in line. Maybe make you drop your objections to the way he's cutting costs on National Health Insurance. Or your reservations over Health Maintenance Organizations. Who knows why he wants it? But that's how the game is played, you know. You're not dealing with doctors-turned-politicians now, Dan. You're dealing with consummate pros! And their politics can be downright cutthroat in an election year. Except for putting a few curbs on how far they could go, Watergate didn't change that."

"No, I suppose not. Still, you'd of thought Nels could've—"

"Could've what?" Jimmy cut in sharply. "Nels is the President's man, not yours! And don't you forget it. Even if he did sponsor you for the job, you can't count on him for a damn thing. In fact, now that your reputation's come under something of a cloud, he's probably backing off fast, trying to put some distance between the two of you. If push comes to shove he'll recommend the President drop you faster than Nixon dropped John Knowles."

Dan nodded glumly. "Damn it!" he muttered. "If only I had an inkling of what they're after, I might not be so uptight about it."

"You want the job that badly?"

"Not at first, I didn't. It just flattered me. You know how they soften you up: the phone calls asking your advice about this and that, the increasing mentions in the press, all the little personal touches. Then capping it off with the invitation to dinner at the White House. Even Kris enjoyed that. But she wasn't taken in by any of it for a minute. Told me I'd be a fool to even think twice about the job. That even if I got it, the political pros in the health field would chew me up alive. I should've listened."

"Then why didn't you?" After Nora, Jimmy considered Kris the most intelligent and appealing woman he knew. Her separation from Dan grieved him deeply.

"Why? The challenge, I guess. The fact that I'm pushing fifty and it's the top job in medicine; my one chance to make a lasting contribution to the profession. Hell, I almost flunked out of medical school, remember? It took me a long time to convince myself I even belonged in the doctor business, let alone that I was any good. If it hadn't been for Gundersen—" Dan paused to look up at his former mentor's portrait on the wall and suddenly went groggy with fatigue. He stumbled back against his desk, steadied himself, and, waving Jimmy off, sank into the leather-upholstered swivel chair.

"You know, Jimmy," he said after a moment, "I sometimes wonder who the hell I really am. No, I mean it. Maybe it sounds self-pitying, but I've hardly ever done anything for myself—always as a reaction to someone else. When we were kids, it was my brother Pete, not me, who wanted to be the doctor; would have too, if he hadn't been killed in World War II. Then after all the slaughter I saw in Korea, I started thinking that way myself. But even in medical school I didn't set my sights too high. I would've been content to be a good GP. Then I met Gundersen, grew to admire his skill so much that I followed him around like a puppy dog trying to model myself after him. When he ditched me, sent me packing off to Springfield like he did, I vowed I'd show the bastard up. Be an even better internist than he was someday." An irrepressible yawn overcame and silenced Dan. Was it his torpor, his fuzzy-headed fatigue, that was making him so talkative, he wondered. He hardly ever talked this revealingly to anybody, even Jimmy, his closest friend. It wasn't his nature.

"Anyway," he continued, "that gives you the picture. Marrying Kris was the one and only thing I've ever done solely for my own happiness, and I've just about blown that. So you see, Jimmy, this health job means a lot—only not for the reasons you might think. The fame and power that goes with it isn't worth shit to me. It's the work. The back-breaking work! You know how some men go to pieces under pressure? Well, I go to pieces without it. All I get from leisure time is insomnia, an unhealthy craving for sleeping pills, and a good case of the jitters. And lately it's been growing worse."

"That bad, huh?" Jimmy looked at him with perplexity and concern.

"Bad?" Dan hissed. "Yeah, it's bad. You know how I'm beginning to see myself? Like some deep-sea creature afraid to emerge from the depths into the thinner atmosphere of ordinary living for fear of collapse. Total disintegration. Why do you think I don't go back to Kris? God knows, I miss her and worry about her enough. But I can't let her see me like this. She has before and it tears her up. I've got to wait until this health post thing's settled, one way or another, so that maybe I can settle down with it. Take a vacation. See a shrink. Decide what I really want to do the rest of my life."

The next moment the phone buzzed. Dan picked it up and Jimmy saw his face brighten.

"Kit!" he exclaimed. "How the hell are you? . . . Oh, all right, I guess. . . . Yeah, tomorrow's the day, if no last-minute hitches develop. . . . Well, none that I know of for sure, but there are rumors . . . No, I haven't spoken with him lately. Freiborg either . . . When? You want me on your show Friday morning? . . . Yeah, I guess so. Here or New York? . . . No, I can fly in late Thursday evening easy enough. You free for dinner? . . . Good. . . . What hotel?" He sounded aggrieved and then grinned. "I was sort of hoping you'd offer the same arrangements as before. . . . Okay, we'll talk about it. Pick you up at your place around nine? . . . Good. See you then."

He hung up the phone and turned to Jimmy. "Kit Colbine," he said needlessly. "This'll make the third or fourth time she's had me on her show. We're old friends."

"So I gather," Jimmy said dryly.

"Old *platonic* friends," insisted Dan, remembering

Jimmy's puritanical streak. "More coffee?" he said to change the subject.

Jimmy glanced at his watch. "No, thanks. I better be getting out to the airport. If I'm going to be any help to you, I ought to get on it right away. I'll phone you the minute I come up with anything. Where'll you be, here or at home?"

"Home, most likely. I'm going to try and catch some sleep if I can wind things up here."

"Good. I hope you do. You look ready for the intensive care unit yourself. Oh, by the way," he said as Dan walked him to the door, "anybody on your staff looking after Charles Cheverton these days?"

"Cheverton? Let me think. . . . He used to be a patient of Gundersen's, I know, since I saw him myself once when Gundersen was out of town. But I haven't heard any doctors here mention seeing him. Why? Is he sick?"

"I'm trying to find out," Jimmy said. "Appreciate it if you'd check it out for me."

"Sure. There must be a file on him someplace. You know, of course, that I can't tell you what's in it."

Jimmy nodded. "I'm not as interested in *what* ails him as I am in whether or not it could land him in the hospital in the near future. Because it's my hunch that's where he'll be. You can tell me that much, can't you?"

"I suppose," Dan said reluctantly.

"Thanks. And about dinner Friday night, think you'll be back from New York by then?"

"Should be. If not, we'll have to make it early next week. All depends . . ."

"On what?" Jimmy asked.

"The FBI. If what they turn up is damaging enough, I could have all sorts of free time ahead of me."

As they shook hands in the doorway Jimmy scrutinized his friend. The spreading crow's feet and baggy lids and open-pored, almost cobblestoned crescents of skin underlying his orbits—the encroachments of advancing years that marred Dan's handsome face—were now so accentuated by fatigue, by grayish bristles of beard shading upward into sallow cheeks and bloodshot eyes, that they gave Jimmy pause. For the first time in all the years he had known Dan he could see what old age was going to do to him. "Listen," he pleaded, "let me get to the bottom of this FBI crap. Just put it out of your mind and get a little sleep, huh?"

Chapter Eight

Following a long noon meeting with his board of trustees and a shorter one with the committee seeking a replacement for him as general director, Dan left the hospital around two o'clock and was asleep in his South Shore apartment an hour later.

At five Nels Freiborg phoned from Washington. "Dan? Did I wake you?"

"Sort of," he mumbled. "Up with a patient most of last night."

Freiborg grunted ruefully. "I wish I'd known. Haven't gotten much sleep myself lately, so I'm sorry as hell for disturbing yours. Also for what I'm about to spring on you. It's awfully short notice, I realize, but could you possibly fly down to Washington for a meeting tomorrow afternoon?"

"Tomorrow! What kind of meeting? With whom?"

"Oh, a few people. Nothing for you to sweat over, I assure you."

"Then why *am* I sweating?" Dan's thick-tongued sleepiness was gone now and his voice hard-edged. "Look, Nels, even if it is short notice I can come to Washington if you really feel it's necessary. But there are one or two matters I want cleared up first."

"Like why the FBI is investigating you so intensively?" Freiborg said, deftly anticipating him.

"Yeah. For openers."

"Fair enough, Dan. That's what the meeting's about. Only it's something I'll have to explain in person. I'm not at liberty to discuss it over the phone."

"Oh, come on, Nels!" he fumed. "Even if I don't have the vaguest idea what's going on, I can't believe national security is involved."

"I'm afraid," Freiborg told him, "that's exactly what is involved."

The measured words, momentarily stunned Dan, making him press the phone receiver tighter against his ear. The notion that he or any of his close friends were security risks seemed so implausible as to be absurd. But it was also frightening. Freiborg, a tough-minded Swede, was neither an alarmist nor a man given to overstatement, and hearing it from him sent a spurt of bitter bile up Dan's throat. "I see," he muttered, trying to collect his thoughts, coax Nels into telling him more. "Then it has nothing to do with my nomination, I take it?"

"No," said Freiborg. "Not directly. The President still plans to announce it in the morning as scheduled. In fact, the press release has already been sent out."

Dan sighed audibly. "Well, that's a relief. All right, tell me when and where you want me tomorrow and I'll be there."

"Four P.M. The old Justice Department building on Ninth and Pennsylvania. The FBI Director prefers his former quarters there to his new ones in the J. Edgar Hoover building. Call my office in the morning to let me know when your flight gets in. I'll try to meet you at National myself to fill you in a little ahead of time. But in case I can't, I'll send a limousine and you come on along."

"Okay," Dan agreed reluctantly.

"One more thing," Freiborg hastily added. "I'd just as soon you keep our meeting place a secret. If your secretary needs to get hold of you, have her call my office."

"Jesus, Nels! Now I'm really chewing my nails. Don't tell me the AMA has a contract out on me?"

Dan expected his quip to at least draw a chuckle, but Freiborg replied soberly, "No, not on *you,* they haven't . . . Now go on back to sleep. I'll see you tomorrow, Dan."

Before he could call out for Nels to wait, not hang up on such a mystifying note, the line went dead.

Slowly Dan sank down on his bed, still holding the

receiver. Had it finally happened, he wondered: had some critical limit of collective tension been exceeded and everybody in Washington gone mad? What could Nels possibly mean about the AMA? For all Dan's differences with them he considered the AMA an honorable organization, composed of decent, responsible men and women. And even though the money squeeze on federal reimbursement of physicians' fees was making the AMA look increasingly like just another trade union, the notion that its leaders might try to eliminate anybody, other than politically, was laughable. So what the hell was Nels hinting at? And how could it possibly involve national security?

Dan had barely hung up the phone when it rang again. He recognized the caller by his distinctive voice: courtly, wheezy Dr. Wiley Weathersby, retired Louisiana surgeon and vice chairman of the AMA Board of Trustees.

"Dr. Lassiter, sir," he drawled breathlessly. "Sorry to disturb you at home, but your secretary thought you might just want to hear from me."

"I do, indeed," Dan answered politely, wondering what the elderly, emphysematous, gray eminence of the AMA's reactionary wing wanted. His first name fit him well; he was as sly and cunning a political animal as ever lived, Dan knew. The two of them had clashed many times in policy-making councils of the AMA though never head-on, face to face. It wasn't Weathersby's style. He preferred to sit back, puffing and hacking on his corncob, while his well-rehearsed stooges spoke for him. For Wiley to call him directly could only mean that he had heard the rumors about the FBI and was hastening to take advantage of his vulnerability.

Or so Dan surmised as he patiently waited for Weathersby to gather the breath to continue.

"Well, first of all, Dr. Lassiter, let me compliment you on your fine performance before our board yesterday morning. Yes, sir, I want to personally commend you for your courtesy in flying all that way just to talk to us and for the deep understanding you showed for our side of the issues. Oh, you know how us old-timers like to put labels on people, particularly you young ones. But you certainly convinced me you were no flaming liberal. Not when it comes to preserving the integrity of our noble profession, you're not! You surely put my fears to rest on that score."

"Thank you, Dr. Weathersby," said Dan, stifling a yawn. "I'm glad to hear that."

"Well, even though we've seldom seen eye to eye on things, the program you outlined seemed to me like it had the makings of a pretty fair compromise. And when I got through telling my wife, Martha, about it, why she thought so too. Martha runs her own doctors' investment counseling outfit here in N'Orleans, so she understands about these things. I even told Martha that we needed an energetic, fair-minded man like you looking after our interests in Washington and you know what she told me? She said, 'Wiley, if you think he's the right man for the job, why don't you help him get it?' Well, as you can imagine, that took a little ponderin'. There's more separatin' us than you being an internist and me a surgeon. Still and all, I told myself, anyone who can run one of our country's finest private hospitals as well as you, can probably do just as good a job nationally, given half a chance. But I guess I don't need to remind you, Dr. Lassiter, you got some powerful enemies."

"No," Dan sighed. "You don't."

"Well, don't you go losin' heart, 'cause you also got some powerful friends. Me, among them. Yes, sir! Though I know damned well it'll raise a few eyebrows, I intend to help you—if you'll let me."

"And how's that?" asked Dan, bracing himself.

"Any way I can, Dr. Lassiter. Any way I can. But I just don't swing the same kind of weight with the organization like I used to. I'm too damned old. You know, well as me, that the only reason they've kept me on as vice chairman is in deference to my past services. Oh, I'm not totally without resources, understand? There's still more'n a few on that board owe me favors. But I'm like an old bulldog who's lost his bite. I'm not the man who can help you the most."

"I'm sorry about that, Dr. Weathersby."

"No more than me. Nothin' I'd like better than to pack my bag and go to Washington to help you fight all those Socialists in the Congress. But even if I'm no longer fit to do that myself, I know just the man who can."

"And who might that be?"

"Why, my nephew Emory. You know Dr. Emory Oswell, of course, but maybe you didn't know we were kin. Well, we are. He's Martha's sister's boy. And we're all mighty proud of Emory. Not only is he past president of the Dade County Medical Society, but in line for the presidency of his State Society. Especially after that fine job he did of making sure all those Florida doctors met them new relicensing requirements. You agree he did a fine job there, don't you?"

Dan almost laughed out loud. The Florida Legislature had been one of the nation's first to pass a medical relicensing law based on the Canadian model: one that required each physician to show proof that he had taken a minimum of fifty hours of continuing medical education courses annually or else take a recertification exam every five years to demonstrate his competence. And much as individual members of the Florida State Medical Society railed at the statute, their leaders remained curiously mute. The relicensing requirement was the price the legislature had exacted from them in return for some desperately needed reforms in the state's malpractice code. But to make sure the new law did not curtail the livelihood of more than a flagrantly errant few, the medical society got the Governor to appoint Oswell chairman of the Florida Board of Registration in Medicine. In this capacity he and his cronies on the board judged which physicians had kept up their medical education and which had fallen short, thereby subjecting themselves to the risks of the recertification exam. This they had done, discharging their duty with dispatch and with results that reflected an extraordinary degree of compliance among Florida's doctors or else an extraordinary tolerance by the Oswell-led board. Out of 12,800 physicians in the state, a mere two hundred or so had failed to qualify for relicensing. And nearly ninety percent of those failing were foreign-trained doctors, mostly Cubans, which implied a bias bordering on bigotry on the part of the board members.

These results were officially known only to the National Board of Medical Examiners of which Dan was a member. When they were released to the public, they were bound to cause a furor. It was already rumored that Oswell had taken bribes or sought political preferment, and with the storm about to break over his head Dan could easily understand why he might want to find a post outside of Florida.

"Well," Weathersby went on, "I know how you're always harping on our need to police ourselves, make sure we keep up-to-date on medical advances, and Emory certainly has a lot of experience in that field."

"He certainly has," Dan agreed readily. Just as Willie Sutton had a lot of experience in the banking business. "And—uh—how do you suggest I make best use of it, Dr. Weathersby?"

"Why, by appointing Emory your right-hand man, Deputy Secretary of Health. He'd sure hate leaving his Florida home and that wonderful practice he's built up, but I just know he'll do it if you ask him. He's got a real sense of duty, that boy."

"I'm sure he does. Well, thanks for the suggestion, Dr. Weathersby. I must admit that your nephew never occurred to me as a possible candidate for that slot, but now that you've brought him to my attention, I'll certainly give it serious consideration."

"Well, now," said Weathersby, "to tell the truth, I was sort of countin' on you being a mite more definite . . . If you know what I mean?"

"I'm afraid not," Dan answered. "But maybe that's because I'm so bushed after being up with a patient all night that I'm not thinking too clearly. So suppose you spell it out."

Weathersby hesitated. "This little talk of ours isn't being tape-recorded by any chance, is it?"

"No, not by me, it isn't! You have my word on that."

"And I accept it," Weathersby replied after a particularly sonorous wheeze, rattling cough, and gruff throat-clearing. "Well, I guess what I'm proposing is a little horse trade. Promise me you'll appoint Emory your deputy and I'll promise you the backing of the AMA Board of Trustees. Their full endorsement. In fact, I'll even get them to announce it right after the President formally nominates you. After that you'll be a shoo-in."

"That's promising a lot, Dr. Weathersby. You sure you can deliver?"

"Sure as I am this emphysema of mine's going to kill me. Ain't nothin' surer than that," he cackled.

"All right," said Dan, wondering if Weathersby still held that much sway with the board and why a man of his reputed craftiness would make so blatant a proposition, yet curious to know what his alternatives might be. "Suppose I agree to go along with your little horse trade. What guarantee do you have that I'll keep my end of the deal once I'm confirmed?"

"Oh, come now, Dr. Lassiter," Weathersby purred. "If I didn't think you were a gentleman of your word I wouldn't be wasting my breath on you. I don't have it to waste."

"No, I suppose not. Well, Dr. Weathersby, since you trust me that much, the least I can do is be equally forthright with you. As of right now, I'd have to say your nephew would be my second choice for deputy."

"Ahem . . . I see . . . And who, if I might be so bold to ask, would be your first?"

"My first is Dr. Cottrell."

"Cottrell! Why he's in jail on income tax fraud."

"That's right. If I really wanted a crook for my deputy, I'd just as soon have a seasoned one."

Weathersby's loud harrumph was all Dan could have hoped for. "I'm afraid I fail to see the humor in that," he said stiffly.

"That's too bad. Because I've certainly seen the humor in your proposal."

"You are makin' a *big* mistake, sir," Weathersby growled between wheezes.

"I probably am. But so are you. You're assuming I want that job so badly I'm willing to go to almost any lengths to get it, and that's a faulty assumption."

"That so? Well, whether it is or isn't, we've got you blocked and you know it. I just hope you accept defeat more gracefully than that fellow Knowles did."

"Don't count on it," Dan replied coldly. "But if you really think you've got me blocked, you'd better let the President know to save him future embarrassment."

"The President will know soon enough. If he announces your nomination after what our friends in Congress are prepared to tell him, he's a bigger fool than you are. But look here . . . Maybe I'm just raising your hackles by pushing you too hard and too fast on somethin' this delicate. Why don't you mull it over awhile. Give me your answer in the morning?"

"No, thanks, Dr. Weathersby. I'm not so sleepy that I can't tell a shady deal when I hear one, and come tomorrow morning I might be so mad I'd forget to be civil. So consider this answer final and spend your time on the President. Tell your nephew Emory that I don't really have any use for his type of talent, and tell Mrs. Weathersby, with all respect, that I'm beyond help. Some people are, you know."

"Yup, some are," Weathersby agreed with surprising tranquility. "It's an impossible job anyway, Dr. Lassiter. Didn't matter in the least who you made your deputy. But I guess you've already given up hope of gettin' it."

"Wrong again," Dan said. "All I've given up is a chance to get it the easy way. But thanks all the same for making me feel so virtuous. I know I'll sleep better because of it. Good night, Dr. Weathersby."

Dan did not gloat as he hung up the phone. Even if he had been tempted to, Weathersby's parting sigh stopped him. The sigh was a summing up, not of their conversation, but of the man: the indescribable weariness in his voice; the murmur of approaching death in his every breath; the cruel curse of a still agile mind slowly being suffocated by a diseased, decrepit body. I was wrong about him, Dan realized: Weathersby doesn't know about the FBI investigation. His wife probably pressured him into making the call to help her bumbling nephew and in the process he had committed a humiliating blunder. The old fox had finally been run to ground.

From Kinsella to Weathersby, all his ancient adversaries seemed to be dropping, Dan reflected. He derived no solace from the thought. A man's enemies helped define his goals, his convictions, his competitive edge, and he felt diminished by their loss. It also depressed him to realize how little he had learned from Weathersby's call. It clarified nothing, not even what pressures the AMA might bring to bear.

Yawning deeply, Dan rubbed his eyes and gave up conjecturing. All that seemed worth deciding now was whether to get up, make coffee, and read, or take sleeping pills and go back to bed.

He called the hospital to check on Matt Kinsella, make reasonably certain there would be no immediate need for his services. Then he called Kris, assuring himself she was all right and promising to visit her when he got back from Washington. Finally he rummaged in his medicine chest for a near-empty bottle of Dalmane and swallowed four 30-milligram tablets, twice the recommended dose.

Strangely, when he slept this time, he dreamed of bicycling through the verdant Berkshire Hills surrounding his hometown of Williamstown, Massachusetts, in the company of a five- or six-year-old boy. Whether the child was his own son or someone else's was never made clear, and there were other indefinable aspects to the dream: a clarity of detail and yet an otherworldliness about it, a world he had never before inhabited, even in fantasy. Yet the outing with the boy was so pleasant that Dan wished it could go on and on, relinquishing the dream images reluctantly after the bright morning sun on his closed lids had wakened him.

PART TWO

"DEVIL-A"

Chapter Nine

Hot, humid air enveloped Dan as he descended the Whisperjet ramp at Washington's National Airport. He almost felt smothered by it. Rivulets of sweat stung his eyes and wilted his shirt collar as he crossed the fifty yards of tarmac to the terminal building. He had forgotten what a sweatbox Washington was in the summer. But the weather did not irritate him nearly as much as his discovery at the gate that Nels Freiborg had sent one of his laconic underlings to meet him. Any of a number of reasons could have prevented Nels from coming, but to Dan the most likely was that he meant to keep him in suspense till the last minute. Jimmy was right: the FBI did not have the slightest shred of incriminating evidence against him. It was all a setup, a devious Washington-style tactic to intimidate him into tractability; make him amenable to compromise or outright surrender on certain key health issues.

He had spoken to Jimmy twice since last seeing him, early this morning and five minutes ago from an airport pay phone. Between calls, Jimmy had doggedly made the rounds of offices, bars, and other oases of information. He had even met clandestinely with two high-level officials, one from Justice, the other from the Attorney General's office. But none of it revealed what if anything the FBI had on him. I'll know soon enough, Dan thought gloomily as the car he rode in crept through downtown Washington traffic and pulled up in front of the old Justice Department building on the corner of Ninth and Pennsylvania.

A blue-uniformed security guard at the reception desk telephoned word of Dan's arrival to somebody, and another security guard escorted him to a fourth-floor suite of offices where he used his passkey to admit him to its anteroom. The door to an inner office was closed and the guard did not approach it. Politely he asked Dan to wait until someone came for him, and departed.

Another time the room might have interested Dan. A long, glass-topped case contained such relics of past FBI triumphs as John Dillinger's plaster death mask and the hollowed-out nickel in which Soviet masterspy Colonel Rudolph Abel had concealed strips of microfilm. But Dan was too edgy now. He had pushed himself hard to make the early afternoon flight from Boston for this 4:00 P.M. meeting, and he resented being made to wait while those inside were probably concocting some last-minute strategy to use against him.

At last the inner door swung open and Nels Freiborg bustled out. "Dan!" he cried heartily. "Good to see you!"

Dan eyed him critically as they shook hands. From his hypertensive coloring to his stocky build and Type-A-plus personality, Freiborg was a textbook example of the coronary-prone male. He was also a masterful, totally dedicated public servant. Dan gave him that, whether he was now friend or foe.

If Freiborg sensed the coolness in Dan's greeting he did not show it. "Hey, I almost forgot!" he exclaimed. "Congratulations on your nomination! The President announced it at the end of his noon news conference. You're not in yet, of course—you still have a tough senatorial confirmation hearing to get through—but at least you've got a foot in the door."

"Thanks," said Dan dryly. "That's *one* door. Now suppose you tell me what's behind the one you just came out of?"

"Oh, that." Freiborg shrugged. "Nothing much, I hope. I tried to meet you at National to fill you in a bit. Honest, I did! Trouble was, too many things came up at the President's press conference that he wanted dealt with right away, and I couldn't get free. But now that you're here I'll let the FBI Director do the explaining. C'mon in and I'll introduce you."

Dan followed Freiborg through the door and across forty feet of deep-pile carpeting to where the FBI Director sat behind a huge mahogany desk with miniature furled American flags at each end and a replica of the FBI seal in the center.

The FBI Director was a craggy-faced, barrel-chested Irishman in his early sixties with an easy smile and a paunch he seldom bothered to suck in or conceal under a suit jacket. Dan had heard that he was extroverted, fair-minded, and unflappable in crises. But as he came closer he spotted the same telltale look in the Director's eyes that he found endemic among high government officials these days, particularly those responsible for the public safety and well-being. It was a weary, lusterless, take-one-problem-and-one-day-at-a-time look—as sure a sign of an overstressed nervous system as jaundice was of an overstressed liver.

The FBI Director stood up and smiled as Dan approached. Two other men rose too: a youngish one with red hair and a swimmer's broad-shouldered tapering build; the other nearer Dan's age, slim and poised-looking in his scholarly wire-rim glasses, hand-knotted bow tie, and Paisley jacket. Dan studied their faces, recognizing neither. Looking past them, he caught sight of a carousel slide projector on one end of a long conference table and its viewing screen on the far wall.

"Well, Dr. Lassiter," the FBI Director said, crunching Dan's knuckles in his calloused, ex-farmboy's hand. "Pleasure to meet you. This young fellow here is Darryl MacBride, head of our special projects section, and this guy who won't take his jacket off to let us see what hardware he's toting is Gus Damon, deputy director of the CIA."

"CIA, eh?" Dan said doubtfully.

"That's right, Dr. Lassiter." Damon gave him a limp handshake. "I gather you're not exactly sure you approve of my being here. Don't feel bad. You react the way most people do nowadays."

"And how's that?" asked Dan.

"Nobody likes us anymore. We're the snoopers and the bumblers. I usually tell people at cocktail parties

I'm an Internal Revenue agent. That keeps them from snickering behind my back. Anyway, nice to meet you. To prove I'm a regular guy, I might even try to wangle some free medical advice from you before we part. What's your specialty?"

"Internal medicine. What's your problem?"

"My specialty. Counterintelligence."

"Can I offer you something, Dr. Lassiter?" the FBI Director interjected. "Iced tea or a soft drink?" From the edge in his voice, Dan got the impression he did not care for Damon's banter either.

"No, thanks," Dan said. "All I really want is an explanation."

"Fair enough. Why don't you sit here?" The FBI Director pointed to a chair at the near end of the conference table. "And we'll get started." He pushed a button on the wall that automatically drew the window drapes and darkened the room. "Ready, Mac?"

"Ready, sir!" the FBI agent replied.

Dan blinked as a bright-colored slide flashed on the screen and the towering figure of Lem Harper loomed up before him. Lem was standing under the arched entrance of Nairobi University, looking curiously professorial with a briefcase in one hand and an umbrella in the other. Beside him stood Kenya's late political genius Tom Mboya with his distinctively boyish face. Mboya was smiling; Lem, his eyes squinting from the bright sun, characteristically was not.

Except for the squint, Dan mused, Lem's bulging, mud-brown eyes would likely show the same look of grim resolution he had seen and suffered so many times in the past, particularly in the early days before Dan learned what a serious and single-minded man Lem was.

"Do you know the man on the left, Dr. Lassiter?" MacBride asked.

"Does he have a name?" Dan said so testily it surprised even him.

"He has," MacBride said. "Several."

"Several, huh? Give me one."

"Well, no disrespect intended, Dr. Lassiter," the FBI agent said pointedly, "but that's a jumbo-sized Nigra up there on the screen and if you know who he is we'd prefer you tell us."

"A jumbo-sized what—?" Dan demanded harshly. "What'd you call him? Nig-ra?"

"Well, yes. That's what we call them back home."

"Is that so? And I'll bet the folks still call you a G-man back home. Nowadays, though, people that color have made it clear they prefer to be called blacks. Maybe 'cause it's less likely to get mispronounced that way."

Stiffening, the FBI agent looked to his boss for guidance. "All right, Mac," the Director said mildly, "you stand corrected. Now tell Dr. Lassiter his name and let's get on with it."

"Yes, sir!" MacBride snapped. "The man's name is Lemuel Duvalier Harper, a black, native-born American male, age 51. Do you know him, Dr. Lassiter?"

"I know a Lem Harper," Dan said casually, "and that's either him or his twin."

"How well do you know him, Dan?" asked Freiborg.

Dan turned to him with a derisive stare. "Is that what this is about, Nels? All the secrecy surrounding this meeting, the mysterious murmurings about national security—how well I know a black man named Lem Harper?"

"He's no ordinary black, Dan," Freiborg explained. "Not ordinary at all—as you're about to learn. In fact, he's got us all worried as hell. But that *is* what this meeting's about."

Dan sighed exasperatedly. "Well, in that case you can relax, Nels. I don't know a damn thing about Lem Harper that worries me in the least. I haven't seen nor heard from him in years. So if you're afraid my knowing him might make the Senate Finance Committee consider me unfit to be Secretary of Health, forget it!"

"Well, that's reassuring," Freiborg said. "But let's backtrack a little. You won't mind answering a few questions about your relationship, will you?"

Dan shrugged. "What do you want to know?"

"Suppose you start by telling us when and how you two met?"

Dan answered the when almost immediately. The *how* stuck in his throat.

"So it was back in '54," Freiborg mused, "which is a fair length of time. But we're still a little curious about *how* you met. I'd appreciate your telling us that too."

"No big mystery. A mutual friend introduced us."

"What friend?"

"A musician named George Robinson," Dan lied. It couldn't possibly matter to them, he reasoned, that he had sought Lem out to satisfy his obsessive curiosity about his cadaver, and he did not deign to divulge it. "George had a Dixieland combo that used to play at a long-gone Boston nightspot called the Savoy. I kept dropping in to listen. So did Lem. Eventually George introduced us. That's about it."

MacBride spoke up, "You sure? I'm not doubting your word or anything, but from what we know of Harper, he's a real loner. He doesn't make friends—even black friends—easily. So how come he chose you?"

Dan glared at him. Tact certainly wasn't MacBride's strong suit. Impulsively he asked, "Do you like Bach?"

"What?"

"Bach," Dan repeated patiently. "The composer, not the beer."

"Oh, *that* Bach!" MacBride sounded perplexed. "Yeah, I guess so. Much as I like any organ music. Only I fail to see what—"

Dan cut him off. "To answer your question: Both Lem Harper and I were Korean War vets. Both of us liked Dixieland music and hung out at the Savoy. I don't exactly know why he took a shine to me—maybe because I was studying medicine and he had a natural interest in that subject after getting shot up in Korea and damned near dying of a bone infection as a result. Or maybe it was my winning ways. I never asked. I liked him because he was smart and opened my eyes to a few things."

"We know he's smart," Freiborg affirmed. "Too damned smart! He seems to know a hell of a lot more about us—right down to the time we put the cat out of the White House at night—than we do about him. That's why we asked you here. It has nothing to do with your nomination. Maybe later on it will, as I'll explain, but right now it doesn't. We simply have to know more about Lem Harper than we do, and you just happen to be one of the few people we can ask. So please don't be offended, and don't spare the details. Okay?"

Dan hesitated. He felt adrift in confusion about this intense interest in Lem, with Freiborg's attempts at clarification his only compass points. Finally he sighed and nodded. "All right, Nels, ask away."

"You say Harper opened your eyes to a few things. What kind?"

"Black-white relationships mainly. It was because of him that I got involved with Charles Evers back in '69. I made my first trip down to Fayette more or less as a favor to Lem."

"Did you and Harper meet down there?"

"We were supposed to, but after setting it up Lem suddenly got called away. Even Evers didn't know where."

"When was the last time you *did* see him, Dan?"

"In April 1972. I can be exact about the date since Kris and I were on our Paris honeymoon at the time. Lem couldn't make it all the way from Kenya to Boston for the wedding, so we met there instead. We all had dinner together. Talked most of the night."

"About what?" Freiborg pressed.

"Oh, Christ!" Dan groaned. "That's hard to pinpoint after so long. About all I remember is kidding him about his professorship in political science at the University of Nairobi and being kidded back for marrying a woman doctor smarter than me."

Suddenly Damon, who had been slumped in his chair sucking on an unlit pipe, perked up. "Did Harper tell you how he happened to get his professorship?"

"Not in so many words," Dan admitted. "But I knew

that after serving in Korea he'd spent several years as a troubleshooter for Kenyatta and that, plus his voracious reading habits, made him a natural to teach. So I just assumed that's how it came about."

"I see," said Damon, resting his chin on his clasped hands and giving Dan a searching look. "Then you didn't know he was considered one of the world's foremost revolutionary theorists by that time? Certainly the top black theorist. That while jokers like Carmichael and Brown were trying to incite riots, and passions in their white girlfriends, your friend Harper was being invited to address the Politburo in China and North Korea. You knew none of this, Dr. Lassiter?"

"No, I didn't," Dan said, shaken. "I'm not even sure I know it for a fact now."

"Oh, it's a fact. A hard one!" Damon declared. "We have it well documented. As will soon be apparent to you, we've amassed a lot of material on Lem Harper. We keep a running check on the countries he visits and the organizations he maintains contact with. But all we've come up with so far is a series of isolated facts with no clear way to piece them together, no grand design. We know he's not after political power—he spreads himself too thin for that. Nor does he seem interested in personal gain. Apart from the house he built in Martinique he doesn't own a thing. All the planes and cars he uses for his round-the-world jaunts are borrowed. So what's he up to? We simply must know what motivates a will-of-the-wisp like him in order to predict his ultimate goal. Because it's our hunch his foreign adventures are just about over and he's coming home to stay. His next move will be aimed squarely at us and might turn out to be one of the gravest internal security threats this country has ever faced."

Dan heard the FBI Director suck in his breath and guessed Damon had gone too far. "Oh?" he said, taking quick advantage. "And what sort of threat might that be?"

The CIA official looked flustered. "Maybe I got a little ahead of myself there. If it's all the same with you,

Dr. Lassiter, I'll hold that bit of speculation in abeyance for a while."

"And if it's not all the same with me?" Dan countered.

"What Gus is trying to say," Freiborg hastily interjected, "is that we're trying to get this whole story across to you in some kind of sequence so it'll make sense. Believe me, Dan, a hell of a lot's at stake here and your cooperation is important."

"Oh, I believe you, Nels," he said wryly. "After all, this man's an old, trusted friend of mine. You wouldn't want to turn me against him or against you too early. That way I might not be so open to your questions or be so floored by the punch line you're doubtless saving for your clincher. So play it your way. You've kept me on tenterhooks for two days now; made me relive and regret every sin I've ever committed. Another few minutes isn't likely to make that much difference."

"Now look, Dan," Freiborg began, trying to sound conciliatory.

"No, you look!" Dan flared. "I may be your boy when it comes to the health post, but in all other respects I'm still a private citizen and I resent being subjected to that intensive FBI investigation you never bothered to explain. Nor do I much care for the little guessing game you've got me playing now. All these vague hints, vague threats, vague predictions. Jesus! I could get more definite information from an astrology chart!"

"Well put, Dr. Lassiter," the FBI Director said. "That happens to be my problem too. Let me give you an example. Right now the Bureau has about two hundred black agents. And you'd assume—as I did—that they're not only loyal members of this organization but knowledgeable about the nation's black community, wouldn't you? Well, this might surprise you, but when we questioned them individually, only a dozen knew Lem Harper's name. Imagine—only twelve of two hundred black agents ever heard of the man that we, along with the internal security agencies of damned near every country, consider to be one of the world's leading revolutionary experts. Now you're a doctor who knows something about human nature. Why do you suppose this is?"

Dan did not know how to answer. Were these things really true of Lem Harper? It hardly seemed possible. For years now he had considered Lem a close though seldom seen friend, and although Dan had always confided more to Lem than Lem to him, he rationalized this as a conditioned response on Lem's part: a sort of racial paranoia that kept him from totally trusting any white man. Now in view of the startling revelations these powerful men were doling out in bits and pieces, he didn't know what to think.

The FBI Director ended the silence by answering his own question. "We're not exactly sure ourselves. Either they, like most white Americans, have never heard of Lemuel 'Devil-A' Harper because he's taken great pains to keep it that way. Or else—and this I shudder to contemplate—he has so indoctrinated my black agents to his cause that they feel a stronger loyalty to it than to us or to this country. That's the horribly vague predicament I face. So share my frustration, Dr. Lassiter. And even though you've not yet been confirmed as a cabinet member, we assume you will be and intend to give you a full and complete briefing. That is, if you choose to hear it?"

The FBI Director's smile was meant to reassure Dan, to welcome him into this select, superpatriotic group of counter-conspirators, but instead it made him feel like a fly trapped in an intricate web of words. That they meant to use him more as a pawn than a partner, Dan had no doubt. "All right, gentlemen," he sighed, "let's hear what you have to say. If it turns out that my old friend, Lem Harper, represents the clear and present danger to the United States you seem to think, I'll do all I can to help you stop him."

"That's good enough for us, Dr. Lassiter," said the FBI Director. He nodded at Darryl MacBride who took a sheaf of typewritten pages from a manila envelope stamped TOP SECRET and began to read aloud: "Lemuel Duvalier Harper, also known by the code name 'Devil-A', was born in Boston, Massachusetts, in 1928. His father, a Floridian by birth and a machinist by trade, was killed in World War II. His mother—"

"Who killed him?" Dan interrupted.

The FBI agent looked up sharply. "Beg your pardon?"

"You said Lem's father was killed in World War II, right?"

"Yes, sir." The papers rustled in MacBride's hands.

"And I asked by whom? The Germans or Japanese?"

"According to our records," MacBride said stiffly, "he was killed in Louisiana."

"Louisiana! Who were we fighting down there?" Knowing from Lem the tragic and shameful circumstances of his father's death, Dan wanted to make certain they were not glossed over.

"How about it, MacBride?" asked Freiborg, perplexed by Dan's acerbity. "What's the story?"

"Well," MacBride replied, "according to the official report of the investigation board, Pvt. Joshua Harper was shot to death during an otherwise peaceful protest demonstration by black tank crews in training at Camp Claiborne, Louisiana, in 1942. The fatal bullet was fired from an army M-1, possibly discharged accidentally in the dark by an unknown sentry."

"You knew this, Dan?" Freiborg asked.

Dan nodded. "Lem's father led that protest and it worked. Virtually all the black tankers' demands for equal treatment were granted by the Inspector General's office. That enraged enough white bigots at Camp Claiborne to make Lem's father a doomed man. His death was *hardly* accidental."

"I see." Freiborg stroked his chin. "And yet he went ahead and volunteered for the Korean War. Won the Silver Star for heroism. How do you account for that?"

"Lem told me he had a white friend in his youth named Rick Ferrar; that they were close as brothers. When Rick got drafted, Lem just upped and enlisted. To be with him, I suppose."

"Hmmm," Damon muttered. "We never heard of this Rick Ferrar. What else can you tell us about him?"

Dan hesitated. "I never knew him. He was a professional boxer who died from ring injuries before I met Lem."

"But a relationship that close . . . With a white man," mused Damon. "Was it—could it possibly have been—homosexual, do you think?"

"Oh, for Chrissake, Damon!" Dan exploded. "Even if that was the least bit pertinent—which it isn't—you can't possibly believe *that's* the kind of liberation Lem Harper's dedicated his life to!"

The CIA official shrugged. "Don't take offense, Dr. Lassiter. It's a routine question. Like you asking a new female patient if she's ever had venereal disease. There's really no delicate way to put it. But to get back to the briefing . . . Harper's Korean War record is an unusual one. For example, did you know he served as a prison guard on Kojedo Island for six months?"

Dan could barely conceal his surprise. "I don't recall if he ever told me or not. But I do recall Kojedo had the reputation of being one of the worst assignments in Korea. More a punishment than a duty."

"Yes," Damon agreed. "It was that, all right. Yet the record shows Harper actually volunteered to serve there. Any ideas why?"

Dan shook his head.

"Neither have we. But we do know he got on pretty well with the Commie prisoners he guarded, including their top man, General Pak Sang Hyen. Although we have no proof that Sgt. Lemuel Harper collaborated with them in any way, evidently he and Pak struck up quite a friendship—one that has lasted to the present day. Mac, let's see the next slide."

The FBI agent clicked on the slide projector and a picture of Lem and a white-goateed Oriental in army uniform riding together in a pedicab appeared on the screen.

"We took this shot several years ago in Pyongyang," Damon explained. "The man with Harper is Pak—then as now North Korea's Defense Minister. He's a political philosopher as well as a military man: a dedicated Marxist who believes that the best hope for world Communism lies not with the bastardized Russian version, but an alliance of Africans and Asians. We have rather convincing evidence that Lem Harper was in both North Korea and mainland China that year to drum up support for the liberation movement he was helping foment in Portuguese West Africa. And there's every indication that, thanks to his old friend and mentor General Pak, he got what he wanted."

"Is that hard fact or supposition?" Dan asked.

Damon smiled tolerantly. "Let's just say it carries a high order of probability. Do you have any reason to doubt it, Dr. Lassiter?"

Dan fell silent. Lem had never once mentioned his Kojedo duty and he could understand why. Barren, overcrowded, all but lawless except for the prisoners' own kangaroo courts, the small cruciform island was not only the site of the largest POW encampment in Korea, but to its 150,000 inhabitants the very personification of hell. No halfway decent soldier was ever sent there; it was reserved for raw recruits and misfits. And although Lem's motive for serving there now seemed clear—even then he was embarked on his revolutionary mission and trying to build up his foreign contacts—he had never trusted Dan enough to explain that. It made him wonder if the close friendship they had known at the beginning would have ever come about had he not done Lem a service by accidentally killing one of the hoods who had murdered his great friend Rick.

"Didn't you say that you first met Lem Harper in late 1954?" said Damon.

Dan nodded.

"That had to be between his release from Fitzsimmons Army Hospital and his departure for Africa six months later. He landed at Mombasa where, we believe, he looked up a Chinese merchant whose import-export business was a front for East African gunrunning. Pak probably advised him to contact this man who, in turn, sent him on to Kenyatta. He became old

'Burning Spear's' trusted counselor through all the in-fighting that led to eventual Kenyan independence; became so valuable to him that in April 1966 Lemuel Harper went to Peking as Kenyatta's personal spokesman. He even got to address the Chinese Peoples Congress, an honor never before afforded a black man and certainly not a black American. With the example of the Belgian Congo bloodbath to point to, he managed to persuade the Chinese that the stability Kenyatta offered would be more valuable to them in the long run than any ideological advantage from Kenyatta's Communist rivals. That's a brief summary of why Lemuel Duvalier Harper is so highly regarded in East Africa."

Dan slowly shook his head as the CIA deputy director spoke, wondering if he knew the Lem Harper who was the confidant of high Communist and African leaders at all. He watched numbly as Damon showed slides of Lem with Kenyatta in Nairobi, with Mobutu in Kinshasha, with Zambian President Kenneth Kaunda, at a futile peace conference with Rhodesia's Ian Smith, with Mozambique President Samora Machel in riot-torn Lourenço Marques, on and on. However much Damon might exaggerate his political influence, there could be no doubting Lem's ubiquitous African activities.

Damon paused to sip water and continued, "Which brings us to some of Lemuel Harper's suspected terrorist acts here at home. But I'll let Mac tell you about that since his men did the investigating."

The next picture flashed on the screen was a police mug shot—front view and profile—of a man whose identity read: Hubbard "Hub" Bryson, Sheriff, Birmingham County, Alabama, and it made Dan wince. With the corneas of his eyes clouded, Bryson was obviously blind.

"Two summers ago," MacBride said, "four Southern sheriffs were mysteriously blinded. Maybe you heard about it, Dr. Lassiter."

"I read the newspapers," Dan said curtly.

"Each man," MacBride informed him, "was heavily

drugged beforehand. They never saw or heard anything: no warnings, no threats, nothing! All were bachelors who lived alone. Three owned watchdogs, but they were poisoned. From what little they could tell us, each went to sleep the night before with perfectly good eyesight and woke up blind. That's it! We examined an eye from one after infection necessitated its removal, and its entire central retina was congealed. All the pathologists we've consulted agree only a laser beam could produce such a lesion, Dr. Lassiter, so we're certain that's how it was done."

"But what makes you think Lem Harper had anything to do with it?" Dan demanded.

"Nobody said he did," Damon interjected.

"No, but Lem Harper has been the sole topic of discussion for over an hour now and suddenly you show me this sadistically blinded policeman. Either there's a connection, or your job's made you so schizoid you're suffering flight of ideas."

Damon smiled thinly. "Lemual Harper usually travels with his own private physician, a Dr. David Farragut Brattle. Do you know him, Dr. Lassiter?"

"No, never met the man. But I've heard about him from friends of Lem. A black surgeon, isn't he?"

"He *was* a surgeon," Damon replied. "A brilliant one who graduated near the top of his class at Howard and took his surgical training at the Medical College of Virginia. Afterward he came back here to practice: teaching appointment at Howard, surgical privileges at D.C. General and Washington Center Hospital, a thriving referral practice. Then calamity struck. His mother, to whom he was devoted, was accidentally killed in the rioting that followed Martin Luther King's assassination, struck by a hail of police bullets in her top-floor apartment during a shoot-out with snipers trapped on the roof. Brattle suffered a severe nervous breakdown after that. Spent three months in St. Elizabeth's mumbling incoherently about retribution. Seems he felt his mother's death was all his fault for selfishly trying to better himself instead of his people. Apparently to someone with Brattle's deep religious convictions, his mother's slaying so soon after King's, his spiritual father, proved God had singled him out for punishment. Finally he calmed down enough to be released from the hospital, but he never went back to his old life. Abandoned his black wife and three kids, gave up his surgical practice and began working emergency rooms around town, particularly those treating a lot of street shootings and knifings."

"So?" said Dan, impatient for Damon to make his point. "More than one doctor's doing that these days. They get sick of the paperwork and other hassles of office practice."

"Which is understandable," Damon said. "What wasn't was that Brattle's black patients seemed to fare better than his white ones, particularly white cops he was called on to treat. No proof, but we strongly suspect he knocked off a few by delaying or withholding the proper treatment in ways a doctor would know. An anonymous telephone call from some woman tipped us off. But even after examining all the ER records we couldn't pin any criminal charges on him. All we really had were mortality statistics on white cops that were so far out of line the Police Commissioner assigned an undercover police surgeon to work the same emergency rooms and keep a close eye on him. Next Brattle was accused of raping and nearly beating to death a hospital nursing supervisor, a white woman in her late thirties who lived alone. They jailed Brattle for it briefly but had to let him go."

"How come?" asked Dan.

"Because the woman refused to press charges. Claimed they were lovers and it was just a lover's quarrel that got out of hand. What she neglected to mention was her heavy morphine habit that Brattle probably helped her meet. She was also scared to death of the little man. No amount of persuasion could make her talk, so they released Brattle and rousted him out of town. He drifted south after that and three or four years ago hooked up with Harper somehow."

"I see," said Dan bitingly. "So you therefore conclude because one, he's a doctor, two, hates cops, and three, is Lem Harper's personal physician, that this same David Brattle must've blinded those Southern sheriffs. Hell, Damon, if you can't convict him, why don't you just lynch him?"

Dan's barb drew a faint pout from the CIA official. Shrugging, he said, "Let's just call it a presumptive diagnosis, Dr. Lassiter. You must make them yourself when you lack objective proof for a definitive one?"

"Sure I do. But you still haven't connected Lem Harper with anything. All I've heard so far is speculation and innuendo, and I'm getting a little tired of it. Maybe I don't know much about intelligence work, but I do know enough psychiatry to diagnose an obsessional neurosis, and frankly, Damon, you sound as if Lem Harper obsesses you."

"Perhaps you're right," the CIA official said quietly. "Perhaps I am obsessed, or at least overly concerned with him. But I've been in this business a long time, Dr. Lassiter, and this is one man who has learned to wield terror unlike anybody I've ever encountered before. More like a scalpel than a sledgehammer and with scalpellike precision. Doubtless you've heard about the Detroit Massacre?"

"Heard about it!" Dan exclaimed. "Good God, how could I not! It's practically become a national industry, all the books, TV documentaries, and movies it's spawned."

Dan's assessment was not exaggerated. A year and a half before, a masterfully planned and executed series of raids by the Detroit-based DDD had swept through the city's west end, killing or maiming scores of dope dealers in a single night and sharply curtailing the hard-drug traffic there ever since.

"What was it they called chopping off a street pusher's finger joint to mark him for life?" Dan asked.

"The 'Marzette Method,' " MacBride answered. "After Henry Marzette, an ex-cop who became Detroit's dope czar before he died."

Dan spread his hands. "Hate to lose the tip of my index finger. Make it damned difficult to dial a telephone."

"Or pull a trigger," Damon added. "It was a nice touch. As was strewing those raw hog guts around. But there were other touches to that operation. Like the myth the Detroit DDD did all the dirty work themselves without outside help. We know better. They had reinforcements, foreign ones. Not a great number maybe, but enough to leave their Mau Mau trademark."

"Oh, really?" Dan said skeptically. "Were you at the oathing?"

"No, but we *do* have an Immigration Department, Dr. Lassiter, and it does keep records. There were almost a hundred young male visitors from Kenya in the Midwest around that time—two to three times the usual number. They could easily have converged on Detroit that night. But to get back to my original point: how Lem Harper—if he's the leader we think he is—uses terror with such devastating impact and accuracy. Four Southern sheriffs were blinded, but from the shock waves it sent through lawmen, it might as well have been four hundred. How many dope dealers do you think were slain in the Detroit Massacre? Make an estimate."

Dan shrugged. "A couple of hundred?"

"Yes, that's the popular belief. Actually it was less than sixty—all big-time drug wholesalers. See what I mean? The more vivid the terror, the more it grows in the imagination."

Freiborg yawned openly and Dan caught the contagion. Damon spoke sharply, "Look, Dr. Lassiter, a lot of people think intelligence types like me just loll around Langley playing silly games, and they're half right. We fancy them up with names like Situational Analyses and Contingency Planning, but all they really amount to are sophisticated versions of 'what if' games. And right now the one my section's working hardest on is this: If the trend toward racial separatism continues in this country as it has worldwide, what type of leader might inspire black Americans to risk everything in open rebellion? In other words, now that they've already had their Gandhi in Martin

Luther King, who will they follow next: a puritanical black Mao or a black Hitler? Get my gist, Dr. Lassister?"

"I think so," said Dan, intrigued.

"Well, people tend to forget that Mao and Hitler were basically military men, so that's what the blacks will need too. Not necessarily a professional soldier, but someone who can count on massive support from the black militants here as well as foreign powers close as Cuba and far away as North Korea. And the only man we know with that broad a power base is Lemuel Harper."

Dan stared distractedly at the CIA deputy director. No longer was he merely accusing Lem of fomenting African revolutions and having powerful Communistic allies, with blinding white lawmen and masterminding the Detroit Massacre, he was accusing Lem of plotting the overthrow of the government of the United States! And making it all the more frightening, Damon had made the accusation in the presence of two of the country's most important men. Why didn't Freiborg, the FBI Director, cough, choke, try to regurgitate the bitter pill the CIA man was making them swallow? Or had they already swallowed it and were waiting for him to follow?

Dan drew a deep, calming breath before daring to reply. "Now wait a minute. So what if Lem Harper does possess such a power base? The problem's still entirely theoretical. This country's not on the brink of any racial revolution, is it?"

Damon smiled faintly. "Maybe not on the brink, Dr. Lassiter, but close—so close that the next election could push us over."

"How can you possibly conclude that?" Dan protested. "The Vietnam War is over. The economy is picking up. There hasn't been a major race riot in two decades."

"Because of the progressive deterioration in our culture's two most basic units: the family and the cities. Our economic resources are so overextended providing health care, national defense, school support, welfare, we simply can't add anymore without collapsing like a house of cards. We are reaching a point where we can no longer serve the most fundamental function of a democracy: protecting the rights of its minorities. The blacks know this, of course, and want to protect themselves against the day the government handouts stop. They're running more candidates than ever in the coming election, but the novelty of black politicians has worn off, and they haven't proved that effective. We predict that most black congressional candidates and their white liberal supporters will be soundly defeated this time. And when that happens," the CIA official said gravely, "the psychology that will overtake such a frustrated group is clear."

Dan nodded, feeling suddenly weary. "You've made your point. But why tell me all this? I'm a medical man. I obviously don't have any brilliant solutions to offer. I don't even know Lem Harper as well as I thought. You've made *that* abundantly clear."

"But you *do* know him, Dr. Lassiter. You're one of the few whites who does. And he knows you." Damon turned to Nels Freiborg as if cuing him in.

"Dan," Freiborg began haltingly, "there's a strong possibility that Lem Harper will contact you soon. He's back in the country now, heading for Washington this very minute. . . . And afterward Boston. If he does come to see you, it's vitally important we know everything he tells you at once."

Dan gave Freiborg a cold, cutting look. "If I understand correctly, you want me to pass on to you everything Lem has to say, even in confidence. In other words, to betray a friend I've known for almost half my life."

"That's exactly what we're asking, Dan. Obviously we have our reasons."

"Reasons!" Dan rasped. "Reasons are exactly what I haven't heard!"

Freiborg looked to the FBI Director for help, but his face remained impassive and Freiborg's sagged. Sighing deeply, he said, "Dan, we can't tell you yet.

We simply can't! Those are the President's explicit instructions and we must obey them."

"Well, I'm still a civilian and under no such restraint. If Lem Harper does try to contact me, I'll let you know. As for telling you anything he confides to me, I'll exercise my own judgment. After all, I've only heard your side of the story so far—and that's pretty biased. I haven't heard Lem's. Nor seen any real proof he's masterminded any of the fiendish atrocities you charge him with. Those slides you showed hardly constitute a prima facie case."

Suddenly the FBI Director broke his long silence. "To what extent you cooperate with us, Dr. Lassiter, is strictly up to you. We have no hold on you." He smiled ruefully. "Not that we didn't search hard for one. But we knew there'd be slim pickings from the start! Ah, the virtues of the medical profession! But you're still a white man, and nothing you were taught in medical school nor picked up since gives you any clear insight into a black man's mind. Neither have we, of course. Not collectively. But we do happen to have a pretty good grasp of the mentality of one of them. So before you decide where you stand on the question of friendship versus patriotism, maybe you'd better have it too." He sighed as if forced to do something distasteful. "Mac, play the tape for Dr. Lassiter."

The FBI agent put a typewriter-sized tape recorder on the table and plugged it in. The spools began to whir, and after a series of clicking and rustling noises Dan heard Harper's deep, unmistakable voice:

"What do black men want? Same as everybody else, you say? Same as white folks? Well, you're wrong! It ain't enough. What we want, need, got to have if we're ever goin' to be at peace with ourselves, is to atone. Not revenge, not reparations for the past wrongs done us, but atonement!

"We all got to atone: For our dumb forefathers ever gettin' on those slave ships. For believin' there were

corn-fritter trees and gold nuggets in the gutters of America. For ever lettin' those slobbering, diseased white sailors and plantation overseers rape our black women to breed mongrel children for the market place. . . . Atonement for our pitiful political ignorance and docility in Reconstruction times. For lettin' those Klansmen burn our barns and lynch our brothers and ride off to do it again. For not risin' up and banding together and cracking their skulls like pecans. We should've turned their hooded sheets into blood-soaked shrouds, those burning crosses into flaming funeral pyres for them. But we didn't do none of that, just huddled in churches singin' hymns! So we got to atone.

"The Jews know all about atonement. They not only turned Israel into a land of Spartan fighters but wired it with atomic bombs. That's how the Jews atoned for the millions that died in the Nazi gas ovens; for the sheep in their ranks who kept on tryin' to rationalize, not riot, even as they smelled the first whiff of poison gas. That's atonement that counts! And now the world knows, or better know, that if Israel goes so goes all the rest in one nuclear holocaust.

"But the white man doesn't understand this. They still think us blacks are dumb, slothful, irresponsible. That instead of wanting to work, better ourselves, pay our dues for living now, all we're interested in is handouts. Welfare, reverse quotas, separate but equal—they don't realize all those sops they throw us ain't enough, will never be enough, because they don't understand the extra burden each black man bears: the need to prove not only his own worth, but the worth of his race.

"Why don't they understand? Because they figure they took care of all that by givin' us religion, by spoon-feeding us a steady diet of their Christian propaganda ever since we were old enough to toddle off to church. Since we all God's chil'ren, we need to atone only to Him. The Lord sent us His only Son, who He just happened to make white, but give it no

mind. Peace Child came once and when he comes again He's bringin' better times.

"You say you had a dream, Martin, that you seen the Promised Land, and I say a dream is all it was. The Church has carried us far as it can, far as we want to go. Fanon is right. Now we got to go with the Devil. We fell from grace like him, so we got to learn to live in the same lake of fire with him, till we atone.

"And don't tell me I'm being blasphemous, that violence ain't God's way. We already got enough prayerful niggers kept in line by their Christian ethic: the best protection the white man ever had. You really believe all that singin' and prayin' of theirs is finally going to get God to say, 'All right, chil'ren, I know I been neglecting you and you been takin' your lumps, but beginning tomorrow that's going to change. I'm going to make those white folks love you and treat you like brothers'? Because I know better. I had enough of that jive. Even if there is a God, why must we go on thinkin' of Him as being good or just or even rational? Do the animals in a zoo think of their keeper that way? Far as God is concerned, we might be nothin' more than a bunch of dumb animals in His zoo. 'Cause that's where we are, you know. Some of us may be lions and tigers, but long as we go on believin' God is going to look after us, we're all in a cage. A cage where we can't get back at those who hurt us or get out of till we make do for ourselves.

"I been to the mountain too, Martin. And after following this blind path and that, I finally hit on a way to the top. Oh, I ain't going to get there alive either, but I got a glimpse of the peak. Now Einstein he got a glimpse of something too. A Unified Wave Theory, he called it. He never saw it clear enough to prove, only to know proof was possible, and what he tried to do with different kinds of waves I'm trying to do with people. All colored people: the blacks in Africa, the Orientals in Asia, the Aborigines in Australia. Time the white man came to realize the truth about himself: That he's not only outnumbered and out-

gunned, but with all his wasteful ways, nothin' more than a parasite on this earth. That if he and his kind expect to survive they got to learn to accommodate, take only their fair share of the fruit and honey, or else we're going to shit them out.

"But if that's what we must do, we got to start preparing now. We don't need no more Lumumbas or Tshombes; no revolutions we can't handle. The twenty-five million American blacks could no more rule the two hundred million whites than a bushman could fly an airplane. So we got to wait, plan, get ready.

"Remember this, brothers, and remember it well. Even if the angels ain't on our side we got somethin' almost as good. Change! *We on the side of the wind and the waves, not the crumblin' rock. Nothin' can hold back change and nothin' can hold us back either. We goin' to keep coming, keep rolling in like a gigantic wave against the rocky beach. Ain't nobody who's powerful enough to stop us or turn us around. Can't nothin' break us up, except ourselves.*

"The future may not be ours long, brothers, but it won't be ours at all unless we quit all our pleadin' and prayin' and be willin' to fight and die for what we want. That might not be your way, Martin, or even God's way. That's white men's way. They didn't get all they got now through prayer, but through slaughter. And that's no blasphemy either. . . . Oh, Lord, if you can hear me, tell them it's only your supplicant, Lemuel, talkin', tellin' these others what you put in my mind: That we got to atone for ever being anybody's nigger but Yours! . . ."

Lem's voice trailed off into the whir and hum of the tape recorder. Dan waited for other taped voices to speak, but the silence continued unbroken. Glancing at the others in the room, he saw their faces were as somber and preoccupied as he imagined his to be. Lem's bitterness and obsession with atonement, his goals for his people, which Dan feared could only be attained through violence, stunned and saddened him. The FBI Director was right. No white man could understand that kind of ethos. Finally he asked, "When did you tape this?"

The FBI Director hesitated. "Around four, five years ago. We bugged the bedroom he was using at a foreign embassy here in town. It was legal then."

"I thought for a while he was talking to Martin Luther King. But King was long dead by then. Who was he talking to?"

"We don't know," said the Director with a gesture of futility. "To himself, I suppose. We played that entire tape many, many times. There are no other voices on it."

Chapter Ten

Back in the Mystère after spending the night and most of that day in Durham, Lem Harper strapped himself down securely for takeoff. He took a gulp of the bourbon Monique had brought him and then slumped back, knowing it would be a long, tiring trip to Washington and later Boston, even longer before he could return to Martinique where his ancestral roots were, where simple hillfolk still whispered tales of his grandfather, Auguste Duvalier, the original "Devil-A."

Lem's maternal grandfather had died on the gallows of a military prison in Martinique. But before that he had led a bloody insurrection of descendants of slaves and Carib Indians against the island's oppressive French rulers. Barely literate, with no military training at all, Auguste Duvalier and his ragtag band had ambushed and outwitted and outfought a vastly superior French militia for almost a year. Eventually he was betrayed and defeated, but until he was actually hanged his enemies had feared him like Lucifer himself.

From early childhood Lem could remember climbing on his grandmother's lap to hear stories of this seven-foot-tall "Black Samson of the Antilles" in her soft, French-accented voice. These tales so thrilled Lem that he would sit for hours on the stoop of his family's Boston tenement house and dwell on what it meant to have the blood of such an extraordinary forebear in his veins. Was he destined to match his grandfather in size *and* in deeds? Could he ever travel to far-off Martinique and find the jungle hilltop house Auguste Duvalier had built for his wife and daughter?

Years later he did. In the dense mountain foliage at

the northern end of the island, atop a verdant slope, Lem not only discovered the crumbling ruins of his grandfather's house, but something far more precious: the remedy for his restless spirit.

That had been after the civil wars in West Africa were finally ended, and for the first time in many tumultuous years Lem could let himself relax. On the site of his grandfather's home he built his own comfortable, well-guarded hideaway, and in the rain-forest stillness found a degree of peace he had never known before. But now, however reluctantly, he had to leave it. There was work to do in the United States.

The upcoming congressional elections would be the most crucial for black people since 1964. The new President had finally begun to curb inflation and pull the nation out of economic stagnation through the most stringent tax reforms in recent history. Big business, having been hardest hit by the new tax laws and fearing more of the same, was determined to deprive the President of his legislative majority by electing congressmen of its choosing.

They would have too, mused Lem, except for one man, a black mathematical genius named Artemus Hill who worked for the Department of HEW and had been assigned the task of projecting federal health expenditures for the coming year. It was Hill's job to compute how much in excess of estimates the National Health Insurance program would be costing the taxpayers and he had done just that and more, giving his political bosses the one thing they wanted least in an election year: proof of an enormous scandal.

Washington was as fertile ground for fraud as for cherry-blossom trees, so government swindles were nothing new. The bigger the departmental budget the more likely they were to occur, and for a long time the Defense Department with its cost overruns and boondoggles and kickbacks led the field. But with the advent of Medicare in 1966, and Medicaid a year later, the Department of HEW had begun to gain on Defense as the top spender, and with the enactment of National Health Insurance now far surpassed it in expenditures. So it was not too surprising to Lem that they should spawn their share of swindles too. But at 1.9 billion dollars, the theft that Hill had uncovered was the biggest ever. The biggest and the most reprehensible, since the pilfered funds were not meant for the support of friendly foreign despots or increasing the megadeath potential of MIRV'd missiles, but for the care of sick people!

Even more astonishing to Lem was that, despite HEW's vast army of employees, its thousands of cost analysts and auditors and field inspectors, it had taken one man playing around with a computer to tumble to it. It was also obvious to Lem that he was something more than a computer virtuoso. It had taken great courage for Hill to report his findings to the authorities, since Washington officials, like ancient kings, had a nasty habit of eliminating the bearers of bad tidings.

Lem would've liked to have met this Artemus Hill, to use him as a special consultant for his operations, but that was no longer possible.

As Lem later learned, Hill had left Washington for his two-week spring vacation safely and on schedule. His idea of blissful relaxation was to sit out on the porch of his cabin in the Blue Ridge Mountains and listen to the wind in the pines while trying to master some avant garde mathematical concept. This time he had brought along a treatise on computer technology so exciting he could hardly wait to get back to Washington to test it out.

But he never got back. When his former professor at Duke came up to spend the weekend, he found Artemus Hill dead in bed, a victim of carbon monoxide poisoning. The vent of his gas heater had somehow been plugged.

That would have been the end of Artemus Hill and his brilliant detective work for the Department of HEW had he not been so proud of it and the highly innovative methods he had devised to confirm his findings that he had sent a duplicate of the report to his old friend and mentor. Forewarned, the professor, a Harlem-born black himself, had needed only a glance at the oily rag the local sheriff pulled out of the cabin vent pipe to realize how and probably why Artemus had died. He knew better than to share his suspicion with the sheriff, or any other white man, but on his way to a consortium of mathematicians in Paris the following week, he stopped off en route at Fort-de-France, Martinique. There was a man there a black colleague at Duke had told him about once. He had said that although Lemuel Harper was himself a theorist, he was not one who dealt in abstractions alone. His field was the gore and glory of revolution.

I got your report, Brother Hill, mused Lem drowsily as the Mystère bored northward toward a smoky summer dusk, and it's going to shake up the politicians in this country like nothing since Watergate. Gonna shake their eyeteeth out, as George Wallace would say.

The seat-belt sign flashed on and Lem came full awake. They were making their penetration toward Dulles International where a limousine with diplomatic plates would whisk him to the Republic of Kenya Embassy, his preferred place of residence in Washington. Al Beal didn't like it; he had stayed there too many times before, and if a hit man was stalking him he'd know just where to go. But Lem remained undeterred. The embassy was a fairly secure building, and once inside he didn't intend to stray. "Anybody come for me, they come," he told Al laconically. "They take their chances, same as me." "A man, maybe, not a bomb," Al argued, reminding him of the listening bugs they'd once found planted in his bedroom. Still Lem was unmoved. But when Al persisted, told him the place gave him bad vibes, Lem gazed at his chief of staff pensively. Al was four or five inches shorter and ten years younger than he, but almost as broad-shouldered, almost as smart and cunning. Fifteen years of police work, the last ten as detective, had given him the same astute instinct for impending danger as Lem's, and it unnerved him that Al was picking up bad vibrations too. Important as tomorrow's meeting was to his plans, maybe he ought to heed Al's advice and move on? But Lem wavered only momentarily before deciding against it. He simply could not let nameless fears sway him. It was like the jitters he got from airplane travel; if he ever gave in to them he could never fly again. Moreover, he was morosely aware of how badly he was slipping, physically and emotionally. There were so many signs of it: his deep reluctance to leave Martinique, his persistent preoccupation with death and betrayal. If he let himself slip any further, his men were bound to sense it; then he truly would be expendable. That settled it. While his followers scattered on assigned errands, he and Andy would go on to the embassy.

Chapter Eleven

A little after 3:00 A.M. a footfall outside their bedroom door made Andy stir. At the soft knock that followed, he moved with catlike quickness, throwing off his covers and reaching for the holstered gun on the chair by his bed. But Lem, who was awake and reading, thrust him back and went to the door himself. As he expected, it was the Ambassador, Joash Ndegwa, his close friend and confidant. "I saw the light on," Joash said apologetically.

Lem smiled at the trim Kikuyu with the bushy grayish-white hair and tribal scars on his ebony face. "You know my sleep habits well."

"Shall we talk now or in the morning?" Joash asked in his faintly British-accented voice.

"Now," said Lem. "I'll get a robe."

Downstairs in the Ambassador's book-lined study, Joash poured whiskey and sodas from a portable bar. "I've completed arrangements for the reception tomorrow night," he said. "It shall be exactly as you requested."

Lem nodded. "How many did you invite?"

"Over eighty. A diverse enough group to provide cover for the ten you wanted."

"Good. Time is short. To achieve maximum impact, we must act fast."

Joash did not question him. From what little he knew of it, the coup Lem planned involved American politics exclusively and was none of his concern.

"Mzee always wanted you back, you know," he said after a reflective pause. "The other old men too. Would you come? Any title you want is yours for the asking."

"And cattle? Wives?" Lem inquired straight-faced.

"What of those? Titles cannot be milked nor cuddled in the night."

"A hundred cows. Five wives." Joash grinned. "Surely you would not want it reversed?" Then turning serious he asked, "Will you return? After your goals here have been accomplished?"

"My goals here!" Lem's eyebrows rose. "Those will take another generation. Another lifetime! First, because the problems are so vast, so complicated, I can concentrate on only one or two at a time. Keep brushfires from becoming conflagrations that could turn back and consume us. And second, because I'm hindered by my own personal sense of involvement."

"How does that hinder you?" Joash asked.

"It's a state of mind. To engineer effective revolution one must be objective, think only of the end result. I could do that in Kenya. It's a whole lot tougher for me here. How can I remain indifferent when black school children are still being spat on in the same South Boston slum as I was?"

"I understand," Joash said softly.

"But equal or not, education alone is not the answer. Being hundreds of years behind, it would take too long for most black folk to catch up. No, our children, our future leaders, must be educated, but the rest must look elsewhere to better their lot."

"But where? What holds any real hope for them? Politics?"

"Not entirely. We keep jabbering about black power. But those who jabber the loudest got none, none that's meaningful, or if they do, let it go to waste."

Joash sighed. "Regretfully I must agree. It is as our late friend Julius Hobson once said: 'Too many black politicians are tasteless, colorless, and odorless.' But what does that leave?"

"It leaves two tired old friends trying to solve the problems of the world," Lem said wryly. "Look, it's late and you're in no mood to hear me lecture."

"Why not?" Joash protested. "You are a teacher, are you not? Some even call you a *moruji,* a diviner and prophet whose knowledge of men transcends mere psychology."

"They call me a lot of things," Lem mocked.

"Oh, I know how you feel about the old superstitions. But please go on. *Moruji* or not, I am anxious to hear what you have to say."

Lem shrugged. "Well, then, consider how a city resembles a human being. Whatever it consumes for energy makes waste it has to eliminate. Stop collecting a big city's garbage and you constipate it. Cut off a city's arms and legs and it can't feed itself. I'm talkin' about its labor force, its unions. Control of the unions has been our main goal for a long time now, and we've made enough false starts: The League of Revolutionary Black Workers, D.R.U.M., the Black Workers Congress. No sooner'd we get one of these set up when a power struggle between a bunch of greedy bastards inside the organization splintered it apart. But we're a lot smarter and quieter in how we operate now. That's why we had to wipe out Detroit's dope traffic. Dope was a tapeworm keeping our black brothers there weak and apathetic. Once we ripped it out of their guts we—" Lem suddenly faltered and gritted his teeth in pain. Thrusting his hand in his robe pocket for two pink capsules, he swallowed them down.

Joash hastily replenished his drink. "The hip again?"

Lem nodded. "That and my kidneys. They're so weak I got to sleep with a pisspot by my bed."

"You've seen a doctor?" Joash asked worriedly.

"Besides Brattle, you mean? Yeah, two. The specialist in Fort-de-France told me my urine's loaded with albumin."

"Albumin? That's egg-white, isn't it?"

"For an egg-eater, maybe. For a man it's a bad sign. He wanted to stick a needle in my kidney and snip out a piece he could examine under a microscope. But I wouldn't let him."

"Why not?"

"Because he agreed with Brattle as to the most likely cause, and there's no cure."

"None?" Joash exclaimed in dismay.

"None that're safe. Brattle wants me to try some new Russian drug, but I can't risk it right now. Too much to do."

"But you must!" Joash urged. "You must do everything possible to preserve your health. You're much too valuable to our people—here, in Africa, everywhere! I know no man is indispensable, but it takes years and years to develop the contacts, the trust, the insights you have. . . . My old friend," he said in a voice husky with emotion, "I shudder to think what we would do without you!"

Lem smiled sardonically. "Well, go easy on your grieving. I ain't dead yet. What I got don't kill you sudden-like, I'm told. I'll be around a while longer—unless, of course, a bullet finds me."

Joash frowned. "You say that as if you'd had an omen. As if you already knew . . . It makes me shiver."

"I don't feel so good about it either. But there's a long list of candidates to shoot that bullet. More than one of my Afro brothers wants to make a martyr of me. But they don't worry me so much as what my own government might do to put me away."

"The United States?" Joash said, surprised. "Why would they want to arrest *you?*"

"Not arrest—kill. It's possible, you know. We've stolen a lot of documents from their files and it's a safe bet they know it. Which leaves them just two choices: admit the scandal I know about publicly and hope it doesn't wreck their health program, lose them control of the Congress; or else stop me from it."

"But they wouldn't actually kill you! Your own government?"

"Not directly. They wouldn't have to. I put enough dope dealers out of business that all they'd have to do is tip some Latino or ex-Jones man where I was at. They'd do it for sure if they knew what my next move was. . . .

"Which is why the reception tomorrow night is so important," Lem went on after gulping whiskey. "To make sure our key people are filled in so when we do break the news it'll have the desired impact. As a white doctor-friend of mine once told me: 'even though a lot of otherwise decent white folk are social bigots, they draw the line at mistreating sick colored people.' "

"But I don't understand how this will help blacks politically."

"By creating a diversion. Who cared about race prejudice while Watergate was going on? Nobody! But afterward, when the recession came along, white workers suddenly took a hard look at the blacks working next to them on the assembly line and wondered which would get laid off next. Back in the old days, the all-white union bosses would've made sure who. But not now. So that makes them close ranks against us and vote for a 'black get back' type. We got no big business leaders to protect us, so we need the politicians—black or white don't matter, long as they're honest. And the way to elect honest politicians is to create an outcry for them like Watergate did."

"I see," said Joash, impressed by Lem's reasoning but more concerned about his health and safety. Never before had he seen his old friend look so tense and haggard—almost as if the death he spoke of might be a welcome relief from the burdens of physical pain and racial responsibility he had borne so long. It grieved Joash deeply.

Lem finished his drink and rose clumsily to his feet. Joash rose with him and extended his hand. "Sleep well, my friend."

Chapter Twelve

When Lem returned to the room Andy Sims was sitting up in bed reading. "What'd Ndegwa want?" he asked.

"Just to talk."

"Everything all set for tomorrow night?"

Lem nodded.

"Be good to see some of the gang again. Especially Barney Carter and Kelso." Carter was Detroit's black Chief of Detectives and Gordon Kelso had succeeded Andy as head of the DDD. "Except for the coke tooters, I hear the town's as clean as a fresh-bathed baby's ass. Least for black folk it is."

Lem lowered himself to his bed with a grimace and a grunt.

"Hurt?"

"Like hell a while ago."

"Want me to call Brattle to come over and give you a shot? He's stayin' with his lady in Georgetown."

"Naw, they don't help much anymore. Built up a tolerance to them, I guess. Only one thing ever really killed the pain and I'd sooner die than get myself hooked again."

"Oh, yeah. I'd forgot you were hooked once. How long?"

"Three months. I never knew that's what those North Korean doctors were givin' me till I got to sneezing and shaking so bad on the plane home I thought I was goin' to shake apart."

"That why you hate dope so much?"

"No, that ain't why. Three things in my life still give me the jitters just thinkin' about: One was a Mau Mau oathing that crazy bastard, Kimanthi, dragged me to. One was seein' what was left of a friend of mine after a bunch of medical students had about finished hacking up his corpse. And the last was a tour of Detroit dope houses that Barney took me on just before you and me met. Mainly hole-in-the-wall shootin' galleries, but they were bad enough. All rat and roach infested. And the women! Some not bad-lookin' either, but layin' around like zombies with lice crawlin' through their Afros. And all so a few high-flyin' nigger pushers could drive flashy cars and wear fancy duds."

"Yeah," said Andy. "Zette didn't like what you said about that. Especially after you'd just hit him up for a hundred grand for your African club members in the OAU or somethin'. He sent me to straighten you out."

Lem looked at him hard. "He sent you to do more than that. He sent you to kill me."

The flat accusation took Andy by surprise. He squirmed and shook his head. "Naw, he didn't either . . . Not exactly. Zette gave me the option, I got to admit. But not a direct order."

"Enough jivin', Andy!" Lem growled. "I said, *enough!* He sent you to kill me."

"You askin' or tellin' me?"

"Tellin' you!"

"Yeah?" said Andy defensively. "Then how come you gave me such an easy shot at you? Leavin' them two African guys you was with and goin' to that Bethel Baptist Church with me to hear the gospel singin'?"

" 'Cause you used to sing there yourself. Your Mama took you every Friday and Sunday."

Andy was visibly stunned. He stared incredulously at Lem for a long moment and rasped, "You knew that! Shee-it, how could you know that? I was just a little kid then. I'd damned near forgot it myself till we got there."

"You forgot!" Lem mocked. "You didn't forget nothin'! Two minutes inside that church and you were gettin' teary-eyed. You weren't goin' to kill *nobody* that night!"

"No, I guess not," said Andy, sounding wistful. "But how'd you know to take me there? Must be dozens of those small churches in the west end of town."

" 'Cause I made it my business to know. After Zette told me you'd be the one droppin' off the money, I called around about you. Found out where you grew up, ran numbers, your outfit in Nam and the medals you won there. Even how long you went straight after discharge before hooking up wth Marzette—who was your brother Carl's old sidekick on the cops before he got himself killed. Yeah, I researched you pretty good. Enough to make sure you weren't so kill-crazy I'd be a sittin' duck."

Andy shook his head in bemused wonder. "Man, you *are* a devil! But that was all three, four years ago. How come you bringin' it up now?"

"I got my reasons," Lem told him. "And I'm askin' you one last time: Did Zette order you to kill me or didn't he?"

Andy got out of bed in his underwear and poured himself a glass of water from the pitcher on the table. Lem saw sweat glistening on his face despite the air-conditioned coolness of the room. Finally Andy turned, squinted at him with anguish, and nodded. "Yeah, he ordered me to. Bet your goddamn ass he did! It took plenty of fast-talkin' to explain why I didn't. Nobody ever crossed Zette and got away with it. Savin' your life meant puttin' mine on the line. I thought I was goin' to get the Marzette treatment for sure. Lose a whole handful of knuckles before convincin' him I was tellin' the truth."

"Which was?"

"Uh uh," Andy said, shaking his head. He was a taciturn man who rarely expressed even mundane feelings. But Lem's stare bored into him. "Aw, c'mon, man," he pleaded. "It's sort of embarrassin'."

"Never mind that. Go on!"

Andy glared defiantly. "Goddamn it, why you askin' me this?"

" 'Cause I got a feelin' somebody close is fixin' to

kill me and I want to make sure it ain't you. That you already had your chance."

"Me?" Andy gasped. "You know damn well it ain't me! I'm your bodyguard, for shit's sake! You whacked right out of your skull to even dream I'd turn on you. But if it's spookin' you that much, I'll tell ya. When Zette told me what he wanted done, I said okay. All I knew was that you were some back-to-Africa nut goin' around sayin' the dope business was black cannibalism and kingpins like Zette were vultures pickin' the bones of the kids they poisoned. Wild stuff like that. But I don't just go waste people. I like to know about them first. So I did some nosing around about you too. Found some Afro at Solidarity House who told me who you were and how some places they called you 'Devil-A'. Man, that really gave me a laugh 'till he told me why—how you got next to those big-shot Communists in Korea and how you helped Kenyatta and were always using that psychology stuff you got out of books. I guess I realized then you were no ordinary nigger."

"Would you have killed me if I were?"

"Not for no reason. I never killed nobody didn't deserved to die. The only two men I ever wasted for Zette were killers themselves. Like that Red Trombley. Man, he was mad-dog crazy, killin' fifteen people in six months like he did. I just put him out of his misery. But you—" Andy looked embarrassed.

"What about me?"

"Aw, c'mon, man, lay off! Talk about somethin' else for a change," Andy growled. But the look on Lem's face was unrelenting. "Well, if you really got to know, I just never had no hero before. After belly-crawlin' around the rice paddies in Nam for a whole year tryin' to stay alive, who gives a shit if some nigger can catch a football or knock out another nigger in Zaire. That's kid stuff. I needed a black man I could look up to and learn from and do things for, and I realized you came closest when we were in that little Bethel Church together. Which shows how smart you were takin' me there. Zette just laughed himself sick when I told him how I felt. But I guess he understood 'cause he never sent nobody else after you. Being hitched to that kidney machine of his twelve hours a day gave him plenty of time to think, and he was about ready to pack it up and move to Grand Bahama Island anyway. I remember one day just before he died. He showed me a picture in the paper of this ten-year-old black kid who OD'd on 'H'—a real clean-cut kid from the looks of him—and then he said, 'Remember that black Jesus or devil or whoever the hell he was you let live? Well, he's an old dogface too. We crossed paths once in Korea. If he's still around, have him come see me. Tell him if he wants to do more than just mouth off about black vultures and shit like that, I got a military operation to talk over with him.' "

"Yeah," Lem recalled. "I was down South when I got the word, but he was dead before I could see him. So, figuring you were in line to take over his operation, I tried gettin' hold of you. But you were long gone."

Andy smiled. "Yeah, man, I was all over. Mexico City, Marseilles, Ankara, Singapore—you name it. Me and Barney had got together by then and decided to do somethin' about the dope problem, and since I had the names of all the big foreign suppliers from Zette, I wanted to get a good look at the whole network. Maybe find the weak links in it. Took a year. When I got back, me and Barney sat down and worked out what we were goin' to do down to the last detail. It was like Zette said, a military operation. That's when the two of us got together again so you could give our plan the once-over and supply reinforcements." Andy suddenly grinned. "Man, some of those Mau Mau types you sent over gave even me the creeps. The blood-drinkers! Ugh! And they sure made a mess with all them hog entrails they left around. Truth is, neither Barney nor me was all that sold on those psychological touches you added. Even if they did work on a bunch of ignorant Africans, it was really stretchin' a point to expect that Halloween stuff to go over here. But you were right and we were wrong. I'd of never believed those tough young bandidos would get so spooked over such far-out stuff as wrappin' the throats of each dead dope dealer with hog guts and the eye-gougin', but they did—worse than our dumbest niggers. Way I hear it, they're still so psyched out they won't come near Detroit, which is why the town's so clean."

Andy leaned back in his chair and rubbed his bleary eyes—a natural response, but one he purposefully tried to avoid whenever he could. Even if he and Lem hadn't been discussing it, the gesture would have reminded him of "Pig Blood Monday," as the Detroit Massacre was known locally, and the gut-churning revulsion he had felt long after.

It had been agreed beforehand that whoever opened the door of the drug pad, whether supplier or junkie, would have to die: a mandatory death sentence meted out to protect the "hole man"—the regular customer and DDD accomplice whose face in the peephole gained the raiding party entry. It had also been agreed that every corpse would be disfigured and draped in exact accordance with Lem's instructions. The eye-gouging and mutilation of animals, even the intermingling of certain of their body parts and fluids with that of humans, had long played a symbolic role in Mau Mau rites, but that was not their purpose here. Lem had not ordered it to gain favor with *Ngai,* the jungle god, or other warrior spirits, but to gain massive newspaper coverage.

Some forty drug pads, quarter houses, and shooting galleries were hit in rapid order that night. Andy had personally led three raiding parties, killed five dope wholesalers, but gouged out only one pair of eyes. One was enough. Their gelatinous consistency and blood-soaked sockets gagged him with repulsion and he ordered one of the Afros in his team to do the rest.

For a week street skirmishes between the DDD and professional gunmen imported by the surviving dope kingpins flared throughout Detroit's West Side, while from every pulpit and meeting hall in the black community praises rang out for the vigilantes. By tacit consent of the Commissioner and the Mayor, the police watched from the sidelines, depending on Barney Carter to tell them which killings were dope-traffic related and which ought to be investigated.

The Mexican families who controlled the pipeline for brown heroin into the United States hastily conferred in Acapulco. Initially their patrónes agreed something had to be done, but after much bickering over what retaliatory strikes should be undertaken by which organizations, nothing was. These men of Mestizo blood were not cowards; their chosen profession did not permit it. But the unparalleled savagery of the DDD onslaught, the eye-gougings and knuckle-choppings, haunted their Latin imaginations and filled their hearts with mystical fears. For once it seemed better to forego the code of vendetta and let the black animals without souls keep their Detroit jungle for themselves—which was precisely what Lem Harper's terror tactics had been intended to achieve.

The only unfortunate outcome of the operation was that Michigan's predominantly white legislature denounced the DDD for encouraging anarchy and mob rule and succeeded in having it listed by the U.S. Attorney General as a subversive organization. Otherwise Lem's plan had worked to perfection, even though Andy Sims could never again rub his eyes without being reminded of the loathsome acts he had committed that night.

It was almost dawn when Lem broke off reminiscing with Andy. He reached for the bottle of Chloral on his nightstand and downed two of the oversized capsules with water, knowing he needed more sleep, needed it now because he was unlikely to get any in the coming night. Long before midnight, when the embassy reception ended, his private meetings with the ten men he had summoned there would start and go on into the early morning hours. The ten comprised a diverse and talented group: lawyers, accountants, newspaper editors, law officers, even an army brigadier general. Most of them were Washington-based and all were reliable. What continued to plague him though was that the man he needed to play the most important role would not be there. Nor could Lem count on him to do as bidden.

That Dr. Daniel Lassiter was a man of conscience he had proved many times over. But as Lem well knew, questions of conscience were subject to interpretation. And change. Many God-fearing people had once considered it conscionable to roast witches and lynch niggers on flimsy charges of rape. Most such decisions depended less on principle than on a weighing of alternatives. And the alternative he had to offer Dr. Daniel Lassiter was neither pleasant nor advantageous.

At last Lem's eyelids grew heavy and he lapsed into a half-sleep, one in which street noises and fragments of conscious thoughts kept intruding, and he wished, almost willed, his mind to transport him back to Martinique, to the haven he had found there late in life and the wellspring from which he derived his strength.

And, as often happened, out of this twilight sleep came the mumblings and sometimes clear language that only Andy Sims was privy to and did not dare interrupt: rambling monologues from his old speeches or writings, or else dialogues with unseen figures of the past, most of whom were long dead and entombed in the special pantheon for murdered men of peace and vision, but whose ghosts lay dormant in Lem's mind only to take shape and grow animated from the mind-distorting mixture of alcohol and sleeping pills and maddening pain.

If there is a God, then we are His only priests; our lives are the prayer. That was Lem's proposition and his chant. And there to argue the pros and cons of it with him were an ethereal congregation of men, some of whom—Martin, Dedan, Julius—Lem had known well; some—Malcolm, Medgar, Fanon—only in passing.

Was it madness, mania, a miasma of paranoiac hate in hallucinatory combination with drugs and kidney toxins? Or was it the incipient revelations, the life review, that he had heard men who were soon to die experienced. Its exact nature didn't much matter to Lem; he knew his mind was its own place of which he was sole proprietor. Yet if what he was experiencing almost nightly now were mere dreams, not actual communications with the dead, why were they so vivid and mind-clearing that he emerged from them as from a particularly edifying sermon with his goals in sharper focus, his resolve strengthened, and his impending date with destiny even more certain?

PART THREE

DOCTORS AND DINOSAURS

Chapter Thirteen

Dan came awake feeling the warmth and weight of Kit Colbine's arm and knee across his body. Had they made love? he wondered. An absurd question. Here he was in bed with one of America's most famous and desirable women and couldn't even remember! After all his months of celibacy too. He might have found the memory lapse amusing except for what it told him about his muddled state of mind.

Thinking back, Dan tried to reconstruct the evening. He had arrived at Kit's 57th Street apartment around 10:00 P.M., shared a couple of drinks, a steak, an hour of relaxed conversation with her, and then . . . He vaguely recalled their discussing sleeping arrangements, the guest bedroom or her own, taking a shower and reclining on her large, comfortable bed while she bathed. That was all. Except rooted in his mind was a dim, insistent memory of the tingling touch of tongues, of deep penetration, of rocking pelvises. He had made love to some woman, but was it Kris in a dream or Kit in reality? Good God, he thought, wide awake now and staring into the blackness of the bedroom, I'm really in bad shape.

With his wristwatch somewhere in the bathroom, Dan had no notion of the hour except that it was not yet five, when Kit's alarm clock would ring. No matter how late he got to bed, his overburdened brain seldom let him sleep past dawn. He wondered how many others shared these desolate early-morning hours with him. One man he felt sure did was the FBI Director.

Again Dan recalled the telltale look in his eyes on first meeting him: the subtle reflection of the same depressive state Dan had recognized in himself after trying to cope with the ceaseless frustrations of running a large hospital. What he saw in the FBI Director's eyes told him that this was a man who drove himself sixteen to eighteen hours a day, then staggered home to a drink and a newspaper and the gut-gnawing knowledge that the success he had achieved, the fulfillment of his boyhood dreams, had been so eroded by change as to become nothing more than a cruel, demoralizing deception: a killer, first of the dream, then of the spirit, finally of the man.

It seemed to Dan that nearly every person he knew in a position of high responsibility was afflicted by the same malaise nowadays. Like all clinical depressions, it represented a bogging down: in a bureaucratic system that had grown too unwieldy for any one man to master or move it; in a cult of bigness that had turned hospitals, federal agencies, city welfare departments, into lumbering dinosaurs too sluggish to harness for useful work, too big to kill off, demanding constant feeding and coddling lest they rise and rampage through the swamps of city slums. They were man-made but self-perpetuating and indestructible monsters that would last until their food supply, the federal fodder sustaining them, finally ran out.

But such brooding thoughts were swept from his mind when Kit suddenly pressed her nude body tightly against his and muttered, "Damn you, Dan Lassiter!"

It took no mental feat to deduce why he was being damned. "Do you want to now?" he asked.

"Hmm," she murmured. "Last night I did. Last night you kept looking me over with such a lustful gleam in your eyes. Times when a woman likes being looked at that way, especially by a man I've always considered not an ex-lover but a loving friend. So I thought, why not? I got really turned on by it. But you—you overworked doctor and VIP—what did you do? I leave you alone for five minutes and you pass out on me!"

"Kit, I'm sorry," he groaned. "I really am." He reached for her breasts and belly to soothe and arouse her, arousing himself. She gave him a dry-mouthed, early-morning kiss, but when his hand slipped between her thighs she tensed and drew back.

"Oh, Dan," she lamented, "you've got me all confused. I don't know whether you want me because you want me or just to make amends. Nor do I know how you really feel about your wife. And you're not the most communicative person. So much as I might like you to—"

Dan cut her short, hugging her so tightly she gasped for breath. The feel of her made him tumescent, and he pictured her auburn hair and hazel eyes and wide, sensual mouth in his mind's eye. But that was the Kit Colbine millions of TV viewers saw on the *Today* show. What attracted Dan most was the inner person: her incisive mind, her sensitivity, her lack of pretenses. And now she was showing him, gifting him, with something extra: total, self-deprecating honesty.

The nobility of friendship, he thought.

And suddenly he did want her, did love her, although not in the same way he loved Kris, not with the same commonality of being. The crack his wife had made in the tough tegument over his emotions belonged exclusively to her. But there were other, less penetrating cracks, and one had just opened to Kit.

"Kit, listen to me," he whispered. "The hell with second-guessing why, I do want you, want to make love to you, to . . . to . . ."

"To start the day with a bang?" she said mockingly but not bitchily. "Then why didn't you just do it without all this talk? Now if you want to get back in my good graces, forget about making love and make coffee. Go put a pot on while I lie here and wonder why I ever let you sleep over; get me so *farmisht,* as Barbara Walters would say."

Obediently Dan got out of bed. "Coffee all you want?"

Kit reached for her alarm clock to read its luminous dial. "Oh, God, it's barely four!" she moaned. "I could've slept a whole hour longer if it weren't for you! So it's more than coffee I want. Juice, toast, two poached eggs, and sausage. And bring it to me in bed. . . . In *bed!*" she repeated imperiously and twisted around to bury her face in the pillow. "After all," she mumbled, "you may be a doctor, but I'm a television star."

An hour later, having cooked a breakfast Kit enjoyed, shaved, and dressed, Dan sat in her bedroom going over the questions a staff writer had prepared for Kit to ask him. He knew from previous *Today* show appearances that after the first few she would likely drop the others and continue the interview in the unpredictable way that made her such a successful TV personality.

But as Dan tried to concentrate on the list, Kit kept distracting him. He watched her brush her hair in her special swaybacked, straddle-legged way before the bathroom mirror. Periodically she would emerge in her slip and his eyes automatically followed.

She was a stunning woman at forty: tall, trim, full-breasted, and more desirable than ever because her beauty was enhanced by maturity of mind. The mystery was why she had never married. Dan knew she came of a broken home, a mother now on her fifth marriage and a brilliant, magazine-editor father who drank himself to death. Maybe that had something to do with it. Or maybe she had never felt the need. Did she now? If the split between Kris and him became permanent . . . But that thought was too painful to pursue.

"Zip me up, will you?" Kit asked after slipping on her dress, and Dan did. Then turning her, he kissed her ardently.

"Well, Doctor!" she gasped. "What was that about?"

"About six hours too late. About the way I feel toward you."

She gave him an intense, almost anguished look, but all she said was, "It's past six. The limousine's waiting."

Kit was running late when they reached the NBC studio, so she went directly to her hairdresser, leaving Dan in a small lounge off the show set. Her secretary brought him two papers to sign: the first declaring that he had neither been coerced nor had he bribed anybody at NBC to arrange his appearance; the second that he was aware of the federal law prohibiting him from accepting any reward for promoting any product, service, or venture. This last gave him brief pause, since in a sense he was promoting himself for the post of Secretary of Health. It also made him acutely aware of the need to choose his words so as not to stir up needless controversy. Any senator on the Finance Committee watching the show would already be familiar with his credentials, his views on national health care, his political pluses and minuses—particularly his appeal or lack of it to certain powerful lobbies and groups. Most of the press, the leaders of academic medicine, and the more liberal congressmen supported his nomination; most of the conservative members of Congress and the AMA opposed it. So the battlelines were pretty clearly drawn and nothing he could possibly say, no matter how inspired, stood much chance of changing any minds or votes. Not that his detractors would be watching indifferently; they would seize upon and fuss at anything controversial he said—which unhappily left Dan no choice but to stick to those public positions he had previously taken and bore the ass off everybody who had heard them before. Either that, or liven things up by making a grab for Kit's ample bosom on camera.

Shortly before seven Kit appeared freshly coiffured to ask if he felt calm and collected, gave him a peck on the cheek for luck, and left to open the show. Fifteen minutes later, Dan was seated beside her under a constellation of reflector lights suspended from the studio ceiling and seeing himself in the monitor behind the front of the interview desk.

"Dr. Lassiter," Kit began, as he knew she would, "as one of the nation's leading medical authorities and now the President's nominee for Secretary of National Health, do you think the American health care system is sick enough to need a doctor?"

With his eyes burning and his throat so sore from ten hours of almost nonstop talking that he had to keep clearing it, Lem Harper watched Dan on television from his room in the Kenyan Embassy. With him sat Andy Sims and Alphonso Beal.

Soon he found himself studying Dan intensely. Almost from the instant his image had appeared on the TV screen Lem sensed some subtle, worrisome difference in his old friend. With every cautious answer he gave to Kit Colbine's provocative questions, Dan Lassiter sounded less like the dedicated doctor he believed him to be than some slick politician running for office.

At the end of the interview Lem ordered the TV set shut off. The bark to his voice told Al Beal he was troubled. "You heard something you don't like, right?"

"I ain't sure," Lem rasped. "But we damned well better find out! So we're leaving Andy behind to take care of things here and headin' straight for Boston. You fix it up and find out where Lassiter's living. I want to see him tonight."

Chapter Fourteen

An NBC limousine transported Dan to La Guardia airport, a shuttle flight to Boston, and a taxi to Commonwealth General. With each leg of his journey the momentum seemed to increase. Although all he needed to do that day was complete a grant renewal request and catch up on some correspondence, he felt an unaccountable sense of urgency to return to the hospital.

The taxi dropped Dan off at the emergency room entrance and he strode down the connecting corridor to the bank of elevators beyond. It was a heavily trafficked intersection and often a time-consuming trap. If Dan was forced to linger there too long, somebody was sure to engage him in conversation, usually a garrulous hospital employee or peeved physician. Now only a few people waited beside him for an elevator, none in hospital garb. But his relief was premature. The next instant Gene Detwiler banged through the swinging doors of the emergency room, head down, fists clenched, face so contorted with rage that even the tips of his moustache twitched. Such a look of unbridled anger in the aloof, slyly argumentative cardiology fellow he remembered from their recent run-in on the intensive care unit seemed so out of character that Dan's curiosity was aroused.

Detwiler's eyes met Dan's and he saw a glimmer of embarrassment, and possibly hope, in them. They stared silently at each other, Detwiler reluctant to admit he needed help, Dan reluctant to get involved in whatever had enraged him. Finally Dan felt compelled to speak. "Gene, old boy," he said lightly, "you look mighty bothered."

Detwiler nodded ruefully. "Yeah," he muttered. Then more forcefully, "Shit, yes, Dr. Lassiter. I am!"

Dan was about to ask if he wanted to talk about it but reminded himself that he was the cardiologist's superior, not his advisor. Instead he said, "Tell me."

Detwiler looked flustered and then broke into a surprising smile. "Well, if you really want to know, I got me a little problem—only not so little. A three-hundred-pound black dwarf who's dying of a pulmonary embolism."

"You got what?" exclaimed Dan, unable to suppress a smile.

Detwiler spotted it and nodded. "Go ahead and smile. So did I when I first heard about it. But I'm not smiling now. I'm stuck with him!"

The elevator door before them slid open but Dan ignored it. Taking Detwiler's arm he drew him into a corner. "What do you mean you're stuck with him?"

"Exactly that," Detwiler retorted. "Nobody else seems to give a damn whether he lives or dies. Not the squeamish intern working the emergency room, nor his attending man, and especially not that Limey bastard Cartmill in the cardiovascular lab."

"And *you* do give a damn?"

"That's right!" Detwiler growled. "He's grotesque. Jesus, is he ever! Makes you wonder what kind of Creator plays pranks like that. But he's still a human being and he's dying and *somebody* ought to give a damn!"

"Yes," said Dan softly, impressed and intrigued. "Somebody should." He would not have guessed the cardiology fellow had such a humane side. Yet who was his outrage really directed at? Unfeeling house officers? Or himself for lacking the courage to let a patient die? A three-hundred-pound black dwarf, marveled Dan, trying to visualize such a freak, incapable of imagining what a miserable life he must have led. "All right," he said. "Where is he? Let's take a look."

"Bed one in the critical care area," Detwiler replied. "His chart and X-rays are in the conference room."

Tolliver "Tolerable" Turner was a forty-two-year-old achondroplastic dwarf who stood a little under four feet and weighed two hundred ninety pounds. The "achondroplastic" designation meant that his head and trunk were disproportionately larger than his limbs, and his nickname sprang from his habitual answer when anybody asked how he was feeling. His life, from its beginnings as a foundling in a public orphanage to his progressive invalidism from arthritis and obesity, was a testimony to human endurance.

As Dan listened in morbid fascination to Detwiler's recital of Turner's case history, he found himself unable to assimilate it, having no point of comparison within the realm of his own experience. Tolliver Turner was clearly the victim of a lifelong series of dirty tricks for which only he would be made to pay.

Dan did, however, appreciate the desperate medical straits the dwarf was in. His blood pressure was low, his breathing rapid and rattling, his tissues so dangerously deficient in oxygen that his lips and nailbeds had a bluish tinge. As described by Detwiler, he was obviously *in extremis* and Dan grew impatient to see him while he yet lived. "All right," he said, abruptly silencing Detwiler in the midst of reading off a long list of laboratory test results, "I've heard enough. He's certainly in right heart failure. But are you convinced he's had a massive pulmonary embolus?"

"Aren't you?" Detwiler challenged. "Have you the slightest doubt after all I've told you?"

"I've been fooled before."

"Maybe so. But all the clinical signs point to pulmonary embolism and if I learned anything from you in handling the Kinsella case, it's to trust my clinical judgment."

"Lead on," Dan said.

In all his years of medical practice Dan had never before seen anybody like Tolliver Turner. His head was at least twice normal size and peculiarly shaped, its bossed brow, snoutlike nose, and protruding lower jaw making him look more anthropoid than human. A miniature Gargantua. His stubby arms barely reached his waist and appeared flipperlike in comparison to the rest of him. His abdomen was immense, so distended with fluid from within and larded with fat that thick layers of flab hung in apronlike folds over his flanks and groin. His legs were ankleless and elephantine, their chronically stretched and swollen skin thickened into hide and badly ulcerated. With his swaybacked deformity and enormous buttocks, Tolliver Turner looked more like he was balanced, egglike, on top of the bed than lying in it.

Dan was both repulsed and fascinated. His geneticist friends had taught him that nature often revealed her secrets through her mutations. But what, except her innate perversity, had she revealed here?

Numerous plastic tubes penetrated Turner's body, the most important having been inserted via an arm vein and threaded through the right side of his heart into the pulmonary artery to measure the back-pressure of blood trying to perfuse his lungs. Its free end was attached to a recording device mounted on the face of a portable cart beside his bed. Also attached to the instrument panel were a host of other tubes and wires that continuously monitored blood pressure, electrocardiogram, pulse, and respiratory rate. Additional instruments on the cart could measure brain waves and pulmonary function, if necessary, to tell the emergency-room physicians everything they needed to know about the patient except his feelings, which very few wanted to know.

Bending over him, Dan saw that Tolliver Turner was awake, his spaniel eyes wide with terror. Recoiling slightly from the intensity of the look, Dan wondered if the cause of his terror was fear of dying or fear of further cruelty from his fellow men.

After examining him briefly Dan led Detwiler back to the conference room where they could confer in private.

"Well," Detwiler said, "do we try to save him or don't we?"

Dan scowled. Much as that question preyed on his mind, he did not like hearing it spoken. "What have you done for him so far?"

Detwiler shrugged. "Mainly try to get him in good enough shape to survive the trip up to the intensive care unit. But it's been a losing battle so far."

"How so?"

"Well, when he first came in he was puffing and wheezing like an old locomotive and bluer than the waters of the Bay. Or would you prefer a more scientific description?"

"I get the picture," Dan said curtly. "Go on."

"Okay. A bolus of heparin and mask oxygen helped relieve his wheezing and he pinked up a little, only not too much. So with both his blood pressure and oxygen tension low, I decided to slip a Swan-Ganz catheter into his pulmonary artery. I almost wish now that I hadn't."

"Why's that?" Dan asked.

" 'Cause his pulmonary artery pressure was over eighty—which either means he's had a massive pulmonary embolus or a shower of smaller emboli superimposed on chronic pulmonary hypertension. Either way, with a PA pressure that high, he's not long for this world."

"No, he's not," Dan agreed. "So what'd you do next?"

"For a mad moment I thought of calling in the cardiac surgeons and letting him die on their service. But I knew damned well none of them would touch him. One look and they'd laugh in my face. I also thought of starting a streptokinase drip in the hope it might open up his pulmonary artery a bit, but—" Detwiler shrugged futilely. "He's allergic to it."

"How do you know that?"

"The computer said so. He had a hell of a reaction to the stuff when they gave it to him at City Hospital six months ago. Went into such severe bronchospasm they had to do a trach on him."

Dan nodded. One of his first official acts as general

director had been to install a computer system for instant retrieval of all hospital records, providing his staff physicians with immediate access to valuable information, particularly drug allergies, and sparing their patients unnecessary duplication of laboratory tests. Initially the computer contained data only on Commonwealth General patients, but at Dan's urging, other local hospitals joined in, so that now the medical records of every Bostonian were included in its memory banks. Tolliver Turner was merely the latest of countless beneficiaries of Dan's innovative system. But now that they knew he was allergic to the most potent clot-dissolving agent available, what more could they do for him?

"All right," Dan said. "So surgery's out, streptokinase's out, and heparin is obviously not enough for him. So all that leaves is to call in the clergyman of his choice and bow out. Agreed?"

"I suppose," Detwiler muttered dejectedly.

"You suppose!" Dan mocked. *"Do* you agree or *don't* you?"

Detwiler shifted uneasily under his stare.

Exasperatedly Dan said, "Well, I'll be damned! You don't agree at all. If you had, you wouldn't have been spoiling for a fight a while ago, and you wouldn't have asked me to see your patient." He shook his head disdainfully. "A three-hundred-pound dwarf, for Chrissake! Kicking up a fuss over a patient like that leads me to believe you were either a circus-freak fancier in your younger days or else there's one more thing you want to try on him. So how about letting me in on it."

"Thrombolysin," Detwiler said. He knew Dan was familiar with the experimental drug, having seen him at the recent research conference where its merits were discussed.

Dan paused thoughtfully. U-6685, otherwise known by the resurrected name of 'thrombolysin,' was a synthetic polypeptide currently being tested for clinical efficacy by several of the nation's leading medical centers. He remembered little more about the drug other than the results obtained from the eight desperately ill patients it was tried on here: four had promptly improved and four had bled to death. Thus the outcome for any given patient was as predictable as a coin toss. Nonetheless, Detwiler was right. Thrombolysin represented Turner's only hope to continue his blighted existence. Without it he would almost certainly perish within the hour. With it he might meet his Maker even sooner—unless his Maker had reasons of His own for postponing their encounter.

"Hmmm," Dan mused, "it's risky as hell. But what've we got to lose except several pints of blood when he starts to hemorrhage. Still, as Nan Forrester's fond of saying, it's easier to treat bleeding than clotting. Easier, and often a lot messier, especially when there's no known antidote to stem the bleeding. But—" He nodded permissively. "If heroics are your style, go ahead and give it. I'll back you up."

"I can't!" Detwiler blurted.

"Why not?"

"'Cause Cartmill won't release any. Not without a pre- and post-infusion pulmonary arteriogram to document its effects."

"And you won't risk the arteriogram, I take it?"

"Damned right, I won't! Not with his pulmonary artery pressure so high. Just one squirt of dye through his Swan-Ganz catheter could finish him off."

"It could," Dan agreed. "So?"

"So I was headed up to the cardiovascular lab to have it out with that English prick when I ran into you."

"I see," said Dan. "And now you want me to intercede on your behalf."

"I do."

Dan smiled wryly. "I'm beginning to wish that I'd never said more than 'Good morning' to you. I don't mind doing a little arm-twisting when the occasion demands, but what are we really trying to accomplish here? Save the life of a three-hundred-pound dwarf who probably can't be saved and might be better off dead?"

"Something like that. But how do we decide?"

"We ask him," Dan said.

Detwiler blinked. "Ask him whether he wants to live or die? Gawd!"

"I doubt God ever asked him. Want me to do it?"

"Yes, Dr. Lassiter," Detwiler said without hesitation. "I sure do."

Walking from the conference room back to the critical care area, Dan wondered why he had involved himself in such a hopeless case when he already had so much else on his mind. What was he trying to prove? That he was a worthy mentor to his house staff, a healer nonpareil, a Christ-like savior? Or could it be that by trying to rescue Tolliver Turner he was also rescuing himself? Every pivotal moment in Dan's life had occurred in the presence of death or near-death: the Korean War slaughter that led him to study medicine, the chance selection of a young cadaver that led him to self-revelation and whatever medical greatness he had achieved, Gundersen's funeral that led him to Kris. Yet what could he possibly learn from this pitiable dwarf that transcended the medical aspects of his case and applied to Dan's unresolved conflicts over the Secretary of Health post, Lem, his wife? What possible lesson, insight, epiphany, could emerge through Tolliver Turner to enlighten him on the nature of God, love, and death—the three great mysteries that intrigued Dan most, even though he was certain of the existence of only one of them? Was the sole purpose of their encounter merely to enforce Dan's already deep-rooted cynicism? He hoped not. From almost his first glimpse of Tolliver Turner a feeling had begun to grow that they were meant to interact in some significant way. Had not dwarfs been housed by ancient kings because they were believed to be bearers of good luck?

Dan arrived at the critical care area, with Detwiler

lagging a few steps behind. This time he drew the curtains surrounding Tolliver Turner's bed and removed his oxygen mask so they could converse. "Mr. Turner, I'm Dr. Daniel Lassiter," he began, "and if you're up to it I'd like to talk to you."

Slowly, painfully, Tolliver turned his massive head in Dan's direction. He wet his lips, swallowed several times, and between gasping intakes of breath managed a barely audible whisper. From what little Dan could make out, Turner had heard of him and what a good doctor he was from a cousin down in Mississippi.

Dan thanked him and went on. "Mr. Turner," he said gravely, "I believe in telling my patients the truth about their condition, hard as that can sometimes be on them, so listen carefully. You've thrown another blood clot to your lungs, a big one, and I'm not sure we'll be able to save you this time. But we'll try, if you really want us to."

Tolliver Turner looked uncomprehending.

"Do you want to live, Mr. Turner?"

"Do—I—want—to—live?" He mouthed the words with great difficulty. "That what you askin'?"

Dan nodded uncomfortably.

"Huh," he grunted. "No doctor ever asked me that before. Not once in all my years. Well, let me tell you—" Suddenly he was seized by a paroxysm of harsh coughing. Frothy, blood-tinged spittle welled up in his throat and trickled out the corners of his mouth. Trying to swallow it down he began to choke. Dan grasped him behind the neck and attempted to sit him up so he wouldn't aspirate, but couldn't budge him. He ordered Detwiler to grab the suction tube off the wall and suck him out while he elevated the head of the bed mechanically. Once that was done, Turner's throat-rattling gradually ceased and his breathing calmed. Dan took a cloth from the bedstand and gently wiped the sweat from the dwarf's face. He was about to replace the oxygen mask over his nose and mouth when Tolliver Turner drew back and shook his head. His plaintive look told Dan that even in his enfeebled condition he did not want to lose this chance to talk, and by straining his ears and reading Turner's lips Dan got the gist of what he had to say.

"I know what I look like," he told Dan. "What I am. But I've had my good moments too. I like to read and watch TV, and best of all I like to go on trips. Not real ones, mind-trips. Give me a picture book to look at and I can be gone for hours. But you ask me a tough question, so let me ask you one: You're a doctor; you've seen lots of people die. Do you think there's anything more?"

"I don't know," Dan answered. "I think so, but I'm not sure."

"Me, neither," Tolliver said wistfully. "Lord, wouldn't it be nice to look like everybody else. But I got to die and be reborn to do that, and since nobody knows for sure if that happens, I guess I better hang on long as I can. So do the best you can for me."

Dan promised him that he would and started to move away, but Turner caught his arm. "Thanks for talkin' to me, Doc," he rasped. "Good to know my feelings count for something too."

In the conference room Dan phoned Cartmill, the co-director of the thrombolysin project in charge of dispensing the drug, and summoned him down. He appeared within minutes, a cloth-covered ledger in one hand, a black satchel in the other. Seated at the far end of the table Dan beckoned him over and stared hard at the tall, gaunt-faced Englishman before rising to shake hands and offer him a chair. Cartmill sank into it and listened attentively, if uneasily, to the general director's arguments for giving Detwiler's patient the drug now. Yes, Dan told him, he was thoroughly familiar with the requirement of a pulmonary arteriogram on each recipient; he himself had approved the research protocol. And yes, he realized that making exceptions, for any reason, was not only poor scientific practice but against FDA regulations and so illegal. But science was passionless, Dan reminded him, and men were not. He simply could not stand by and let a patient in this hospital die when, in his considered judgment, thrombolysin therapy offered a slim chance of saving him. Cartmill looked properly sympathetic, but not until Dan told him he would assume full responsibility did he hand over the satchel containing the drug along with instructions on how to administer it, and depart.

Minutes later, Dan joined Detwiler and the ER nurse at Tolliver Turner's bedside. The heparin he had been anticoagulated with earlier had now been neutralized and a glucose solution containing the thrombolysin dripped directly into his pulmonary artery via the previously placed Swan-Ganz catheter. If Turner were as allergic to it as he had been to the streptolysin he would have reacted violently by now, Dan surmised. But he still had to surmount the risk of massive hemorrhage. Would he? Did Dan really want him to? The healer in him did; the existentialist philosopher was not so sure, since it was one of the few times in his medical life he could view his old adversary, death, as more liberator than destroyer.

Together with Detwiler, Dan waited the full forty minutes for the thrombolysin infusion to run in. In his mind's eye he could picture the drug working on the clot in Turner's pulmonary artery; loosening and splitting the peptide linkages on its surface until entire strands of fibrin began to unravel and fragment and be dispersed into the circulation. But Dan also knew the drug attacked indiscriminately, digesting old blood clots as well as new ones, the essential along with the injurious, and soon Tolliver Turner began to ooze blood from his nose and needle-puncture sites.

Tensely Dan watched as Detwiler inserted a nasal pack to stem the nosebleed, and the nurse applied pressure dressings to the stigmata on his limbs. Suddenly Turner jerked his arm free from the nurse's grasp, ripped off his oxygen mask, and coughed up a mouthful of blood clots onto the bedsheet. As Dan rushed to suction him, the two exchanged strained looks. Tolliver Turner was close to death, was probably even welcoming it, Dan realized, but even so he brusquely ordered the nurse to have him typed and cross-matched for ten units of fresh blood and transferred at once to the shock unit.

Chapter Fifteen

When Dan finally got back to his office that afternoon, there was the usual stack of telephone messages, memos, and urgent letters awaiting him, along with a remarkable discovery for which Jimmy Dallesio was unwittingly responsible. Dan had promised to review the outpatient record Gundersen had kept on Charles Cheverton for him and just before departing for Washington had asked his secretary, Hedley, to locate it and leave it on his desk. To her surprise it was missing from his files. She had spent hours futilely searching for it, then on a hunch phoned her predecessor, Paula, now living in quiet retirement on Cape Cod, and learned that Gundersen had kept a special cache of VIP patient records safely hidden from prying eyes in the main hospital vault. Dan's phone call gained her entry into the vault where she quickly found the green metal lockbox Paula had described and brought it back to the office triumphantly. Together they hunted out the right key from those Gundersen had left scattered in his desk drawers and Dan opened it. It held about two dozen patient charts, some so old that the file folders were yellow and curling at the edges.

Dan spotted Cheverton's at once and was about to remove it when he was suddenly distracted, nearly stunned, to read the name on an adjacent folder, a name as famous as any on earth. This was a patient that he had never heard Gundersen mention: a former Boston resident who was now President of the United States.

Dan's hands shook slightly as he lifted the President's folder. Although he had inherited the record from Gundersen with the rest of his medical domain, he was guiltily aware that he might be violating the man's privacy by looking inside. But knowledge is power, Dan knew, and proven medical knowledge can be the most powerful of all.

Ten minutes later he had read both men's records. Cheverton's revealed little of significance. But the medical history of the young man who was destined to become President contained one of the best-kept secrets in the annals of American politics.

Dan's scalp prickled and his gut stirred at the immense medical, political, even personal consequences of his find. Pushing the button on his intercom that signaled Hedley to hold all calls, he meticulously reread Gundersen's crabbed notes. Then he leaned back, propped his feet on his desk, and ruminated over its many imponderables.

Did the President know so revealing a record still existed? Had Gundersen promised to destroy it and for some unknowable reason reneged? Did other physicians, particularly any AMA stalwarts, know enough of the man's affliction to make veiled threats to expose it? Most puzzling of all, how could anybody so closely scrutinized as a United States President keep such a condition hidden all these years when he couldn't even renew his driver's license legally without disclosing it?

Dan knew the disease the President suffered varied widely in severity and he probably had a form of it that did not impair his ability to function at all. So he left no great compulsion to reveal it to the press for the protection of the American public. But what of Dan's own protection? What would he do if ever his sense of medical morality clashed head-on with that of the President's?

The memory of the tense two hours Dan had spent in the FBI Director's office yesterday afternoon still rankled. From the outset he suspected that everything these high-level officials confided had been carefully scripted to manipulate if not mislead him, and their refusal to divulge why Lem Harper wanted to contact him confirmed it. When Nels Freiborg finally admitted that they were withholding this information by direct order of the President, Dan had felt powerless to protest and more than a little resentful.

Well, he was powerless no longer. Because Jimmy Dallesio had asked for a bit of journalistic information he had stumbled, perhaps unethically, upon a secret with enormous power to further his own ambitions in the health field or thwart those of the President's. He could now strike back if necessary; the medical file in his hands provided him the weapon, and if pushed to the wall by any political steamroller he might just use it, regardless of the consequences. But before he faced that awesome decision he would first have to learn where and how far the President and his obedient accomplices were leading him.

Dan returned both charts to the filing box, relocked it, and summoned Hedley to take it back to the hospital vault for safekeeping. His preoccupied look prompted her to ask if he were feeling well. He assured her that he was, wished her a pleasant weekend, and followed her out of the office for the intensive care unit.

Matt Kinsella was sound asleep and snoring so sonorously when Dan entered his cubicle that he did not wake him. Instead he reviewed his hospital chart and was relieved and gratified by what he saw. Kinsella's doctors had been able to reduce his daily cortisone dosage from 300 milligrams to the much safer maintenance level of 30 milligrams, and his serial chest X-rays showed no increase in heart size, indicating that the blood Dan had removed from his pericardial sac as a life-saving measure had not reaccumulated. Seeking out Sanbar, Dan confirmed that the chart accurately reflected Kinsella's still serious but steadily improving condition and then reluctantly headed for the shock unit to check on Tolliver Turner.

Suddenly the door opened and Detwiler came out looking more like a butcher in a meat-packing plant than a doctor. The front of the cotton gown he had donned over his white coat was splattered with blood, the sleeves nearly saturated, and the expression on his face bespoke their failure to keep the pathetic dwarf alive.

Detwiler approached within a few feet of Dan, grimaced, and said, "Turner died a few minutes ago."

"What happened?"

"He bled out. Christ, I never saw anything like it! We pumped all ten units into him, along with every clotting factor in the blood bank, but none of it did any good. A massive brain hemorrhage finally finished him off."

Dan gestured. "It was a good try."

"Yeah," Detwiler growled through clenched teeth. Then more philosophically, "Yeah, I suppose it was. Thanks for your support, Dr. Lassiter. I'll tell Cartmill so he can fill out his little report," he added and walked away.

Dan watched him remove his gown and deposit it in the hamper outside the nursing station before going inside to wash the blood off his hands.

The next moment he saw a nurse, her gown even more bloodied than Detwiler's, come out of the shock unit. "God," she groaned, "is it ever a mess in there! I'll need a mop and pail to clean it up. I don't dare ask the orderly to do it. He's from Haiti and believes dwarfs can put a hex on you."

"Even dead ones?" Dan asked.

"I don't know. I'll ask Juan that, if I ever see him again. You going to want a post?"

"Yes, if we can get one."

The nurse snorted and shook her head. "The pathology boys will love you for that! Ah, well, at least they'll have a bloodless corpse to cut up. His blood's all over the bed and floor."

"I can imagine," remarked Dan, content to do just that. He already knew what a live three-hundred-pound dwarf looked like and had no desire to see a dead one. After the nurse had moved on he thought back to his brief but memorable talk with Tolliver Turner, to the uncertainty they had shared whether he could or should be saved, and was glad that he had finally found release from his repulsive form. One aspect of his death bothered Dan, however. As if it were not enough that he had been born and lived out his life as a freak, Tolliver Turner had not even been allowed a natural death. Instead he had died from the complications of a medical experiment. The dangers of the drug he was to receive had been explained to him and he had signed the required consent form, making it all perfectly legal. Medical science had even benefitted from his death. Just how much, Dan would learn from Cartmill's next progress report on thrombolysin.

But the most the experience had done for him was reinforce an old conviction. The Lord giveth and the Lord taketh away just one thing: *life*. For better or for worse, that was the extent of His involvement in mankind, and Dan refused to ponder further the mystery of His ways. It was all in the book of Job and numerous lesser tracts, and he had nothing new to contribute after unsuccessfully trying to save Tolliver Turner's life.

The cool breeze blowing in his face and his anticipation at seeing Kris again brightened Dan's spirits as he walked to his car in the parking lot. Instead of troubling his conscience, his near-seduction of Kit Colbine had the opposite effect, reaffirming his deep devotion for his wife. So much had happened since seeing her last Sunday that he hardly knew where to begin to tell her about it. But before that he would ask about her, her happenings, lest he arouse her resentment over his being the freer, more active member of the marriage. It was a lesson Dan had learned late but well in their relationship and diligently applied to ease the unspoken but evident strain his visits produced in her.

Hilde, Kris's housekeeper, met him at the front door, exchanged pleasantries, and gave him one disturbing bit of news before he went on alone to the combination library and family room in the west wing of the house. Kris, wearing a pale yellow dressing gown, was lying on the couch by the fireplace when he entered. She opened her arms to him for a lengthy hug and brief kiss.

Dan drew up a chair and they stared appraisingly at each other. Kris's long straight blonde hair looked particularly becoming. But her face was pale and her eyes, once so prominent and gleaming with vivacity, now appeared sunken beneath swollen lids and dulled by orbital shadows.

"Hilde tells me you've been doing some bleeding," Dan said casually, trying to mask his concern.

Kris frowned. "Hilde talks too much."

"Wasn't she supposed to?"

She shrugged. "I don't recall whether I specifically told her not to or what. But she should've had the good sense to let me decide."

"Are you bleeding much?"

"Not really. Just enough for Jim Neubeck to advise I stay off my feet until it stops—which it seems to be doing."

"Good," Dan said and smiled reassuringly, even though her facial twitches told him more than her casual dismissal. "How *are* you feeling?"

Kris hesitated. "Oh, about the way you look. Terribly restless and tired. But not as bad as you! Haven't you been getting any sleep?"

"Not much," he admitted. "Except for a few nights ago when I had to go to the hospital after midnight to see an emergency consult—Matt Kinsella of all people —I don't even have a reason. I just can't sleep."

"How's Matt doing now?" Kris asked with professional curiosity.

Dan told her.

"Nan tells me you made yourself look pretty good by the expert way you handled his case." She winked. "Like a real clinician. Rare praise from Nan. Made me a little envious."

"How so?" asked Dan, pleased.

"Oh, you know. Wondering if I'd have been as sharp and sure of myself as you apparently were."

"I wasn't sure at all! Just lucky to remember that

adrenal hemorrhage was a rare complication of coumadin overdosage. Believe me, it was touch and go all the way."

"Even so, it must've given you a good feeling to know you're still smarter than the residents. It always did me."

"Miss it?" Dan said softly.

"The hospital? The action? Of course, I miss it. But—" she hesitated, her frown telling him she wanted to drop the subject. "Why don't you fix us a drink? There should still be ice in the bucket."

Dan went to the bar between the bookcases and poured whiskeys and sodas. "Did you catch me on the *Today* show?"

"Uh huh. Not only you, but those big eyes Kit Colbine had for you, even when what you were saying wasn't all that fascinating. That hasn't started up again, has it?" she asked pointedly.

Dan shook his head, loathe to speak even a partial lie. But Kris's skeptical stare forced him to. "I swear it hasn't. I haven't been with any woman since we split. Never mind why. I just haven't."

"You might sleep better if you did?"

"Maybe," he conceded. "But I'll stick with Dalmane a while longer. It's gone when you wake up."

"What else have you been doing or not doing?"

Dan was tempted to tell her about Tolliver Turner but held back, afraid that the unrelieved tragedy of the dwarf's life and death might depress more than fascinate her. Instead he sketchily filled her in on his week's political activities: his meeting with Jimmy over the unusually thorough security check run on him; his tense, top-level meeting in the FBI Director's office yesterday afternoon; even some of what he had been told about Lem. He realized this was violating a strict confidence, even national security, but she was still his wife, there was no one whose judgment he trusted more, and he wanted her to share the deep dilemmas in his life.

"Good God!" she exclaimed when he had finished. "What do you make of Lem now? I can hardly believe he's the same man we had that marvelous evening with in Paris. He sounds so damned ruthless and sinister."

"I know," Dan said. "I had a hell of a time believing all they accused him of myself."

"Did you?"

"Most of it. At least his role in blinding those sheriffs and the Detroit Massacre. The FBI was damned convincing about that. As for the rest—the part about his plotting racial warfare if the upcoming elections go against his people—I couldn't believe that."

"Why not?" Kris asked.

"For one, they were contradicting themselves: making Lem out to be hardly more than a madman when all along they'd been telling me what a masterful revolutionary strategist he was. I'm also pretty sure they had an ulterior motive for trying to prejudice me against him."

"What motive?"

"I don't know. But if the FBI's forecast is correct, I expect I'll be finding out soon. From Lem himself."

Kris stared at him worriedly. "For God's sake, be careful. Be very careful, Dan. I want our child to have a live father, you know." Impulsively she reached out to squeeze his hand, relinquishing it reluctantly. "Damn, I wish . . . I only wish—"

"You wish what?"

"Oh, lots of things," she said vaguely. "That I wasn't so fat and lazy and pregnant. That I could be more help to you right now. Mostly, that the time hadn't passed when we could really talk."

"Has it?" he asked wistfully.

"I don't mean to hurt you, Dan, but I'm afraid so. I'm not happy about it either; in fact, pretty miserable. But there are certain flaws in our relationship I've simply had to face. Some things I *do* understand about you. Better than you might think. Better than even you yourself. But there's still so much that I don't. Especially what you want and need to be more at peace with yourself. I'm not even sure how you feel deep-down about women."

"Women!" Dan protested. "What difference does that make? You're the only woman who's ever meant anything to me, Kris. The only one who's ever given me roots, a home, a sense of belonging to one person and one place. All the things I lost when I was still a kid and never found again until you came along. Don't you know you've given me the only really happy years of my life?"

"Dan, don't!" Kris cried as she saw the moisture in his eyes. "Oh, come here," she urged, taking and holding him tightly in her arms. "Oh, Dan, I *do* know. I've always known. That's why I kept on loving you even when you were so busy we hardly talked for days. Why I could bear the terrible frustration I felt while you tossed and turned beside me in bed all night, knowing how driven by demons you were but never getting you to open up enough for me to understand them. Maybe help free you from them. That's why I wanted something more in our lives."

"A child, you mean?"

"Yes, a child. But you've never really tried to understand all it could mean to us and I've never been able to explain. Not when you kept so busy all the time. And now I can't explain; I simply don't have the strength. So you'll just have to go on believing I was acting selfish, deceitful—anything you wish—until it happens."

"Maybe I could understand it better if you weren't jeopardizing your life."

"It's my life, isn't it?"

"But I'm still your husband. Part of the responsibility for it belongs to me."

"Maybe once," she conceded. "Not for a long time."

"When did it stop?"

"When?" she said wryly. "When it was no longer enough to even fill your leisure time let alone your needs. When you had to have more and more outside challenges to keep you chasing after Gundersen's ghost."

"But we shared so many good times together. Don't you miss them?"

"Of course, I miss them. Just as I miss medicine. Just as I miss you pressed against me in bed at night. I miss all of it. But not as much as I'd miss this," she said, patting her stomach. "What's growing inside of me—kicking the hell out of me. What's going to happen to me soon—to both of us, really, if only you let it."

Dan was moved by the look she gave him, so tender and hopeful yet mysterious, beyond his masculine ken. But the warm, wifely feeling it imparted, missing so long from his life, only accentuated that void; made him so aware of how despondent and depressed and lost he was without her that he was on the verge of capitulating, of begging her to take him back. But he hesitated and the chance was gone.

The next moment Kris said, "Oh, I almost forgot. Mother's coming to stay with me for a while."

Dan's eyebrows lifted. "All the way from Norway?"

"That's right. Her wanting to come surprised me too. But she is. I'm expecting her next week."

In seven years of marriage Dan had met Kris's mother only twice: once at their wedding and once at a medical meeting in Copenhagen. He had liked and admired Marta as a woman of keen intelligence, wit, and conviction. But it was hard to picture her as anybody's mother. As Kris, her only child, ruefully acknowledged, motherhood had more or less befallen Marta as an accident, as had a marriage to a top amateur American tennis player named Jack Torvald, which had begun almost simultaneously with her pregnancy and barely outlasted it.

And now after so many years Marta was coming to visit, to fill as best she could the unaccustomed role of mother, and Dan resented it.

"You don't look too happy about Mother coming," Kris remarked.

Dan feigned astonishment. "Why should that make me unhappy? She's a great lady. How about you?"

"I'll be glad to see her. She's certain to liven things up around here. Especially with all she'll have to say about the political mess this country is in. But I can't help feeling you look disappointed. Why, Dan?"

He almost told her, almost let the last buttress to his pride fall and confess how much he missed and needed and wanted to come home to her. But how could he possibly do that with a Senate confirmation hearing next week, with all the administrative problems he had to solve before leaving his job at the hospital, with his mysterious reunion with Lem coming up? How could he even promise Kris he'd be there to drive her to the hospital when the time came for her to deliver?

"Why?" he began haltingly, almost bitterly. "Because you happen to be right about my leading such a full, useful life—useful to everybody but myself. I tried to explain it to Jimmy the other day: how, except for marrying you, I've never done anything for myself because I wanted to do it, but always as a reaction to someone else, the demands they place on me, or me on myself. How, like some Kafka character, I'm turning into more of a machine than a man. But you know all that, don't you? It's the thing you despise most about me."

Kris's face creased with anguish. "I don't despise you, Dan. Not anything about you. You're the most decent and admirable man I've ever known. It's just that you've pieced yourself out to so many people you're no longer a whole person. Not your own person anyway. Maybe I did have the biggest piece of you for a time, but even that wasn't much. Oh, don't you see, Dan," she implored. "Don't you see how little of your life belongs to you anymore?"

Ruefully he admitted, "I'm beginning to."

"It's almost—oh, I don't know if this is really fair of me to say—but it's almost as if you've carried the way you practice medicine to the same extreme. You're not only dedicated to saving your patients' lives, it's as though you're determined to die—die slowly—along with them. That's a form of self-murder, you know."

"Oh, Kris, that's not true," he protested, but held in the grip of sudden revelation he was no longer sure. His mind flashed back to a mass burial of cadavers in a medical school cemetery outside of Boston; to the final laying to rest of the scraps of flesh and bone left of the cadaver he had dissected and the profound insight that had struck him as he personally shoveled clods on Rick Ferrar's pine coffin. It was through that one symbolic gesture, the returning to earth and to nature what had sprung from it, that Dan's long-repressed bitterness toward death for robbing him of his entire family by age sixteen, his personification of it as the archenemy, had finally surfaced. The perfection he strove ever after to achieve in medicine had begun there.

But he thought he had overcome all that, grown more detached toward death. Their pitched battle had gone on so long it had bred mutual respect, even intimacy, between them. Maybe Kris didn't understand that. Or maybe she understood only too well that he had given away so much of himself that even death, much as he might feel its fatal lure at times, was having a hard time claiming him. Could that be the source of his driving ambition: that lacking self-love he was making a bid for immortality, "the love of anonymous people," as the next best thing? But it all seemed so unnatural and self-defeating. How could he be such an expert on the problems of preserving life and such a novice on the problems of living? Especially living with himself?

Kris broke into his reverie. "Hey, remember me? I'm here too," she said. "And seeing as little of you as I do, I want to be talked to. So quit your brooding and talk to me. At least, fix me another drink."

Dan did and settled back in his chair.

"When's your Senate hearing set for?" she asked.

"Next Wednesday or Thursday."

"How's it look?"

"Nels is fairly optimistic. Based on his latest head count he figures I ought to end up with three or four votes to spare. That is, unless the AMA pulls something at the last minute to turn the committee against me."

"Much chance of that happening?"

"Not as far as I know."

"Then it looks like you'll be our nation's first Secretary of Health in another month."

"Looks that way," he said tonelessly.

"Oh, Dan, I'm sorry," Kris lamented. "Sorry to put such a damper on everything you've worked so hard to get. Put you through the mental torture I did tonight. As if you didn't already have enough on your mind! But somehow you finally seemed ready to listen." Her face suddenly brightened. "How 'bout coming out for Sunday brunch? I'll have Hilde fix her special *apfelkugel* and promise I won't be so hard on you. Can you come?"

Dan smiled. "Far as I know. In fact, I'd love to."

Kris hesitated, looking sheepish. "Want to feel the baby? Oh, I know it's rather a silly ritual, but do it anyway to please me."

Gently Dan placed both hands on her protuberant, vein-streaked abdomen until he felt a few vigorous movements. Then he knelt to listen for fetal heart tones on her lower right side, pretending to count them at one hundred forty beats per minute.

He left shortly afterward, comforted by Kris's high spirits but worried by her haggard appearance and that her vaginal bleeding might presage another dangerously low-lying placenta. Still, if she were as certain as she claimed about her last menstrual date, she was within a week or two of the critical seventh month when even if the baby had to be delivered by Caesarian section it stood a slim chance of survival. The thought consoled him as did the prospect of spending a pleasant Sunday with Kris.

But after leaving the dirt road for the two-lane highway, Dan suddenly felt tense and tired, as if every blinding headlight flash from oncoming cars was meant to remind him that no matter how carefully he drove, his life was still on a collision course—one he'd set for himself so long ago that he had virtually no chance to escape and only the barest chance to survive.

But it was not the possibility of premature death that troubled him so much as its inevitable huckster, its forerunner: demoralization. He recognized its heavy hand in the dreariness of his leisure moments, his growing aversion for meeting life's eternal demands.

What Dan felt went far beyond his ability to contend, to cope, to hope to win out; he no longer even cared. He had already won one for the Gipper, and another, and a third—enough to know it was never-ending. That winning itself was illusory and the Gipper, however inspirational he was for young people, most of whom lost not won for him, was the foil of disillusionment and ultimately death.

Dan depressed the gas pedal, speeding up to 80 mph, as he reached the coast road. With the vast black void of the Atlantic on one side and the lights of homes and tenement houses merging into a blurry streak on the other, he was suddenly impatient to get back to his apartment, even if all that awaited him there was the usual soul-sapping loneliness, the inescapable toll that self-sufficiency or, more precisely, *self,* exacted from him.

Chapter Sixteen

Dan had been inside his apartment only long enough to take off his coat and tie when the phone rang. "Dr. Lassiter?" said the caller in a raspy-deep voice.

"Yes. Who's this?"

"Well, let's just say I'm callin' for a friend."

"What friend?" asked Dan brusquely.

"Well, now, this friend of mine would just as soon not have his name mentioned. But he said you'd know who he was if I told you he once had a buddy named Rick."

So it was Lem, thought Dan, his stomach muscles tightening. But why would Lem use an intermediary? Because he was afraid the FBI has his phone tapped? "Tell your friend I remember him now," he said. "What does he want?"

"To see you. On important business. Tonight."

"Tonight? Jesus, it's pretty late. Can't it wait till morning?"

"Afraid not, Dr. Lassiter. It ain't safe for him to be in any one place too long. So it has to be tonight. That is, if you're willin'."

Dan sighed deeply. "I suppose so. Where's he now?"

"Near enough to make it out to your place in about an hour."

"Okay, I'll be expecting him then. Need directions how to get here?"

"No, I drove out earlier this evening but you weren't home."

"You might've saved yourself a trip if you'd called first."

"Yeah, I know. But I wanted to look around a little."

"Like what you saw?" Dan said dryly.

"It's a real tony neighborhood, being close to the ocean and all . . . Well, don't want to tie you up on the phone with idle chatter. I'm Al, by the way. I'll be drivin' your friend out, but you won't meet me. He wants to talk to you alone."

"All right," Dan said resignedly. "Tell my friend I'll be glad to see him again."

"He'll be glad too, Dr. Lassiter. He thinks a lot of you. I'll have him at your place in another hour."

Dan hesitated. "Okay, but be careful driving. It gets pretty foggy around here this time of night. Drifts all the way up the coast from the Potomac."

"Don't worry 'bout that. I'm always real careful when he's in the car. But thanks for warning me about the fog. And thanks for seein' him. He's goin' to appreciate that. Good night, Dr. Lassiter."

Dan hung up the phone and sank into a chair, nervous excitement temporarily sweeping the torpor from his brain. Lem had contacted him earlier than he or the FBI had expected—which suggested that his "important business" had grown more urgent. And from the nature of the phone call, Lem was probably aware the FBI was watching him. But what could he possibly want? Was Lem seriously ill and wanted Dan to treat him? If only that was the crux of his visit he would oblige gladly. But Dan's instincts told him that something far more consequential, even perilous to himself, was involved. Otherwise why would Freiborg have acted so threatened by what Lem might reveal?

Wearily Dan rose from his chair and went into the kitchen to put on a pot of coffee. From there he shed the rest of his clothes and wandered into the bathroom to shower. His fatigue, returning with a rush, so stupefied him that each sudden movement made him giddy. Mentally he tallied up the amount of sleep he had gotten since they called him in to care for Matt Kinsella on Tuesday: twelve hours in four days! No matter how physically fit he was, he knew he couldn't keep this up without doing irreparable harm to himself.

He stayed in the icy shower spray until his shivering became uncontrollable. Two cups of strong black coffee helped dispel his mind-buzzing fatigue further. Then he dressed in shirt and slacks, tuned in an FM station to soft music, and sat down with a newspaper to wait. An hour had passed since the phone call and Lem was due. He listened for sounds of his arrival amid the faint hum of the air-conditioner unit and the muted melodies on the radio.

The doorbell roused Dan from reverie. The electric clock on the mantle showed 2:20 A.M. High time, he thought irritably and went to the door. Lem stood huge and shadowy in the hallway.

"Come in," said Dan and stood aside for him to enter.

"Lock it," Lem said curtly, closing the door behind him.

"It locks automatically." Dan turned to face him. Physically Lem was as imposing as ever: a hulking giant almost seven feet tall whose great breadth of shoulder was further emphasized by his flat stomach. But he had aged strikingly in the years since Dan last saw him. His stubbly hair and beard were nearly white and his erect, military carriage had become stooped, favoring a stronger right leg. Most disturbing of all to Dan's professional scrutiny were his eyes: bloodshot, darting furtively about, displaying an intense but inner-directed gleam uncomfortably reminiscent of the look chronically ill patients developed almost as a reflection of their flesh-eating diseases. Lem *was* sick. Seriously. Did he know it?

"Well, Doc," Lem said, forcing a grin. "How're you?"

"Tired! Of waiting too. I expected you two hours ago."

"Yeah, I know. Traffic held us up."

"At *this* hour?"

"Traffic behind us. It got a little heavy when we

first started out. But Al Beal, the guy who phoned you, finally managed to put some distance between them and us. Look, I'm pretty tired myself. Mind if I sit down?"

"Please do." Dan pointed to an easy chair.

Lem stumbled forward, caught himself on the arm of the chair, and settled into it. "Gettin' clumsy as hell in my old age," he grumbled. "Like they say, the bigger you are, the harder you fall—*apart.*"

"You falling apart?"

Lem grinned. "In some ways that maybe I'll get around to later. But I didn't come for no free medical consultation."

"What did you come for?"

"We'll get around to that too. Wouldn't mind a drink first, if you're offerin'."

"Still whiskey and water?"

"Yeah, if it's handy. Otherwise saki, vodka, so-chu —whatever's available."

"I'm drinking Crown Royal. That okay?"

Lem nodded. "How's that pretty doctor-wife of yours?" he asked as Dan handed him his drink.

"We're separated," Dan replied tersely, not intending to elaborate. But seeing Lem wince, remembering what close friends they had once been, he explained briefly.

"Well," Lem said, "I sure hope you work things out."

"What about you? Did you ever marry?"

"Not me!" Lem scoffed. "Never planned to. But havin' a kid at your age! That must be an experience to look forward to. I sure wish you and Kris a healthy one."

"Thanks," said Dan, yawning.

Lem took a long swallow of whiskey. "Yeah, I could envy you that, having no kids of my own. None I know of, anyway. I might've planted one in some native gal in my younger days. But if I did, she never told me."

"I'm surprised."

"About what?"

"That any African girl bearing your baby wouldn't tell you. Ought to be quite an honor having 'Devil-A's' child."

Lem peered at Dan over the rim of the glass. "How'd you know some places they call me that? I never told you."

"No," Dan said. "You sure as hell didn't! There's a lot you never told me about yourself. Some of it pretty fascinating too. Trouble is, the 'Devil-A' stories I've heard have reached near mythologic proportions. Makes it hard to separate fact from fiction. Also makes me realize how little I know about the real *you.* Practically nothing, which is a pretty sad commentary on the state of our twenty-five-year-old friendship."

Lem squinted appraisingly at him and slowly nodded. "Yeah, I can understand how you might feel that way. But you sure you want to know? That kind of inside stuff about a friend can get pretty heavy. Hard to carry around in your head without feelin' the urge to unburden yourself a little. Or maybe a lot, by tellin' the authorities. Not that I don't trust you; wouldn't be here if I didn't. But a lot of what I did over the years ain't nothin' to be proud of. Just had to be done, that's all. I'm no doctor, but I been responsible for a lot of lives too. My people's lives. We ain't too different in that respect, and if what I got in mind works out, we goin' to get a lot closer. But before comin' to that, I want to clear up any real doubts you got about me or my past. Tell you anything the FBI Director couldn't."

"You knew about that?"

Lem shrugged. "Not for a fact, I didn't. Not till you called me 'Devil-A'. But I knew a meeting between you two was bound to happen, especially after that big security investigation he ran—which was actually aimed more at me and certain things that worry hell out of the President than you personally. So I figured he'd be calling you in."

"How come you know so much of what goes on there?"

Lem shrugged. "You know how it is. We got informers in their organizations and they in ours. Which is okay. Up to a point, we *want* them to know what our aims are, so they don't scare hell out of everybody in Washington gettin' them wrong."

"What are they?" Dan asked.

"What they always been: fair treatment through fair elections, out of which will come better homes, better jobs, a better life. Which means we got to keep gettin' the right people elected. A racist Congress could stop us cold, like so many times before. All they need to do is cause more job layoffs, more cuts in welfare and unemployment benefits, and the big cities would erupt like wildfire."

"So what happens if you don't elect enough of your people to stop them from moving that way? What will you recommend then?"

Lem's eyes glinted mockingly. "What I recommend *then* won't matter none. Mostly I deal with blacks in high places these days. They're a savvy bunch—politicians, professional people, military men—and when I tell them how I see things they listen. But it ain't always been so. In my early days with Kenyatta, I tried talkin' political sense to starvin' Somali tribesmen and it was useless. All they'd listen to was their bellies growlin' and their babies bawlin'. So you see, Dan, hungry, desperate blacks won't listen to nobody, not even a resurrected Martin Luther King doing the miracle of the loaves and the fishes. If living conditions in the cities keep goin' to hell, there just ain't nothin' me or my organization can do."

"Not even cause a diversion elsewhere? Say, in Panama?"

Lem sneered. "That what they told you in Washington? Oh, Panama was a possibility. The political situation there's ripe to exploit. But we rejected it. How we goin' to benefit from a revolt in Panama? Send the white seventy percent of the U.S. regular army down there to crush it while the black troops turn around and take over Washington? That might make a good plot for a movie but militarily it's got the makings of another Yalu River disaster. Only this time it wouldn't be 'yellow hordes' but white who'd swarm all over us. That's the road to race suicide, not revolution."

"What makes you so sure?" Dan said. "After all, you've been involved in successful revolts before."

"Yeah, I been involved in them. But those were in poor, black African countries. Totally different from here. So forget what those Washington experts told you. There ain't goin' to be no all-out race war in this country. None I'm helpin' plan anyway."

"Maybe not," Dan conceded. "But you *do* have some kind of plan, don't you? One that's got the FBI, the CIA, even the President, worried as hell."

Lem smiled sardonically. "Yeah, I got me a plan. And they got good reason to worry, 'cause it's nothin' I dreamt up myself. Their own people did that, out of greed and inhumanity. No small fry or petty grafters either, but high-paid federal officials. And they got caught at it." Lem's eyes glittered disdainfully. "Caught like a thievin' nigger in a hen house. Only this time it happened the other way around. It was a nigger that nailed them, a computer wizard named Artemus Hill, and they killed him for it."

Dan winced. "They murdered him? Are you sure?"

"Damned right! Tried to make it look like an accident—carbon monoxide poisoning—but they were too late. Didn't know he'd sent a copy of his findings to his old math professor at Duke University who—"

"Now wait a second," Dan interrupted. "You're getting way ahead of me. *Who* murdered him and why?"

"We ain't exactly sure who yet, but we will be soon. We got it narrowed down to three top lawyers in the General Accounting Office. But explainin' the why's goin' to take some time, and before I do, I got to get something from my car."

"Jesus, Lem," he pleaded, "can't this wait till morning? I'm so tired I can barely see straight, let alone think straight. I'd much rather hear about it in the morning."

"Morning!" Lem jeered. "By morning I'll be halfway

home to Martinique and you'll be tied up on the telephone."

"The phone?" Dan puzzled. "To whom?"

Lem shrugged. "All depends—"

"On what?"

"On you and your conscience; whether you're your own man or the politicians'. Dependin' on that you'll either be phoning doctors you know down South to confirm what I'm going to tell you or else spillin' your guts to Freiborg and the FBI. That's a chance I just got to take. Like the big one I took comin' here."

"Okay," Dan sighed, "so it won't wait till morning. I suppose with more coffee in me I can stay awake a while longer. Go get whatever's in your car you want to show me. You want coffee too?"

Lem nodded. "Yeah, believe I do. 'Spanish Coffee,' " he added, rising to his feet. Suddenly he staggered sideways, knocking over a lamp and falling to his hands and knees.

Dan leaped up and knelt beside him. "Lem! You all right?"

"Yeah, fine," Lem grunted. "Foot fell asleep, is all."

But the sweat pouring from his forehead and the forceful throbbing of his neck arteries told Dan differently. "Roll on your back so I can examine you a little," he ordered, and gripping Lem's upper arm levered him into that position. He opened Lem's shirt collar and took a pulse reading from the carotid artery under his jaw. Its bounding character indicated high blood pressure.

"When's the last time you saw a doctor?" Dan asked.

"I travel with one."

"David Brattle?"

"Yeah, Brattle. You know him?"

"Not personally," Dan replied, withholding from Lem what he knew about him. "Is he downstairs now?"

"No, at the airport."

"When did he last check your blood pressure?"

Lem shrugged. "A week or so ago."

"And?"

"It runs a little high."

"How high?"

"Around 180, I think. He's got me on meds for it."

"What meds?"

"One's called Ismelin; the other's a water pill."

Ismelin! Dan reflected: an older, generally outmoded but powerful antihypertensive drug, notorious for producing steep postural drops in blood pressure and sudden dizzy spells like the one that had just felled Lem.

"What else's wrong with you?"

"Hip still gives me fits. Hurts so much at times I can hardly get around."

"Then why the hell haven't you had it replaced? They're doing total hip replacements in virtually every major hospital in the world these days."

Lem could have told him that his mysterious kidney ailment made the extensive hip operation too risky in the opinion of the orthopedic surgeons he had consulted, but he held back, realizing their time together was too limited to go into his state of health now. "It ain't all that bad," he lied. "Nothin' I can't live with."

"All right," said Dan, helping him up and back into his chair. "You rest here while I go get whatever you want out of your car. That okay?"

"Guess it'll have to be," Lem muttered. "It's a silver Lincoln Continental parked at the gas station on the corner. Walk toward it slowly and Al Beal will intercept you. Tell him I said to give you the leather suitcase locked in the trunk."

"And if he refuses?"

"Send him up. I'll tell him myself."

Dan nodded, but instead of moving toward the door stood shaking his head ruefully.

"Now what's the matter?" Lem asked exasperatedly.

"Oh, nothing. Just thinking how if you hadn't armtwisted me into studying for a final exam once I probably never would've become a doctor. Then I'd be of no use to you, the government, or anybody else right now. I'd be in bed!"

"Lord, wouldn't you know!" Lem sighed. "Let a well-meanin' nigger do a honky a favor and he never stops havin' second thoughts about it."

"Never does," Dan said cheerfully and left.

Chapter Seventeen

Dan was about halfway to the darkened gas station on the corner when he saw a bulky black man crossing the street diagonally toward him. They met at the base of the large Mobil sign jutting up from the driveway.

"Dr. Lassiter?" the black man said.

Dan nodded.

"Lem okay?"

Dan briefly described the dizzy spell he had suffered, assured Al it was not serious, and told him what Lem wanted. Al got the suitcase out of the car trunk and handed it over. "He trusts you a lot, Doc," he said after Dan had thanked him and started to turn away. "Try to do right by him."

The suitcase, though medium-sized, was surprisingly heavy. Dan lugged it up to his apartment, laid it at Lem's feet, and went into the kitchen to prepare a tray of coffee, whipping cream, and brandy.

When he returned Lem had a black cardboard-covered folder in his lap. Dan served up steaming cups of coffee laced with cognac and then settled back in his own chair, ready to listen.

"You know you'll be takin' on one big mother of a job as Secretary of Health?" Lem began.

"Yeah," Dan said wryly. "I *do* know. I lie awake nights worrying about it when people like you aren't keeping me up telling me."

"Okay, Doc," Lem said, taking command of the conversation. "You should also know you got a 1.9 billion dollar swindle in misused federal health funds to worry about!"

"W—what!" Dan hastily lowered his rattling cup and saucer to the table and leaned forward. "What did you say?"

"You heard right. 1.9 billion dollars. An impressive sum, ain't it? Bound to impress even the most professional swindlers. Only the bunch behind this were amateurs, and what's worse, they stole the money from sick people. That worth your stayin' up a while longer to hear about?"

Dan stared at him in consternation. "Damned right. If you can prove it."

"Oh, I can prove it," Lem said confidently. "Wouldn't be wasting your time if I couldn't. It took months to put together, but the proof's all here." He patted the suitcase. "A lot of it's been photocopied illegally, some even stolen, but we didn't have no choice. Not after they murdered Artemus Hill, the black man I told you about who first tumbled to it. Here's why." Lem handed him the cardboard-covered folder. "That's a copy of his report to the legal department of the GAO last April."

Dan leafed through the contents of the folder. Except for a few pages of narrative at the beginning and end, it consisted almost entirely of graphs, tabulated figures, and statistical analyses. "You understand what all this means?"

"Not at all," Lem admitted. "At first I couldn't understand ten words. But I made it my business to. Had each page explained to me by experts."

"Then maybe you'd better give me the gist for now."

"Glad to. The gist is that a large gang of health field professionals—doctors, dentists, druggists, hospital and HMO administrators, you name it—banded together to bilk the government out of a little of the two hundred twenty billion or so it doles out for health care each year. We don't really know how or where it got started, probably as some small-time operation. But somebody told somebody else and it didn't stay small-time for long. It was Hill's estimate that ninety-two counties in eight southwestern states were involved in the network. That's most likely a minimum figure. One thing's for sure, the scandal's spreadin', not shrinkin', which is what happens when people get the notion the federal government can be had. That they're givin' away money faster than their bookkeepers can keep track of it, or else feel so overworked and underpaid they don't give a damn. Sure, they know their duty as a law-abidin' citizen, and as a federal employee the procedure they're supposed to follow in such cases is all spelled out. But what if their own supervisor is on the take? What if the top men hired themselves a gang of enforcers? They could not only be riskin' their jobs but their lives. So who cares if the government gets ripped off? Who even cares if the loot's comin' out of federal funds for the sick when it's only a measly one percent? . . . Well, Artemus Hill cared. Only he put his trust in computers, not people. Computers don't lie, don't cheat, don't get bought off. So he was safe for a while. He probably thought he was still safe after he sent his findings to the General Accounting Office. After all, he was dealin' with one of the most reputable outfits in Washington: Congress's own watchdog agency. Well, being the math wizard he was, Hill probably didn't make many miscalculations, but this one cost him his life."

As Lem paused to sip coffee the incredulous look on Dan's face gradually gave way to scowling indignation. "How many HMOs are there in those ninety-two counties?"

"Almost eleven hundred."

"That many?"

"Some pretty big cities like Dallas and Miami are included. But as a round figure eleven hundred's right. Divide it into last year's estimated 1.9 billion take and it figures out to over a million and a half dollars per HMO. 'Course, that's got to be spread among quite a few people—maybe hundreds in each place—but it's still a tidy sum, being tax free and all."

Dan shook his head in disgust. "But I just don't understand how they got away with it. Sure, the National Health Insurance program's a bureaucratic nightmare. But it's still the federal government's single biggest expenditure. Two hundred twenty billion last year and climbing. Hell, that's the reason the HMO concept was pushed, why the medical profession finally came around to supporting it. They knew that the money squeeze was really on, and as the only segment without fixed expenditures or union protection they were going to get squeezed the hardest. Much as it grated them, they gave in on the HMO issue to take the pressure off those who chose to remain in private practice. Otherwise the local medical societies never would've allowed so many community hospitals and group practice clinics to be converted into HMOs. That was supposed to cut costs, redistribute physicians to needy areas, produce all sorts of public benefits."

"Well, it sure benefitted some—the ones runnin' the HMOs."

"But good Christ!" Dan erupted. "I know the law that created them. I helped draft sections of it. There was a whole slew of safeguards in it against just what you're describing: a lot of local, state, and regional supervisory boards all the way up the line to a special section of the Department of HEW. You can't expect me to believe that the entire health officialdom of ninety-two counties were bought off!"

"Naw, you know better'n that. You know well as me how a bureaucratic system operates. It's the people at the bottom—the cashiers, clerks, bookkeepers—who make the costliest mistakes. That's where if a decimal point gets misplaced it usually stays misplaced. Unless the auditors pick it up, no supervisory board can catch those errors. Not without checking every invoice against the ledgers themselves. And that bottom rung can be bought cheap. A free trip to some meetin' or an extra week's vacation. As for the auditors . . . well, it must get pretty dull checking columns of figures day after day. A lot of them turn to booze and gamblin', I hear. Or shrinks. All of which cost money. So most of them got their price too."

Bleakly Dan nodded.

"Ain't like they'd hit on anything new," Lem pointed out. "Same thing's been goin' on in nursing homes and mental institutions for years. Not so long ago, as I recall, it happened with the 'Medicaid mills' that claimed to be takin' care of twenty-five million people. Took nearly a dozen years before Congress tumbled to them and got the states to crack down. The only surprisin' part's the number of doctors in cahoots with them, or else lookin' the other way. But I guess you're a pretty disgruntled group these days."

Dan ignored the slur. "Does the President know about this?"

Lem's thick lips spread in a smile that was almost a sneer. "Bet your ass he does! He, the Attorney General, the Secretary of HEW, they all know. But except for some quiet checkin' by a team out of the Attorney General's office they ain't movin' on it. And they ain't goin' to till after the elections."

"How come?"

"How come?" repeated Lem bitterly. " 'Cause the President doesn't dare. Not if he expects to hold on to all those congressional seats he picked up in the South and West last time. He's lookin' to get his kind of people elected same as me, which makes for a battle between us."

"Yeah, I can see that," Dan said, suddenly perceiving his pivotal role in their forthcoming struggle. It made him uncomfortable. "Since you seem to be so much on top of things," he said, "tell me why I wasn't told any of this the other day. By Freiborg, the FBI Director, somebody!"

Lem pondered the best way to phrase his answer. He knew their discussion had reached the critical phase; that he had Dan dangling on the rope of uncertainty. But he was rapidly running out of fresh facts to disclose, so its slack was nearly played out. What he said next might prove conclusive in gaining or losing Dan's cooperation. "Well," he finally replied, "I ain't claimin' to know for sure, but a couple reasons come to mind."

"Like what?"

"Like if they really laid it on the line, made clear all the housecleanin' and congressional investigations you'd be lettin' yourself in for, you might just decide you wanted no part of the job."

"That's certainly a possibility," Dan admitted. "What's another?"

"They might not want you."

"Why not?"

"Not if you feel like me: that stealin' money supposed to keep poor folk healthy and make sick folk well ain't just another form of corruption—it's in a class by itself. Like beatin' up on the crippled or robbin' the blind. That no President, no matter how crucial he sees it to all his future plans, got the right to cover up somethin' like that. Or let it go on for a few months, even a few days, longer than it ought to. What do you think that big FBI check was all about? They wanted a hold on you. Only instead of findin' one, they came up with somethin' to worry them more—you knowin' me."

Dan gazed pensively at him. Everything Lem had said thus far had the inherent ring of truth. But he could not escape the feeling that, despite all Lem had confided, he was deliberately omitting some key element, some crucial disclosure. Dan felt so certain of this he could almost visualize it as the missing piece in a jigsaw puzzle, one whose shape he might have recognized if his mental faculties were less blunted by fatigue.

"Anything else?" he asked.

"One more thing," Lem said somberly. "Maybe the reason they didn't tell you was 'cause they wanted you to hear it from me first."

"Why you?" asked Dan, feeling he already knew, but hoping Lem's answer might tip him to any hidden motives.

"Lots of reasons. That way they could find out from you how much I really knew. They probably figured that was a sure bet. Wouldn't matter what promises you made me, not even what loyalty you owed me as a friend, your sense of outrage would keep eatin' away at you till you blew. Why do you think I ain't asked you to keep what I told you so far confidential?"

"Suppose you tell me?"

"First off, 'cause it wouldn't be fair. How the hell could I blame you for breakin' such a promise when as Secretary of Health it'll be your responsibility to get this mess straightened out? That is, if you're still interested in the job. So that's one thing. The other is, I'm pretty sure they tried their best to poison your mind against me. They did try, didn't they?"

"They did," Dan answered and saw a baleful glint in Lem's eyes.

"Sure. I expected it. That way you might not buy what I'm tellin' you—not all of it anyway—or figure I had some ulterior motive."

Suddenly Dan grasped the elusive insight he had been chasing. "More coffee?" he asked, wanting extra time to examine it.

"Yeah, maybe a little," Lem said, appearing put off by Dan's lack of response to his last remark. "Make it straight, though. No brandy."

Dan poured coffee into both cups then settled back to sip and think. Lem had just supplied the answer to a question that had been haunting him ever since his session with the FBI Director. He now understood the urgency, the high-level nature, most important of all the unspoken intent behind the meeting. Lem was right on both counts: they *had* wanted to find out how much he knew of the hushed-up health scandal as well as prejudice Dan against him. But by putting his mind to rest on that question Lem had raised another, the one Dan had been trying so hard to frame for himself. Why, he wondered, after all these years, was his old friend being so remarkably candid with him? He knew Lem could be as ruthless as any ideologically driven man. But devious or direct, racist or humanitarian, what did he hope to gain that apparently only Dan could provide?

"All right, Lem," he said, putting down his cup and saucer and facing him with a look of grim resolution. "You just raised an interesting point: ulterior motives. We all have them—me for wanting to be Secretary of Health, you for being 'Devil-A'. So let's get down to the gut issue, the real reason you risked coming here tonight and telling me all that you have. What do you want me to do about it?"

"Lord!" Lem sighed. "It took a long time in comin', a lot of missed sleep on both our parts, but we're finally at the plunging-in point—the point where we either swim against the tide together or pull each other down. What I'm askin' is going to make you take a long, hard look inside yourself, like Rick once made you do. Maybe test you like you never been tested before. You got a Senate hearing comin' up end of next week, right?"

Dan nodded.

"Well, between now and then I want you to go over all the documents in that suitcase, prove to yourself everything I told you is true, and then—" Lem paused for effect. "Then I want you to go before that Senate Committee and those TV cameras and tell the whole country about it."

"Do you?" Dan said wryly. "I figured as much. I can even understand what you want to accomplish. To resurrect Watergate's ghost. So refresh the public's memory of it that they'll go back to demanding honesty and morality in government again. What I don't quite get is why you've picked *me* for your spokesman. Your sacrificial lamb. Because we both know that's what I'll be. If the President ever got wind of it he'd withdraw my nomination instantly. He'll do it for sure if I mention one word of this to the Senate. Don't you want me to be Secretary of Health?"

Lem shrugged noncommittally. "You'd make a good one, I got to admit. But whether or not I want you in the job ain't important. The big question, I suppose, is how bad *you* want it."

"You suppose nothing! You had this all figured out days, maybe months ago. But why me, Lem? Why shoulder me with the responsibility when you could just as easily tell all you know to the press? If you've got the kind of conclusive proof you claim, you shouldn't have the slightest trouble selling them on the story. Hell, you'd have visions of Pulitzer Prizes and bestsellers dancing like sugarplum fairies in their heads. So why not go that route?"

"I thought about it," Lem said laconically, "and I'll be thinkin' about it some more if you turn me down. Only that way has certain drawbacks."

"Like what?"

"I already told you we got our hands on most of the documents in that suitcase illegally—which not only makes them inadmissible before a grand jury, but with the new 'shield' laws, too hot for most of the press to handle. But even that ain't my main reason for wantin' you to do it."

"No, I imagine not," said Dan, his sardonic smile a match for Lem's own. "Your major reason is the extra impact I'd add. That's what you're really after. Impact! And what could be more headline-grabbing than the President's own Health Secretary-designate blowing the whistle on him? That's pretty dramatic stuff; bound to increase public acceptance. Otherwise you run the risk of recreating the old Nixon versus the press hassle in a lot of people's minds: Is the health scandal true or not? Did the President try to suppress its disclosure or didn't he? By the time the smoke clears the elections might be over. That's the real reason you want me to do it, isn't it?"

"Ain't it reason enough?"

"Not entirely. I'm a white man, remember? An old friend but a white one just the same. And don't try to tell me that doesn't matter. If it didn't, how come tonight's the first time in all the years we've known each other you've really leveled with me. Take Kojedo, for example. You could've told me about that. I would've understood—or at least tried to. But no, you never trusted me enough for that. Not even after killing a man for me—for both Rick and me. Well, I guess you've a right to your prejudices too. So I have an alternate proposal. You've got a damned fine black man sitting on the Supreme Court. Why not take your suitcase-full of documents to him?"

"That's a possibility too," Lem allowed in a low, flat voice. "There's all sorts of ways we can go if we have to—some better than others. No need to worry your head about one thing, though. Whether you do it or not, the story is goin' to get told. The most your refusal can do is slow us down. But never mind that. Never mind why I'm askin' what I am, which you pretty well guessed anyhow. Never mind even that I'm black and you're white. That ain't what's makin' you squirm. You know well as me that no matter how much we talk about or around it, it still comes down to a question of right and wrong: What means more to you—satisfyin' your ambition or your conscience?"

"Why not both?" Dan countered. "Why not let me get confirmed and then break the scandal? That way I could conduct the cleanup from the inside."

"Yeah," Lem reluctantly admitted. "I thought of that. Considered it carefully and turned it down."

"Why, when the most it would mean is a month or two delay? It'll still get out before the elections."

"No, it won't," Lem stated flatly.

"Why the hell not?"

" 'Cause you ain't goin' to get confirmed. You might not even make it to the Senate hearing next week."

"Oh, really?" Dan bristled. "And what makes you so sure of that?"

"The way things been shapin' up. Why do you think your friend Freiborg didn't tell you any of this before? 'Cause the President gave him strict orders not to. He's no fool that man. He knew how you were likely to react. He damned near decided to drop your nomination once the FBI Director told him you knew me. He and Freiborg had a helluva row over that. He only went ahead with it 'cause Freiborg managed to convince him he'd have more of a hold on you if he kept dangling that cabinet job in front of your nose."

Dan's eyes narrowed. "You seem to know a hell of a lot about what goes on in that Oval Office. I thought the bugs went out with Nixon?"

"Not the black ones. Believe anythin' you want, but what I just told you is the truth. Now all you got to do is call Freiborg and repeat it, especially the part about using the Senate hearing as your forum, and see how long it takes for the President to drop you. This ain't no little game between him and me—it's war. And the stakes are damned high. So what the hell does the President care about your sense of moral indignation? No, you go ahead and call Freiborg tomorrow. You'd better anyway, since chances are he knows about this meeting. But be careful what you tell him, else you're out. And I wouldn't want that to happen, Dan. Believe me, I wouldn't."

"Even if I refuse to do what you're asking?"

"Even then. 'Least that way it's *your* choice, not the President's. Facing up to a tough choice is almost as important as makin' the right one, and I want you to have that chance."

"Why?"

Lem scowled and shifted uneasily in his chair. "I ain't exactly sure. Honest, I ain't. Maybe it's got somethin' to do with what we went through together in the old days; how we both felt about Rick. Or maybe it's got to do with myself. My hatred of injustice—white men's injustice—runs so deep and hard that it's carried me a long, long way. Maybe too far. But I need somebody like you to prove that to me."

"To prove we can be trusted?"

"Somethin' like that."

Dan whistled softly. "Man, you're really laying it on me tonight! I'm going to try to ignore that last part—or at least not let it influence me. But I agree with you on one thing. However I decide, it's going to be my choice. Mine alone. I can promise you that. I may be a rank amateur when it comes to playing cutthroat politics, but I still have a few cards in my hand and one of them's a trump. So don't worry about what I tell Freiborg. Or even the President. Funny thing about the President. Despite all you've told me, I still think he's a good man. He just faces the same dilemma that I imagine you did when ordering certain terrorist strikes and that I'm facing right now. It's an ages-old dilemma. Old as mankind. Does a man—any man—ever have the right to commit an immoral act, no matter how great its potential benefit to others? Obviously the President thinks so or he wouldn't be so intent on his Party winning the next election. And obviously you do or you wouldn't have spilled the blood you have. Me, I'm not so sure. Being a doctor I've never really had to come to grips with it before. I'll have to think long and hard about it."

"You do that," said Lem, rising slowly, clumsily, to his feet. "You can let me know your decision in a few days."

"How?"

"I'll be in touch. Maybe in person, maybe not. Al will call to tell you which." He yawned and stretched. "Another long, tirin' day. Been a lot of those lately. A lot more to come."

"Yeah, I know," Dan commiserated. "Makes me wonder if it's worth all the wear and tear?"

"That ain't for us to decide."

"Who then?"

"History. Kids, if you got any. God, if there is one. Mainly what keeps me going, though, is a feelin'—a feelin' that maybe the universe ain't so big or death so long."

At the door Lem stared penetratingly at Dan for a moment. "G'night, Doc. Sleep well. Hard days ahead."

Chapter Eighteen

In the abrupt silence, the palpable release of tension, that followed Lem's departure, Dan tried to collect his thoughts. Lem was so sinister and commanding a figure yet so appealing in his human touches that his exit left a peculiar sense of void in the room. Bone-weary as he was, Dan felt that he could have gone on talking with him all night. But could he trust him? Could he trust any man who had seen and contributed to so much slaughter that one more life, whether a friend's or Lem's own, meant little to him?

As Dan loaded the serving tray and carried it into the kitchen, his mind continued to dwell on the mystery that was Lem Harper. Of all the terrorist acts the FBI and CIA had accused him of, Dan had meant to ask him specifically about one: the blinding of those sheriffs. Then why hadn't he? Because he was reluctant to make Lem reveal that ugly side of his nature full-face? Or because he felt that he already knew? Dan had learned long ago in Korea what usually justified man's murderous impulses toward his fellow-men: *Haunting mental images.* The reason he had been one of the few soldiers in his company who took deliberate aim before firing his rifle in combat was to assuage and avenge and put to rest the ghosts of comrades this same enemy had slain: to erase their haunting images.

So he could at least understand if not condone Lem's extremes of violence. You didn't have to be black to share the sickening sense of outrage at pictures of the bullet-torn corpses of Medgar Evers or Martin Luther King. Or even more obscene, the six daintily dressed young black girls whose bodies had been sundered by the senseless bombing of a Birmingham church in the early sixties. Had that been in Lem's mind when he ordered those blindings? Possibly, Dan mused, since the sheriff whose photo MacBride had shown him was from that county.

Exhaustion combined with sleeping pills made Dan yawn and reel as he pulled back his bed covers. But the black leather suitcase Lem had left with him loomed large in his mind, eliminating any immediate hope of slumber. Dan had a sudden, unnerving vision of its contents pulsating, straining to burst the lock and spread its testaments of human greed over him like a paper shroud as he slept.

Impulsively he phoned Jimmy Dallesio at his home. "James? This is Dan," he announced heartily on hearing his friend's sleepy voice.

"Dan!" Jimmy exclaimed. "Where the hell you calling from—a D.C. jail?"

"If I were I wouldn't be wasting my one phone call on you. I'm back in town and I've got to see you."

"When? Not at this ungodly hour, I hope?"

"No, in the morning. Nine o'clock. Stop off someplace on the way and pick me up some breakfast, will you? I intend to sleep till you get here."

"That's nice. Being Saturday and all, I'd planned to sleep in myself. But I wouldn't want you to miss breakfast. Anything else I can do for you?"

"Ask *not* what you can do for Dr. Daniel Lassiter, but what Dr. Lassiter can do for you. Or have I got it ass-backwards?"

"You have. But never mind that. What do you want to see me about?"

"Your next Pulitzer Prize. I've got it waiting right here for you in a suitcase."

"Dan?"

"Yeah?"

"You sure you're all right? *Really* all right? You haven't tied one on or anything?"

"No, I'm fine. Fuzzy-headed from sleeping pills but otherwise fine. I don't hand out Pulitzer Prize-winning material every day, though, so get your ass over here by nine sharp. At five after nine it all goes to Jack Anderson."

"Okay," Jimmy sighed. "If you say you've got a Pulitzer Prize in a suitcase for me the least I can do is come over and take a look."

"Attaboy. See you at nine," Dan said and hung up.

As sleep overcame him Dan tried to recall the names of certain of his medical colleagues who practiced in the South—men he had gone through residency training with or had trained himself and knew particularly well. Out of the gallery of faces that flashed before him he chose three—Ed Clay from North Carolina, Charlie Humphrey from Mississippi, and Jim Calhoun from Texas—intending to call each in the morning to find out what they knew of Lem's accusations.

Jimmy arrived at Dan's door shortly before nine, a brown paper bag in one hand and a cardboard-covered platter of breakfast food balanced on the other. Dan mumbled his thanks and, in the kitchen, between mouthfuls of food and sips of black coffee, filled Jimmy in on his meeting with the FBI Director. But he said nothing about his talk with Lem until he had shaved, showered, and felt more clear-headed.

In the living room Jimmy listened attentively as Dan described the almost cloak-and-dagger atmosphere that had surrounded Lem's early-morning visit. But when he got to Lem's charges of swindled health funds Jimmy reached for his notepad and pencil. Dan's sudden frown made him pause.

"Oh, go ahead and take notes if you want to," Dan told him. "But hear me out carefully."

Jimmy's eyes widened at the presumed murder of Artemus Hill, and he whistled at the estimated 1.9 billion-dollar take from the health swindle. Upon learning of the President's suspected cover-up his mouth fell open.

"Marrone!" he groaned and shook his head. "That's one big bombshell you got handed. You really believe the part about the President?"

"Do you?"

"I'm having trouble with it. It's so out of character for him. I can maybe understand that with his own investigation pending and the real possibility of scaring you away from the health job he wouldn't want Freiborg to tell you about it now. But to conceal it deliberately—" Jimmy grimaced. "That'd be taking one hell of a risk, wouldn't you say?"

"Not yet it isn't. But it will be once more people know about it. Right now, if anything gets out, he could always claim he has the Justice Department gathering the necessary proof before going public with it. But according to Lem he's known about it since April."

"How, if the report Hill sent the GAO got buried along with him?"

"Whether or not Lem ever gave the President a copy of Hill's findings he didn't say. But he swore he'd made sure news of its existence reached him. And I believe him."

"So do I," Jimmy said. "I kept picking up hints something like this was in the wind while trying to track down the reason for the big FBI investigation of you. People at HEW and the Attorney General's offices have been getting a lot of anonymous tips lately that some such shenanigans were going on. But the ones I talked to didn't seem too concerned about them. Claimed they came mostly from doctors fed up with so much government paperwork or disgruntled patients. But when I tried to bluff them by saying I'd heard the FBI was digging into it, they clammed up in a hurry. So something's got them shook up. But a two-billion-dollar rip-off! And so much of it involving doctors!" Jimmy shook his head doubtfully. "You sure Lem Harper's not exaggerating all this for reasons of his own?"

"I'm not sure of anything," Dan admitted. "Nor

would I put it past him. According to that CIA guy, Damon, this election is just as crucial for black people as it is for the President. But why go on speculating when we got the proof right here?"

"You mean the suitcase?"

Dan nodded.

"Well, then, let's get it opened so I can see if my next Pulitzer's inside!"

Three hours and two pots of coffee later, having looked at less than half the hundreds of invoices, annual fiscal reports, and the like that the black suitcase disgorged, Dan and Jimmy gave up in despair.

"Well," Jimmy said after a moment of somber reflection, "that was a real bust! Humbling too. Here I am, an investigative reporter, and here you are, a hospital director, and neither of us knows enough about statistics to predict that the sun'll rise tomorrow!"

"No, we sure don't. But finding that out doesn't help me one damned bit. Not with a Senate hearing in four, five days. So what do I do now?"

Jimmy pondered briefly. "Obviously you need expert help."

"Obviously," Dan said dryly. "But where do I get it? I can't call in my friendly neighborhood CPA. I can't even go to my own accounting people at the hospital. Not if I expect to keep this hushed-up. Besides, even if I were willing to risk it, I'm not sure how much help they'd be."

"Why not?"

"Because we're a private hospital, not a Health Maintenance Organization. They wouldn't be all that familiar with the federal forms. No, what I need—and quick—is somebody special. Somebody shrewd as hell, with a real mastery of the ins and outs of running a HMO operation, who I can trust to keep his mouth shut."

"That's a pretty tall order. Know anybody like that?"

Dan stroked his chin in silent deliberation. "I think

so," he said at last. "One man fits that bill pretty well. But—"

"But what?"

"I don't know if I dare ask him. He and I haven't been on the friendliest of terms until recently when he fell ill. In fact, he's still in our intensive care unit."

"Not Matt Kinsella!" Jimmy gasped in amazement. "Sweet Jesus, wouldn't that put quite a strain on him? Even kill him?"

"It might. But if we're lucky, not before he tells us what we want to know. Which would be ideal."

"You've got to be kidding!"

"Oh, maybe about it being the death of him. I'd keep a damned close eye on him to make sure there's little chance of that. But not about Matt Kinsella being our man. I've never known anybody who had a better head for figures. He can quote you from memory the price of any hospital item from an Engstrom respirator to a box of paper clips. Also, there's a certain poetic justice in my using him this way, since he drove me nearly crazy with such minutiae for five years!"

"Then he's our man?"

"That he is!" Dan declared.

Neil Robinson and Shafeek Sanbar were surprised to see Dan enter the ICU conference room on a Saturday. "Good afternoon, Dr. Lassiter!" Sanbar said, hastily rising to his feet. "Here to check on Mr. Kinsella?"

Dan nodded. "How's he doing?"

"Fine." Sanbar beamed. "He's really recovering quite marvelously, thanks to you. If you're going in to examine him, we'll go with you."

"No, I'd prefer you didn't. There are a few personal matters I'd like to discuss with him. But stick around. If he's doing as well as you say, I'll probably want to change some orders on him."

"Well, well," Matt Kinsella rasped through a voice box still raw from the insertion of an endotracheal tube, "if it isn't the *famous* Dr. Lassiter. I was wondering when you'd finally get around to showing your face here. Not that I'm ungrateful to you for missing a night's sleep on my account. But where the devil you been since? Can't you spare a little time between all your newspaper and TV interviews to visit your patients?"

Same old Matt Kinsella, thought Dan: impenitent, unfazed by near-death, as big an ingrate as ever! It reassured him that Kinsella had suffered no significant brain damage from his cardiac arrests, and was certainly the right man for Dan's needs. He gestured apologetically.

"Don't misunderstand me now," Kinsella went on. "Isn't that I haven't been properly cared for. You've a fine bunch of young house officers here. But as for Dr. Forrester—well, you know how I feel about women doctors . . ."

"I know," Dan said, remembering all the female interns at Holmes Memorial Hospital Kinsella's tirades had reduced to tears. "But you'd better make damned sure Dr. Forrester doesn't."

"How long you planning to keep me here? At $350 a day!"

"That's what I came by to talk to you about."

"Good! Talk."

"Well," Dan spoke hesitantly, "so happens I've a little favor to ask of you."

"Do you now?" said Kinsella, perking up. "Well, go ahead and ask. I can't deny that I owe you one."

"Well, it's like this," Dan began and watched Kinsella's facial expression change from intense interest to dour disgust as he described the alleged health swindle. But his eyes took on a special twinkle when Dan finally made his request. "Well, what d'you know," he sneered. "So those so-called health experts in Washington got themselves taken for a ride. A two-billion-dollar ride! And not by just a bunch of shady administrators, but doctors too! Doesn't surprise me any. I never did believe sainthood was conferred along with an M.D.

degree. And now that so many are working for wages—"

Dan cut him short. "Well, what do you say, Matt? Think you're up to that big a job? Physically, I mean."

"Up to it!" Kinsella snorted. "You bet I am! My biggest fear these days is being bored to death. Besides, according to what Dr. Forrester told me, there wasn't all that much wrong with my heart to begin with. It was the rat poison that old geezer from Hartford kept giving me that caused all the trouble."

Dan smiled thinly. He hadn't heard coumadin called "rat poison" for some time, though originally it had been developed for that purpose. Nor did he deign to rise to the Hartford cardiologist's defense by reminding Matt of his own culpability in the matter.

"That's the truth, isn't it?" Kinsella demanded. "Oh, don't worry. I've no intention of suing him. Wouldn't waste my time. But before I agree to go over all that stuff for you, a little negotiating's in order."

"What kind of negotiating?" asked Dan dubiously.

"Aw, nothing you can't handle with ease. First, transfer me out of this fishtank to a private room. Second, put a stop to all those tranquilizers and dope shots I'm getting. A single 500 milligram Chloral Hydrate tablet at bedtime will do just fine. Third, I'll need a good old-fashioned adding machine. And lastly, I want your okay to call Hutchinson, my assistant administrator at Holmes, to bring me last year's set of books so I'll have something to compare the annual expenditures of those HMOs to. Don't worry about Hutch. As far as he'll know, I want those ledgers for light reading. All that agreeable to you?"

"It is," Dan said, "long as you're careful not to overtire yourself."

Kinsella nodded vigorously. "I will be, I promise. One thing you can be sure of—I intend to see this thing through. After all the nickel and diming I've done in my lifetime, I wouldn't miss the chance to pin a two-billion-dollar swindle on a bunch of government crooks for the world, now would I?"

No, indeed, thought Dan, watching Kinsella rub his hands with actual glee.

"So go ahead and get me transferred. Then bring me that suitcase so I can get going on it."

"Okay. I'll have it for you in a couple of hours."

"Good! The sooner the better. Oh, and one more thing," Kinsella said and faltered, his face contorting in what Dan took to be a mixture of discomfort and embarrassment. "Thanks . . . Not for saving my life. That's just doing your job. But for trusting me to handle this other business for you. That makes me feel good—as if all the time I spent trying to teach you how a hospital should be run wasn't entirely wasted."

Dan waited until he was out of Kinsella's sight before shaking his head at the incredible gall of the man; his knack for always twisting things in his favor. Fists clenched, he remembered the many times he had been on the verge of punching his bulbous nose in, glad now that he hadn't. He might have other uses for that ballsy Mick in Washington.

That evening, after delivering the suitcase to Kinsella's spacious new room in the VIP section of the tenth floor, Dan tried to call Nels Freiborg in Washington. Unable to reach him at home, he tracked him to a diplomatic reception at the White House. No, he told an aide in a gruff tone of authority, he did not wish to wait for Mr. Freiborg to return his call; he didn't give a damn if he had to be dragged away from the dinner table or the dance floor or the arms of the Sheik's bosomy bride, he wanted to speak with him *now*. On a matter of the *gravest national urgency,* Dan advised, a little ashamed of using that pretentious phrase but liking the way Freiborg's aide blurted "Yes, sir!" and left the line to do as bidden.

Nels Freiborg answered the phone calmly. Too calmly. Not the slightest hint of irritation or curiosity in his voice. But Dan was wise to the ways of wily politicians like him: show temper in dealing with minor matters, calm in weightier ones.

So he spoke briefly and to the point. He had been contacted by Lem Harper, Dan told him, and they must meet to discuss it as soon as possible. No, he was not willing to return to Washington; this time Freiborg would have to come to him. No, tomorrow morning was inconvenient—he was having brunch with his wife—and Monday too late.

With Dan maintaining the same note of haughty insistence and Freiborg the same strained calm, they finally arranged for a seven o'clock meeting the following evening. As his one concession, Dan agreed to meet Freiborg at the airport.

At the bar of a roadside inn in Silver Springs, Maryland, Douglas Corcoran was rapidly getting drunk. He had never handled liquor well, nor women. Now he was trying to ease his excruciating torment with both.

Corcoran, a high-level government attorney, had never been in more trouble in his life. He was not a naive man; no matter how meticulously he had planned and executed every step of the gigantic swindle, the possibility of being caught had so preyed on his mind that he had prepared his escape well: two million dollars stashed in a Bahamian bank, a phony passport, a Costa Rican hideaway. But his downfall had come with such stunning rapidity that they now seemed as far out of reach as the stars.

Three days before, the Attorney General had asked him to drop by for a chat. There was nothing unusual in that and nary a hint of what was to be sprung on him in their opening minutes of casual conversation. Then the knock on the door, heralding the hard knocks to follow. A trio of assistant attorney generals had trooped in, attaché cases in hand, and barely seated themselves before firing accusation after accusation at him. Each had investigated different phases of the health fund fraud and recited the charges against him in tones of righteous indignation. But toward the end of the long session Corcoran thought he could detect a note of grudging admiration in their voices. After all, he had perpetrated the biggest government theft of all time, and bigness, whatever its nature, impressed Washington bureaucrats. In the process of ruining his reputation these men would be building their own, making legal history.

Fortunately they did not appear aware of his connection with Artemus Hill's murder, otherwise they never would've given him a week of freedom to gather evidence against his cohorts. Half of the week was already over, and while going through the motions of complying, Corcoran thought only of deserting his wife and grown children and fleeing the country. But no exit was open to him. Teams of FBI agents had him under constant surveillance and he was expressly forbidden from using any telephone outside his home or office. They had him boxed in tight, frantic as a trapped animal scurrying around the confines of his cage looking for escape, near physical and mental collapse. So Douglas Corcoran was at this roadside inn near his home, desperately seeking diversion from his troubles by drinking heavily and conversing with the handsome, tawny-skinned female seated next to him.

Corcoran had been married to the same woman for twenty-four years. To his friends, most of whom had been divorced at least once, the longevity of their union was impressive, but he seldom bragged about it. From the beginning his wife, a prim, passionless woman, had submitted to his sexual advances with teeth so clenched and body so rigid that he could hardly kiss or penetrate her. A brief fling with a young typist in his office, an hysterical type, had proved he was not impotent but cost him financially and emotionally when he tired of her and her incessant avowals of love and broke it off. After that he had forsworn sex, steered clear of unattached women. But the delectable one beside him now had made the initial overture. She had occupied the adjacent bar stool, ordered a rum drink and, in a sultry, Spanish-accented voice said, "Allo. My name's Monique and I'm what you call direct. When I see a man who interests me I talk to him. You interest me."

Surprised and suspicious, he turned to her and asked, "For God's sake, why?"

"Your eyes . . . Look at them."

Blearily he glanced at his reflection in the bar mirror, at his dark-circled eyes set in his condemned man's face, and was momentarily overcome with remorse. How, in God's name, had it happened? he asked himself. He had never even tried to get a traffic ticket fixed, so what'd possessed him to do it? Because it had been done successfully before by doctors? For five years Corcoran had served as chief legal counsel for Senator Alvin Balbridge's subcommittee on health and heard tale after tale of flagrant Medicare and Medicaid fraud. Only three to four percent of all doctors participating in the programs were implicated, but of the hundreds he had helped prosecute, fewer than sixty were convicted and a mere fifteen sent to jail. At first Corcoran had been outraged, then had turned cunning and calculating. If dishonest doctors were treated so leniently, why not take personal advantage of this inequity, especially when he knew the names of their cleverest operators? So he had, to his ultimate regret.

Corcoran and his alluring bar companion were soon deep in conversation. She had studied law for a while herself at the Sorbonne, she told him, and proved it by asking informed questions. After that their talk turned more intimate and they moved to a booth. Monique confided that she had recently broken off a long affair with a married man and because of it were her unmet physical and emotional cravings for a man. Corcoran had never heard a woman talk so explicitly about her sexual appetites before, and despite his distracting legal problems, she aroused him mightily. Although aware the FBI would tail them, one overriding thought prevailed: he was headed for jail, homosexual heaven, and this was his last chance to enjoy a woman for a long time. When Monique finally suggested that he accompany her back to her motel, he agreed at once.

Drunk as he was, Corcoran insisted on driving his own car and had just turned onto the highway when a loud crash of colliding metal somewhere behind him made him hit the brakes. Twisting around, he saw that a Yellow Cab had sideswiped another car near the end of the driveway. He watched the drivers, one black, one white, leap out of their cars and stand head to head in argument until Monique urged him on. Further down the highway he looked back, saw no headlights behind him, and wondered if the cab could have collided with the car carrying his FBI watchdogs. If so, he was temporarily free; he could drive to a marina he knew on Chesapeake Bay and hire a small boat to take him to the Bahamas. But Monique was snuggled against him, caressing his neck and thigh, promising sexual pleasures no woman ever had before. He knew it was unwise to delay his escape even an hour, but her whisperings made him feverish with desire.

"Honey, wait!" he pleaded as she wrapped her arms around him, darted her tongue expertly in and out of his mouth. "I can hardly hold on to the wheel."

She laughed throatily. "Hold what you want, Douglas, and so will I." Impulsively she unzipped his fly, nimbly exposing his erection. He moaned with pleasure.

"Pull over!" she suddenly insisted. "Pull into that clearing ahead."

He started to protest. The neon sign of a motel shone in the distance. But her fingers, hard on him, transmitted her sense of urgency and he obeyed. He cut the motor and headlights and immediately she was upon him, kissing him long and hard. As they fell back against the seat he thought he heard a faint click, a rustling movement, but with Monique's hands covering his ears, her luscious mouth and body immobilizing him, he couldn't be sure.

"Oh, now! Do it to me now!" he groaned and pushed her head down.

"Yes, now," she said harshly and disengaged herself. Suddenly Corcoran sensed the presence of another person in the car and sat up. Near paralyzed with fright, he caught a brief glimpse of a black man, teeth bared like some vicious dog, before powerful arms wrapped around his neck.

The rest was nightmare.

Chapter Nineteen

Dan went to the hospital early Sunday morning to see Matt Kinsella. He found him hunched over a table, bifocals partway down his nose, busily sorting through stacks of papers. Crankily he interrupted his work to disrobe and get in bed for Dan to examine him.

"Well, if you're finally satisfied," he said after Dan put his stethoscope back in his pocket, "maybe you'll let me ask you a few questions. Where the devil did you get this stuff? It's dynamite!"

"From a friend," Dan answered vaguely. "He felt I ought to know about it."

"I can understand why," Kinsella sneered. "You take that job in Washington, you'll have one hell of a mess on your hands. But I can't see anybody in HEW handing you this stuff out of the goodness of his heart. It's been stolen, right?"

Dan admitted it.

"I thought so," Kinsella said smugly. "Making me an accessory if I don't report it."

"It'll be reported," Dan assured him. "Soon as you tell me what it all means. When do you figure that'll be?"

Kinsella shrugged. "Another day at least. I've barely gone through a quarter of the pile so far. But there's no mistaking where it's going to lead: to the biggest government scandal of all time. Take this annual report, for example." He reached for a slim folder on the tabletop. "From a HMO in Charleston, South Carolina. According to them 3,800 of the almost 22,000 patients they saw last year had Pap smears and 900 sigmoidoscopies—which strikes me as a wee bit peculiar when eighty percent of their clinic load happens to be kids!"

But flagrant as this was, it merely represented one of many such fraudulent practices, as Kinsella went on to demonstrate. In addition to all the old tricks used by the Medicaid "mills" to defraud the government: padded travel expenses and consultant fees, kickbacks from commercial pharmacies and laboratories for overordering costly drugs and tests, "ping-ponging" patients by referring them on to all of the other specialists in a clinic—this new breed had added even bigger money-makers by taking advantage of certain medical advances.

As Kinsella had suspected and Dan confirmed, there seemed to be a disproportionately high amount of coronary, renal, and carotid artery surgery at these HMOs compared to similar-sized ones elsewhere. Even their autopsy rates were higher! Although Kinsella was not yet prepared to estimate the exact number of health-care facilities involved in the swindle or the overall size of their take, its mere existence was no longer in doubt—leaving Dan only one major uncertainty to grapple with: how much of this did the President know, and what if anything was he doing about it?

That crucial question haunted Dan the rest of the day, even during the hours he spent with Kris. After their frank and revealing talk of the other night, his preoccupation distressed her. It distressed her even more when he explained its cause. They discussed it quietly until Kris, feeling helpless to advise him, withdrew into her private self, finally giving him an excuse to leave by announcing that it was time for her compulsory afternoon nap.

Having dallied at the hospital helping Hedley, who had come in special to photocopy the contents of Lem's suitcase, Dan arrived at Logan Airport twenty minutes after Nels Freiborg's flight.

He found Nels in a phone booth off the Eastern Airlines lobby, possibly trying to call him. Freiborg spotted him and emerged from the booth. "Where're we going?" he asked Dan as they shook hands.

"My office, if that's private enough."

"Fine." Flushed and tense, Freiborg stared at Dan's equally grim expression and forced a grin. "Hey, Dan, remember me? Your old Washington drinking buddy? We used to be friends."

"We used to," Dan said flatly. "Maybe we will be again, once this is settled."

"Then let's get it settled, for Chrissake! Things are hot enough—here, Washington, every damned place I go! I don't need extra heat from you."

Inside his car, Dan started the engine and turned on the air conditioner. "That cool you off a little?"

Freiborg nodded.

"Good. Let's keep it that way till we get to my office."

"So that's what's got you so hot and bothered," Freiborg said with remarkable composure after Dan told him in full about his talks with Lem Harper and Matt Kinsella. "Damned if you don't sound like some kind of medical Mary Poppins who narrowly missed getting gang-raped by a bunch of Washington louts."

Dan's eyebrows arched. "Do I? And here I thought I was Horatio at the Bridge."

"Sorry to disappoint you, but all the would-be Horatios are at the Pentagon. So use your umbrella to come down to earth and maybe we can make sense out of all this."

Dan glared. "Goddamn it, is there a health swindle or isn't there?"

"Apparently so," Freiborg admitted, "since you've a suitcase-full of hard evidence proving it. But you don't really believe the President is conspiring to cover it up, do you?"

"Somebody is."

"I grant you that. But not the President! Do you think the man's a total idiot? That Watergate never happened and for the sake of a few extra congressional seats he's willing to out-Nixon Nixon? Power-hungry he may be—all Presidents are or they'd never run for the office. But not power-mad! And it would be sheer madness for him to try to cover up something as contemptible as this. Think who the victims are: not a bunch of rival politicians, but sick people! Hell, he'd not only be impeached, but lynched!"

Dan fell silent. He had expected Freiborg to respond with a hedging admission of foreknowledge of the swindle or a spirited defense for delaying its disclosure, not outright ridicule. "All right," he sighed, "so somebody is lying to somebody: Lem Harper to me, or the President to you. How do you propose we find out which?"

Freiborg shrugged. "You tell me."

"So far I'm undecided. I can understand Lem Harper blowing up the story out of all proportion, but at least he's given me proof there is a story. All I've gotten from you are words."

"What more can I give you?"

"Answers, honest ones, to a few key questions. Like, how long has the President known about this? Did he get a copy of Hill's report last April or didn't he?"

Freiborg faltered, frowned, finally nodded. "I know damned well this isn't going to make me look too good, but I can't answer that. I wasn't even aware such a report existed until you showed it to me a few minutes ago. Nor do I know for sure this Artemus Hill was murdered over it."

"You don't doubt it, do you?"

"No, frankly I don't. Not after seeing its contents. But any chance we might've had of proving that is probably now gone."

"How so?"

"Because, unless I miss my guess, Lem Harper and company made sure of it. Last night around midnight our chief suspect, a man named Corcoran, one of three senior counsels for the GAO, drove his car off a Maryland bridge. The blood alcohol level they got on him postmortem was almost too high for him to be conscious, let alone behind the wheel of a car. So whether he drove himself off that bridge or was driven off is up for grabs."

"I see," said Dan, shaken. "So that disposes of a possible kingpin named Corcoran. But whose fault is that—Lem Harper's for finally taking the law into his own hands or the Justice Department's for not apprehending him earlier?"

"There's something called 'due process,' you know."

"So I've heard. But Artemus Hill was killed in April and it's now August. How long does it take you people to put a case together?"

"Longer than you might realize. Especially when so many key pieces of evidence are missing. That's right, Dan. A lot of the documents Harper handed you aren't copies of originals, they *are* the originals. And Justice will be damned glad to get them back. It'll certainly expedite their getting to the bottom of this mess."

"No doubt it will—if that's their intention. But how do I know that? And why wasn't I given a hint earlier that something like this was going on? Why was it left for Lem Harper to tell me?"

Freiborg's face twisted into a tight scowl. "Yeah, I knew I wasn't likely to get out of here without your sticking me with that. Well, you were set up, all right. There's no denying it. I argued like hell against it, but the President wouldn't listen. Not after the FBI Director told him how well you and Harper knew each other. That damned near decided him to kill your nomination right then, but I managed to persuade him to go through with it. Unfortunately," he added, "at a price: the one you just paid. We simply had to find out how much Lem Harper knew and how he intended to use it, maybe even get back some of the documents his people stole. And you were the only person we could use for that purpose. So we used you. We knew you'd resent it, that your feelings were bound to be bruised, only not too badly, we hoped. We also hoped you'd see we had no real alternative once you knew the score. In fact, the President told me to tell you he owes you one for this. You can decide how you want to collect after you've been confirmed as Secretary of Health."

Dan stared hard at Freiborg for a moment before rising, coffee cup and saucer in hand. So there it was, he thought: the pitch, the plea for understanding, the package from Washington all neatly tied up and ribboned. The President never intended to cover up the health fund swindle, he simply lacked the necessary evidence to expose and convict the culprits. So Dan had been set up to get the missing pieces back for him, and as a reward the Secretary of Health job was his, along with an unspecified bonus. What more could he possibly ask of such dedicated, high-minded men? To get them all under oath, make them tell the truth, the whole truth and nothing but the truth? Or was that too perilous a condition to impose on any politician, especially a President?

Dan went behind his desk to refill his cup with frothy-hot coffee from his espresso machine, then garnished it with a piece of lemon peel from the refrigerator. Between moves he stole side-glances at his visitor fidgeting on the couch. Finally Dan returned to the chair opposite him and faced Freiborg with a wry, forbearing look. "Neat, Nels," he said. "Very neat. You were treading on pretty thin ice there for a time, but now you seem to have made it to safer ground. Or so you might think. Let's review. As far as my feelings being bruised—" He shrugged. "—they were. But I'll get over it. And I'm genuinely glad to have aided the cause of justice by returning stolen government documents. It had crossed my mind to turn them over to the newspapers, but I'm no Daniel Ellsberg. Now I've no reason to even consider such a course, have I?"

"What do you mean?"

"What I mean is, you can tell the President he has until Thursday, the day of my Senate confirmation hearing, to break the news of the HMO scandal to the public. I realize that's pushing the Justice Department pretty hard, but they've got the staff. The least they can do is get indictments against most of the big-time swindlers by then. Because I can promise you this, either the President publicizes what's going on or I do!"

Freiborg's flushed face finally paled. "You can't be serious!"

"Dead serious," Dan warned.

"The President will never stand for it!"

"Our good and fair-minded President who rode to victory two years ago promising to combat all the sickness in our society? *That* President would not want to see justice done?"

"Come on, Dan!" Freiborg said gruffly. "Stop kidding around. You know damned well these things take time. You can't draw up indictments against half the health field personnel of eight states in just four days. Not if you expect to make them stick, you can't! You've also got to take into account all the consequences."

"What consequences?"

"To the medical profession, for one. You people haven't exactly had the best press in recent years. Not after all those strikes and job actions you pulled over the malpractice situation. If you really want the public so riled up against doctors they'll demand full-blown socialized medicine, this'll do it. Christ, will it! Is that what you want to be remembered for? If so, just go ahead and make good your threat. 'Cause I can tell you right now the President won't even consider it."

"Why not?" argued Dan. "He'll get the credit."

"Sure he will. But at whose expense? The entire medical profession's? Make three hundred thousand doctors suffer for the misdeeds of a few? That's pretty irresponsible, wouldn't you say? No, the only way to put a stop to such a massive swindle and still salvage something of our present medical system is to give you doctors the chance to clean up the mess yourselves. Wait till you're confirmed as Secretary, then call the leaders of organized medicine together and get them to demand a congressional crackdown.

Believe me, Dan, that's the sensible way to handle it. It'll get you a lot farther than issuing ultimatums to the President!"

"I see your point," Dan admitted. "I just don't happen to agree with it."

"Why don't you?" Freiborg snapped.

"Because, sensible as it sounds, your way takes time. And under these circumstances time can cost lives. Maybe only a handful, but I don't want them on my conscience." He gestured uncertainly. "I admit I've no idea whose version, yours or Lem Harper's, is closest to the truth. All I *do* know is that HEW is being robbed blind of health funds and the sooner it's stopped the better. I trust the public to put the blame where it belongs, on some doctors, not all. But I can't answer for them, only for myself. My actions. So my original proposal still holds. Either the President makes a public disclosure of the swindle before Thursday or I do."

"I see." Wearily Freiborg rubbed his face and fixed Dan with an inimical stare. "That's assuming, of course, that you'll have a Senate hearing."

Dan gave him a contemptuous look. "That's right, Nels. But regardless of what you might think, it's a pretty safe assumption. After Thursday the President can do whatever he wants with the nomination, but not before. Not until I've had my say."

"Oh? And what's to stop him?"

"How well do you know the man, Nels?"

"The President?" Freiborg's face creased in confusion. "As well as anybody, I guess. After working ten years for him."

"As well as Bob Talberg?"

"What's his personal physician got to do with it? Far as I know, the President's in perfect health."

"As far as you, *or anybody else* knows, he is," Dan said pointedly. "With two exceptions. Talberg and me."

"What are you driving at?"

Dan paused, disliking what he was about to do.

But Freiborg clearly was trying to intimidate him and he had no recourse but to reply in kind. "Nels," he said heavily, "the President's not as healthy as you think. In fact, he's an epileptic; has been ever since he fractured his skull in an auto accident in his early twenties."

Freiborg drew back, stunned. "He's a what? An epi—leptic?" He stumbled over the word. "Jesus! I can't believe it."

"Can't you? Ever see him swallow any gold-striped capsules?"

"Yeah," Freiborg reluctantly admitted. "For migraine headaches, he said."

"The name of the pill is Dilantin and it's for epilepsy, not migraine. My guess is he hasn't had an attack in years, but Talberg keeps him on them just in case."

"How could *you* possibly know that? Not from Talberg."

"No, not from Talberg. Nor from any idle medical gossip I happened to have picked up. You can assure the President on that score. You can also assure him I not only know he's epileptic, but can prove it."

"How?"

"By his hospital and office records. You see, Nels, it happened while he was living in Boston and Gundersen was his doctor. I've got Gundersen's entire medical file on him safely locked away. Not another soul need know about it, provided I remain the President's nominee for Secretary of National Health past Thursday."

Freiborg shook his head. "I can't believe this. Any of it! Not only that the President's epileptic, but that you'd threaten to use it against him."

"It was the President's decision to keep his condition secret in the first place," Dan pointed out. "Epilepsy doesn't carry the same public stigma it once did. Especially latent epilepsy, the form the President has. What he does about it now is up to him. His secret is as safe as my nomination."

"You shock hell out of me, Doctor."

"Why? Because you figured I was so consumed with ambition I'd be a pushover? That all you'd have to do was mention dropping my nomination and I'd cave in? Well, you'll simply have to face the fact that you've finally met up with an amateur who can play politics as rough as any professional, if the stakes warrant it. And this time I believe they do." Dan smiled ruefully. "The funny part is, I'm not even sure I want the goddamn health post anymore."

"Then what's making you act like such a bastard over it?"

Dan shrugged. "Who knows? Maybe it does me good to know I'm complete master of my fate for once? Or maybe I'm headline-happy? Just remind the President what story, if any, I break is up to him."

Rising abruptly, Freiborg said, "I'll be *sure* to do that." He took a last, searching look at Dan, lifted Lem's black suitcase off the desktop and turned to leave. "You'll be hearing from me soon."

"Don't you want a ride back to the airport?"

"No need," Freiborg huffed. "I can catch a cab."

"Suit yourself," said Dan. "Just out of curiosity, though, how's it feel?"

Freiborg wheeled. "How does *what* feel?"

"To be on the receiving end of a power play for a change?"

"Shit! You make it sound like that's how I get my kicks. I thought you knew me better than that."

Dan gazed at the hurt, disgusted look on Freiborg's face. "I do, Nels," he said contritely. "I'm sorry."

"So am I. I just hope you know what the hell you're doing—for the medical profession's sake as well as your own. But that's your worry, not mine! I'm going to have my hands full with the President. I only hope he throws one of his regular fits, not an epileptic one. What do I do then?"

"Just keep him from biting his tongue."

"It's my *ass,* not his tongue, I'm worried about!" Freiborg growled and strode out of the office.

Back at his apartment Dan was about to shut off his bedlamp and go to sleep when the phone rang. It was Dr. Charles Humphrey returning his call.

"Charlie, how are you?" Dan said.

"Mighty fine, old buddy," he answered in his Mississippi drawl. "Mighty fine. How's yourself?"

"Oh, fair to middling. But I've got a question for you: How come you left that HMO you were working for in Jackson and went back into private practice in Hattiesburg?"

"Oh, you know how those things go. I gave it a pretty fair try, only things didn't pan out. The working hours weren't bad, but all that paperwork finally got to me."

"All what paperwork, Charlie? Like, for Pap smears and sigmoidoscopies that never got done?"

"I kind of figured this wasn't no little social call from my old chief, but that's gettin' a mite personal, don't you think? I mean, even if we are good buddies, and you're up for that big health job, there're certain things you got no right to ask."

"I realize that, Charlie, and I apologize. But I've simply got to get some line—and quick—on what's going on down there."

"Well, you know I'd never lie to you, Danny, but I got a kid brother still working there, so there ain't much I care to tell you. Let's just say I'm doing a lot less of those procedures now and liking myself a lot better."

"I understand, Charlie. Incidentally, I tried calling Ed Cole in Raleigh today but couldn't reach him. Remember Ed? Well, he's evidently left the HMO he was working for there and gone back in private practice too. As for that kid brother of yours, get him out."

"That an order, chief?"

"It is. *Stat.*"

"Stat, you say!" Humphrey sounded impressed. "Well, I'll certainly make sure he takes heed of that. Thanks for the advice. And if you find yourself down this way be sure to drop in. The bass are biting bet-

ter'n ever, though 'less I miss my guess you're after bigger fish. So be damned careful, and God bless, hear?"

"Thanks. Same to you, Charlie," Dan said and hung up.

Dr. Charles Lee Humphrey had been one of the best interns Dan had ever trained at Commonwealth General: bright, tireless, so unfailingly good-humored that some of his corn-pone expressions even made Gundersen chuckle. A Korean War vet, a star halfback at Ole Miss, a staunch individualist, Charlie was no country hick, and Dan's relationship with him had ripened into firm friendship. He had even been Charlie's best man at his wedding. But close as they once were, would Charlie ever forgive him if he were to bring on socialized medicine? And suddenly Dan knew. For the first time he understood why he would even blackmail a President of the United States before backing off from the decision he faced. The answer was as simple as it was self-revealing. He was no machine now, no Gundersen protégé who made diagnoses and prescribed treatments almost by rote. His patient was not a person but an entire medical system for which he was doctor of last resort. Rather than cow him, it made Dan feel more alive.

PART FOUR

DEATH TO LIFE

Chapter Twenty

Monday morning at the hospital passed interminably for Dan as he waited for the call he knew must come from Washington. Finally, a little before noon, it did.

"Good morning, Dan," Freiborg began blandly. "The President sends his greetings and hopes you might be able to join him for lunch at the White House tomorrow."

"Lunch?" Dan was mildly surprised. Masterful a politician as he was, the President was also notoriously hot-tempered, and he had not expected such a cordial approach. Potential blackmailers rarely became White House luncheon guests. A condemned man's last meal? The spider-fly imagery again?

"Can you make it?" Freiborg asked.

"I think so."

"Good! The President will be happy to hear it. He feels certain any differences between the two of you can easily be worked out."

"Let's hope so," said Dan. "Anything else I should know?"

"Well, even though he realizes the Freedom of Information Act doesn't apply to medicine, he'd appreciate it if you brought a certain medical record along."

Dan smiled inwardly. "I understand. Perhaps he'll return the favor by making certain progress reports from the AG's office available to me."

"I'll certainly request it. Will you fly down tonight or tomorrow morning?"

Dan glanced at his desk calendar. "Late tonight, most likely."

"In that case I'll book your usual accommodations

at the Shoreham. The President will be expecting you around noon then. Good luck!"

Dan replaced the phone with a half-pleased, half-wary look on his face and went to lunch with Jimmy at Vittorio's, an Italian café owned by Jimmy's uncle. After much discussion they agreed that the next move was the President's and in the meanwhile to split another bottle of wine.

In the early evening, Dan spent long enough with Matt Kinsella to scribble all the factual information Matt could feed him into his pocket-sized notebook and then went home to pack for his trip. When he entered his apartment the telephone was ringing. It was Al Beal, and although Al lacked Lem's intimidating manner, the call produced a steep upsurge of tension in Dan.

As casually as possible he told Al he had carefully examined the documents Lem had left behind but reached no decision as yet; wouldn't until after his talk with the President tomorrow. The rest of the phone conversation consisted mainly of long, ominous silences from Beal, who wouldn't say where Lem was but that Dan would probably hear from him before Thursday. He concluded on a surprisingly sympathetic note. "Well, I know you're in a tight spot, Doc. But like my old mammy used to tell me: 'Do right, and fear nobody.' "

Dan hung up, poured himself a stiff scotch and sat staring into his cold fireplace pondering Beal's call.

The soot-black fireplace, gaping like the mouth of a mountain cave, reminded him of other black holes, and his thoughts wandered back to Mississippi, to the free medical clinics he and his associates had established in the Fayette-Port Gibson area and the steady flow of neglected humanity that crowded in to get their first medical examination ever. Their shy, curious looks were faintly amusing; their illnesses were not. Extreme degrees of anemia, hypertension, and diabetes were so prevalent that their discovery soon ceased to evoke much excitement, or even comment, from Dan's colleagues. But the case of a ten-year-old black boy profoundly affected them all. Although he was in the second grade of school, no one had ever heard him speak an intelligible word. The reason became obvious as soon as Dan looked into his mouth: he'd been born with only half a palate. It took the plastic surgeon Dan had flown in from Boston a scant fifty minutes to repair the defect, but the memory of that once mute boy and the unimaginable torment he must have suffered would stay with his doctors forever.

Dan had no doubt which of his choices would do the most for the poor blacks of America's rural South. But he knew equally well that men in his position seldom made isolated decisions. Every choice, like every nerve fiber in his brain, connected to thousands of others. What seemed best for a given group at a given time might be disastrous for others later. However guilty organized medicine was for failing to recognize and remedy the gross inequities in our present health care system, Dan knew that total governmental control of it would make matters infinitely worse. Trust the bureaucratic monster to aggravate the most minor problem into a major crisis.

But why go on deluding himself into believing that the powerful political forces in this country would actually leave so important a decision to him? Did the rainmaker, no matter how much noise he made, really believe he could shake the heavens with his absurd little dance?

Dan got his garment bag from the bedroom and was about to leave for the airport when the phone rang.

"Daaan!" a woman's voice shrieked in his ear. It was Kris, drunk or hysterical. But before he could speak she screamed he must come home at once, she was losing the baby, and hung up.

Afterward, Dan was never able to remember clear details of his wild ride to Sudbury. Vaguely he recalled weaving through city traffic at insane speeds; of coming off an exit ramp of the crosstown expressway on two wheels; of seeing his speedometer quiver at 100 mph as he drove, blowing his horn ceaselessly down the Interstate; of narrowly missing an oncoming car as he swung, dust billowing up behind, into the dirt road to his house. To his dismay there were no other cars in the driveway. Not Jim Neubeck's nor an ambulance, not even the Volkswagen microbus of the Kramers, the live-in couple who kept house for Kris.

Hearing her scream his name as he burst through the front door, Dan rapidly climbed the stairs to the master bedroom. There he found Kris sitting doubled-over by the side of the bed, her hair stringy and disheveled, her face ashen, her forehead glistening with sweat. She stared strangely, almost wildly, at him for a moment and then began to gag and retch saliva into a wastepaper basket by her feet. Dan noticed an empty pint bottle of vodka and a near-empty one of tonic water on the bedstand and understood instantly. Hoping to halt her labor contractions, Kris had drunk herself sick.

"Oh, Dan," she moaned before retching again. Suddenly she threw herself back on the bed, her face contorting in a mixture of panic and pain, and gripped her mounding belly with both hands. "Dan, make them stop!" she pleaded. "Please make them stop."

Dan pried her fingers loose from the sides of her abdomen and placed his hands there to feel the strength of her contraction. Gradually her flesh grew firmer and tauter until it felt rock-hard. Looking down, Dan saw that the underpants Kris wore below her silk pajama top were blood-stained. To his further horror, reddish-pink liquid spurted from her vagina at the height of the contraction and ran down her thighs onto the bedsheet. Trying to sound calm he asked, "How long's it been since you ruptured your membranes?"

"Huh?" she mumbled and reached up to wipe away blood trickling from her left nostril. Her retching had probably caused the nosebleed, Dan realized, but the crimson smear on her cheek and hand made her look even more ghastly.

"Kris, listen to me!" he cried.

"Yes!" she snapped, drunkenly obedient. "I'm listening."

"When did your membranes rupture?"

"My what?"

"Your membranes! Your bag of waters, for Chrissake!" Dan growled, resorting to the lay term in a desperate attempt to make himself understood.

"Oh?" she said. "Oh, those . . . Around six o'clock, I guess."

Almost four hours ago, he thought with a quiver of apprehension. "Have you called Jim Neubeck?"

"Jim?" She looked uncomprehending. "Why Jim?"

"Kris! For God's sake, pay attention. You're in labor!"

"No, I'm not!" she insisted. "I am *not* in labor. It's too early."

"Where are the Kramers?"

"They went into Boston for the day."

"Both of them?"

"Heine had to get a bunch of teeth pulled and Hilde drove him to the dentist."

"Leaving you alone?"

"I told them it would be okay. That I'd be perfectly . . . Oh! . . . Oh, damn, I'm having another one!" She gasped in pain.

Dan looked at his watch, estimating her contractions at three to four minutes apart but wanting to time them precisely.

He mopped her brow with his handkerchief, squeezed her hands, talked soothingly to her until the pain passed. Despite this being Kris's fourth pregnancy, she was technically still a primipara whose unstretched pelvic muscles would likely make her labor last several more hours, Dan reckoned. Even so, he decided he'd better examine her.

"Your medical bag still in the bedroom closet?"

She thought for a moment and nodded.

Dan took it from the shelf, tore open a paper package of sterile rubber gloves, and slipped one on.

"Lie back with your legs spread apart," he told her, removing her underpants.

Smiling shyly, demurely, Kris complied. Dan parted her matted pubic hair and spread her labia when suddenly she protested, "What are you doing?"

"Examining you!" he said gruffly. "Lie back and relax, for God's sake."

Gently he slipped his index finger in to feel for her cervix. But Kris kept squirming, trying to push his hand away, and he felt nothing.

Determinedly he thrust his finger in its full length and moved it around to locate the cervical prominence. Except for a thin residual rim, the cervix was no longer there. She was fully dilated.

"Dan, stop! Please take it out!" Kris cried as another contraction began, and to his heightened horror Dan felt the baby's head touch the tip of his finger.

Hastily he withdrew his finger, peeled off his glove, and dialed the telephone operator, asking to be connected with the nearest ambulance company. To his annoyance she insisted that he tell her which one he wanted. Having no idea, he made her name some, picking the service run by a funeral home located nearby. At last the operator put him through and he gave the dispatcher his name and address, explained his urgent need of a delivery kit, and begged them to hurry. Rattled by Kris's low, whimpering moans, he grasped her hands to comfort and reassure her. When the contraction eased, he seized the phone again to call Commonwealth General. Not knowing Jim Neubeck's home telephone number, he asked the hospital operator for it. Dr. Neubeck was there, she said, and connected him with the labor and delivery floor.

To Dan's consternation the nurse who answered informed him Dr. Neubeck was in the OR doing an emergency Caesarean section. Choking back a tightness in his throat, Dan told her to notify Dr. Neubeck that they were on their way to the hospital by ambulance.

Shakily he hung up, cursing his wretched luck and Kris's negligence. Why hadn't she called Neubeck earlier? But he knew why, and the reminder sent a shiver down his spine. Kris was not a doctor now, but an expectant mother who, having brutally lost three previous babies, was incapable of acting rationally with her fourth. Unless she had improbably miscalculated her last menstrual date, she knew she was only in her sixth month and no fetus that immature could survive. So, except for trying to stop her labor pains with alcohol, she had temporarily forsaken reality.

Dan sat slumped by the side of the bed, overwhelmed by feelings of love and sadness for his wife and her futile quest for motherhood. His mental image of the dead, possibly macerated, fetus she would soon expel sickened his stomach. He was about to embrace and comfort her when her piercing scream chilled his blood. Swinging around he saw her arch her back, spread her legs wide, begin bearing-down pains. The baby was coming.

"Kris, don't!" he cried, clasping her hands. "Breathe through your mouth. Pant, don't push!"

"I can't help it!" she groaned. "It hurts so!" Breaking free of his grasp, she reached in back of her to grip one of the loops carved into the wood headboard. Dan's eyes widened as he saw her entire bottom, from gaping vagina to hemorrhoid-swollen anus, begin to bulge.

At the peak of the contraction her face flushed purplish-red, her nose started to bleed again, and her perineum ballooned out as if about to burst, drenching the bedsheets with a mixture of urine and pink-tinged amniotic fluid. "Kris, don't!" he pleaded. "Not yet. Don't push, pant!" To his immense relief she slumped back on the bed and her tense abdomen relaxed.

Pulling the pillowcase from the other pillow on the bed, Dan used it to wipe sweat and blood from her face and feces from around her rectum. Then he folded it over and tucked the clean half under her bottom, grateful for this momentary relief from unbearable tension, yet knowing it would only last a minute or two. There was no denying it; her next contraction would almost certainly push out the baby. Like an earthquake or erupting volcano, it was an irresistible natural force that no prayer nor incantation could stop. It had happened to billions of women before and would again. But to this woman at this time, it was much less likely to yield a miniature new life than a blighted product of one, not a renewal but a disposal, as the latest fulfillment of Kris's curse. His heart heavy with grief, Dan's eyes moistened.

Amazingly Kris spoke to him calmly, rationally, in the lull between contractions. "It's going to come now, isn't it?"

He nodded dully.

"Oh, Dan, I'm sorry! Sorry I acted so stupidly. I should've called Jim, but I couldn't. I didn't want him here. Only you! I must be crazy, but I wanted you with me tonight more than I've ever wanted anybody before."

"It's all right, baby," Dan soothed. "Everything's going to be all right."

"No, it's not! I should be in the hospital, not here."

"It's okay. I can handle it."

"I know you can. But I want this baby so much. You'll never know how much. And there'll never be any others." The thought, a twinge of pain—something—made her grimace. "Will it, do you think it will—"

The question went unfinished as if she were loathe to hear the truth or the lie he would have to tell her instead.

"There's a chance," Dan said. "Maybe a good one. You're awfully big for six months."

"Am I?" she said hopefully.

He watched her wince, fight back another paroxysm of pain, as if determined to hold her contraction in abeyance until she finished what she had to tell him. "I wanted this baby so bad I was willing to risk everything—my life, our marriage—for it. And you never even knew why, did you?"

"No," he said heavily. "Tell me."

"I wanted it—" Abruptly she broke off, her face twisting in an agony that transcended mere physical pain. "Oh, God!" she moaned. "Oh, dear God, no! Oh, Gaaawd—" Again her back arched and she gripped the headboard with both hands. Her eyes squeezed shut and her nostrils flared. She gulped, panted, drew deep, sniffing breaths of air. Then wetting her lips, she again tried to speak. Finally the words came. "I wanted it—" Suddenly her abdomen quivered convulsively, cutting off her breath. She gasped and screamed as she felt something rip loose inside her. Dan heard a pistollike crack as the loop of headboard she held snapped in her grip. Her legs went spread-eagled and her triangular introitus, from hoodlike clitoris to base of vagina, gaped wide. For a moment Dan saw its pink-glistening membranes fill with a fistlike blackness that rapidly receded.

"Oh, Dan!" Kris groaned. "It's coming, I can't stop it."

"It's all right," he told her. "Go ahead, push."

"But I wanted to tell you—"

"No, don't talk. Push!"

Again the black fist appeared at the introitus as if trying to punch its way out. Dan inserted both index fingers into Kris's vagina to spread its lips, help ease the baby's passage. As if from a distance, amid all Kris's grunts and yelps, he heard her scream at him, "I wanted it for you! To give you something more to live for."

Dan tried to grasp her meaning, the profound message of her words, but there was no time. He was too busy. And more . . . With the baby's birth imminent, with the extreme tension he labored under exceeding his capacity to absorb it, Dan suffered a sensory overload. A certain detachment, an almost self-hypnotic calm regulating the flow of nervous impulses from the motor cortex of his brain to his hands, overcame him. It was a phenomenon, a splitting of personality into master and robot with which he was well familiar, having experienced it in the midst of medical crises many times before. But this particular schism was incomplete, unlike any he had ever known. Instead of his brain blanking out all extraneous thought, all interfering emotion, to allow total concentration, he seemed caught up in a puzzling *déjà vu*. Then it came to him. Years before, under similar harrowing conditions, he had delivered a black baby in Mississippi and now his mind flashed back to it, recapturing that experience so vividly that it became inseparable with the present one. . . .

The middle-aged black mother giving precipitate birth to her fourth child in the stretcher two white nurses were using to wheel her into the delivery room . . . The dusky-pale male infant slithering out between her legs, his tan skin stained with greenish-brown meconium, the bowel material fetuses excreted into the placental sac, the signal of a baby in trouble . . . The loops of umbilical cord tightly wound around its scrawny neck . . . Dan quickly unwinding them, clamping and cutting the cord, trying to get the baby to breathe, urgently asking for oxygen, suction, appalled to learn neither machine worked; appalled even more by the uncaring attitudes of the two nurses, their perfunctory shrugs at the equipment failure, the clear impression their pursed mouths gave that they really didn't give a damn, nor felt he ought to, if this helpless black infant lived or died . . . Trembling with barely suppressed rage, Dan was determined to do his utmost to make this baby live . . . He dangled it by its feet, slapped its backside hard, then seeing its purplish face darkening further, placed it back on the stretcher to give it mouth-to-mouth resuscitation. Again and again he emptied his own breath into the baby's lungs to inflate them, start it breathing on its own, to no avail . . . Finally he grabbed the rubber catheter from the delivery kit, stuck it down the baby's throat and sucked stringy mucus from its mouth into his own before spitting it out on the floor. The nurses looked disgusted, the black mother amazed, but Dan kept it up until he managed to suck a large glob of mucus from the baby's windpipe. At that, it gave a weak gasp, a feeble cry. He forced more deep breaths into its lungs, held it upside down, and gave it another whack across the back. This time it let out a short, shrill yelp . . . Not good enough. He whacked it twice more until he got what he wanted:

a lusty squall and a flush of healthy color. It bawled, it pissed on his shirt front, it lived!

And now, unbelievably, Dan heard the same squalling cry again, only it came from no black baby in faraway Fayette, but his own; from the doll-sized head that had slid out between his fingers and twisted its neck sideways.

It wasn't possible. He could hardly believe his ears. In all the hundreds of deliveries Dan had performed, he'd never before heard a newborn cry the moment its head popped.

Gently he freed its left shoulder and shouted for Kris to push hard. She did and the rest of the baby slid out, trailing its thick, ropy umbilical cord. A gush of amniotic fluid nearly engulfed it. Grasping its feet, Dan raised it up to behold the miracle granted them. What he held was little more than a foot long and weighed at most two pounds. With its thatch of blood-matted scalp hair and hairy back and meconium-stained hue, an impartial observer might think it more nearly resembled a newborn monkey than a human being, but that never occurred to Dan. Captivated by its perfectly formed face and hands, he thought it was the most exquisite creature he had ever seen. Almost incidentally he glanced at the key piece of anatomy between its legs and immediately started thinking of it as her. Kris had given birth to a daughter, their own little girl.

Nearly teary-eyed with wonder, he looked up at his wife, at the exhausted, tight-eyed, almost prayerful expression on her face and announced, "It's a girl, Kris. You had a little girl."

Her eyes opened to gaze deeply, tenderly, into his. "A girl! Oh, Dan, how wonderful," she said, yet did not ask to see her.

Dan understood. "She's going to make it, Kris. I swear to God she will!"

"Oh, Dan, please!" she implored. "Please make it live."

Enough talk, he thought. He had things to do. He rested the baby between Kris's legs and reached for her medical bag. Impatiently he inverted it, dumping its contents onto the bed, and grabbed for a package of sterile gauzes to wipe away mucus from her mouth and nose. Then he broke open the suture kit and removed its two surgical clamps and scalpel. Lifting the baby by the feet again, he milked whatever small but important quantity of blood remained in the umbilical cord into her circulation before applying the first clamp approximately six inches from her belly. He placed the second clamp higher up and severed the cord with a swipe of the scalpel. Then balancing the baby on the back of one hand, momentarily letting her flop and flounder until he could grasp her behind the neck and hold her head-down in the crook of his arm, he used a rubber-bulbed ear syringe to suck more mucus out of her mouth and nose. That started her squawking again, much to his delight. It also affected Kris who suddenly said, "Oh, Dan, give it here. Let me see her."

Dan took one more look at her perfectly rounded head and incredibly black, bird-bright eyes and handed the baby over.

Despite its long, erratic hours, Dan had always liked obstetrics as a medical student; liked it especially for the unique phenomenon he often saw in the delivery room: the distillation of pure love on the mother's face when she first glimpsed her child. Regardless of what the cynics said, love did exist in this world. He saw it again now in the surpassingly tender way Kris regarded their baby girl.

A moment later Dan heard the front door open and close. Assuming the ambulance crew had arrived, he shouted, "Up here!"

"Hey, what do I do with this?" Kris pointed to the length of umbilical cord protruding from her vagina.

"Leave it," Dan said. "It'd be safer to remove the placenta once we get to the hospital."

Looking down at her nakedness, at the pool of urine and blood and amniotic fluid she lay in, Kris said, "Jesus, I'm a sight! I hope those ambulance drivers don't shock easily."

Surprisingly they did, particularly the younger of the pair, a freckled-faced lad of seventeen or eighteen. Dan saw him stop short, gulp, grow wide-eyed and slack-jawed as he entered the bedroom. Taking a backward step, he collided with his partner, a thick-set, older youth, repulsively modish in tinted glasses, shaggy sideburns, and shoulder-length hair.

Dan introduced himself and Kris, accenting the *doctor* prefix to their names, and ordered them to return with a portable stretcher and incubator. They carried no incubator, he learned in dismay, but at least they had an oxygen tank he could use.

While waiting for the pair to return, Dan dialed the hospital again and asked for Dr. Bryce Baker, chief resident in pediatrics. Having no time now to individually marshal the various experts he wanted to attend Kris and the baby at the hospital, he delegated that task to Baker. The list was a lengthy one. In addition to Jim Neubeck, it included Henry deJong, chief of their neonatal intensive care unit; Jack Ormand, a pediatric radiologist; Fred Hale, chief of the clinical laboratories; and Ted Swerdloff, director of the pediatric research program and one of the nation's foremost authorities on blood-clotting problems. Dan knew too well that the battle to keep their immature infant alive would begin in earnest once they reached the hospital and was never more grateful for his position of authority there. Though his promise to Kris that their daughter would live was beyond his—or any mortal's—capacity to insure, she would at least have the benefit of all that one of the country's leading medical institutions could offer.

The ambulance attendants lumbered up the stairs and into the bedroom with their portable stretcher. Reluctantly Kris passed the baby to Dan and slid onto it, still spread-eagled and nakedly exposed.

"Wait! Cover her with the bedspread!" Dan ordered and the ambulance drivers obeyed before carrying her down the stairs. He then went into their closet and pulled a heavy wool sweater off the rack to bundle the baby in before following.

Dan sat in the jump seat beside Kris as they made the ten-mile ride into the hospital. Those eyes! he marveled, while holding the plastic oxygen mask an inch or so from the baby's face. Those incredibly bright eyes. He could hardly take his own from them.

Kris noticed it and remarked, "Hey, the way you're looking at her is beginning to make me jealous."

Dan grinned. "With good reason, Mrs. Lassiter . . . With good reason."

But his banter merely served to conceal his true feelings. Fear, fear of sudden death, rode every foot of the way with him. He could hear its mocking murmurs in the unnerving *ooh-aah* of the ambulance sirens. Yet he refused to be daunted. Tiny as she was, this was no ordinary little girl, he reminded himself. Ordinary little girls didn't cry out the moment their head hatched. Dan remembered his boxing days and smiled. This Lassiter kid had come out fighting; angry to live. If she should make it, she would grow up to be a tough one. And if she should not—? But he wrenched that morbid thought from his mind. The experience of becoming a father was still too new, too exhilarating, for him to think that way. Or let Kris suspect that he was. He understood her obsession now; her saying she had done it for him. It was the most precious gift he could ever be given and he wanted to accept it, would accept it, with love and devotion once he was reasonably sure it was his to keep. Until then he tried to hold back, to face up to the slim chance this tiny creature in his arms had of surviving or growing up normally—*tried,* but couldn't. Her eyes would not allow such detached doctor-thought. For once his heart held sway over his head. He could not think, only feel, under the spell of his daughter's mesmerizing eyes.

Chapter Twenty-One

At last the hospital tower loomed into view and the ambulance sped around its circular drive to the rear. Baker had done his work well and Dan could see an entourage of eight or nine hospital personnel waiting for them under the hazy glare of the emergency room lights. The instant the ambulance came to a halt Dan opened its back doors and, holding the baby tightly in one arm, jumped out.

Jim Neubeck was the first to reach him, followed closely by two nurses carrying a portable incubator.

"Jesus, Dan!" he blurted. "What happened?"

A superfluous question, thought Dan, in view of the bundle he held in his arms. "We had a baby. That is, Kris did. I just delivered it."

"She never called," Jim said, puzzled.

"I know. She wanted it to be a family affair. Don't worry, you'll still collect your fee. But you'd better check Kris. The placenta's still in her."

"Right," Jim said and ducked past him to climb into the ambulance. A moment later he reappeared and ordered two hospital orderlies to take Kris directly to the delivery room.

Dan went slightly weak-kneed as he passed the baby to a nurse to put in the incubator but rapidly recovered and started to follow them inside. To his astonishment, one of the ambulance drivers stood blocking his way. "That'll, ah, be ninety-five dollars, Doctor," he said.

Dan looked hard at him. Mercenary bastard, he thought. Had he enough money in his wallet he would have thrown it at the man.

The ambulance driver fidgeted under his glare. "Eighty for the ambulance ride and fifteen for the use of the oxygen," he explained.

"All right, send me a bill. My insurance will cover it."

"I'm supposed to collect it when we get to the hospital."

Dan had to hold his seething temper in check. He had heard how exorbitant private ambulance fees were but not how crassly they tried to dun patients or their families for it.

"What if I can't pay? Do you take the baby as collateral?"

The ambulance driver shrugged. "Just following orders, Doc."

"All right, come to my office in the morning and my secretary will give you a check."

The driver looked dubious. "What office is that?"

"Just ask for the head of the hospital," Dan snapped and strode past him to overtake Bryce Baker.

"Good job," he told Baker. "Is Henry here?"

"In his office."

"Already? That was fast."

"He came in for morning rounds and never got to leave." Baker shook his head. "We've had a rough day."

Dr. Henry deJong was a short, intense man of mixed Dutch-Indonesian ancestry. He was also a perfectionist, a stern task-master to his residents, and an authentic genius. Although Henry had been at Commonwealth General for years, Dan really did not know him well. Few members of the hospital staff did. Henry came in seven days a week but confined himself almost exclusively to his particular bailiwick: the neonatal intensive care unit on the west wing of the nineteenth floor. He seldom ate in the hospital cafeteria or mingled with his fellow doctors in their coffee lounges; he saw no need. His exotic-looking Balinese wife packed a lunch box with his favorite soup and curried rice each day and his secretary brewed a pot of imported mint tea for him the first thing every morning and again at four. It was not that Henry was antisocial; he simply showed little interest in anybody weighing over five pounds or older than six months. Newborn babies were his métier, his clay, and no other pediatrician in the country could match his sure and delicate touch with them. Thanks to his organizational genius and Ted Swerdloff's research, Commonwealth General had one of the finest neonatology units with one of the lowest infant mortality rates of any hospital in the world.

Henry was on the telephone when Dan entered his office. "That was the nursery," he said upon hanging up. "Your little girl weighs one pound twelve ounces. Roughly 800 grams."

Dan grimaced and sank heavily into a chair. He had guessed higher. "That's not good, is it?"

Henry looked at his worried face and tightly clasped hands and said smilingly, out of kindness not conceit, "No, it's not. But I am! So chin up and let's take a look."

Donning a sterile gown in the nursing station next to the neonatal ICU, Dan followed Henry through the door. The rectangular-shaped room was brightly lighted, with Walt Disney animal characters adorning its yellow walls, and noisy. Incredibly noisy. The chirping signals issuing from its many monitors made it sound like an aviary of young birds at feeding time. A double row of plastic-topped Isolette incubators ran along each side of the room, leaving little walking space. A black monitor box, the size of an ordinary suitcase, sat on a shelf above each Isolette, its two speedometerlike dials continually registering the infant's heart and respiratory rates. Between them were two small bulbs, one yellow, one red. The chirping noise was synchronous with the flashing yellow light and sounded approximately once per second to indicate all was well. The red light was the danger signal. It did not chirp but buzzed if the infant's heartbeat or breathing rate fell outside certain limits. On a lower shelf a pair of tube-connected, water-filled bottles bubbled with oxygen streaming through them to acquire the necessary humidity before flowing into each Isolette.

Dan caught glimpses of premie infants of various sizes, shapes, hues, and postures as he followed Henry down the narrow aisle between incubators. Some of the sicker ones lay on their backs, their heads enclosed in bowl-sized plastic oxygen hoods, rubber endotracheal or feeding tubes protruding from their mouths, IV solutions dripping into their arms or umbilical veins. The healthier ones lay on their stomachs, their diapered bottoms sticking up insouciantly in the air.

The eyes of several babies were tightly bandaged to shield them from the panel of bright, predominately blue-spectrum fluorescent lights shining down on them. Their function was to reduce the level of bilirubin, a breakdown product of red blood cells, in the infant's blood and so prevent the brain damage excessive amounts of this substance could cause.

Initially Dan was fascinated by all he saw, visualizing the neonatal intensive care unit as a combination chick hatchery and baby-repair factory. But the group of grim-faced doctors and nurses huddled around the incubator in the corner where his baby lay filled him with dread. Two nurses stepped back from the Isolette to make room for Henry and himself. Dan felt a stab of tenderness as he gazed down at his little girl. She looked considerably different now that the nurses had scrubbed her clean of blood and pink-tinged amniotic fluid, trimmed and disinfected her umbilical stump, and attached a pair of button-sized pressure sensors to each side of her chest to record the rate and depth of respirations. But the other changes he observed troubled him. Her color had darkened from pink to a fleshy reddish-brown, her breathing appeared more labored, and instead of making pumping motions her tiny arms and legs twitched. Even the look in her eyes seemed duller.

Bryce Baker, a slim metal probe and pair of tweezers in his hands, looked up at Dan and asked, "Would you rather that Dr. deJong did the umbilical artery catheterization, Dr. Lassiter?"

Dan glanced fleetingly at Henry and said, "No, go ahead. You're perfectly capable." Actually he would have preferred that Henry do it, but he did not want to slight Baker's ability, rob him of the self-confidence so necessary in a chief resident. Dan's mere presence placed enough added pressure on him.

Baker nodded and resumed probing for the pinpoint opening in the pale, finger-sized cross-section of cord. Finally, thinking he had located it, he grasped one lip with the tweezers, threaded the tip of a slim plastic catheter through the slit, and pushed it forward a few inches into what he hoped was the main aorta. To his relief bright-red blood back-flowed through the lumen of the catheter, confirming the correctness of his placement.

"Good job!" Dan said and watched Baker attach a 5cc syringe to the catheter's free end to draw blood for multiple laboratory analyses.

Dan was momentarily startled to see the red danger light flash on and a nurse give a quick finger flick to the soles of his baby's feet to start her breathing again. "Don't worry, Dr. Lassiter," she said. "That happens all the time with these tiny ones. All it takes is a little stimulation to get them going again."

"I see," Dan replied. But his shaken look did not escape Henry. Draping an arm around Dan's shoulder he said, "Why don't you get out of here? Go visit your wife or something and come back in a half hour or so. We'll have the results of her lab work by then and can tell much more."

Dan looked doubtful, prompting Henry to lead him a step away. "Don't worry," he said confidently. "I promise you she'll still be here when you get back."

From the nursing station Dan phoned the delivery labor floor and spoke with Jim Neubeck. The placenta was out, the minor cervical tear Kris had suffered repaired, and his wife was fine, Jim assured him. But she was asleep right now and he advised Dan to let her rest a while longer.

Dan nodded at the telephone and hung up. A bit dazed, he wandered out of the neonatal unit into the corridor, paused to orient himself, and mounted the stairs to his office.

It was well past midnight now and pale moonlight shone through the windows. He stood before one, feeling drained but restless, hopeful but wary, unable to steel himself against the possibility of his daughter's death, unable to rid his mind of it. Would he rather she die now, if nature meant her to, or be saved by Henry's wizardry only to grow up hopelessly handicapped? It was a Solomonic choice, a nerve-shattering one, and Dan knew he must not dwell on it further in his state of near-collapse.

He telephoned Jimmy's home to tell him and Nora the news.

Jimmy was astounded and elated. "You had to deliver her yourself?" he repeated. "Wow! That must've been quite an experience. Too bad you folks couldn't afford a regular baby doctor. But home deliveries are back in vogue, I hear. And the baby's doing okay, you say? When can we see her?"

"Nora can see her in the morning."

"What about me? I'm the godfather!"

"I dunno. Between your eyesight and her size I doubt you'll be able to see her at all."

Jimmy chuckled. "Okay, wise guy. Give Kris our love and tell her we'll be up in the morning."

Next Dan phoned Nels Freiborg to cancel his luncheon date with the President.

Nels, too, was amazed and sympathetic. "Don't worry about the President, Dan," he said. "In fact, don't worry about anything right now except that little baby of yours." But ever the politician, he added, "However, if this changes your thinking on any of the matters under discussion, please let me know."

Irked, Dan replied, "I'll do that, Nels. All it's changed so far, though, is my availability to Washington for the next several days. So, see if you can move that Senate hearing ahead a few weeks, will you?"

"Of course. That's pushing it close to their summer recess, but I'm sure something can be arranged. And the President will still want to have his private talk with you beforehand."

"He will, Nels. He will. I'll keep you posted," Dan said wearily and hung up.

The look on Henry's face when Dan entered his office forewarned him that the news would not be good. "Sit down, Dan," he urged.

"Not yet," Dan said and steadied himself with both hands on the desktop. "She's still alive, isn't she?"

Henry nodded vigorously. "Yes, she's alive. But it doesn't look too favorable. Do you want me to go over all the lab results we've gotten so far?"

"Later! All I want to hear right now is what her chances of making it are."

"Oh, God," Henry groaned. "If you only knew how I hate playing the Lord's oddsmaker. But I do know the statistics, and they're not good. Not good at all. Her AGPAR's slipped five points in the last half hour. And her blood gases show—"

"Never mind those," Dan interrupted. "Just tell me her chances."

"Okay. . . . Right now, even if her lung function doesn't deteriorate any further, I'd have to say no better than one in ten."

"That bad, huh?" Dan slumped into a chair. Clearing a sudden fullness from his throat he asked, "And that's with you going all-out, doing everything you possibily can to save her?"

To his surprise, Henry shook his head. "No, it's not. That's only using presently accepted methods. There's one thing more we can try to maybe better those odds. As I've already indicated, her main problem is pulmonary—it usually is in infants so immature. But not hyaline membrane disease."

"What is it then?"

"Bleeding. Either into the lungs or brain. Their capillaries are so fragile that the least trauma, even a hard jar of the incubator, can rupture them. The Vitamins K and C we inject usually help reduce the bleeding tendency in more mature infants but don't work worth a damn in those under a kilogram."

"So?" Dan prompted.

"So, if you'd taken time to attend some of our pediatric research seminars, you'd know Swerdloff and I have been working on this problem for the last five years. Ted phoned me around ten minutes ago from the airport. He's chartered a helicopter and ought to descend on us momentarily. And since this is primarily his work, I really should let him tell you about it. But I can see the state you're in, so I'll go ahead and give you the gist myself. Essentially what Ted has done is isolate a platelet factor ten times more powerful than anything previously tested in reducing capillary fragility. It's so new we haven't even given it a name or number yet, just call it NHF—*Neonatal Hemostatic Factor*. But our hunch is, what we've isolated may well be the platelet's cement substance in pure form."

"How extensively have you tested it so far?"

Henry frowned. "That's the catch. The stuff is so damned hard to separate that we've only had enough for limited trials." He laughed harshly. "Limited, did I say? That's hardly the word." He spread the fingers on one hand. "Five immature rhesus monkeys! That's our total animal trials to date."

"And humans?" Dan asked anxiously. "Have you tried it on them yet?"

"Three—all weighing under a kilogram. Only one survived. But I'm almost positive our salvage rate would've been higher if only we'd had the guts to give it earlier—as we did with the last one. The autopsies on the first two showed massive brain hemorrhage. Nothing could've pulled them through at that stage. We saved four of the five monkeys, though."

"How early did you give it to them?"

"Practically as soon as we got them out of their mothers' bellies."

"And the one infant you saved?"

"Within two hours of birth."

Dan looked at his watch. "In other words, around now?"

Soberly Henry nodded. "That's right."

"What about side effects?"

"None, so far. But who's to know what'll turn up when we test it more extensively? The one kiddo we were successful with ended up being exchanged—mainly as a precaution—but so do a lot his size." Henry compressed his lips. "I only wish it was somebody else's kid we were talking about using it on."

"But it's not! It's mine—Kris's and mine. The only one we'll ever have. And I'm grateful for even this much hope. After all, one in three's a damn sight better than one in ten."

"I agree. But if anything goes wrong and it turns out to be the fault of the drug—" Henry blinked and sighed. "I don't know how I'd ever forgive myself."

"If anything goes wrong, it goes wrong, that's all!" Dan said supportively. "I'm all for using it. The only thing is—" Suddenly he faltered, an anguished look on his face. "The thing is, I suppose I ought to talk to Kris before giving you the final okay. God, how I hate breaking it to her, but—"

"But it's still experimental and she has a right to know."

Just as they heard the whir of helicopter blades above them, the phone rang. Henry picked it up, listened a moment, and winced. "All right," he said brusquely, "we'll be right there."

Turning back to Dan, Henry was startled by his ashen face. "No, no, she's still alive," he said hastily. "It's just that her pulse and respiratory rate keep climbing and Baker feels she ought to go on a respirator."

Dan followed Henry out of the office into the adjoining neonatal ICU at a fast pace, almost a trot. His first glimpse of his little girl—she really needed a name, he thought—clutched at his stomach. Her color was distinctly duskier, especially her limbs, and she was breathing so rapidly her chest and abdomen appeared to be fluttering. But her eyes were wide open and her tiny hands kept flailing out as if wanting to grasp something. Her daddy's hand? thought Dan wistfully and the words burst from him: "Give it to her, Henry! Give it now. I'll sign the forms; take full responsibility."

Henry nodded and spoke crisply to Baker. "Go ahead and intubate her. I want her on a controlled-cycled respirator. She needs the rest. Then draw 2cc of blood for baseline platelet function studies. We'll be following the NHF protocol." Turning to Dan he said, "Forget the formalities. You can sign the papers later. Go get some rest. Take a drink, a tranquilizer—anything. You're just in the way here."

Reluctantly Dan nodded. "Ask Ted to come to my office when he can. I'd like to know more about his platelet stuff."

"I will, Dan," Henry assured him. "Now go!"

Dan resisted the urge to take a last look at his infant and left. He ought to go to Kris, but he couldn't face her right now. Not with his nerves so strung out. He knew he was only postponing the inevitable, that before the night was over he would have to tell her how desperately their precious little girl was battling for life, but he simply couldn't now. Later maybe, but not now . . .

Weighed down by despair, Dan trudged back to his office, hoping Henry would send Swerdloff to him soon. He couldn't bear having to wait alone in here too long.

Moving to the bank of windows, he gazed out at the dark and endless firmament—all else had a beginning, an existence, however brief, a finitude, except possibly that.

Heavenly bread, he thought. *Please God, grant me Heavenly bread and I'll forego all material kind.*

Oh, God, enter into this temple of science and let it be You in Your wisdom that governs our earthly affairs, not the immutable laws of probability.

Chapter Twenty-Two

Dan was stretched out on his office couch when Swerdloff appeared at the door. "Dr. Lassiter?" he inquired uncertainly.

"Come in, Ted! Come in," Dan urged. "The light switch is on your right. I've been resting, only not too well. I'd much rather talk."

He rose to shake hands and offer coffee. Swerdloff was a medium-tall, thick-set man in his early fifties. With his round face, aquiline nose, and thin hedge of hair rimming his bald pate like a laurel wreath, he reminded Dan of a Roman Senator. It had been almost six years since he had interviewed Swerdloff for a staff position and he could scarcely recall speaking to him again. Like Henry, he was another of the many brilliant men at Commonwealth General that Dan had never taken time to know well, though he was officially their chief. The realization chagrined and humbled him.

"Well," Swerdloff said, "we injected the NHF around an hour ago. We ought to know soon how effective it'll be."

"How soon?"

Swerdloff shrugged. "Around three, four hours. We should be picking up a trend in her coagulation studies, particularly her bleeding time, by then." Observing Dan's grim expression he remarked, "That's a real cute little kid you got, Dr. Lassiter. Hate to say it, but I think she looks more like her mother."

Dan smiled weakly. "You do, huh?"

"Afraid so. I have four girls myself—no Y chromosomes, I guess—and they all look like my wife, which is a blessing."

Suddenly Dan remembered that Swerdloff was married to a once famous New York stage actress and was an accomplished amateur actor himself: a man of diverse talents.

"Henry said you wanted me to tell you more about the research we're doing—which I'm happy to do, since we're planning to hit you up for an extra $25,000 in supplemental funds for next year."

Dan's eyebrows lifted. "Are you? Well, in that case I'd better learn all I can about it to make sure it's approved while I'm still director. But not now, Ted. Not now. Let's talk about flying, stage plays, how the hell to revive basic research in this country—anything to keep me diverted until it's time to draw the next set of lab studies on the baby. Think you can do that?"

"Me?" Swerdloff said immodestly. "Don't you know that the med students say I have an inherent capacity for instant bullshit. Just add water, or preferably beer, and—presto—an hour's talk!"

The students were right. For three hours Swerdloff kept up a constant flow of chatter, making Dan laugh, ponder, occasionally dispute him on a wide range of medical and nonmedical topics. It also made him wonder if the person they were seeking to replace Dan as general director of the hospital might not be sitting across from him.

At 4:00 A.M. they descended to the neonatal unit to watch the bloodletting. The rubber endotracheal tube taped to his little girl's nose and chin made it almost impossible for Dan to see her face. He winced when a lab technician stuck a metal stylet with a quarter-inch-long point into her tiny earlobe, and clicking on a stopwatch gently wiped at the trickle of blood with filter paper until the bleeding stopped.

"Five minutes and five seconds," the technician informed Henry who had come up behind them.

"Is that good?" Dan asked.

Henry smiled. "Not bad. Not bad at all, considering it was almost double that four hours ago."

As they were removing their gowns in the nursing station, Henry asked, "Have you spoken to Kris yet?"

Dan shook his head. "I'm waiting for something more favorable to tell her. Otherwise I know damn well she'll insist on seeing the baby right away. When do you think she might be able to come off the respirator?"

"Oh, by morning. We'll start weaning her in another hour or so to see how she does."

"Good. I'd prefer that Kris sees her when she's off, if possible. Well, what do you think now?"

"You want me to play oddsmaker again?" Henry chided.

"No, just human being."

"Hmmm . . . Well, as a fellow human being I'm exhausted, humbled, and cautiously optimistic. We still have infection, heart failure, hyperbilirubinemia, and a dozen other potential complications to worry about, but right now I'm going to brew myself a strong cup of tea. Care to join me?"

"Thanks, maybe later. I guess I'd better go tell Kris."

But first Dan went to his office to shave, bathe his bloodshot eyes in eyewash, and put on his best face for her—to no avail. He had barely wakened her and begun to describe their little girl's battle to stay alive when he choked and tears filled his eyes. Kris took him in her arms and hugged him tightly until he could go on. Finally he managed to tell her all of it.

Kris took it stoically, almost as much concerned about Dan's health as their infant's. "Here," she said, sliding over to make room for him on the bed. "Slip off your shoes and lie down for a while. You need to rest."

Ignoring hospital regulations, Dan did, snuggling his head against her breast.

Soothingly Kris caressed his face and brow. "Our Dana's a brave little girl," she said softly.

"Is she ever!" Dan sighed and drew away to stare at her. "What'd you call her?"

Kris smiled. "You heard me! No arguing about it either. Mothers get to pick their daughters' names, and this one's Dana Lassiter. Has sort of a nice ring to it, don't you think?"

"Lovely," mumbled Dan and fell asleep with a grin on his face.

Thanks to Jimmy, the Lassiter baby made the front page of Tuesday's *Boston Globe* and was picked up by the national wire services. His column the next day, relating the circumstances of her birth and the dramatic new treatment she was receiving, won a vast readership. Not since the ill-fated birth of the Kennedy infant in 1963 had the public shown such interest in so tiny a tike. Even though the Lassiters weren't Catholic, special Masses were held for Dana's well-being. Telegrams, cards, bouquets of flowers, but only an occasional gift—people being superstitious about giving gifts until a baby's survival was assured—poured into the hospital in huge quantities. The first thing day-shift workers at Commonwealth General asked the night-shift was, how much did the Lassiter baby weigh, and showed dismay to hear she had dropped another half ounce or so. But that was to be expected. All newborn babies lose up to ten percent of their birth weight in the few days of life before stabilizing and slowly regaining it over the next several weeks.

Although wishing it were otherwise, that Henry could somehow feed her more glucose or protein hydrolysate to flesh her out without overloading her heart, Dan and Kris accepted the weight loss philosophically. By Friday, Dana had leveled off at one pound six ounces, and with her skin color turning from pink to flaming red, she began to resemble a broiled lobster without claws.

The many visitors who streamed past the display window of the neonatal ICU to peek at the Lassiter baby and *ooh* and *ahh* at her tininess mistook this bright complexion as a sign of health. But Kris and Dan knew better. On closer inspection, her crimson color was developing an orangish tinge that grew more pronounced as her serum bilirubin level climbed a gram or two each day.

That Friday afternoon Henry met them in Kris's room to discuss the complication.

"What's her latest report?" Dan asked.

"Nine-and-a-half grams," said Henry. "I've placed her under a bilirubin lamp in the hope that'll lower it."

"And if it doesn't?"

"Then we'll have to resort to exchange transfusion. The frustrating thing is, we still don't have any solid data on what's the danger level for infants that immature. Not like we have for full-termers."

"What's your hunch?"

Henry made a wry face to remind Dan scientists preferred to talk in terms of known facts, not hunches. But in this case there simply weren't any. "My policy's been to go ahead and exchange them whenever their bilirubin level gets much over 10."

"Ten!" Kris exclaimed. "She's awfully close to that now."

Henry nodded. "I'm hoping the phototherapy will stop, if not reverse, the climb."

"When will you know?" asked Dan.

"I've scheduled another test for 4:00 P.M." He shrugged. "We'll just have to wait and see how it turns out."

"And if it isn't any lower?" Dan persisted. "What then?"

"I'll have no choice then but to exchange her," Henry said. "Nonetheless, I must warn you: It's always a touch-and-go business in these real tiny ones, but in Dana's case the risks may be even higher."

Dan and Kris exchanged anxious looks. "How so?" he asked.

Henry nervously cleared his throat. "Because of the NHF we gave her. We process our material from pooled human platelets, you know, and it may have sensitized her to them."

"I see," said Dan. "Would it help any if you took the blood from me since we're both the same type?"

Henry shrugged. "It might, if you want to give it."

"Why not? I'd never miss it. Hell, I must've sweated off that much by now."

"Well," Henry said, "let's hope the phototherapy

makes this whole discussion academic." He paused, as if trying to think of something more reassuring to say, then shrugged. "We'll know at four."

Much as it pained him to see it, Dan went down to the neonatal ICU a little before four to watch the lab technician stick Dana's already badly bruised heel with his stylet and squeeze out enough blood for a bilirubin determination. Then he followed the technician to the laboratory to wait for the test result.

"Hey, Dr. Lassiter!" the technician suddenly exclaimed. "You're going to like this: 8.5 grams on the nose!"

Elated, Dan rushed to tell Kris the good news. He found her on the telephone, talking to her mother in Norway. Since Dana would be in the hospital at least three months, they had agreed for Marta to postpone her visit until she came home. "Oh, wait, Mother. Here's Dan," Kris said. "It's what? 8.5! Oh, how wonderful! Do you hear that, Mother? it's 8.5 grams. . . . What is? Her bilirubin level. What do you think I've been trying to explain for the last five minutes? Yes, Mother, I know you're not a doctor. . . . Yes, Mother . . . look, I'll call you back around the same time tomorrow, okay?" Kris said and hung up. "Oh, Dan, that's great. Simply great!" she enthused. "When will they be checking it again?"

"At midnight."

"Then go home—our home—and get some sleep. You must be as tired as I am of these hospital beds. So go ahead. I'll get Nan to keep me company this evening."

Dan stopped by his office to pick up his shaving gear and tell Hedley the good news about the baby.

She beamed on hearing it. "But before you resign your job here, I want a raise. A substantial one. I'm going to need it to afford flying back and forth to Washington every weekend to see little Dana. Oh, Dr. Lassiter," Hedley suddenly added, "I almost forgot to tell you: Mr. Freiborg called. I asked him if he wanted to speak directly to you, but he said it wasn't necessary. Just to let you know your Senate hearing has been rescheduled for next Friday and your luncheon with the President for the day before. If that's not satisfactory, he wants you to phone him at his home tonight. Otherwise he'll call tomorrow to confirm it personally. Do you want me to try and get him back on the line for you now?"

"No need," Dan said. "Next Friday sounds fine. But call Mr. Dallesio at his Washington office and tell him. Also tell him to quit trying to sound like a Wop Dr. Spock with all that joys of fatherhood drivel he's been writing lately. If he's not careful he'll drive up the birth rate."

"I'll do that, Dr. Lassiter," Hedley said, hiding a grin. "Maybe not in those exact words, but similar."

Just before his alarm clock was set to ring at eleven, a terrifying nightmare woke Dan abruptly. Fearing what if might bode, he telephoned the hospital to be assured by the night nurse on the neonatal ICU that Dana's condition remained unchanged. Maybe the now forgotten dream had something to do with politics, with some imagined danger to himself from Lem, or from the health fund swindlers, Dan speculated. Whatever its origin, it left him with a lingering sense of unease, of imminent peril, that long years of medical experience had taught him not to ignore.

At ten after twelve he found out what it was. Inexplicably Dana's bilirubin level had jumped to 11 grams. Henry ordered an immediate repeat, which came back only a fraction lower, and told Dan he was proceeding with the exchange transfusion at once. Bleakly Dan nodded and went directly to the blood donor area of the laboratory to have them draw the necessary amount of blood from him.

The problem of what to tell Kris so preoccupied him that he barely flinched when the technician jabbed the large-bore needle into his arm vein. Finally he decided to tell her nothing until the exchange was completed.

Disregarding the technician's warning, Dan jumped off the table the moment the needle was withdrawn, waited for his head to stop swimming, and headed for the small OR off the neonatal unit to join Henry. He was grateful to find Bryce Baker and Ted Swerdloff there too—Baker to assist with the procedure, Swerdloff to lend moral support.

"Did you helicopter in again?" he asked Ted.

"No, I was already in town. Having the ass bored off me by some archbishop expounding on the ethics of human experimentation at Harvard Med School. To hear him tell it, us pediatric researchers are getting damned close to original sin."

The next moment Dana was brought in by a nurse and laid on a special strapboard, usually used for circumcisions, that was already on the operating table. With her arms and legs drawn up and her belly flesh so wrinkled, she looked pathetically tiny and fragile, and the feeble cries she uttered when her limbs were wired with EKG leads made Dan's heart ache. Though her umbilical cord remnant was shriveled and charred, its vessels would have to be used again, and after disinfecting and draping it and assuring Dan it would be painless, Henry amputated it close to her abdomen. The spot of blood oozing out of its upper half indicated the site of the vein. Henry threaded a long polyvinyl catheter into it, secured it with a mattress suture, and flushed its lumen with a heparinized salt solution to prevent the blood flowing back and forth through it from clotting.

The plastic bag containing the 125 cc of blood Dan had donated was then removed from the sink where it had been sitting in warm water and hung on the IV pole. "Test the temperature," Henry told the nurse and she let a few cc run into a special cup wired to a thermocouple.

"Thirty-seven point four centigrade," she announced and Henry nodded.

Almost sternly he turned to Dan. "I don't object to your being here, but I must warn you we're in for a hair-raiser, there's no possible help you can give us, and I'd really prefer that you leave."

"Thanks for the out, Henry," Dan replied, "but I'd

rather stay. She's my baby and it's my blood and I'd like to see what you do with them."

"Suit yourself." Henry made a final check of the EKG and monitor readings and said, "We'll use 5cc exchanges."

Baker nodded. He reached into the transfusion tray for the glass syringe that would serve as receptacle for both the blood taken from and transfused into the baby, fit a three-way stopcock to its nozzle, and attached the plastic catheter in Dana's umbilical vein to it. Gently he drew back on the handle until dark-red blood filled its barrel to the 5 mark. Watching intensely, Dan thought he saw Dana pale perceptibly. Baker then moved the stopcock a quarter turn and emptied the blood into a run-off basin. Again he refilled the barrel, this time with blood from the plastipack, and slowly, 1cc every thirty seconds, injected it into Dana's circulation. With less than half the barrel-full in her, she began to shiver violently and her heart rate climbed to 170 beats per minute.

"Stop!" Henry barked.

"What's happening?" Dan asked.

"She's having a reaction of some sort. What do you think, Ted?"

Swerdloff shrugged. "We've seen it before in some of our monkeys. More of a febrile than a hemolytic one. I'd try some hydrocortisone."

"All right," Henry said doubtfully and ordered the nurse to inject 25 milligrams of Solu-Cortef.

She did and gradually Dana's shivering ceased.

At a nod from Henry, Baker injected the remaining 3 cc of blood without any adverse effect.

With this Dan's tense muscles relaxed, and he diverted his attention long enough to make a quick calculation. With each 5cc exchange taking about five minutes, the procedure would last at least two more hours. He hoped his nervous system could stand the strain.

The next several mini-exchanges proceeded uneventfully, further reducing the collective tension of the group. But as Baker injected the sixth syringeful, the red monitor light flashed on and Dana's pulse fell to 100 beats per minute.

Again Henry ordered Baker to halt. "I warned you this would be a hair-raiser," he told Dan. "Now it's her heart. It's not adjusting to the changes in intravascular volume as well as we'd hoped. Also her abdomen is distending, pushing up her diaphragm and further reducing cardiac output."

Dana let out several feeble cries as Henry grasped her tiny face between his thumb and forefinger and forced a plastic tube down her throat into her stomach. The nurse took the free end, attached a bulb-topped suction syringe to its tip and began aspirating small amounts of gastric juice and air with it. Henry then detached the syringe from the umbilical catheter and held it straight up until the back-flow of blood stopped rising and he could measure the height of the column with a ruler. "Venous pressure 14 centimeters," he announced.

"Meaning what?" Dan asked.

"Meaning her heart is failing. Not bad, though. We can try digoxin, but it's not all that effective in these circumstances. Or, if you prefer, cardiocyclase?"

Dan pondered. For two centuries digitalis leaf, the parent compound of digoxin, had been the *only* cardiotonic drug known to medicine. Recently a new experimental agent, cardiocyclase, had begun to replace it but not without increasing the risk of cardiac rhythm irregularities.

"For God's sake, Henry," he finally said, "do whatever you ordinarily would if I weren't here."

Above his face mask Henry's eyes crinkled in a sympathetic smile. "Twenty micrograms of digoxin IV," he told the nurse.

The injection was given, successfully lowering Dana's venous pressure after a time, and Henry decided to continue the exchange transfusion.

The next hour and a half passed without incident. With his gaze on Dana's gnomelike head and face, disproportionately large in comparison to her underdeveloped limbs, hearing the faint sucking sounds she made against the tube in her mouth, Dan felt his eyelids grow heavy and he drifted into drowsiness. Only Bryce Baker's periodic announcements after each 10cc had been exchanged intruded upon his reverie, and when 90cc, the three-quarter mark was reached, Dan relaxed further. The long procedure would soon be ended, he told himself confidently. His spunky little girl, now more than ever a part of him with his blood in her, had shown her mettle again. The worst was over.

But it wasn't.

Vaguely Dan heard Henry tell the nurse to draw up the calcium solution that was needed to counteract the citrate added to the blood he had donated to prevent it from clotting in the bag, and watched him slowly inject it.

Suddenly the flashing red light on the monitor jolted him out of his lethargy. Dana's heart rate, which had been holding steady at 160 beats per minute, had dropped below 100. To Dan's horror it kept plummeting until the dial hit zero. At the same instant that her heart stopped, she gave a faint gasp and ceased breathing too.

On the verge of fainting, Dan had to steady himself on the operating table. Through a veil of bitter tears he blearily watched the trio of doctors huddled around Dana. But neither their shouts nor frantic activities registered in his brain as the reverberations of a single thought drowned out all else: how could he possibly tell Kris?

Chapter Twenty-Three

With one hand Bryce Baker held the triangular rubber mask of the Ambu bag tightly against Dana's face and with the other kneaded its bladderlike attachment to force air into her lungs.

"That's it!" Henry cried. "Keep bagging her." With a sweeping motion he grabbed a fluid-filled syringe from the nurse and plunged it into the center of Dana's chest. He drew back on the handle until dark blood showed in the base of the syringe and then thrust it in, injecting a mix of epinephrine and cardiocyclase directly into her heart cavity.

A brutal sight, thought Dan. He had used the same last-ditch measure on innumerable dying patients himself, but never in one so tiny that the syringe affixed to her doll-sized body reminded him more of a voodoo than a medical ritual. His chest heaved and his heart raced as he shared the blackness, the smothering sensation, produced by the Ambu face mask. As adrenalin jolted Dana's nervous system, it also jolted his in some empathic fashion. It was as if his soul had mingled with the child's to make her suffering his own. For a transcendent moment they felt as one, they were one, imprinting an indelible memory in Dan. However long they had to live, he knew that from this instant on a special affinity would bind him and his daughter. Then abruptly, shiveringly, his trancelike state lifted and he heard Henry growl, "That damned calcium! I knew I should never have given it. Should've used heparinized blood instead."

"Why didn't you?" Dan asked.

"Because one of the lab monkeys who got NHF bled intracranially after we transfused him with it. He might have anyway, but I didn't want to chance it. So we used the usual ACD anticoagulant to collect your blood."

"Jesus, Henry, what are you going to do now?" Dan managed to say in a voice choked with strain.

Henry looked up at the monitor. Although Dana's heart beat hovered around the 180 mark, she was breathing on her own now and her color had pinked up. "Let's get a set of blood gases," he proposed, "and if they don't look too bad finish up." As the others nodded, he shook his head. "Christ, how did I ever get into this line of work! I should've been a tugboat captain, a tulip grower—all the things I wanted to be as a kid." He gave Dan a sharp glance. "How you holding up under all this?"

Dan tried to smile. "Well, I haven't fainted yet."

Dana's blood gases—the critical measurements of her internal oxygen and carbon dioxide content—were near enough to normal for Henry to continue the exchange transfusion. The process consumed another half hour, the longest of Dan's life, a profoundly reflective time for him and a pivotal point in his existence.

Had he ever before fully appreciated how indomitable the human spirit could be until his tiny daughter had showed him? Unable to see, barely able to hear or think in her inchoate state, this bundle of raw instinct had refused to yield to death's onslaught. Something more powerful than medical science, more purposeful than chance, had protected her: the inherent will to live. Knowing nothing of life, of its joys and woes and inevitable decline to dust, she seemed fiercely determined to experience it all for herself, as if intuitively certain that in balance it would prove worthwhile. A sense of awe and reverence, more moving than any he had known before, overcame Dan, filling him with self-doubt. Had he ever really thought of his own life as being so beneficent or himself deserving of its best?

Unlike the masses of adults who spent so much of their time trying to deal with their death anxieties by seeking religious succor or sensual diversions, he had reacted differently. Instead of trying to deny death's existence, push his almost daily glimpses of its devastation from his conscious mind, he had personified it.

Death had been his shadowy companion ever since it had claimed his mother and father when he was twelve, his older brother four years later, and the many army buddies whose corpses he had helped plant in the rocky beaches of Inchon, Korea, at age twenty-two. Then had come medical school and his obsession with his cadaver. Though the gross anatomy course had lasted only six months, it seemed to him as if the gloom, the stench, the charnel house horrors of the dissection lab had never really left him. Each autopsy he watched, each sleepless night he spent, invariably brought back traces of it.

First as an archenemy, then as a sometime friend to his tormented, terminally ill patients, most recently as a smiling succubus tempting him to take the plunge into eternal peace or eternal oblivion, he had been enthralled by death. He had allowed his fascination with it to worm its way deep inside him, eroding his spirit and draining his strength of will.

But no more, he vowed.

Never again could he reconcile such morbid thoughts with the memory of the valiant battle this tiny creature he had sired, this bare pound of human being, had waged to live. In giving him this child, his loving wife had aroused an overwhelming curiosity in him to watch her grow from infancy into flourishing girlhood and womanhood. Both wife and daughter had shamed him by their examples, made him deplore his death-haunted years.

"Well, that's it!" Henry sighed in tones of tremendous relief as the last cc of blood had been exchanged and the nurse reported to him that Dana's bilirubin level had fallen to 8 grams. Failing to draw even a nod from Dan, Henry gave him a quizzical glance and spoke louder. "I said, that's it! That's all the blood she's getting tonight since her bilirubin's down to 8. Weren't you listening?"

Dan shrugged apologetically. "Guess not. Must've been daydreaming, or maybe praying."

Henry nodded. "Well, if it was praying, keep it up.

Maybe you've got a knack for it." Wearily he stripped off his rubber gloves and wiped his sweating forehead with the towel the nurse handed him. "You understand, of course," he advised, "that all we did was remove the circulating bilirubin, not that already fixed to her tissues. So we've got to expect the level to rise a gram or two in the next twenty-four hours. But the phototherapy should take care of that."

Swerdloff looked at the overhead clock and yawned. "You guys realize it's three in the morning? What I could use right now is a good, stiff drink. Anybody care to join me? Oh, not you, Henry. I know you're a teetotaler, with the emphasis on tea! But how about it, Dan? I've got a bottle of Jack Daniels in my office."

"Thanks, no," said Dan. "God knows I could use it, but I'd better go tell Kris." He turned to Henry. "You don't expect any more trouble tonight, do you?"

Henry's mouth twisted as if he were about to wisecrack. Instead he replied, "No, not really. Not from Dana anyway. But I still have twenty other babies in the unit to worry about, so I'll be around."

Dan nodded gratefully. He had never felt such total dependency on a fellow doctor before, not even when Kris had nearly hemorrhaged to death with her last pregnancy. At least he knew most of the right therapeutic measures to take in that type of emergency and could watch over her care like a mother hen. But he was almost totally ignorant when it came to treating the neonates inhabiting Henry's Lilliputian world. "Listen, I can't even begin to tell you fellows how much—" He paused, seeing the faint flush of embarrassment on their faces. "Well, what I mean to say is, thanks. Just thanks. From Kris too."

"Think nothing of it, Doctor," Henry replied. "Glad you finally caught our act. It's what you pay us for."

Kris's eyes were red-rimmed and puffy when he entered her room. "You knew?" he asked, surprised and chagrined.

"Of course, I knew!" she said crossly. "I phoned the neonatal unit around two hours ago to find out how

Dana was doing and the nurse told me. I could barely restrain myself from leaping out of bed and rushing down there. How is she?"

"Fine." Dan smiled. "Just fine."

"Oh, sure! God, what a rotten liar you are! Look at you, so dead on your feet I'm surprised you managed to stagger down here without collapsing. And you expect me to buy that?"

"She's okay. I swear, she is. Henry did an incredible job. Just incredible! It was a professional pleasure to watch him."

"I believe you," she said impatiently. "Now sit down. Or better yet, lie here beside me and tell me about it."

"I'll lie down. Gladly!" Dan said. "As for telling you . . . Well, you know 'Murphy's law,' don't you?"

"You mean the one that says: 'If anything can go wrong, it will'?"

He nodded vigorously. "That's the one! Well, it ended up okay, but until then it followed Murphy's law all the way." In clinical terms, Dan described the two moderately severe and one near-fatal complication their daughter had survived, but nothing at all about his personal reactions to them. With his mind still in turmoil from the harsh self-truths he'd faced, from at last coming to terms with himself, his life, and what he valued most in it, words failed him. He could not even begin to tell her about that now, or possibly ever. It was something he would simply live by.

When he had finished, Kris did not reply with words but with tender hugs and kisses. "Oh, darling," she whispered, "the absolute hell you must've suffered! Thank God it's over. The worst is over, isn't it?"

Dan nodded. "Henry's pretty sure nothing more'll happen tonight."

"Oh, I'm glad. So glad. About that and everything."

"Me, too," said Dan, and heard the hoarseness in his voice as he prayed Henry would be right.

But no sooner had he offered up such a prayer when the strident ring of the telephone threatened to make a mockery of it. He knew nobody would casually call either of them this late at night, so who could it be? What possible calamity could it portend? Had something gone wrong with Dana: something that Henry, brilliant but fallible human being that he was, had failed to foresee?

Kris seized the phone, listened a moment, and passed the receiver to him. Gripping it tightly, Dan heard the hospital operator tell him he had an emergency call from a Mr. Alphonso Beal and instructed her to put it through.

"Doc! Dr. Lassiter!" Al shouted. "Listen, man, you got to get here quick. It's Lem. He's dying, looks like. Havin' one convulsion after another and gushing blood from his nose and mouth. Oh, Lord Almighty, Doc, it's awful! You got to come. Right now!"

"Now calm down, Al. Calm down!" Dan urged. "Talk so I can understand. Where are you?"

"Dorchester. A motel called the Colonial. Right on the main drag."

"The Colonial," Dan repeated. "Okay, slowly now, tell me all you can about Lem's condition. Slowly!"

"Ain't no time for that, man!" Al cried. "I tol' you he's dyin'! Brattle's here, but Lem won't let him near. Keeps yellin' Brattle poisoned him or somethin'! Jesus, we can't hardly hold Lem down, he's convulsin' so! And bleedin'! Look, Doc, I can't talk no more. You just gotta get here. Lem keeps callin' for you by name, so you gotta come, hear? He's a goner if you don't do somethin' quick!"

"Okay, I'll be right there. With an ambulance," Dan said and hung up.

"It's Lem," he explained to Kris while hurriedly slipping into his shoes. "He's in status epilepticus."

"My God!" she gasped. "From what? Any ideas?"

He shook his head at her and dialed the hospital operator back. "Call the ER," he ordered. "Tell them to have one of the cardiac-care ambulances waiting for me. I'll be right down." Hanging up he turned back to Kris. "Hypertensive encephalopathy, most likely. At least I hope so, bad as it is. Look, I've got to go. See you later."

"Dan, be careful!" she shouted after him. "You could be in danger!"

Her warning surprised and baffled him as he fit his key into the lock that summoned the emergency elevator. And then he wasn't baffled at all. He already knew Lem was ill, so he couldn't believe Beal was trying to trick or bait a trap for him. But if any of Lem's enemies were lying there in wait, they might mark him for prey too.

To safeguard himself against that possibility, Dan used the two-way radio in the ambulance to request a police escort.

Chapter Twenty-Four

The police patrol car intercepted the ambulance Dan was riding as it came off the Interstate to swing north on Bluehill Avenue. With both sirens blaring out of synch, the caterwaul cleared a wide swath through traffic up the center of the street and sent early-morning stragglers scurrying for shelter.

The two vehicles traveled most of the length of the avenue until its storefronts thinned out and the gateway of Franklin Park loomed ahead. Just below and to the left stood the Colonial Motel: a pair of three-story white wood and brick structures with columned entrances linked by a bar and restaurant whose neon-garish trim clashed with the Early American decor. A vine-overgrown fence and wooden archway separated the motel grounds from the street. The ambulance jounced along a potholed driveway and pulled up in front of the reception office. Dan instructed the two paramedics to wait for him in the vehicle and the police officers to look around the premises while he went inside. Then grabbing the oversized medical bag from its rack in the rear of the ambulance, he jumped out.

Hearing someone call his name, Dan looked up to see Al Beal leaning out the window of a corner room on the second floor. "Up here, Doc!" he yelled. "Room 220. Come alone."

The motel room Al led him into was a shambles: chairs and lamps tipped over, drinking glasses and water pitchers smashed, a mix of blood and booze and vomitus staining the bed linen and beige rug. Lem lay motionless on one twin bed, his breathing sterterous, a thin trickle of blood running down the side of his mouth, his tan slacks soaked in the crotch from loss of bladder control. A tall black man with a gun in a shoulder holster sat on one side of him and an attractive middle-aged woman on the other. Both stared grimly at Dan before shifting aside to give him access to Lem. As he reached in the medical bag for a stethoscope, Dan was startled to see a slim, light-skinned black man stretched out on the floor between the bed and the wall. His eyes were glazed, the side of his jaw freshly bruised, and blood crusted his nostrils. "Who the hell is that?" he asked Al.

"David Brattle. Lem slugged him pretty hard a while back. He's still out cold."

Dan nodded; he could tend to Brattle later. He pried open Lem's lids to observe his pupils, took his pulse, tested his limbs for paralysis, and then said, "Before I go any further, suppose somebody fills me in on what's happened?"

"Okay," Al said. "The story is this. We flew in around noon. Lem hadn't been feelin' too hot the last couple of days—even got airsick on the plane—but insisted on comin' anyway. With all's been going on in Washington lately, he felt he had to talk to you. Anyhow, around an hour ago, after complainin' about his head hurtin' all day, he suddenly grabbed hold of it and cried it was splittin'. So Brattle gave him some kind of pain shot. A couple of minutes later, Lem's hand, then arm, then whole left side started shakin' and his eyes rolled around in his head. Brattle rushed over to him, saw he was convulsin', and was about to go for his bag when Lem reached up with his right hand and caught him by the throat. He looked at him meaner than I ever saw Lem look at anybody before and snarled, 'You Judas! You poisoned me!' And when Brattle didn't say nothin', didn't even shake his head, he gave him a helluva backhand. Knocked him clear across the bed and against the wall. He's been out ever since."

"And then?" Dan asked.

"Then Lem really convulsed. Bit his tongue, wet his pants, the works! Took me and Andy all we could do just to hold him down."

"How long did it last?"

"Seemed like forever!" Al groaned. "But five, six minutes would be my guess. He's had three or four shorter ones since then. I took a look in his mouth and his tongue ain't bit too bad."

"Was he conscious between attacks?"

"Just the first time. That's when he said again Brattle done poisoned him and to call you. Not to let nobody treat him but you."

"Anything more you can tell me?"

"Nothin' much. 'Cept I know he's been to see some specialist in Martinique about a kidney ailment."

"What kind of kidney ailment?"

Al shrugged. "Somethin' rare, I heard him say. But that's all I know. Maybe Andy can tell you more. This here's Andy Sims, by the way . . . Andy, Doc Lassiter."

Recognizing the name, Dan studied the handsome young black's face as they shook hands. The look in Andy's eyes was the same he had seen in other proud, fearless killers with a cause: a grudging respect for the medical knowledge that ceded authority to him under such circumstances. "Well—" Dan prompted, "you know the name of Lem's kidney condition?"

Andy looked uncertain. "I heard him mention it once. Amy-something. Amy-lord? That sound right?"

Amyloid, thought Dan, making the connection between it and Lem's chronically inflamed hip at once. Amyloidosis was a rare, poorly understood disease of the body's connective tissue in which a proteinlike material infiltrated and destroyed various vital organs progressively and relentlessly. If that's what Lem had, he was probably doomed.

Seeing the somber look on Dan's face, Andy asked, "What kind of condition is that, and how bad?"

"Later," Dan said. "Right now I want to finish my examination." Removing the blood pressure cuff from the bag, he wrapped it around Lem's upper arm, fit his stethoscope to his ears, and took a reading. The dial on the attached gauge went up to 300 millimeters of mercury and Lem's systolic blood pressure nearly topped it. The more important diastolic pressure, that point where the transmitted sound of Lem's pulse faded out, was also dangerously elevated.

"How high is it?" asked Al.

Dan grimaced. "I get 290 over 180, which is high enough to burst a blood vessel in his brain, if it hasn't already. I'll have to give him something to lower it right away."

"Do what you got to, Doc," Al said heavily.

Dan removed a vial-filled leather case from the bag and was relieved to find it contained an ampule of a powerful antihypertensive drug. He snapped off its narrow neck with his fingers, drew up its liquid contents in a syringe, and slowly injected it into Lem's arm vein. Then he told Al and Andy to undress Lem so he could examine him more completely.

As they complied, the tawny-skinned woman sidled over to him. "I'm Monique Bouchet, Dr. Lassiter," she said. "Lem's traveling secretary, among other things."

Impressed by both her composure and sleek attractiveness, Dan wondered what the "other things" might include, suspecting that Monique was of far more value to Lem than a secretary or even a bedmate. "Nice to meet you," he replied, and was about to extend his hand when Al said, "Ready, Doc."

Holding the handle of an ophthalmoscope with one hand and Lem's right eyelid open with the other, Dan advanced the head of the instrument until it was almost touching his eyeball before peering through its tiny aperture into the interior of the eye—the one place in the human body where its smaller blood vessels can be viewed directly. What Dan saw alarmed him further. Instead of the normally round, flat optic nerve disc in the center of a network of nutrient arterioles fanning out from it like spokes of a wheel, Lem's disc was swollen and misshapen and the surrounding retina splotched with flame-shaped hemorrhages—indicating that his high blood pressure had entered the "malignant" phase where its body-damaging effects were severe and extensive.

The rest of what Dan's examination disclosed was

equally discouraging. As he listened to Lem's heart he could hear a scratchy sound, like cellophane crinkled between the fingers, coincident with each beat. The medical term for the distinctive noise was a "friction rub," and though its potential causes were numerous, in Lem's case it most likely represented advanced kidney failure.

Suddenly he stirred as Dan pressed the flat of his hand into his abdomen to feel for his liver. Opening his eyes, Lem focused them with difficulty on Dan and tried to speak through his swollen tongue. "Hey, Doc," he finally managed to utter, "where's it at?"

"It's at the hospital—where I'm taking you," Dan said. "Any objections?"

Lem looked up and around at Al and Andy. Slowly he raised his hand, pointed a finger at Dan, and mumbled thickly, "T—Trust!"

The two men nodded. Lem's meaning was clear.

After giving Lem a second injection to prevent further convulsions enroute to the hospital, Dan sent Andy to tell the ambulance crew to bring up a stretcher and portable oxygen. Then he fixed Al Beal with a penetrating stare. "Level with me. Is Lem in any danger from outside?"

"Not for now, I'd say. Not with that cop car you brought along. But we ain't goin' to leave him alone for a second at the hospital. You gotta arrange that, Doc."

Dan nodded and at last turned to Brattle, unconscious on the floor. His cursory exam assured Dan the man was not seriously injured and roused him to the point where he could mumble a few answers to where he hurt. Dan did not press him further. "Pack some ice cubes in a pillowcase that he can hold against his jaw to cut down the swelling," he told Al, "and then bring him along. There are a lot of questions I want to ask Dr. David Brattle."

For the second time that week Dan rode the jump seat in the rear of a siren-wailing ambulance to Commonwealth General. Lem was taken directly to the intensive care unit and placed in a monitor bed. Though his blood pressure had dropped to 260 over 140, he was no longer responsive, not even to such painful stimuli as pinching his Achilles tendon or thumb pressure against the bony ridge over his eye, making Dan fearful that he might have suffered a cerebral bleed in the interim. Sanbar and Robinson had joined him at Lem's bedside by then and he ordered them to perform a lumbar puncture.

To Dan's intense relief the fluid spurting out the nub of the eight-inch needle inserted into Lem's spinal canal was clear and colorless, making the possibility of a cerebral hemorrhage unlikely.

It turned out to be the only encouraging piece of information that Dan got on Lem all night. He was anemic, severely acidotic, and in heart failure. The catheterized urine specimen they drew from his bladder was loaded with albumin and pus cells, and both his serum creatinine and urea nitrogen levels, the two standard blood measurements of kidney function, were markedly elevated—establishing that he had advanced and probably irreparable kidney disease. Clearly Lem was close to death, and though they could probably forestall it there seemed little hope he would ever leave the hospital alive.

Dan was still staring glumly at the lab slips pasted on Lem's chart when the nurse called him to the telephone.

It was Kris. "Dana's fine. I just checked. How's Lem?"

He told her.

"I'm coming up."

"What for?" Dan asked without thinking.

"What for!" she exclaimed in mock indignation. "I'm a doctor too, remember? Maybe I can help."

"Maybe you can at that," he cheerfully conceded and hung up the phone. He was still smiling when the nurse returned to tell him that a black gentleman wanted to talk to him in the visitors' lounge. Al, thought Dan, and went to him. "Where's Brattle?" he asked.

"Monique and Andy got him in the cafeteria. Either the man's innocent or a damned good actor 'cause he's really shook up by what Lem accused him of. Just keeps ramblin' on and on 'bout it. But I brought what you told me." Al reached down and handed him Brattle's doctor satchel and a paper sack full of pill bottles. Dan quickly sorted through them. Two of the bottles lacked labels, but the rest were commonly prescribed painkillers and antihypertensives. Just on the off-chance any were mislabeled, though, Dan sent the entire batch to the toxicology lab for analysis.

Finally Al summoned up the courage to ask how Lem was.

"Bad," Dan replied and explained why.

"That kidney condition of his," Al said somberly. "Ain't nothin' can be done for it?"

"Oh, sure. Quite a bit. We can get his blood pressure down and clean the waste products from his system by dialysis. Putting him on an artificial kidney machine."

"Oh, yeah," said Al. "Andy told me all about those. A guy he used to work for was on one at home. How long would Lem have to stay on it?"

"Hard to say. Maybe forever."

"Forever! Oh, Lord!" Al moaned. "He ain't gonna, you know. He as much as told me so. He once spent eighteen months in a hospital and he ain't ever goin' to stay long in one again."

Dan gestured futilely. "Unless we can come up with something treatable on him, or maybe a transplant, he won't have any choice."

"He still got one," Al reminded him. "To die. I know it's what a lot of others would wish for him; even make happen, if they could."

"Explain that," Dan snapped. "You'd better, if you want my cooperation in his security arrangements. And after you get through with that, there's another matter I want cleared up."

"Well," Al began, "I don't know how much Lem told you about his African activities, but there's damned little goin' on behind closed doors over there he hasn't got a line on. So he got a lot of schemin' generals and bribe-takers plenty worried 'bout what he knows. There's also that bunch of dope peddlers he disenfranchised in Detroit gunnin' for him. And if none of them get him, there's always the chance some 'dirty trick' specialist in our own government will."

"That's the other thing I want cleared up. According to what I heard a few nights ago, a man named Corcoran, one of the chief suspects in the health fund swindle, drove to his death off a bridge recently. And the person who told me that didn't think it was any accident either. It's his hunch you people killed, or should I say executed, him. What about that?"

Al scowled. "Man, you askin' me if we hit Corcoran is really puttin' me on the spot."

"So you're on the spot. Talk!"

"Tell you one thing," Al said, thrusting out his jaw. "Bet you whoever the government guy was told you that didn't tell you a whole lot else. Like, how we know for sure Corcoran ordered Artemus Hill's death, and so does the Attorney General. He and three of his top assistants spent most of a day grillin' Corcoran about it last week. They couldn't pin Hill's murder on him, a'course, since hired killers did that, but they sure nailed him on the health fraud. So what you think they done—lock him up? Hell, no! After all, he wasn't no nigger con man, just one of their own kind who'd gone wrong. So they let him cop a plea; told him they'd consider naming him a coconspirator, instead of a codefendant, providin' he came up with enough evidence to indict the rest of his gang. They gave him one week to get it together."

"You know all that for a fact?"

" 'Course, we do! We got witnesses seen him go into the AG's office at one o'clock and come out at six. They had the same goods on him we did, so how come they sent him home, not to jail? Did we kill a creep named Corcoran? Damned right we did! His life wasn't worth shit compared to a genius like Hill's, and we avenge our own."

"How many more do you plan to kill?"

"Depends on how many more they kill of us." Al shrugged. "Like it or not, that's good, Old Testament justice, Doc. Who knows how many sick black people they already killed? By faked tests, by unnecessary surgery, by God knows what?"

Bleakly Dan nodded. "Well, thanks for leveling with me. We'll talk more about it later. Right now the life that concerns me most is Lem's."

The next moment Kris stepped out of the elevator opposite them wearing a blue blouse and skirt under her long white coat. Seeing her dressed that way once again stirred deep emotion in Dan. Calling her over, he introduced her to Al Beal.

Al's face suddenly fell as they shook hands. "Oh, Lord!" he groaned. "Here I been fillin' your husband's ear with all our problems and never once thought to ask how that little baby of yours is doin'."

"Just fine," Kris said. "But I wouldn't talk much more about her, Al, or this big, tough doctor here is liable to go all teary-eyed again. Right, dear?" She smiled fondly at Dan.

"Come on, Doctor," he said brusquely, taking Kris's arm. "Let's see if you still remember which side of the bed you stand on to examine a patient."

Dan escorted his wife into the ICU where he introduced her to Sanbar and Robinson. Sanbar pleased him mightily by saying how much he had learned from some of the articles Kris had published on pituitary disease, and Robinson appeared dazzled by her poise and beauty.

Dan left Kris at Lem's bedside and went back out to see Al Beal. "Bring Brattle to my office on the twentieth floor, will you? There are a few questions I need to ask him."

"Right," said Al and headed for the elevators.

"Allow me to apologize for my unsightly appearance," Brattle said once he was alone with Dan in his office and sipping the coffee served him. "I really don't know what got into Lem."

"He seems of the opinion you poisoned him," Dan

reminded the slim, stiffly posed doctor with the bruised jaw and placid, almost detached, look in his eyes.

"So I understand," Brattle said and emitted a high-pitched giggling laugh. "It's ridiculous, of course. I've been Lem's personal physician for almost four years now and my competence, not to mention my deep devotion, has never been questioned before."

"What exactly's been wrong with Lem?"

"Oh, my goodness!" Brattle exclaimed, throwing up his arms. "So many things I hardly know where to begin."

"Suppose you start from the time you first became his personal physician. That seems as good a place as any."

Brattle touched his swollen jaw gingerly and complied, but little of what he said surprised Dan. He already knew about Lem's bad hip, his hypertension, his kidney condition. He had also heard of the new Russian anticancer agent that showed promise in the treatment of amyloidosis.

"I agree, of course," Brattle replied after Dan had challenged his proposed use of the drug, "that ideally the diagnosis should be firmly established in any patient before trying an experimental form of therapy on him. But in Lem's case that wasn't possible."

"Why not? Most places are still doing kidney biopsies, aren't they?"

Brattle gave him an indulgent smile. "Of course they are—when the patient consents to it. Lem wouldn't."

"Why wouldn't he?"

"I really don't know. Perhaps it would be best if you asked Lem that."

"All right, I will," Dan said. "Now what'say you give me a quick rundown on all the drugs you've been prescribing for him."

"To see if there are any potential kidney poisons among them?" Brattle said with an edge to his voice. "I can assure you there are not. But if you insist . . ."

Later Dan repeated the same list to Kris as she sat in his office. She was also interested to hear of Lem's wartime leg wounds and the subsequent osteomyelitis he developed that took eighteen months of intensive therapy at Fitzsimmons Army Hospital to cure.

"Well, that along with TB and inflammatory bowel disease are certainly the leading causes of secondary amyloidosis," she said. "But that's not what I think he's got."

Dan's eyebrows lifted. "Oh, really? Why not?"

"Because he has nothing else to go along with it. No enlarged liver, spleen, tongue—"

"An enlarged tongue occurs almost exclusively with the primary, not the secondary, form," Dan corrected.

"Don't nitpick, dear. I still don't think it's amyloidosis."

"Then what *do* you think it is?"

"I don't know—yet. I'd settle for a working diagnosis of malignant hypertension and attribute his kidney failure to that if it weren't for the heavy amounts of albumin and pus casts in his urine. I still think a nephrotoxin of some sort is possible, don't you?"

Dan shrugged. "I personally went through all the meds he had on him and, unless Brattle managed to slip a little mercury or bismuth into one of them, didn't see any."

"But those are just the medicines he's carrying. Who knows what he might be taking back home?"

"Hmmm," Dan said, conceding the point and acting on it. He phoned the ICU and told the ward clerk to look for a Mr. Al Beal in the lounge and send him up to his office.

Al appeared within a few minutes. "Listen," Dan told him, "we've an important question to ask you. There were four different types of pills in that sack you brought me. Are they all, or does Lem take more back in Martinique?"

"Does he! He got drawers and drawers of them. I never saw so many pill bottles in my life—most with French labels."

"Al, it's important as hell that we get hold of all those pills as soon as possible so we can analyze them. How fast can you get them here?"

"Real quick. Tomorrow afternoon at the latest. I can send the jet we came in for them."

"Good," said Dan. "Do that."

"Sure, Doc. Sure! Only thing is," he said hesitantly, "okay if Monique goes 'stead of me? I don't want to leave Lem now, for reasons we already discussed."

"I understand," said Dan, avoiding Kris's inquisitive stare. "Just make sure she brings everything."

"Don't worry, she will. I'll send her after them right now."

"Well—" Dan said to Kris after Al had left. "Any more bright ideas?"

"One. Getting some sleep. And since that couch of yours won't hold both of us, I'm going back to my room."

"Directly?"

She smiled. "You know damned well not directly."

"Good. I'll go see her with you."

Chapter Twenty-Five

At 8:00 A.M. Dan was giving Matt Kinsella a final check before discharging him from the hospital when Nan Forrester reached him by telephone. "Exactly *who* is this Lem Harper you've dumped in my lap?" she demanded. "And don't you dare tell me he's a hypertensive in uremia. I already know that! What I want to know is why I've gotten two calls this morning, one from the FBI and one from a guy who says he's head of the local Drug Enforcement Agency, wondering when they can question him. So suppose you tell me just who and *what* he is!"

"I will, Nan," Dan said, constrained by Kinsella's presence. "I'll be up in a few minutes and tell you all I know. What are your plans for him?"

"Need you ask? I've already transferred him to the dialysis unit—without consulting you, I might add. And after talking to Kris I agree with her, he doesn't have amyloidosis."

"What does he have then?"

She sighed. "I don't know. That's why I intend to dialyze him today and biopsy his kidney tomorrow. But I doubt he'll turn out to have anything as exotic as amyloidosis—even if he is a friend of yours."

"Okay. Tell me where you'll be ten minutes from now and I'll join you."

"In the renal unit. Putting a shunt in his arm. That's a pretty small operating room they got there, though, and I'm a pretty big girl. What do you suggest I do with those two hulking bodyguards of his?"

Dan laughed. "Talk nice to them, Nan. Real nice. One packs a thirty-eight and the other an old-fashioned straight razor."

"Oh, great!" she groaned in disgust. "Next you'll be

telling me that they believe in the Code of Hammurabi."

"Not so far as I know. But maybe you'd better ask them. I'd hate to see you lose any of your vital parts."

"So would I! Getting sued for malpractice is one thing, but that's going too far! Look, finish up whatever you're doing and get down here quick as you can, huh?"

"Will do," Dan said and hung up.

"Well—you satisfied?" asked Kinsella, dressed in street clothes and impatient to leave.

Dan nodded. "And grateful. Where're you headed from here?"

"My sister's place on the Cape to catch a little sun for a week before going back to Springfield and settling my affairs there. I was due to retire in November, but I'm sure I can get them to push it up a few months."

"And then?"

Kinsella shrugged. "Maybe do a little consulting work for the American Hospital Association, or maybe just sit around listening to my arteries harden. Haven't really thought that far."

"How'd you like to work for me?"

Kinsella made a wry face. "I never much liked working with you, so what makes you think I'd like working *for* you any better? Especially in a madhouse like Washington, if that's where you're heading?"

"Probably—if I get confirmed. I could sure use you to keep me honest."

"Oh, you're honest enough. Which is more than I can say for the gang you're getting in with. Yeah, maybe you do need a wiser head than yours."

"Could be, Matt," Dan said, humoring him. "So think it over and let me know what you decide in a week or so."

"Yeah, I'll do that." Squaring his shoulders Kinsella thrust out his hand. "Well, so long, Danny. I'm not much good at it, but I'll be praying for that little tike of yours."

Dan thanked him and watched him leave with a

mixture of relief and regret. Narrow-minded but never in doubt, the Matt Kinsellas of this world led uncomplicated, uncluttered, almost stripped-down versions of life. He might have envied Matt his insular existence had he not seemed so lonely.

Minutes later, as Dan was leaving his office, he saw Dr. David Brattle sitting in his reception room. "Good morning, Dr. Lassiter," he said, rising. "I hope I'm not inconveniencing you, but I came by to find out how our patient is doing."

Dan caught the slight emphasis on the "our" but resisted comment. Uncomfortable as Brattle made him, he felt obliged to treat the man fairly since neither the FBI's nor Lem's allegations against him had been proven. If only the look in his eyes matched his polite, diffident manner. "Not too well," Dan answered. "Because of his kidney failure, I asked Dr. Nan Forrester, an expert nephrologist, to consult on him and she had him transferred to our renal unit. In fact, I'm headed there now to fill her in on his history while she puts an A-V shunt in his arm. So if you'll excuse me . . ."

"I'd very much like to accompany you, if I may? It's been some time since I've been around a big hospital and I'm a little out of touch with the way they do things these days. So if you don't have any objection . . ."

"No," Dan said reluctantly. "Come along if you wish."

Through the small window in the operating room door they could see Lem's huge frame stretched out on the table, his left arm strapped to a sideboard and his feet overlapping its edge. Unmistakable to Dan, even in her surgical cap, mask, and gown, was the figure of Nan Forrester, sitting on a metal stool and probing the incision she had made in Lem's forearm with forceps and scalpel while Neil Robinson assisted her. Looking up from her dissection she saw Dan outside the door. "Well, just don't stand there!" she growled. "Put on a gown and c'mon in. I'm not doing so hot."

As Dan and Brattle approached the operating table, they could see that Nan had completed the venous side of the U-shaped shunt by inserting a soft plastic tube into Lem's forearm vein but not the arterial.

The two watched in silence as Robinson spread the brownish bellies of two muscles apart with a pair of right-angle retractors and Nan dissected deeper in search of the elusive artery. "That damned radial!" she swore. "Should be as big as a garden hose, but I've been at it for ten minutes now and still can't find it. Well, into the breach once more, as they say."

To Dan's surprise he heard Brattle say, "Mind if I give it a try, Dr. Forrester? I'm a board-certified surgeon and took part of my training in vascular. I can't promise it, of course, but I usually have pretty good luck in catching that wiggling little devil."

She gave Dan a questioning glance and sighed. "Oh, why not? I've certainly had a fair crack at it. Let's see if you do any better."

Quickly but thoroughly, Brattle completed a surgical scrub, slipped on a pair of rubber gloves, and replaced Nan on the stool. Taking the pair of retractors from Robinson, he repositioned them wider and deeper and told the intern, "Like that, if you please." Then after spending a few moments probing the wound, he announced, "Yes, I see the difficulty. Due to the patient's muscular development, the artery's deeper than usual. No problem though," he said almost cockily.

With impressive dexterity Brattle had an inch-long segment of the radial artery isolated, trapped between two encircling ligatures, and ready to be incised in less than a minute. The remaining limb of the plastic shunt was anchored in place and the forearm incision sutured in another few minutes. "That ought to do it," Brattle said, rising from the stool and stripping off his gloves. "Thanks for letting me assist you, Dr. Forrester."

"Thank you!" Nan exclaimed. "You can see why I never considered a career in surgery."

"It's merely a manual skill," Brattle replied gently.

"Hardly compares to some of the brilliant contributions you've made to our understanding of surgical shock. I've read and benefitted by many of your papers, Dr. Forrester."

Nan couldn't help beaming. "Since most of the surgeons I know only read *The Wall Street Journal,* you can call me Nan, Dr. Brattle." Suddenly she turned to Robinson. "Well, what are you gawking at? It'll be a long time before you do anything to earn that privilege, so get back to work. In case you've forgotten, we still have to hitch the patient up to the dialysis machine."

At three that afternoon, after five hours of having his blood cleansed of toxic waste products by the washing-machine-sized artificial kidney, Lem was sufficiently alert and clear-headed to ask for Dan. Leaving Andy Sims behind, Al went to fetch Dan from his office.

"How's that tiny baby of yours doin'?" Lem asked him after Al and Andy had moved into the corridor to permit them to talk privately.

"Just fine," said Dan.

"And the wife?"

"Back to work. She examined you last night while you were still unconscious."

"Yeah? Sorry I missed that. I never been gone over by a lady doctor before." He paused for breath. "Okay, Doc, Al filled me in on what he told you about Corcoran. So you know about that. There are a few other things you ought to know along those lines, which I'll get to later. But I'll tell you now, no matter what else you might hear, you ain't goin' to catch me in no lie. I been truthful in everything I told you so far and I got no reason to change. But first I want you to level with me."

"About what?"

"About the kind of shape I'm in."

"Okay. But why the hell didn't you tell me about your kidney condition before?"

"I sure wanted to. Especially after I nearly fell out at your place. But I was afraid if I told you then you'd stick me in the hospital and I wasn't ready to go. Not till a few more important matters got taken care of."

"What's more important than your life?"

Lem laughed harshly. "You mean what little I got left? A lot of things. The upcoming election for one. Seeing sick black folk down South get proper care for another. I made me a choice how I wanted to live, and die, a long time ago. But unless you can make me feel a whole lot better than I been lately, I guess I'm about played out. Can you, Doc?"

"Maybe." Dan spoke hesitantly. "There's an outside chance. Depends on what's really wrong with you. I want you to sign a consent form so we can biopsy your kidney tomorrow. Find out exactly what's damaged them."

"You mean it ain't what Brattle's been tellin' me it was: this here Amy-loid? That he been handin' me a line all this time?"

"No, I don't. Amyloidosis is still a possibility. But before we go into that I want to know why you accused Brattle of poisoning you last night."

" 'Cause I started to shake all over after the shot he gave me and that's what I thought." He shrugged. "I must've been wrong, huh?"

"You were. The shot he gave you was a harmless painkiller. We had it analyzed. And you can thank Brattle for putting that shunt in your arm. The man's a talented surgeon."

"Yeah? Then I guess I was way out of line. But if I ain't got this amyloid, and I ain't been poisoned, what's wrong with me?"

"The main thing is kidney disease. We should know what kind tomorrow—if the process hasn't gone too far."

"What you mean by that?"

"Well, if all your biopsy shows is what's called an 'end-stage' kidney, the pathologist may not be able to tell what originally damaged them."

"Much chance of that?"

Dan frowned. "Afraid so. Your kidneys are pretty well shot."

"Then what?"

"Then we have to put you on chronic dialysis until we can find another kidney for you to use. A transplant."

Lem ended a brief silence with a shudder, a shake of his head. "No way, Doc. If you can find some way to cure what I got—fine. I'll stick around long enough for you to do that. But ain't no way you gonna get me to stay otherwise. I been crippled once before and it took misery like you'll never know before I overcame that. I got no intention of being another kind of cripple—which is what I'll be if I have to depend on doctors and hospitals the rest of my life. So you just go ahead and take that biopsy. Find out exactly what's ailin' me and if you can fix it. If you can't, say so and let me go. I already picked the place I want to die."

"That's brave talk, Lem. But do you mean it?"

"Damned right! I'm a proud nigger, beholden to no man—nobody except you, Doc, and only for a while. Swear you'll tell me the truth 'bout my condition and that's the last favor I'll ever ask you."

Dan nodded.

"Good! Ain't no white man I trust more'n you. And now we got that settled, you can go about your business. I'm kind of tired now, so let's put off that political stuff till later."

That evening, after visiting the neonatal unit together, Kris and Dan sat in his office discussing Lem. "Everything depends on that biopsy now," he said, still depressed over his talk with Lem.

"What about the toxicology report?" she asked.

"The pills he's been taking are just what they're supposed to be. No traces of heavy metals or other nephrotoxins in them. Monique's due back from Martinique anytime now, but I doubt what he's been taking there is much different. Lem was once a heroin addict, you know."

"No, I didn't," said Kris, surprised. "Tell me."

"Well, according to Andy Sims, it happened while he was hospitalized for pneumonia in North Korea. The doctors there had him believing the pain shots they were giving him for his hip were some kind of herbal extract. What they neglected to tell him was the basic herb was the poppy plant. Lem's been damned careful to make sure what's in the medicine he takes since then. Too bad, in a way. We might have cured him if he'd had toxic kidney disease. But I'm afraid there's little likelihood of that."

Surprisingly Kris said, "I'm not so sure."

"What do you mean?"

"I mean, you may be looking for the wrong thing. An acute nephrotoxin instead of a chronic one. You did say his hip has been hurting for years. And that he steers clear of anything potentially addicting. So . . ."

"Oh, Christ!" Dan groaned, pounding his forehead with the flat of his hand. "Analgesic abuse! It fits like a glove. Now why the hell didn't I think of that?"

Kris grinned. "Maybe because you're not always too bright. You certainly weren't where the baby and I were concerned."

"Okay, okay, don't rub it in. I always said you were my equal as an internist, didn't I?"

"You might've said it," Kris taunted. "But did you really mean it?"

Dan smiled weakly. "I do now—providing number one, your diagnosis is correct, and number two, you don't gloat too much over it."

"Well, as for the first, it figures, doesn't it? He must swallow dozens of pain pills each day. And even though they no longer put phenacetin in the over-the-counter painkillers in this country, they still do in most of Europe. Martinique too, I'd imagine."

"So would I! Let's get hold of Nan and discuss it with her," Dan said eagerly.

"All right, but not right now."

"Why not?"

"Because the last time I saw her she was having coffee in the cafeteria with Andy Sims. In case you hadn't noticed, he's a good-looking man who for some strange reason knows a great deal about kidney dialysis. And he's been fascinating Nan all day with stories of the Detroit DDD."

Al Beal was sitting at Lem's bedside, trying to read a newspaper but gradually being lulled to sleep by the trickling sounds of the kidney machine, when David Brattle entered the room.

"Hey, man!" Al greeted him heartily. "Hear you did a damned good job puttin' that plastic gismo in Lem's arm today."

Brattle smiled. "Where's Andy?"

"Havin' coffee with Dr. Forrester. Why? What's up?"

"I just left Dr. Lassiter. He's on his way to his office and wants you to meet him there."

"Yeah? What about?"

"He didn't say. But you go ahead and I'll stay with Lem until Andy gets back."

Al looked doubtful but acquiesced under Brattle's stare. "Okay. Be back soon as I can," he said and left.

Quietly Brattle moved to the head of Lem's bed to make sure he was still sleeping, then around to the opposite side where he gently lifted Lem's free arm and tightened a leather restraining strap around it, effectively immobilizing him.

The tug of the strap woke Lem and he blinked several times to bring the face above him into focus.

Solemnly Brattle said, "It's time, Lem. You always knew I'd be here when the time came, didn't you?"

When Lem's expression remained uncomprehending, Brattle gave him a mildly disapproving look. "You almost ruined it by what you accused me of the other night. But I knew you were just talking out of your head and didn't mean it. Still, you hurt me bad, and not just physically either. I served you well. For four years I took care of you, did your bidding, even blinded those sheriffs for you. And it hurt me that in your delirium you called for this Lassiter to doctor you, trusted him more than me. But it doesn't matter. It's worked out perfectly this way. How much better that you die now, a martyr to the cause, instead of just another victim of kidney disease. They'll blame Lassiter, of course. Once word gets out that he knew about the health scandal in advance, there'll be rumors your death was no accident; that he had you killed under orders from the government. I'll see to that, along with everything else. I won't fail you. You always knew I was your appointed angel of death, didn't you?"

Wide-eyed, his forehead cropped with sweat, Lem wet his lips and spread them in a sardonic smile. "Yes, David, I always knew that's who you were. I already told Lassiter I'd just as soon die now if I couldn't be cured. But why blame him? He's a good man, a friend—"

"A *white* friend! A devil," Brattle hissed. "Did you really think he'd sacrifice his chance to be top dog to serve our cause? Never! But the way I've got it planned he'll serve anyway. We shall all serve, but you most of all. Your death will be as glorious as your life." He reached for the limb of the plastic shunt in Lem's arm that connected to the larger, blood-filled tube flowing into the kidney machine and held it gently, almost lovingly, between his fingers. "All I have to do is disconnect this joint," he went on, "and you'll bleed to death in a few minutes. There'll be no alarm—I've already shut if off—no pain, nothing except a gradual dimming of vision, and then eternal peace. You'll see, Lem. You'll see."

"David, wait—"

"No! You've suffered enough. Do you think it was easy for me to see you so racked with pain all these years? Now you won't ever have to suffer again. You'll be glorified. Your legend will surpass your grandfather's. Black folk the world over, not just in Martinique, will sanctify the memory of 'Devil-A'. Trust me, Lem. I'm the instrument of your destiny. Oh, yes! Oh, yes!" he said in a sort of chant and began to pry the plastic conection apart with his fingernails.

"Wait—" Lem cried.

"No, time's short. If you want me to stay with you,

it'll have to be done now. You *do* want me to stay till the darkness sets in, don't you?"

"David, listen!" Lem rasped. "You're sick again. You need help. I'll take you back to Martinique with me, make sure you get it."

"Sick!" Brattle smiled cunningly. "Of course, I'm sick. I serve the Devil, don't I?"

Chapter Twenty-Six

"No," said Dan with a puzzled look. "I didn't send for you. Why would Brattle tell you that?"

Al Beal's fleshy face quivered with consternation. "Then we better get down there fast! No tellin' what that crazy bastard's got a mind to do."

"Let's go!" Leaping out of his chair, Dan ran for the staircase outside his office. It was twelve flights down to the renal unit and he prayed they could reach it in time.

But David Brattle had made certain there was little chance of that. Earlier he had taken the elevator to Dan's office, as Al Beal would, paused ten seconds outside the door, and then rushed down the stairs to the eighth floor. With the compulsive attention to detail that characterized most paranoiacs, he had timed it precisely. Nobody could possibly stop him if he acted now, he told himself. Now! But as he dug his thumbnail into the plastic joint to pry it loose, he saw Lem's eyes narrow and his head shake slowly. "Why you doin' that!" Brattle cried. "What you shakin' your head at me for?"

"It ain't meant for you, David," said Lem softly.

Suddenly Brattle shivered at the tickling touch of cold steel against his throat. "Easy now," Andy Sims warned as he pushed Brattle's jaw up and back with his forearm. "Just drop that tube and hang loose. Real loose. No sudden moves."

The next instant Dan burst breathlessly into the room. What he encountered made him blink and stop short. The three men before him seemed frozen in a tableau, like a posed shot for a crime magazine or movie ad. Horror-struck but fascinated too, he stood staring until Al Beal came puffing through the door to break the spell.

"What happened?" Al blurted.

"Nothin'," said Andy Sims, still holding the gleaming blade of his straight razor to Brattle's throat. "I got here just in time to stop it. Damned good thing you called me to come up, Al. Another minute or so and Lem would've bled all over the floor."

"You called him?" Dan asked.

"Yeah," said Al, smiling and shrugging. "My suspicious nature." He turned to Lem. "Now what we goin' to do with him?"

"Nothin' now," Lem replied. "Not till we get him out of here."

"Then what?"

Ignoring Brattle's suffused face and wild-eyed stare roaming the ceiling, Lem said laconically, "After that I'm open to suggestion."

"I say waste him," Andy snarled. "After what he just done, be my pleasure."

"And you, Al? That your feelin' too?"

Al shrugged. "I don't reckon we got any choice."

"Now wait a second!" cried Dan. "This is a hospital, not a back alley, goddamn it! You can't waste people here. Besides, the man's obviously insane. He belongs in a psychiatric ward."

Lem nodded. "You're right, Doc. He does belong in one. And I swear to you it's where we'll put him, only not here."

"Where then?"

"Back in Martinique. You probably won't go for that, and I can't explain, but we got to handle it that way."

Dan was about to argue, insist that Brattle needed immediate care, when Lem's reasoning suddenly became clear to him. If Brattle was to live, Lem could not possibly permit any U.S. law officers to question him about his past activities. "Okay," Dan finally said. "When does he leave?"

"Tonight. On the same plane that's bringing Monique back. Hate to ask you to do it, Doc, but mind givin' him a shot to knock him out?"

"I *do* mind. But I suppose he'd prefer it to Al's gun butt against his head."

Dan found Kris and Nan Forrester waiting outside the room.

"Is Lem all right?" asked Kris anxiously.

He nodded. "But don't go in. Either of you. Brattle went berserk and they're restraining him. I'll explain later. Listen, Nan, do you think you can do that biopsy tonight? I want to get this whole goddamn business wrapped up before I end up on the psycho ward myself."

"I suppose so," said Nan, "if you can get Fred Hale to come in and read it."

"Thanks. I'll get Fred. Go ahead and set it up."

Andy Sims did not take his razor from Brattle's throat until he went limp from the powerful tranquilizer Dan injected into his jugular vein. As instructed, an orderly had deposited a wheeled stretcher outside the door, and Dan used it to transport Brattle to a side entrance where a hearse summoned by Al Beal from a black funeral home was waiting to take him to the airport. Although the ornate black vehicle added yet another macabre touch to the evening, Dan was greatly relieved to see it drive away with its troublesome rear passenger.

"What now, Doc?" asked Al as he stood beside Dan in the muggy night air.

"You must've heard of Willie Sutton, haven't you?"

"Heard of him! I damned near collared him once after a bank heist he pulled in Philly. Would've too, if I'd been smart enough to look closer at the Salvation Army Band playin' across the street. How does Willie figure in this?"

"There's a medical principle we call 'Sutton's law.' Remember the time some bush-league reporter asked why he only robbed banks and he said: ' 'Cause that's where they keep the money'? Well, the same kind of logic applies to medicine too. Instead of screwing around trying to diagnose Lem's kidney condition with more blood tests, we're going directly to what offers the biggest payoff: a biopsy. That ought to tell us what's really wrong, and whether anything can be done about it."

"Any hope of that?"

"Yeah, matter of fact there is. Thanks to a brilliant diagnosis my wife made, we might just find something treatable. Bring Monique to my office as soon as she gets back. I'll meet you there shortly."

After Brattle was spirited out of the room Kris and Nan Forrester detached Lem from the dialysis machine and had him transferred to the "special procedures" section of the X-ray department. Following a brief search, Dan joined them and a staff radiologist named Shah there. Lem lay prone on its metal table, his bare back glistening from the thin coat of mineral oil spread on it to provide a tight seal for the ultrasonic probe Shah would use to delineate the size and location of his kidneys for the biopsy.

Dan watched Shah sweep the probe over every inch of Lem's lower back until both his kidneys were so clearly depicted on the computerized television screen that their distance from certain bony landmarks could be measured. At a nod from Shah, Nan Forrester stepped forward to paint Lem's flanks with strong disinfectant, drape all but an inch-square area above each kidney with sterile towels, and freeze the underlying tissues with a local anesthetic. With a bayonet scalpel, she made a deep stab wound through the skin, gristly-tough fascia, and most of the muscle over his left kidney. She sounded the depth of the wound with a thin metal probe to make certain that less than an inch of subcutaneous fat and muscle lay between it and the capsule of the kidney, and then plunged a biopsy needle with a special cutting edge through the slit up to its hilt.

"Looks like kidney, all right," Nan said with satisfaction after washing the threadlike core of tissue from the lumen of the needle into a specimen jar with a syringeful of saline. She ordered Lem returned promptly to his room where his blood pressure and pulse could be taken every five minutes to guard against the danger of internal hemorrhage, and then, hand-carried the biopsy specimen to Fred Hale in the laboratory.

"Lucked out again, huh, Nan?" remarked Hale, a lank, long-faced, jovial man who had once wanted to be a small-town GP before being forced into the more lucrative field of pathology by his strict Catholic upbringing, an equally devout and prolific wife, and ten children.

"Sure did, Fred," said Nan dryly. "Sorry to drag you out of bed and so forth, but there is a population explosion, you know."

It took Hale less than half an hour to freeze the biopsy specimen in liquid freon, slice it into sections less than six thousandths of a millimeter thick with a microtome, mount and stain the shavings on glass slides, and peer at them under a microscope. Nan, Kris, and Dan crowded around, anxiously awaiting his verdict.

"Well," Hale announced after painstaking study of four of the six slides he had prepared, "the tubules, what's left of them, are atrophic and dilated, and there's a hell of a lot of interstitial fibrosis with round-cell infiltration . . ."

"In other words, chronic interstitial nephritis," Nan said.

"I knew all that pathologist talk wouldn't fool you, Nan. That's what it looks like to me, all right."

"No amyloid?" asked Dan.

"None that stains with crystal violet or thioflavin-t. I can't be absolutely certain until I do fluorescent studies on a paraffin block, but there's no hint of it in anything I've seen so far."

"So 'analgesic abuse' is a good bet, huh?" ventured Kris.

"Well, as you know," Hale hedged, "there are over a dozen different causes of chronic interstitial nephritis. But if you've got a good history to go along with it, I'd have to agree that's the most likely."

Conclusive proof of it was provided by Monique and the large suitcase-full of proprietary medicines she brought back from Lem's home in Martinique. Dan read some of the labels aloud: Acamol, Aparacet, Atasol, APAP—different brand names for virtually identical concoctions of aspirin, phenacetin, and caffeine.

"Well, that clinches the diagnosis, I guess," said Dan with a wan smile.

"What diagnosis?" asked Al Beal.

Dan turned to Kris. "Explain it to them, will you please? I want to go tell Lem."

"All right," she agreed, "but after that we go home —our home. These late hours are really getting to me."

"I didn't know Jim Neubeck discharged you."

"He hasn't—yet. But he will as soon as I get him on the phone. He'd better, or else I'll discharge myself. Any objections?"

"None," Dan said hastily. "None at all."

"Good. Make it fast then."

Dan did, explaining to Lem as best he could how the massive amounts of painkillers he had ingested over the years had damaged his kidneys, but holding out the hope that after a few weeks or months of dialysis they would heal sufficiently for him to come off the machine.

"Sounds great, Doc," Lem said. "But if I can't take no more of them pills, what do I do for pain?"

"There isn't going to be any more pain. Tomorrow I'm going to have Jake Harris, our chief of orthopedics, see you, and soon as you're in good enough shape schedule you for a total hip replacement—an operation you should've had years ago."

"Well, ain't that somethin'!" Lem marveled. "And here I thought I was a goner for sure. I would've been too if Andy Sims hadn't stopped Brattle." He paused reflectively. "I guess this just about evens us up. How you handle that Senate hearing now is strictly up to you."

"That's comforting to know!" Dan snapped. "But exactly how does that even us up? For what?"

Lem smiled sardonically. "For more'n you realize. For tippin' you to that health fund swindle so you'd know what you were lettin' yourself in for if you took that cabinet job. By being ready to step in and save your life, if needs be."

"My life!" Dan looked incredulous. "When the hell was that ever in danger?"

"Since our meeting last week when I handed over that suitcase-full of documents. What makes you think the men who murdered Artemus Hill wouldn't do the same to you?"

"What makes you think they would?"

"Corcoran. My people had a little talk with him before seeing if his car could float on water, and he talked plenty. Though the Feds had enough on Corcoran to lock him up for life, they had little or nothing on those in cahoots with him. Not the ringleaders anyway. And they needed time to either cover their tracks or skip the country—time they would've gotten from the President's slow way of investigatin' them, but not from you. So you were a big threat to them, Doc. Y'ask me, what mainly made them shy away from orderin' a hit on you was that little girl of yours."

"Dana?"

"Yeah, Dana. Wouldn't surprise me none if she saved your life."

Dan gaped at Lem dumbfounded; then struck by the seeming absurdity of his statement almost laughed out loud. "You've got to be kidding!"

"Well, I ain't," Lem maintained. "I nearly sent Al Beal up to keep watch over you. He was all set to leave when news of your daughter's birth reached us. Don't you see, that made you practically untouchable. They didn't dare knock off the daddy of such a famous little kid."

"I'll be damned!" Dan muttered. "I swear, if I were hearing this from anybody but you—" He shook his head exasperatedly. "Hell, even if it is you, I still can't believe it."

Lem shrugged. "Believe what you want. What makes it any harder to swallow than some of the things you saw tonight: Brattle tryin' to make me a martyr; Andy Sims nearly slittin' his throat? Or do you think us uncivilized black folk do that sort of thing to each other all the time?"

"Uh uh," warned Dan. "Don't try to bait me with that stuff. I'm not in the mood. Just stick to the facts."

"Like the two-billion-dollar health rip-off? You know that's a fact. Well, let me tell you another fact. The President's finally ready to move on it. I don't know how you did it, but you forced his hand. Got him to put together a special task force of people from HEW, Justice, and the GAO to crack down on those crooks. Trouble is, people are still goin' to wonder how come the President let the swindle get so big or go on so long. After all, it was his political appointees who were supposed to be lookin' after things, and a theft that size just don't happen overnight. Takes a lot of embezzlers a lot of nights doctoring up the books. So it's bound to cost him votes. Just like the piddlin' grafters in Truman's administration cost him control of Congress, and Watergate got so bad a lot of Republicans didn't even try to run for reelection . . ."

"So?" Dan prompted.

"So, it's my hunch that instead of makin' a big splash with the story, he's goin' to leak it to the press a little at a time. Keep them from findin' out how big the swindle really is till after the elections. That is, if you let him."

"And if I do?"

"I already told you we're even. What you do from now on is between you and your conscience. You ain't goin' to feel no pressure from my end. Truth is, though, I'd sure like to know what you got on the President. I'd a bet anythin' he'd have dropped your nomination by now. And when he didn't, I figured Freiborg must've gotten you to go along. It sure surprised me to find out he hadn't; that you really meant it when you said the final decision would be yours alone."

"I still mean it. But where the hell are you getting all your inside information?"

Lem grinned. "Same place as the President, and not too long after him. But before I get to that, one thing I want to know. You still plannin' on taking that health post or not?"

"Let's say I plan to have lunch with the President on Thursday and show up for that Senate hearing on Friday. After that we'll see. But I'm getting damned tired of being manipulated. What the hell did you really expect of me?"

"No great mystery. Big exposé. Big headlines. Enough maybe to break up that block of Southwestern congressional seats lined up against us. Nothin' I ain't already told you."

"Not quite. You never bothered to tell me so many of those documents you passed on were originals; that by stealing them you really hindered Justice's investigation. You also never told me you planned to kill Corcoran."

"We never would've if he'd been where he belonged. In jail! As for stealin' those documents, that was mainly meant to put the fear of God in them. We knew you'd give them back."

Dan sighed wearily. "That about covers it then, except for maybe one thing. Say I decide the hell with it: to both the job and the Senate hearing—which even if she hasn't said so, is what Kris is hoping I'll do. What then?"

Lem gave Dan's arm a consoling squeeze. "Now I'm really goin' to make it easy for you. Tell you the name of our back-up man, the guy who's been feedin' us all our inside info: Donald Allport."

"Allport!" gasped Dan. "The assistant attorney general? But he's from Alabama. Practically a Wallace protégé, for Chrissake!"

"That don't necessarily damn the man."

"No, I suppose not. But how the hell did you latch onto him?"

"Through that same black professor from Duke who brought me Artemus Hill's report. Turns out Allport was his former student too. And one night, right after the shooting at Mississippi State, Allport came to him with an interesting war story. How he was once trapped by a bunch of Viet Cong while out on patrol and this black chopper pilot swooped down and rescued him. Got Allport back to base even after a burst of machine-gun fire smashed through his windshield and caught him square in the chest. Must've been a hell of a flyer 'cause even with a punctured lung and a slug next to his heart he landed his copter safely. But then his luck ran out and he died during surgery. So this Allport owed his life to a black man and you know how those Alabama hillfolk are. No matter how educated they are or high they climb, they got an old-fashioned code of honor. Look up Allport when you're in Washington. He's a rare guy. We could sure use him right where he is, but he's ready to step in, in case you bow out."

"That's reassuring," Dan said wryly.

"I figured you'd think so."

"You lying bastard! You knew damned well telling me about him would make things harder, not easier, for me."

"Yeah," drawled Lem, grinning. "But I kind of been lookin' at it another way too. With you as Secretary of Health and Allport headin' up part of the investigation, those health swindlers could be put away real quick. Think about it, why don't you?"

Wearily Dan nodded. "Well, I'd better be getting back. I've kept Kris waiting long enough."

"Yeah, you do that. G'night, Doc. Hope you sleep real good after our little talk."

"Thanks!" Dan growled in disgust. "Same to you and your kidney machine."

—

Chapter Twenty-Seven

Early Thursday morning Dan flew to Washington alone. Jimmy was already there and Kris and Nora would arrive tomorrow to attend his Senate confirmation hearing. Unlike Boston's balmy end-of-August weather, Washington was in the midst of another scorcher, and between air-conditioned limousines and buildings Dan spent the day in sticky misery.

His tightly scheduled round of meetings finally ended at six and an hour later Dan sat alone at a window table in the French restaurant atop the Kennedy Center nursing a drink and waiting for Jimmy Dallesio to join him. Jimmy was not late; he was early. After being met at the airport by Nels Freiborg and accompanied, almost bird-dogged, from appointment to appointment by him all day, Dan wanted a little time to himself. Freiborg was friendly although uncharacteristically subdued—almost as if he were viewing Dan with the same apprehension and concern he might feel for a doomed patient who did not know it yet. Certainly Freiborg's somber mood did not seem to match his strong assurances to Dan as to how firmly the President now agreed that the crackdown on the health swindlers should begin at once, and the enthusiastic support his appointment had from the other members of the President's cabinet.

From his first appointment with the retiring Secretary of HEW at 10:00 A.M. to his last with the Attorney General at four, Dan had met with dozens of high government officials, including the President, during the long, tiring day. Yet it was Freiborg, the political figure he had known longest and best, who most preoccupied him as he gazed abstractedly out the window at the dazzling Milky Way of lights sprawling below him. Despite his almost blind devotion to the President, it was Freiborg alone who seemed to mirror truth, not illusion.

"You're early!" exclaimed Jimmy, coming up from behind him and giving his shoulders a squeeze. "How come?"

"I got glad-handing cramps after awhile. Wanted to wrap my hand around a drink instead of another politician's."

"I can understand that," Jimmy said, sitting opposite him. "How'd your day go?"

Dan scowled and then spoke brightly. "Did you know there were thirty-six steps from street level to the entrance to the Capitol?"

"Is that a fact?" Jimmy pretended to look impressed. "I knew there were a lot, having climbed them enough times. But thirty-six. Imagine that!"

"Thirty-six exactly. I counted them."

"Well, that's certainly newsworthy. Might even make a good filler for my column. But being the serious-minded man you are, what deeper nuance do I draw from that informative tidbit?"

Dan shrugged. "It's the only hard fact I learned all day. The rest—well, the rest were soft, even gaseous. Want to know what I ate for lunch at the White House today?"

"I'd rather know what put you in this mood."

"Oh, that . . . Well, you shall. Since Kris won't be here till tomorrow and I trust nobody else but you, Jimmy, you shall. I'm not only going to give you a complete rundown of my day, times and places of meetings, what I discussed with whom, but even throw in a few penetrating insights for good measure. And you, being the great student of human nature you are, will then put it all together for me. Where would you like me to start?"

"With how you feel right now."

Dan laughed harshly. "You mean you want what we doctors call the 'chief complaint'? Well, to sum up: Daniel Lassiter, white, Caucasian, male, age 48, married, father of one, dealt a fairly good hand by fate, nearly a winning one, except for the one joker thrown in. The joker being this job. The President claims that he needs me. Rather desperately. Not that I'm indispensable, nor clearly preeminent in my field—only that my inside knowledge of the health scandal, now that he has decided to go public with it, is a big plus. Saves him the bother of having to explain it to a new man."

"Looks like you won that battle then."

"That's the way it's supposed to look, until you get to the fine print. As the President pointed out, and the Attorney General expounded on at great length, health frauds aren't the easiest cases in the world to prosecute. How can you determine for sure whether a particular patient needed a particular test, drug, or operation, without having ever examined him yourself? Or that doing Pap smears on a thousand girls under eighteen is a waste if it turns up one early cancer? Look at that big delaying action the drug companies fought to keep HEW from enforcing its rule that Medicare and Medicaid prescriptions had to be filled by generic instead of brand-name drugs. There's a hell of a judgmental factor involved. So that's one thing."

"What's the other?"

"Me. My real feeling about the health job. I'm not sure I want or can even stomach it. Not when it's going to take so much time away from Kris and the baby; take me away from the care of sick patients completely. Yeah, I realize it's a little late to be thinking this way. Not only have the wedding invitations been mailed, but I'm not exactly a blushing bride. I knew pretty well what I was getting myself into from the start. Only the personal part of my life didn't matter much until the last couple of weeks."

Jimmy nodded sympathetically and sipped the scotch he had ordered from the waiter on his way in. "Did you tell the President that?"

"Indirectly. But he kept coming back at me with a potent persuader. The future of American medicine. He believes that if we don't clean up this mess just right—with doctors taking the lead—the public will overreact and demand that our whole damn medical system be scrapped. They're sick of arrogant, greedy, holier-than-thou doctors and want to see them taken down a peg. What the hell do most people care about fancy open-heart surgery or diagnosing dime-sized brain tumors with CAT scanners when they can't get a doctor to look at their kid's rash or their old granny's arthritis? And the way the AMA's kept crying 'wolf' about socialized medicine all these years, they might just decide to let the wolf at us. So that's the other thing. The President feels that, for the sake of the medical profession, he can't appoint some nameless bureaucrat to the job. The public wants somebody it knows and feels is on their side."

"Looks like you're hemmed in then. The government wants you, the medical profession needs you, and thanks to that scrappy little baby of yours every mother in America is squarely behind you. No wonder the President's willing to pay your price: exposure of the health swindle now. Buddy, you're in!"

Dan nodded bleakly. "I'm in, all right. In my own grave. I dug it myself. So there's nothing left to do but lie in it and let the weaseling bureaucrats dig me in deeper and cover me over with red tape. Hell, let's eat. You ready to order?"

"In a minute," Jimmy said and gave Dan a speculative look. "One thing you may be overlooking. Even if he *is* the President, how sure can you be that he's leveling with you? That he's really ready to crack down on those health swindlers now?"

"He's certainly done the spadework for it. From the White House I went directly to the Attorney General who spent two hours with a team of his top assistants showing me the proof they've accumulated and the indictments they've drawn up." Dan refrained from mentioning to Jimmy one disturbing detail. Donald Allport was not at the meeting. Somebody told him Allport had been temporarily assigned to Sacramento to head up the prosecution of a former lieutenant governor being brought to trial on bribery charges. Dan had wanted to meet Allport and found his absence worrisome. Had the Attorney General discovered that Allport was Lem's source of information? Worse yet, had Lem's revelation of it to him somehow led to Allport's exposure?

Dan had not mentioned Allport's name to anybody, nor did he see how the FBI could have bugged Lem's hospital room. But with one of their long-range listening devices they wouldn't have had to—in which case Allport's absence from Washington at this time was no mere coincidence. "Still," he said to Jimmy a moment later, "a Presidential double cross remains a possibility. Any way you could check it out?"

Jimmy sighed. "Believe me, Danny, I've tried. But the people I've talked to about it are as close-mouthed as ever. Which worries me."

"How so?"

"Well, whenever any major Presidential statement is imminent, it's nearly always leaked out a little ahead of time. Especially by insiders looking for future favors from the press. All I got, though, was some scared, pleading looks from guys who already owe me; no mention of any timetable."

"Hmmm," murmured Dan, again reminded of Freiborg's subdued behavior. "Do you think I'm being strung along?"

"Maybe for a while. Until the President does some fast fence-mending."

"But that wasn't our understanding, damn it! He promised me he was going to move on it at once."

"In those exact words?"

Dan reflected briefly. "I remember him saying, 'with dispatch.' "

"Dispatch has two meanings, as I recall. One, to carry out promptly. The other, to kill summarily."

"Well, that's sure smart-assed of you!" Dan growled. "But where does it leave me?"

"Did you make clear to the President your intention of breaking the news of the health scandal if he didn't?"

"Not in so many words. Freiborg already did that for me. That's what the President was alluding to, I suppose, when he told me not to worry; that he would personally see to it that the swindlers were dealt with quickly."

"And when he said it did he smile or bang his fist on the table?"

"Jesus! You ask the oddest questions. Smile, I suppose, since I don't remember any dishes rattling. Why?"

Jimmy shrugged. "Just wondering. Even though he's not Italian, the President talks a lot with his hands."

"All right, James," said Dan exasperatedly. "I get the distinct impression that you're leading up to something—probably another dazzling display of your supersleuthing. But I'm too damned tired to play along, so get to the point."

"Well," Jimmy said, "instead of just goddamning the President, let's try to see it from his point of view. He didn't just run against his Republican opponent in the last election, he ran against big business and industry. Instead of candy-coated pills, he forced strong medicine down the corporations' throats. All of which made him mighty popular with the little guy but earned him the undying enmity of the big money men. And the President's a realist. He knows that without their support he's likely to be a one-term President and has more or less resigned himself to it."

"Hey, hold on," Dan protested. "The little people are the majority. So what the hell does he need the moguls for?"

"Because it's the forty percent of the little people who are getting government handouts of one kind or another that this President's going after next. He believes every able-bodied man should earn his own keep. And he knows damned well, as one of your predecessors at HEW, old 'Cap the Knife,' used to warn, that the way things are going half the Gross National Product will go to our domestic social programs by the end of the century. Meaning half the people will be working to support the other half and effectively ending our free-enterprise system. So the President's determined that if he does nothing else before his term ends he's going to get rid of the social welfare mess. And he could well do it too, if he can hold onto his present congressional majority two more years. To make sure of that, he might just be willing to temporize on exposing a two-billion-dollar health scandal. So that's his moral dilemma."

"Yeah, I know," said Dan heavily. "Freiborg's explained it to me enough times. And I can't really fault the President for wanting it. But neither can I convince myself this is one time when the end justifies the means—not when lives of sick people are at stake. So what the hell do I do? Come on, Jimmy, just don't leave me hanging. You must have some sage advice to offer."

A sly smile played on Jimmy's lips. "Matter of fact, I do. But first I want you to concede two points. That smart as you are, I know politics and politicians better than you do. And that, same as in medicine, desperate situations demand desperate remedies. . . ." Jimmy waited for Dan's grudging nod before continuing. "Well, feeling as I do about the President and the sorry straits this country might be in without him, I've often wondered what I'd do if I ever uncovered another Watergate-style scandal."

"What, for Chrissake?"

Jimmy told him.

Chapter Twenty-Eight

Dan's confirmation hearing before the powerful Senate Finance Committee was scheduled for 10:00 A.M. in room 2211 of the Dirksen Senate Office building. He was familiar with the setting, having testified before that guardian body on health-related matters in the past. There was a curved dais for members of the Committee in the front of the room, a table for invited guests flanked by two more tables for the press in the middle, and several rows of spectator seats in the rear.

At 8:30, to the surprise of the Finance Committee staff, a Secret Service team appeared unannounced to give the hearing room an electronic sweep security check. When the staff secretary questioned this precaution, they answered vaguely that a large audience was expected.

Their estimate was right. By nine o'clock the crowd that had been gathering outside the hearing room ever since the building opened so jammed the corridor that the security guards had to rig up rope barriers to herd them behind to keep the passageway open. Crews from the four national TV networks had to plead and sometimes shove their way through the mob to get their equipment into the room. Voices were raised and tempers flared as the stream of spectators, lined up four abreast, filled the block-long corridor from end to end, and late arrivals, apart from authorized personnel, were barred from getting off the elevator at that floor. The size of the crowd, unmatched since some of ex-Secretary of State Henry Kissinger's dramatic appearances, was a puzzlement to staff workers in the building. All they could glean from those reporters who would answer them was that rumor had it something highly unusual was about to happen, although exactly what or by whom nobody was certain. By 9:30, the crowds in and around the building had grown so large and restive that the security chief called the D.C. police to cordon off the entire block.

"Jesus!" Nels Freiborg exclaimed as the limousine carrying Dan and himself turned into First Street and was halted by a police barrier. Rolling down the window, he hailed a mounted policeman to ask what was going on.

"Don't rightly know, sir," said the officer. "Something to do with the Lassiter hearing."

Freiborg's face creased with concern. "There hasn't been a bomb scare, has there?"

"No, sir! No threats of any kind."

"Then what the hell is that mob doing here?"

The police officer reined in his frisky mount and shrugged. "Come to hear Dr. Lassiter's testimony, I guess."

Freiborg looked sharply at Dan. "You know anything about this?"

Dan shook his head vigorously. "I sure as hell don't. But I'm just as anxious to find out as you are."

Freiborg's eyes narrowed. "You planning any surprises I don't know about?"

"No!" snapped Dan. "Are you? . . . Including any delayed ones?"

Freiborg swore softly and picked up the car telephone. "Connect me with the main security desk at the Dirksen Senate Office building," he told the operator. ". . . Hello, Joe. Nels Freiborg. What the hell's going on in there?"

"Damned if I know," came the reply. "But the whole second floor corridor's packed and a lot of damn mad reporters are milling around my desk demanding to be let up there."

"What for?"

"Nobody I've talked to seems to know, or else ain't saying. The rumor making the rounds is some big story's about to break."

"A big story, huh?" Freiborg said. "All right, Joe, we'll swing around the block and come in by the delivery entrance. Send a squad of your men to clear our way." Hanging up, he gave Dan an accusing stare.

"Nels, I swear I don't know any more about what's going on than you do."

Freiborg scrutinized him in heavy silence and then leaned forward to tell the driver where to go. Finally he said to Dan, "Well, that only leaves one person who might—Lem Harper."

"If that's true, which I doubt, then he lied to me. He promised there'd be no pressure from his end."

"And you believed him?"

"That's right!" Dan declared. "I still do. Just as I still believe the President."

Freiborg squeezed his eyes shut to stop them from twitching. "Okay, Dan. I don't really know what you mean by your last remark and I don't want to know. He's still the President and I have nothing more to say on that subject. I'll get you to that hearing room safely. After that you're on your own."

"I always felt I was, Nels," Dan said flatly. "I thought I made that clear."

At 10:00 A.M., the doors of room 2211 were opened and only enough spectators to fill its eighty or so seats admitted, since the rules forbade standing. Orders were then issued to the security guards to clear the corridor and, amid much commotion, they did. Because so many Finance Committee members had trouble reaching the hearing room the Chairman delayed the start of the meeting thirty minutes.

Four policemen escorted Dan and Nels Freiborg up a back staircase and by a circuitous route to the old Executive Sessions chamber adjoining room 2211. To Dan's relief he found Kris and Nora Dallesio there in the company of Senator Edward Brooke of Massachusetts who would formally introduce him to the Committee.

"Dan!" cried Kris. "What in the world is going on?"

"I don't know," he said, kissing her cheek. "But I intend to find out. Right now."

Excusing himself, he moved to a small alcove with a bank of telephones and placed a call to Commonwealth General. Al Beal answered the phone in Lem's room and after chuckling at Dan's predicament put Lem on.

"Hey, Doc!" Lem said cheerfully. "How's Washington? Crowded, huh? Well, I promised you'd be on your own and you are. I never said nothin' about not providin' an audience for you."

"But damn it, this is the Senate of the United States, not a circus ground!"

"Yeah, I know. But tell me this: Who's sweatin' more, you or Freiborg?"

Dan hesitated. "Freiborg, I guess."

"Good! He's the President's official sweater, so let him sweat. Good luck, Doc," Lem said and hung up.

When Dan emerged from the alcove Nels Freiborg was nowhere in sight, sparing him from relating Lem's explanation. But Jimmy was there, red-eyed, hair more tousled than usual, looking as if he hadn't slept much the previous night. "Well—" Jimmy asked. "Any decision?"

"Nope," Dan admitted.

"Still waiting for Divine guidance?"

"Something like that. Makes more sense than that lunatic scheme of yours."

"Oh, well," Jimmy said philosophically, "at least I had fun thinking about it last night."

The next moment the Finance Committee Chairman entered the room, nodded pleasantly at Dan, and said, "All right, ladies and gentlemen. Order seems to have been restored. We can start now."

With the full eighteen-man Committee present, a rare occurrence even for a cabinet-level hearing, the chairs behind the dais were completely occupied. Dan sat at the center table immediately below, with Senator Brooke on one side and Nels Freiborg on the other.

Jimmy sat at a press table an arm's length away, and Kris and Nora in the front row of spectator seats.

Dan scanned the faces of the men on the dais, most of them looking staid and dignified in response to the large audience, until his gaze settled on Alvin Balbridge, the senator from Arkansas. Dan knew exactly where he stood with him. In his previous appearance before the Committee, the elderly Arkansan's antipathy toward him was barely blunted by his courtly manner. The feeling was reciprocated. Balbridge's bald, beak-nosed profile reminded Dan of the eagle on the seal of the United States above him. But instead of arrows and olive branches the man clutched political power in his claws and was not to be underestimated. He was a shrewd, articulate spokesman for Southern conservatism and as knowledgeable in economic matters as his former fellow senator from Arkansas, William Fulbright, had been in foreign ones. But unlike Fulbright, he made no pretense about being a segregationist; he was one. Somewhere in his rural upbringing a racial prejudice had been so deeply implanted that Balbridge had not the slightest doubt of its validity. He was too intelligent to condemn an entire race solely on the basis of skin color, so he blamed the supposed inferiority of blacks on breeding. To his farm-grown mentality, breeding determined quality, and it mattered not whether a man was black or white, if ill-bred he was foredoomed to failure. But he was too cagey a politician to express his biases openly and so the last time he and Dan had clashed on health issues Balbridge tried to expose him as the utopian fool and wasteful spender he suspected him to be. Thus their enmity was sealed.

But to Dan's surprise, when their eyes met now the senator from Arkansas gave him a warm nod and smile.

At 10:40, the Finance Committee Chairman convened the hearing. "I will now call this meeting to order," he said in his pleasant Louisiana accent. "We are pleased to have with us this morning Dr. Daniel Lassiter, general director of the Commonwealth General Hospital and the President's nominee for the new cabinet post of Secretary of National Health. I will ask that a resumé of Dr. Lassiter's credentials, along with the public law that created this position and other pertinent material dealing with the office, appear in the record at this point. I now call on Senator Edward Brooke of Massachusetts."

"Thank you, Mr. Chairman," said Brooke. "It is my great pleasure to appear before you today to assist in the presentation of one of Massachusetts's most illustrious physicians and certainly its most illustrious new father."

Brooke half-turned to acknowledge the audience's laughter with a grin and a nod and then proceeded to give a twenty-minute speech on Dan's medical career, emphasizing his administrative experience, his service on many health-related national advisory boards, and his deep commitment to health care for the indigent as evidenced by the successful medical projects he had instituted in Mississippi and Massachusetts.

The Chairman thanked him and turned to Dan. "Do you have a statement you would like to make to the Committee at this time, Dr. Lassiter?"

Dan hesitated, feeling some remark, preferably humorous, was appropriate in response to Senator Brooke's laudatory introduction, but none came to mind. How humorous would the Committee find it if he told them he no longer wanted the job with its ceaseless round of committee meetings, congressional appearances, and political pulse-takings. That after almost fifty years of confused striving he finally had everything he really wanted from life, though not the bill for it nor any sign from Heaven that the debt was being canceled or called. When he'd tried to express this doubt to Kris all she had said was, "Oh, God, you're positively mystical!" So here he sat, about to make history as the nation's first Secretary of Health, and so bedeviled by indecision that he was practically tongue-tied. Did he have anything to say? "No, Mr. Chairman," he finally replied. "Not at this time."

"As you wish, Dr. Lassiter," said the Chairman. "You'll have ample opportunity to express your views on health issues later on. I was sort of hoping, though, that you might offer some explanation for the unprecedented popularity of this hearing."

"I believe that's mainly my wife's doing, Senator. My contribution was rather limited and months apart."

The Chairman waited for the laughter to subside before adding, "But essential, Dr. Lassiter. Much as I subscribe to the goals of the feminist movement, I would like to remind them that we men are not obsolete yet."

The Chairman's remark drew less of a laugh than a titter. "Well," he said, turning sober-faced, "let's go right to the questions. I'm sure Senator Balbridge, chairman of our subcommittee on health, has some he'd like to ask you."

Dan was sure too. Here it comes, he thought, bracing himself for the onslaught but also relieved that the formalities were over and he and his main adversary were about to collide, triggering the flow of adrenalin through his veins and lifting the mental fog he had been in.

"Thank you, Mr. Chairman," said Balbridge in a homespun drawl he usually reserved for rural Arkansan hustings. "But if Dr. Lassiter is expectin' the same sort of grillin' I gave him the last time he appeared before this Committee let me put his mind at ease. I realize, as we all do, that not only has he put in a busy couple of weeks, but is taking on one of the toughest jobs in all of government and so deserves our support and encouragement." Balbridge paused to look around and prompt nods from his fellow Committeemen, before showing a sly smile. "Now, I can plainly see from the look on Dr. Lassiter's face that my attitude comes as a big surprise. About as big a surprise as if I tried to tell him the Mayflower landed at Little Rock before Plymouth Rock. He just ain't ready to believe me. But maybe he will when he hears my reasons. I've recently read a transcript of the remarks Dr. Lassiter made before the board of trustees of the

AMA a few weeks back, and I was mighty pleased to find that his forward health plan was both moderate in tone and realistic in scope. I would therefore like to request that Dr. Lassiter's speech before the AMA be made a part of this record. That okay with you, Mr. Chairman? . . . Good. I would also like to state that I heartily endorse its principles in most respects. Be assured, Dr. Lassiter, I'll let you know soon enough where we happen to differ, but before getting to that I want to commend you again for your fortitude in taking on such a demanding job."

Dan was more than surprised; he was stunned. Either the AMA had been unwilling or unable to meet Balbridge's price for opposing his nomination, or else he was following some secret scenario. "Thank you, Senator," Dan managed to say after clearing his throat. "I'm not quite ready to relax my guard until I learn exactly where we do differ, but I want you to know how deeply I appreciate your kind remarks." That said, Dan hastily scribbled a note on the pad before him and passed it to Jimmy. Jimmy read it, nodded, and quietly left the room for the old Executive Sessions chamber to use one of their telephones. What Dan wanted to know was which, if any, senators the President had met with that morning. And Jimmy, wondering the same thing himself, was chagrined that he had neglected to find this out earlier when he had visited the White House to place an envelope in the hands of a trusted friend and source person who worked in the office of Paul Jarvis, the President's Appointments Secretary. Phoning her now he learned that the President had breakfasted with Balbridge and four other senators that morning, all members of the Finance Committee and all from the South. The tantalizing question was why. Was it a final attempt on the President's part to persuade them to support Dan's nomination, or was it deal time in Dixie?

When Jimmy returned to the hearing room the Chairman was in the midst of a long-winded description of the plight of the aged in Louisiana. He passed the list to Dan, saw him glance at it without change of expression and continue to nod at the Chairman to assure him he held his attention. ". . . And so, Dr. Lassiter," he concluded, "I ask you: Do you subscribe to the principle that in a democratic society like ours we cannot base the decision as to who shall live and who shall die, who shall be well cared for and who shall be neglected, on economic grounds alone?"

"I do indeed subscribe to that principle, Mr. Chairman. I firmly believe that every citizen should have access to quality health care; that it is a fallacious belief of some health field personnel, including physicians, that good health is not so much a right as a privilege."

"But you are also aware, are you not, of how much the provision of that right can cost?" asked Balbridge pointedly.

"Very much aware, Senator."

"But are you equally aware that such a system is not as equitable as it sounds? That in fact it represents a gross inequity to a sizable segment of our population? In other words, if a man does not have the intelligence, the drive and the ability to earn what another man earns, then the government, through the transfer of payments such as health funds, simply takes from he who has done well and gives it to he who has not. Frankly, Doctor, I not only find that inequitable as hell, but fear it might prove the ruination of our entire economic system. Must we go on providing the same high-priced medical care to the producer as well as the nonproducer? The intelligent as well as the subintelligent? The pie can only be split so many ways, you know."

"I am well versed in the splitting of pies, Senator. I am less certain of the intent of your remarks."

Balbridge's eyes flashed angrily. "Then let me clarify them, sir. You stated before the AMA that since fifty percent of all federal health monies are expended on hospitals that serve less than five percent of the population in any one year, the logical place to cut costs would be there, did you not?"

"I did," Dan said.

"You also pointed out that since empty hospital beds cost almost as much to maintain as full ones we must reduce the size of hospitals as well as their number of admissions. Cut the bed capacity of the big ones in half and convert most of the small ones into outpatient clinics. But most people still believe they get the best kind of medical care in hospitals. That's where they want their babies delivered and their old folks to die. So don't you feel that not only should hospital beds be cut, but some discretion used as to the type of people admitted to them?"

"I certainly do, Senator. The sickest ones! Regardless of whether they're intelligent or subintelligent, as you so quaintly put it."

Balbridge glared at Dan but held his temper in check. "Oh, I may be a little bullheaded on this subject, but I doubt you'll find many others up here who think I'm quaint. It just seems to me you doctors aren't as aware as you ought to be who pays the bills in this society: that instead of rewarding excellence of effort with excellence of medical care, you'll just go on shirking that responsibility and blame us politicians when the money runs out. Isn't that so, Doctor?"

"No, Senator, it is not. When I feel the time has come to stop the life-supporting devices on a hopelessly dying patient, I don't call in the district attorney. I shut them off myself."

"But those are the hopelessly dying. What about the hopelessly living? Can't we conserve some of our hard-earned resources there? How many infections in hard-core drug addicts must we treat before we realize the futility of it? How many illegitimate babies of subintelligent mothers must we support before we say enough?"

Dan started to reply, faltered, rubbed his eyes as if to wipe away the haunting visions that suddenly began to pass before them: black babies left to die at birth or to languish in dangerously dilapidated incubators; mute children missing half their palates; medical atrocities the equal of any he had seen in wartime.

He only half-listened as Balbridge continued his diatribe. The man was baiting him despite himself, despite the deal he had probably made with the President to support Dan's nomination providing the investigation of the HMO scandal in his state was delayed until after the elections. Balbridge couldn't help it; his bigotry ran too deep—as did Dan's humanity. But what of the President's? Was he any less humane trying to stave off what he foresaw as certain disaster for this country? Could Dan break his promise to the President to keep silent on the health swindle, bring personal disgrace and political ruination upon the man, merely over the suspicion that his breakfasting with Balbridge that morning was tantamount to betrayal? So he was stymied, or would have been, were it not for his owlish-eyed, near-genius of a friend and his audacious scheme. Yet audacious was hardly the word; it was outrageous, dangerously reckless, the biggest bluff since a former White House spokesman had tried to pass off the Watergate break-in as a "third-rate burglary." But Jimmy had just given him the barest outline of his plan. And Dan, thinking it more fanciful than feasible, had not bothered to press him for details. So now he would have to improvise. Yet it might just work. It would work if only he could muster the verve, the straight-faced solemnity, the Churchillian ring of righteous indignation to his voice.

Dan began listening more closely to the Senator from Arkansas, waiting for him to wind down.

Finally he did. ". . . So, what I am saying to you, Dr. Lassiter—and I feel I speak for a majority of this Committee as well—is that we not only expect you to do your best to contain expenditures, but make some effort to insure that the most productive members of our society reap the maximum benefit from the health care system that their hard labors have paid for. I hope I make myself clear?"

"You certainly do, Senator," Dan said. "Transparently. Now all I need from you and your Committee is a set of guidelines on how to properly evaluate productiveness. How productive is a newborn baby? My own, for example? If all continues to go well with her—and

I pray to God it will—she should be in the hospital another three, four months. At an estimated total cost of around thirty thousand dollars. I cannot, of course, predict what her future worth to society will be, or that it will justify this initial investment in her. But even if I could, there is another consideration that troubles me far more. Thanks to my position as general director of one of our nation's great hospitals, my little girl got the best treatment available anywhere in the world. Naturally I am very grateful, but I am also deeply humbled by it as well. As Secretary of Health, it would be my fondest hope we could evolve a medical care system so efficient that every newborn infant in this country would receive comparable care. You talk about subintelligence, Senator, as if it were some kind of predetermined affliction. But much of it is produced by birth injuries, improper nutrition in infancy—factors that are clearly preventable if only we made a concerted effort to prevent them. Yet as you point out, the pie is only so big and can only be sliced in so many pieces. So there must be no waste. But there *is* waste, Senator, much more than can be accounted for by sheer bureaucratic inefficiency." Dan drew a deep breath, knowing full well what a sensation his next statement would cause. "I should now like to inform you that I come before you today with a dual purpose. My first, to present my qualifications for the post of Secretary of National Health, which Senator Brooke has so generously helped me do. My second, to act as the President's personal spokesman in making known to you a shocking scandal in misused federal health funds that has recently been uncovered by investigators from the Justice Department. . . . Mr. Chairman, it is my sad duty to inform both your Committee and the American public that due to massive fraud and collusion on the part of certain personnel involved in the running of Health Maintenance Operations in eight southwestern states, that 1.9 billion dollars has been swindled from this year's health expenditures. I wish to make very clear to you that this is a reasonably accurate estimate and that the swindle I speak of has been established beyond a doubt."

As Dan paused to sip water the audience response was instantaneous: from the press a wild scramble to reach the phones in the old Executive Sessions chamber; from the spectators cries of outrage and indignation; from the members of the Finance Committee looks of consternation and chagrin.

The Chairman, appearing equally dumbfounded by the stunning accusation, let the commotion continue until a sharp cry for recognition from Senator Balbridge prompted him to bang his gavel to restore order. The unlucky reporters who had not beaten the security guards to the door of the Executive Sessions chamber were sent back to their seats and the audience warned that no further outbreaks would be tolerated. Though tempted, Dan did not turn around to look at Kris or Jimmy. He did, however, glance at Freiborg, pale and panting, slumped in his seat. "Nels, stop hyperventilating, for Chrissake!" Dan whispered in his ear. "You'll pass out or have a coronary. It's for the best, you'll see."

"If you planned this—" he hissed.

"I swear, I didn't. But if rape is inevitable . . ."

"Yeah, I know," Freiborg muttered between gasping intakes of breath.

"Mr. Chairman!" Balbridge shouted again. "I would surely like to know what Dr. Lassiter is trying to pull here by his unsubstantiated accusation. None of this was on our agenda. Nor have we any proof that he does, in fact, speak for the President. I therefore request—nay, demand—that Dr. Lassiter address himself to these questions."

Dan waited for the Chairman's nod before answering. "I can readily understand the Senator from Arkansas's concern," he said, "since several of the HMOs involved in the swindle are located in his state. But I can assure him that I *do* speak for the President—as Mr. Freiborg will verify in just a moment. Before he does, however, I would like to make clear that I undertook this duty voluntarily and was not coerced into it in any way. Conclusive proof of these extremely grave charges was furnished the President only recently, and he has instructed me to inform you that he intends to make an official report to both the Congress and the American people shortly. Quite possibly at a press conference tomorrow. As we all know, the President is not only a courageous but fair-minded man and so felt obliged to tell me of these facts at our noon meeting yesterday. He did so for two reasons: first, to fully acquaint me with the situation and the enormous extra burden it adds to my cabinet duties should I still wish to be considered for the post; second, to discuss the possibility that I might make more of a contribution to the speedy resolution of this crisis in some other capacity than as Secretary of Health, namely, as head of a committee of nationally known physicians who would work closely with the Justice Department to evaluate these charges and bring the culprits to justice. In addition, the President will shortly request that grand juries be impaneled in every locality where the swindles occurred. Naturally he expects Congress to cooperate fully with him, not only through the General Accounting Office, but through special investigative committees in both Houses. I can assure you, Mr. Chairman, that from what I have heard both the President and Attorney General say, there is going to be a housecleaning the likes of which this country has never seen before."

"All well and good, Dr. Lassiter—if true," Balbridge retorted. "But you still haven't explained—not to my satisfaction anyway—why you saw fit to withhold this information from our Committee until now. Or why, since you no longer seem interested in the post of Secretary of Health, you came before us under false pretenses?"

"Senator, you astound me," Dan replied evenly. "As one of the Senate's leading exponents of fiscal responsibility, I would hardly consider a 1.9 billion-dollar swindle unworthy of your attention."

"You know perfectly well what I mean!" Balbridge sputtered.

"Frankly, Senator, I'm not sure that I do. The tone of your challenges leaves me no choice but to draw one of two rather unpleasant conclusions: Either you think that I have taken leave of my senses and invented this massive swindle, or else am so publicity-mad as to want to preempt the President and grab all the headlines for myself. I can assure you neither is even remotely true. Nonetheless, you have made it clear that before I can complete my rather lengthy report to this Committee without further interruptions I'd better allay some of your doubts, and so I shall. To start, much has been said about the soaring costs of National Health Insurance. It needed saying. It also needs to be said that just as we could barely afford the three-hundred-million-dollar Medicaid swindle of a few years back, we can't possibly afford a two-billion-dollar one now! That is self-evident. What might not be is the potentially disastrous effect such a vast and despicable scandal could have on American health care in general and the medical profession in particular. The President is very much afraid that in the heat of its anger the public might blame all doctors, not the mere handful actually involved in these swindles, and demand blanket retribution. I speak, of course, of socialized medicine.

"In place of the warm, respectful, almost blind trust the American people once felt for doctors, there exists a much more ambivalent—I might even say antagonistic—attitude toward us today. Yet how much of this is really justified? Most doctors keep so busy caring for patients in their sheltered little world of hospitals and offices that they can hardly do more than shake their heads in bewilderment at the harsh criticism heaped upon us. Only a small minority, either because of discontent with the strenuous demands medicine makes on them, or simple greed, have sacrificed their ethics and ideals for monetary gain. Mr. Chairman, I seriously doubt that the individual American will allow *his* or *her* doctor to be punished for the misdeeds of so very few. European-style socialized medicine simply does not fit the style, the premium on individual initiative, the quest for excellence, that has made this country great. If it ever comes to pass—as it might—it will not be the result of any health scandal, even one as vast as this; it will be because of a breakdown in our entire free-enterprise system. And if that should happen, we will be losing the very system that has made American medicine and the American way of life the envy of the entire world.

"It was the President's wish that this plea on behalf of the overwhelmingly honorable members of the medical profession be made and that I, as a physician, make it. I trust that answers one of your questions, Senator Balbridge. I leave the other for Mr. Freiborg to answer."

Pressing the palm of one hand against his cheek, possibly to keep from shaking his head in bemused wonder, Nels Freiborg reached for the microphone. "Mr. Chairman, members of the Committee," he began, "Dr. Lassiter has asked I confirm that he speaks for the President. I would prefer to say that he speaks at his behest. The President, of course, speaks for himself, and you have heard only a small sampling of the wrath that this shocking swindle has provoked in him. You will hear the rest in due time—uh, tomorrow, in fact, as Dr. Lassiter has indicated. But I warn you now that the President expects all the committees of the Congress holding jurisdiction over health matters to move apace with him in this investigation. Yes, he realizes an election is drawing near and that the disclosure and prosecution of the culprits behind this scandal might have embarrassing consequences for congressmen from those states and districts involved. But he advises you that no whitewashes, no cover-ups, no delaying tactics, will be tolerated He wants action and he wants it now!" Freiborg said, banging the microphone stand against the table.

A hush followed, a few scattered handclaps from

the spectators, and then a loud round of applause. "Praise the President!" shouted a woman in the rear. "Amen!" cried another. Nels glanced at Dan, rolled his eyes as if to say, what'd you expect, but turned away from the smile forming on his face.

"And now, Mr. Chairman," Freiborg continued, "if you and the members of your Committee will excuse me, I have to consult further with the President. He will be meeting with the leaders of both Houses of Congress, including several of you, imminently, and arrangements must be made. Dr. Lassiter has been thoroughly briefed by the Justice Department and will now give you a full report of what is known of the size and scope of the health fund swindle. He will also, I'm sure, give you his recommendations as to what steps must be taken to prevent any future recurrences. As he has already mentioned, any action on his nomination for the post of Secretary of National Health will have to be held in abeyance, as it would have been anyway, had you had prior knowledge of this scandal." Nels gathered up his papers and rose. "So, if you will excuse me . . ."

"Uh, one second, Mr. Freiborg," urged the Chairman. "As you must realize, this startling turn of events has left my head spinning. Dr. Lassiter springs a two-billion-dollar health scandal on us and while we're reeling from that you say the President expects us to take action on it at once. That's quite a lot to deal with for one morning. I hope there's not any more."

"No, Senator," Freiborg replied. "Not that I know of anyway."

"And you, Dr. Lassiter? Any more from you?"

Dan shook his head.

"Well, that's a relief! You are therefore excused, Mr. Freiborg. But please hurry back to us as soon as you can. We're all anxious to learn more about the President's plans—preferably in advance of the press."

Nels nodded and left.

"And now, Dr. Lassiter," said the Chairman heavily, "if you'll be so kind as to start at the beginning and tell us what you know of the events leading up to your remarkable disclosure we would all be *most* grateful."

Dan reached into his briefcase for the notebook containing the facts and figures Matt Kinsella had supplied him. He felt a pang of guilt at omitting any mention of Artemus Hill and his crucial rôle in exposing the health fund scandal. But he could leave that to Jimmy and the many columns he would write on the story.

Fifty minutes later Dan concluded his detailed report. Pushing the microphone away and leaning back in his seat, he surveyed the faces of the Committee. The thirteen senators from states untouched by the swindle appeared grave and somber, four of the five others looked distraught, as if contemplating their unpromising homecomings. Balbridge, his fists clenched, stared down at the tabletop, avoiding Dan's gaze completely. He now understood how his younger brother, Pine Bluff's leading gynecologist and philanderer, had acquired his recent wealth. He had suspected as much but never confronted him with it. And even though not a penny of the tainted money had changed hands between them, who'd believe that the Senate's foremost expert on health care did not know his own brother was in on the swindle? He would be branded either a liar or a fool.

Doctors! thought Balbridge in dour disgust. Yesterday the urologist at Bethesda Naval Hospital who had removed his cancerous prostate gland a year ago told him tests showed his operation was not curative after all, and he would have to be emasculated. Now this Lassiter cuts off his political balls! Alvin Balbridge felt like putting a gun to his head and ending the folly of his old age permanently. But before doing that, he was sorely tempted to use the gun on his no-account brother.

In the ensuing silence, as if the Committee were pausing to catch their collective breaths, a nervous shiver overcame Dan as he realized it was over, or almost over. He had yet to hear from the President.

A minute or so later the Chairman asked the Committee if they had any further questions for Dr. Lassiter. Hearing none, he adjourned the meeting, ordering the security guards to clear the room of spectators and reporters at this time. Dan beckoned for Kris and Nora to join him at the witness table as the crowd departed. Kris, looking lovely in a green suede suit, gave him a quick kiss and, holding tightly to his arm, murmured, "I never knew what a crazy man I'd married."

Dan reached out to hug her and Nora to him. "You didn't," he said. "Nora did. It was Jimmy's idea. He concocted the whole scheme."

"My Jimmy!" Nora gasped. "I'll certainly have to have a talk with that boy. Imagine a regular churchgoer like him making up such awful lies!"

"What about a non-churchgoer?" Kris said, nodding at Dan. "He didn't do so bad either—scheduling Presidential press conferences, impaneling grand juries, and the like. The bit I liked best, though, was when you swore the President had not coerced you into any of this. I had to bite my lip to keep from laughing out loud at that!"

Dan saw a security guard approach the Chairman and speak briefly with him. The Chairman nodded, stepped down from the dais, and moved to their table.

Dan rose and introduced Kris and Nora to him. The Chairman bowed and extended his hand to them before turning to Dan. "Well, Dr. Lassiter, you certainly provided this Committee with its most memorable session ever. I'm still not clear about one thing, though. Do you want the Health Secretary job or don't you?"

Dan smiled. "Would you, Senator?"

"Uh uh," the Chairman answered evasively. "That's what us lawyers call 'shifting the burden,' and I won't even attempt to advise you there. But with that new baby of yours and all the President's got you doing, you'll be busy enough either way. Mr. Freiborg is waiting for you in the Executive Sessions chamber.

He'd like a word with you alone before he meets with the Committee."

"Nora and I'll wait for you here," said Kris.

"No, come along," Dan insisted. "I might need protection."

Nels was leaning against the conference table, holding a sheaf of typewritten papers in his hand, as they entered. Jimmy sat beside him.

"Well—" Dan asked uncertainly.

"Well, what?" Nels growled. "I never knew they taught Machiavelli in medical school."

"They don't. But maybe they should, now that the government owns most of the health industry. How'd the President take it?"

Freiborg scowled. "The President *didn't* take it. He gave it—to me. Made me feel like the biggest screw-up since Albert Fall and 'Teapot Dome.' Far as the President's concerned, the Secretary of Health job can go to a chiropractor. It'll be a long time before he'll let any more halo-headed doctors near him."

"That bad, huh?"

Tight-lipped, Nels nodded. Then shrugged. "Could've been worse, I suppose, if it weren't for that cute little ploy your buddy here pulled." His eyes darted at Jimmy. "Just as the President was really getting himself worked up, Jarvis showed up with this." He passed the sheaf of papers he held to Dan. "An advance copy of the popular Mr. Dallesio's column for tomorrow," he explained. "Sweet as maple syrup, if you ask me, but the President lapped it up."

Dan skimmed the first page and could see why. Entitled "The Brave Act of a Brave Man," it made the President sound like a modern-day Moses recently descended from Mount Sinai brandishing a fiery serpent in one hand and a banner of the Eighth Commandment in the other, determined to restore honesty to government even though it might bar him from the Promised Land of a second term.

Freiborg turned to Jimmy with scorn. "Do you really believe that pap?"

"What pap?" Jimmy said innocently.

"Oh, your hunch that the way the Heavenly Court entertains itself is by betting on moral decisions by us mortals instead of pro football games."

Jimmy shrugged. "It's not a bad line. Do you?"

"Jesus, after the morning I just put in, *my* biggest worry is that there might be life after death!"

Dan lowered the papers in his hands. "How *do* you feel, Nels?"

Frieborg faced him with wry resignation. "I figured you'd ask that. Well, if you really must know, relieved. Yeah, relieved. You did the right thing. I have to believe the President would've done it too—that all those airy assurances he gave Balbridge and his bunch over breakfast was just to make sure you got confirmed." He gestured speculatively. "As I say, I have to believe it if I'm to go on working with the man. Now we'll never know, and neither will Balbridge. That bigoted bastard looked like a ton of Ozark muleshit fell on him. So, all in all, I don't feel too bad. Mostly surprised—surprised a reputable doctor like you could tell such outrageous lies. But don't think you're out of the woods yet. Not by a long stretch." He smiled maliciously. "The President wants to see you before you leave town, preferably right away."

"What for?" asked Dan.

"Probably wants to know what further instructions you have for him. Take my limousine. It's waiting for you where we came in. And please," Freiborg added, "steer clear of any more reporters. They're obviously a bad influence on you."

Kris and Dan stepped into the rear of the limousine and settled back in its plush, leather-upholstered seats as the driver pulled away from the curb. Holding his wife's arm, Dan drew what seemed his first full breath all day. The greenery of Capitol Hill Plaza faded from view and the light dimmed as the limousine entered the Ninth Street Tunnel en route to the White House. Halfway through, Dan suffered a sudden qualm. Despite the desperate gamble he had won, he was still a doctor, a public figure; the end of this harrowing episode in his life might merely be the beginning of the next. Even as he saw the glitter of sunlight ahead the doubt remained: Was he coming out of a tunnel or entering one?

ABOUT THE AUTHOR

Physician, writer, teacher, MARSHALL GOLDBERG is full-time chief of medicine of Hurley Medical Center in Flint, Michigan, and professor of medicine at Michigan State University. His previous novels were *The Karamanov Equations* and *The Anatomy Lesson* (the first in the Dr. Daniel Lassiter series and a "cult" book among medical students). He was recipient of the Outstanding Teacher Award at Michigan State College of Human Medicine in 1972 and a past president of the Michigan Association for Medical Education. Dr. Goldberg won the NAACP Humanitarian Award in 1974 for instituting a project which helped provide medical care for Fayette, Mississippi, and serves on the board of directors of the Medgar Evers Foundation. In addition to publishing numerous articles in medical journals and popular magazines, Dr. Goldberg appears weekly on CTV's "CANADA A.M." as their resident health expert. He is currently completing *Skeletons,* the third in the Lassiter series.